P9-ECI-057

# The CEDAR POST

### The Pristine American Dream

### A Principle within a Novel

### Book One

# Jack R. Rose

i

Fifth Edition, 2012
Copyright © 2000 by Jack Randall Rose

All rights reserved. No part of this book may be used or reproduced in any manner whatsoever without written permission of the Publisher. Printed in the United States of America. For information address American Dream Makers, 3305 Cobble Creek Lane, Heber, UT 84032 www.americandreammakers.com

ISBN 0-9706772-0-0

Registered with Library of Congress # Txu 924-213 as Ur, the Great American Dream.

**Cover Design by Christauna Rose Asay**

The Cedar Post, Book One

Tears of Joy, Book Two

Fly Paper, Book Three

Published by:
American Dream Makers
3305 Cobble Creek Lane
Heber, UT 84032
www.americandreammakers.com

" ... one of the most insightful and captivating novels I have read in many years. I will be using this novel to help teach *character development* to the youth I teach in a long-term secure correction facility."
— Joycelyn Timothy, Reading Teacher

" ... very impressed at what a wonderful writer you are. I enjoyed the book thoroughly; it took me on a voyage which ended with a handkerchief in hand. Very good stuff."
— George Ayoub, Film Producer, Ontario, Canada

"I can honestly say this is the best book I have ever read.... This book taught me so many things that, in the mix of life, I had lost. I have failed many times in my life and I have been in the pit of self-hatred for so long because I never realized that I am worth being forgiven, by myself of all people. I never realized that I had that last human right—to choose how I react to every situation."
— Cody (17-year-old youth corrections inmate)

" ...This is a tremendous work of fiction which may one day be considered a classic. The story is impressive. You have successfully intertwined a principle-centered theme with a compelling narrative that will capture the imagination of a diverse readership."
— Laurie Turnblom, English Teacher

# ACKNOWLEDGEMENTS

I must express my deepest gratitude to those who were so willing to read this work and give me feedback.. To Loretta, George, Vicki, Cleo, Brenda, Jack Joseph, Ameri, Tyrene, Christauna, Kenny, Laurie, Peter, Roy and Jessianna, I offer my deepest gratitude.

A special thanks to Doris, who spent about a zillion hours in the critical days before printing to get the grammar and punctuation straight.

My sincere gratitude to my editors and formatters, Karen Belliston and Greg Belliston, whose many hours of work turned a sow's ear into a silk purse.

To my partner, Corbin, who has spent hours listening to me talk about inherent rights. I thank you for your untiring support.

To Ronda, my beloved of 28 years, who has encouraged me and discussed this book with frankness and gentleness.

**Seven sins of the world:**
Wealth without Work
Pleasure without Conscience
Knowledge without Character
Commerce without Morality
Science without Humility
Worship without Sacrifice and
Politics without Principle …

— Gandhi

IT IS IMPOSSIBLE TO HAVE LIBERTY WITHOUT
VIRTUE.

# DEDICATION

---

To Declo, Idaho, for supporting my widowed mother and for including and teaching me during the years of my youth.

To my friends, the deaf and the deaf-blind, who have looked past my "hearingness" and embraced me with their language, culture, and friendship.

To those who have so willingly read my manuscript and offered helpful suggestions.

To my family who have supported this work and willingly sacrificed their own time to help.

Most especially to my companion for her love and steady strength which has kept me going.

A NATION CANNOT GOVERN ITSELF WITHOUT
CITIZENS WHO CAN GOVERN THEIR PASSIONS
AND ACTIONS WITH VIRTUE.

# FOREWORD

This compelling story is not about young romance, high school wrestling, the deaf or the deaf-blind. It is not about terrorism, the holocaust, or understanding death. They are the framework of this moving story about a underachieving high school senior and his best friend, a deaf-blind, legless old man. The old man teaches him how to capture and hold The Pristine American Dream and changes his life forever.

*Pristine:* *"Characteristics of the earliest period or condition: original: still pure: uncorrupted: unspoiled [Pristine beauty]."* *Webster's New World Dictionary.*

Exactly when The Pristine American Dream our Founding Fathers knew disappeared from our culture nobody knows. Like colors fading from a handkerchief long forgotten on a post, the Dream gradually faded from our thoughts, passions and aspirations. The change was imperceptible, yet over time all of the brilliance gave way to the dull, uninspiring and common. Sadly, the American Dream of today is a hue our forefathers not only could not, but would not recognize.

To many citizens, the American Dream is a passionate search for easy wealth by hitting it big in the lottery, sweepstakes, a big lawsuit, or receiving an inheritance. To others it's landing a professional sports contract, achieving prominence in politics, business, or popularity without any thought to maintaining one's inherent rights. As important as these achievements may be to some people, The Pristine American Dream is far superior by any standard of measurement.

This story showcases The Pristine American Dream. And what is that dream? The Pristine American Dream is comprised of unalienable rights and privileges. One must recognize, accept and live by those unalienable or inherent rights guaranteed to all people by virtue of their birth. Simply put, inherent rights are the rights to be and to do good. Everything that is good is a right, an inherent right. Nobody ever has the right to do bad; they only have the power to choose it. One must also be willing to invest the diligence, hard work, and determination required to receive and enjoy the privileges of life.

All rights are defined by a law. It is impossible to have a right without its defining law! The right and the law that defines it are two sides of the same coin. Governments may pass laws that extend rights to citizens but unalienable rights are defined by the laws of common sense. These laws are born within us and are common among all humans.

Goodness is the catalyst that fires the furnace of happiness. No matter what circumstance individuals, families, communities or nations find themselves in, they always enjoy more peace of mind and happiness when they maintain their inherent rights. Privileges are the sweet things of life for which one must work to receive.

This story is fiction. The setting is Declo, Idaho, during the years of 1966 and 1967. All characters are fictional, but like many great fictional characters they may resemble living or dead individuals whose lives have impacted the author. Most family names are indigenous to the Declo community, yet this should not infer that any of the characters are living or have ever lived. There are, however, certain real individuals who make cameo appearances to add color to its historical setting. And although the author may have drawn from some personal experience to tell this story, this is not a story about the author.

Because this book has some deaf characters, it is important to point out that their conversations do not necessarily reflect the grammar of American Sign Language. I have often seen the language of the Deaf transliterated into choppy, awkward English to reflect the grammar and culture of the Deaf. To portray the Deaf in this way to those who do not know American Sign Language is to show them and their language in an inferior light. American Sign Language is a beautiful, graceful language full of rich expressions of feelings and concepts. When the Deaf sign in this book, it sounds like English because that is the language of this book.

The main character is a deaf-blind man named Ur. He has the ability to communicate with hearing people by several traditional techniques, including using his voice. However, the main method he uses to understand what people are saying is by putting his hand to the face of the person with whom he is talking, placing his index finger and second finger along the jaw line with his thumb on the lips. His ring finger and little finger are bent and placed against the voice box. It may amaze some that a deaf-blind person can communicate this way. However, in 1970, the author conversed easily for over an hour with two deaf-blind brothers in San Gabriel, California, who used this technique.

**Read this story for the wholesome enjoyment of it.
Learn about your unalienable rights for the
happiness and peace they give.
Discover receiving privileges for the pure pleasure of
them.**

A PRIVILEGE IS NEVER SAFE IN THE HANDS OF
THOSE WHO DO NOT UNDERSTAND NOR MAINTAIN
THEIR UNALIENABLE RIGHTS.

# TABLE OF CONTENTS

PEACE OF MIND IS THE GATE THROUGH WHICH ALL
MANKIND MUST PASS TO FIND HAPPINESS.

TO WAIVE ONE'S UNALIENABLE RIGHTS IS TO
WAIVE ONE'S HAPPINESS.

# PROLOGUE

At sunrise I stood in the sloping windswept cemetery that rises gently above Marsh Creek in Declo, Idaho. A gentle breeze lifted the river smells and floated them over the nearby farms to where I stood. Squadrons of seagulls quietly waved across the early-morning sky. Their silent morning and evening passing was a ritual as regular as the rising and setting of the sun. Each morning the sun chased them away from the Minidoka Dam to graze on millions of crickets, grasshoppers and grubs, and the evening sun gently shooed them back to their chalky lava perches around Lake Walcott. To the east the sun radiated through orange-ribbed clouds and cast a salmon glow on the distant hills above the old Dewey Ranch. The clouds were the last stubborn remnants of a late May thunderstorm that disturbed the peace of Cassia County during the night. In the glistening wet grass, a killdeer faked a broken wing by fluttering and shrieking a few yards from where I stood.

I must be standing near her nest, I mused as I glanced around the ground. I thought about chasing her like I used to when I was young, but I knew she would miraculously be healed after drawing me away from her nest. A white seed truck with a red spud-bed whined along the Burley-Declo highway. I heard some rail cars lock with a clunk. Lifting my eyes to the tracks a switch engine's roar sounded its intent to pull the cars away from the grain elevator for the slow nine-mile grind to Burley.

Modest headstones, glossy like hard candy, pushed up through the deep green grass around me. Dandelion blemishes freckled the grass here and there while others gathered in small yellow congregations around the granite and marble memorials.

I walked through the cemetery reading familiar names stopping at a modest, dark granite headstone. My eyes swept the treeless cemetery. Buried on this rolling hill were some of the people who stepped in after my father died. These were the founders of the community: the Osterhouts, Okelberrys, Lewises, Prestons, Darringtons, Turners, Woods, Johnsons, Matthews and Andersons. Solid in the basic honest values of rural America, they filled my fatherless void by example and inclusion. As the sun started to break the early-morning chill, I saw there were not any great marble edifices here to make the dead seem bigger in eternity than they were in mortality. These were mostly rural folk, who lived and died with sincere tributes rightfully earned from their posterity and neighbors.

To the north, a plume of dust rose in a long feathery trail behind Osterhouts' Massey Ferguson tractor and harrow. Above the plume, a low-flying crop-duster bee-lined to some weed-control appointment to the east. I reached out and placed my hand reverently on the headstone. "Born September 1, 1909 – Died March 18, 1985"—an insignificant stone for such a significant man. Who would ever guess that foreign diplomats, political leaders, education leaders and even a member of the President's cabinet stood on this little hill to say good-bye to my friend?

Last night at Declo High School's commencement program I spoke about him and my senior year. I tried to tell those assembled what my friend would say had he still been here.

He would say, "No matter what the cost," he would pause, and let this sink in, "capture and live The Pristine American Dream."

Sometimes when I talk about The Pristine American Dream I feel like I did when I poured milk from a bucket into a calf bottle; most of the milk spilling over the sides being wasted. Last night it was different. Last night it felt like I was leisurely pouring into a wide-mouthed milk strainer. The graduates and their families sat enthralled by my story of how The Pristine American Dream wove its strong, gentle cords into the fiber of my young soul. At times they laughed and cried; other times they sat white-knuckled, gripping their chairs in suspense. The best part was teaching about The Pristine American Dream, and I saw understanding in their eyes as they nodded slowly. I wanted them to like my speech, of course, but what I really wanted most of all was for them to catch The Dream.

Afterward, while the graduates lined up shaking hands, back-pounding and kissing relatives, a line formed in front of me too. There were some I didn't know, new move-ins I assumed, but mostly they were old friends, neighbors, and old high school teachers, one of whom was Mrs. Moncur, the most dazzling reading teacher I have ever known.

"Jon, have you ever written that story down?" she asked. "It is really quite good, and the principles are powerful. I wish I had a copy of that story for my classes to read."

I blushed at her complimentary request.

"Please consider writing it. Would you?" She reached out and touched my arm. "Please."

It wasn't the first time that request had been made. I squatted down on my haunches in front of the polished granite and traced the deeply grooved lettering with my finger, UR BABIRASKI. What an odd name.

Ur had requested almost the same thing as Mrs. Moncur. "Jon, write your experience down so others can learn from it."

A morning mosquito was messing with my eyebrow. I slapped at it and felt the old scar and remembered the hard-muscled terrorist that had laid my eye open almost 30 years ago. Had I killed him with that rock, or had the Israeli Army killed him the morning of the attack? I never found out.

A screen door slapped shut in the distant early morning stillness. Looking toward the sound across the highway, railroad tracks and canal, I saw Mr. Johnson, now hunched with age, carrying a milk bucket to the barn. I used to do that. In fact, it was on that same farm my muscles grew into hard ropes of knotted steel as Mr. Johnson worked me in the fields and on the workout bench. I watched him until he disappeared into the sagging, faded red barn. A twist of nostalgia stuck in my stomach.

Maybe it is time to write it. What have I got to do today anyway? My family is all back in Virginia, and Mary doesn't expect me until tonight. I can't write it all today, but I can remember it and write down some notes. I looked at the sky. It was going to be a beautiful day, not too hot, and miraculously little wind. I remembered seeing an electric outlet in the pavilion at the city park where they celebrate Declo Days. Why not, I thought, as I drove purposely to the small grassy park where an old church once stood. I set up my laptop computer. I mused for a minute on how to start, and then I began the story.

When I introduce myself, I say, "I am from Declo, Idaho," but that isn't exactly correct. I would do better to say, "I am Declo." I am the sum of the community that raised me. I am its values, its dreams and its disappointments. Declo is like America. America is mostly made up of small towns, not sprawling urban centers. In these small towns people live the great scenario of life. Each town has its own unique culture filled with its own unique people, its own unique batch of heroes, villains and bystanders. For the most part these people live their lives in a swirl of small town gossip, adventure and romance, tragedy, drama, anguish and secrets. Their lives are filled with "Did you hear?" or "I can't believe … !" The landscape is sketched, drawn and painted with birth and death, marriage and divorce, health and sickness, fear, faith and affection. They laugh, cheer, celebrate, clap, tickle and hug. Each town is a microcosm of the whole world, but to those who live there, it is their whole world.

# CHAPTER 1

## I Have a Right to Prevent Dents in My Life

My outfit was a piece of junk! I mean my car, not my clothes. In Declo, everything driven is an outfit, regardless if it is a tractor, car, pickup or bicycle. Anyway, my outfit was ugly enough to make a train take a dirt road! It was dented, dirty and smelly. I hated to drive it…in fact I'd rather use my boss's pickup to take Moose on dates, if I ever should ask her, than my car. I'm not saying Moose would complain if I used my car. No, she is not that kind of a girl. She would smile just the same perfect smile and sit the same perfect sit while lumping along in my old beat-up outfit. She wouldn't show her discomfort, but mine would be as obvious as a red potato.

My car hadn't always been so ugly a wrecker would refuse to get near it. Actually, when I first bought it, it was beautiful. Oh, it wasn't as beautiful as a new Mustang or an SS 396 Chevelle, but it was beautiful to me. It was a 1963, lime-green Plymouth, four-door with a three-on-the-tree and 226-cubic-inch engine.

I loved people to see me in it. I washed and waxed it nearly every day. I even went out and bought one of those smelly trees to hang on a knob so when Moose was riding with me, if she ever did, she wouldn't have to smell me; she could smell the tree. It had a heater and a loud AM radio. Sometimes I would pull my outfit out on the grass, roll the windows down, turn the front wheels to the left and then just admire how much it looked like the cars advertised in Hot Rod

Magazine. I knew it wasn't Hot Rod quality, but I liked to imagine it was just the same. It doesn't cost anything to imagine.

That was over a year ago and a lot can happen to a car in a year. The beauty of my car started caving in with its first dent 38 days after I bought it. I know it was 38 days because, I remember Fred shouting, "Little-brother, you are dumber than a crow-bar!" He quickly counted on his fingers. "You ain't had that car 38 days and you already wrecked it!"

I decided to let my Moose chasing rest for a weekend and call a girl named Patsy. I met her while dragging main in Burley with my worthless best friend Kenny. I always wanted to date a Burley woman, and since Patsy was from Burley I decided to ask her. I was new at dating then and wanted all the cards stacked in my favor before I asked her out. I remembered seeing a new invention that would probably give me the edge I needed. It was next to the Frosty Freeze hamburger joint down where Overland Avenue crossed the Snake River. It was a telephone that didn't have a booth. You just drove right up to it, rolled down your window and from the comfort and convenience of your own climate-controlled vehicle you could talk on the phone. I decided to use that exceptional phone for this exceptional phone call. I figured the phone would give me the needed advantage to hook up with Patsy.

I gathered my courage like spuds into a 100-pound sack and dialed her number from my car. I laughed while the phone rang because I was actually talking on a phone from my outfit! When she answered, I reminded her of who I was and why it would be in her best interest to accompany me to the Burley Drive-in on Friday. With only the slightest bit of hesitation, she accepted my invite.

Never in my life had a date come so quickly. My little guy-heart was flip-flopping faster than a bucket of live trout. Pitching the phone back into its cradle, I slammed the clutch to the floor and jerked the shifter into first gear and ... The inventor of the phone had put a guardrail to protect the phone from romantic aficionados like me. I cranked the steering wheel left and popped the clutch, catching the end of the guardrail in the middle of my back door. The noise of metal grinding on metal was startling and threw my brain, which was already suffering from romantic overload, into a 50-mile-per-hour jackknife. I knew every cool kid sitting at the Frosty Freeze was gawking at me.

You know how when you do a dumb thing in public it is important to follow up as quickly as possible with another dumb thing to draw their attention away from the first dumb thing. So instead of stopping and backing up, I floor-boarded my car. The screaming metal was so loud it drowned out truck horns. After the guardrail had drug itself down my fender and past my tail light, the screeching stopped. Then I did what I always did when I did something stupid—I pretended nothing happened.

I drove the entire nine miles to Declo without stopping to look at the damage; in fact, by the time I got home I had convinced myself I had not done that dumb thing. So convinced was I that when I got out of my car, I averted my eyes away from my rear fender and walked straight to my front door. Just before entering my house, I glanced back to look and be sure. But I had done it and the fender was mangled and scraped from the middle of the back door to the tail light.

Bellowing in rage I rushed at my car formulating a plan on the fly. I jerked open the trunk and dug under my diddy bag, hay chaps, desert water bag and found my heavy hydraulic jack. In my mind I could see me swinging the heavy hydraulic jack from inside of the trunk against the inside of the fender. I could see the fender popping out and repainting itself. After swinging the jack a dozen times I collapsed in exhaustion. Then I surveyed the repair job. Not only had I not improved the dent, but the sharp corner of the jack's base had made pokey-outie places all over the fender.

From that moment on, I treated my car differently. Where I used to wash and wax it all over, now I just washed and waxed the good side of my car and only hosed off the dented side I was ashamed of that side of my car and tried to hide it from public view. When I parked my outfit, I tried to find a bush or something to hide the bad side. In those days when picking up your date, you always let her in on the driver's side to let her slide across the bench seat, hoping maybe she would get tired about half way across and stop. Then if your hand needed holding, she would be in the neighborhood. But since I was ashamed of that part of my car, I had to let my dates in on the passenger side and then slam the door with the velocity of a spring-loaded barn door, hoping the concussion would drive her over to the middle of the seat. A lot of things got treated different as I tried to hide that part of my car.

The second dent happened as my buddies, Kenny, Sam, Randy, Clyde, Bull of the Woods and I were driving on a black-gravel road one night. The jack-rabbits were thicker than maggots on road-kill. We got crazy and started driving faster and faster, swerving this way and that way at rabbits. I think the rabbits had a plan because they led us into a T-intersection at 70 miles per hour. I jumped on the brakes like a suicide-jockey in a run-away 18-wheeler. We slid through the intersection screaming like first graders at a monster movie and slammed into the borrow-pit on the other side of the road. After getting the outfit out of the ditch, Bull of the Woods said, "Gees, Jon, you dented the good side of your outfit."

I now had a dent on both sides of my car! From that moment on I treated my outfit differently. I didn't spend much money on Turtle Wax after that. If it got dirty, I would just squirt it with the hose or wait for the wind to blow it off, which in Idaho is only about ten minutes.

The car inside's was still in pretty good shape, but even that didn't last long. I had finally secured a date with Moose. Unlike most guys, I had planned the date. I took her to see *Lawrence of Arabia* at the Wilson Theater in Rupert, which lasted longer than the seven-year itch. Then I hauled her over to the Frosty Freeze and fed her. By then it was about 11:30 and I was still intent on getting in the last planned activity of the evening.

Fred told me about a place on the north side of the Snake River in the Big Bend area past the Boon Docks called Lovers Leap. He said the road goes straight for about four miles and crosses a lateral canal. At this point he made his hand swoop up and over the imaginary canal. He explained that if you go over that canal at about 40 miles per hour, it gives you a ticklely feeling in your stomach, like you feel when you are in love. Before taking Moose home, I wanted to share that special feeling with her.

I got my outfit lined up on the right road alright and stopped about two miles short of the canal. Since cars didn't come with seat belts and since I had always been a safety-conscious driver, I installed one seat belt in my car. And since that seat belt happened to be where I was sitting, I went ahead and snapped it on. I glanced at Moose, feeling bad about her not having a seat belt. But I had heard a song once about this guy who got in a real bad crash and his girl friend was all mashed up. He held her in his arms and sang to her while waiting for an ambulance. I figured if we crashed and Moose got mashed up, at least I would be available to do some singing if necessary.

I started the car forward, shifting smoothly, and brought the speed up to 40. The thought occurred to me: If that hill feels good at 40 … imagine how good it will feel at 70! I floored-boarded my outfit. We hit the base of the lateral canal at an even 70. The whole car sagged under the G-force of the climb. When we rounded the top, everything went weightless. In fact, everything including Moose went screaming into the roof of the car.

Back in those days the girls wore their hair different. They would grow it long and then back-comb it or tease it. They did this until it looked pretty mad. Because of the amount of hair spray needed to control their hair, most girls had a sprayer you had to start with a rope. It would pump about 20 gallons of hair spray a minute. Consequently, it only took them maybe five minutes to get the hair all sculpted into something looking like the abdomen of a cat-face spider.

When their hair dried, it was solid as a lump of lava. It wouldn't move! You could go down the road at 80 miles per hour, roll the window down, and stick their head out. You could kill wildlife and knock down fence posts, but nothing would move their hair. You can stand them up in the back of a pickup and go under real low overpasses. Big chunks of cement and rebar would tear from the overpass, but you won't move their hair …. And at dances, after twisting hard to Chubby Checker, something slow would come on, like Andy Williams's *Moon River*. You would bring her in close. First thing you had to do was fight your way through the fumes to get to her hair-stack. Then you placed your sweating cheek down on her hair. The sweat and the hair spray would mix and when they dried there was an adhesive effect. You could actually become glued to your date's head.

Moose had one of those hair styles on when she took on the appearance of a smashed bug in the interior of my outfit. As she was launched from the seat, her knee hit my radio knob and snapped it clean off, cutting her knee. She hit the roof so hard she grunted and her hair-stack actually became a flattop. I was afraid it was going to break her hair right off. As she and me talked about this later I told her I felt bad about her knee and sore neck and all, but they would heal and that knob

9

was broken off forever! After that every time I didn't listen to my radio I thought about Moose and felt she had been careless

I had damaged the interior of my outfit and from that moment on I treated it differently. This was the first damage to the interior of my car, but it wouldn't be the last.

During the summer, my buddies and I were riding around on a Saturday afternoon. We knew all the girls were over at the baseball diamond behind the church messing around. We were trying to think of some way we could show them how much we loved them. Finally Clyde, while digging into his pocket, brought out his big string of Black Cat firecrackers. We decided to drive over past the ball diamond, light off the string and throw the whole thing at the girls. The plan was simple: Randy would light the firecrackers and Clyde would throw the exploding string out the window as we passed. Looking at it later, we thought Clyde probably should have rolled his window down before Randy lit the firecrackers.

It was almost worth the whole painful experience just to see Clyde's face when he realized he had not rolled his window down and the fuse was dissolving faster than shoestring licorice at the movies. He had a look on his face that could only be captured in a cartoon. Suffering from serious brain-freeze, he followed through with what he planned. He tossed the firecrackers at the window anyway and then squished his face up in horror as they bounced back on his lap. Two or three of the tiny incendiary devices went off in his lap before he could move. I think humans scream different when things like that happen to them.

If you ignite one firecracker in a car, it just about blows your ears off, but if you let off a string of twenty it also has the potential of removing your eyebrows and most of your teeth at the same time. You should have seen all of us trying to get out of my car at 40 miles per hour. My outfit had little flowered burn marks all over its interior.

In about a year's time, my outfit had become a piece of junk. I now treated it different from when I first bought it. Now I didn't wash it or wax it. I never greased it or changed the oil. I'm not sure it even had oil, I never looked to see. I would take it out to change the irrigation water and then just throw my shovel onto the back seat. I went banging out through the sage brush and lava beds in it, not caring what happened to my car. You could say I just didn't respect it anymore.

Looking back on it now...I guess in some ways my life was like my outfit or my outfit was like my life, depending on which view you took. I could remember when my life seemed cleaner, happier, and more beautiful—more together, especially before Dad died and Dean left.

Now it seemed like everything was coming apart. I reminded myself of a three-legged dog—going someplace, but looking awkward and disjointed, never quite feeling all-together. The dings and dents of life had taken their toll on me, and I couldn't see any way to straighten things out. I knew I could take my car to a body and fender repair shop and they would restore it, but how does one restore his life? How does one take out the careless dents, the self-inflicted dents, or especially the dents pounded in by mean people? I guess the most important question I was wrestling with was how do I keep the dents out?

Like the dents in my outfit, there were things about me I was hiding from public view; things I was ashamed of or had convinced myself had never happened. I'm not sure I knew then, but now I can see those things were like rocks in my pockets: not really visible, but obvious to everyone. The rocks were always there slowing me down while causing distraction and discouragement with their extra weight. I don't know what would have happened to me if Ur hadn't moved into Declo and into my life that fall.

We have staked the whole future of American civilization, not upon the power of government, far from it. We have staked the future of all of our political institutions upon the capacity of mankind for self-government; upon the capacity of each and all of us to govern ourselves, to control ourselves, to sustain ourselves according to the Ten Commandments of God.

James Madison ~June 20, 1785

# CHAPTER 2

## I Have a Right to Do Good

September 1966

Declo was a small town. Its graveled streets lay on the insignificant intersection of U.S. Highway 30 and State Road 77. This intersection connects Declo to Albion on the south, Rupert on the north, Burley on the west and Malta on the east. On the north side of Highway 30 at the city limits there was a highway sign near an irrigation canal that said "Burley 9 miles," and across the same road to the south side was a green and white "Entering Declo" sign that said "Pop. 262." Two flashing lights hung on two thin cables in the middle of two rough intersections. The lights flashed red one direction and yellow the other. Two grocery stores fed the town while two gas stations fueled it. It had one bar and twice that many churches. I guess to most people driving under our flashing traffic lights Declo seemed a pretty ordinary place, but to those of us who lived there it was everything.

We only knew two famous people who came from Declo: the billionaire J.R. Simplot and a famous jockey named Vosco Parke. Once during study hall I busied myself in a world Atlas and discovered there is only one Declo in the whole world. From that moment on I always thought Declo was a pretty special place, even though there are different opinions as to how Declo got its name. Some say it was supposed to be Delco, but was spelled wrong on the Town Charter. Others say the name Declo came from the names of the first five men who came to the Post

Office for their mail: D-Dethlef, E-Enyert, C-Clark, L-Lewis, O-Osterhout.

Declo did have one other thing nobody else in the whole world had: the actual train car in which the purported mummified body of John Wilkes Booth was exhibited as it traveled around the U.S. The old Pullman car made its last stop behind the Novosel-Mackie house, where it remained as a storage shed.

I was a senior at Declo High School, the home of the mighty stinging Hornets. I liked school—I really did. I wasn't a good student, but I liked it anyway. I think the one thing that kept me in school, other than the girls, was my teachers.

Take Mr. Musser for example. He was a slight man from Tennessee with a masters'degree in History. His skin was leathery and he complained he smoked too much. He had a great laugh that started deep and sounded like gravel swishing around in the bottom of a tin bucket. I knew he liked me because he teased me during class. After I did poorly on a history test, he pulled off his glasses and point them at me saying, "Jon, you bonehead. Didn't you study?"

"I lost my study sheet," I said innocently.

"Well, I'm going to personally see that you are kicked out of school if you don't do better on the next test."

"You'll be doing better than me if you do, 'cause I've been trying to get kicked out of school since I was six years old."

He laughed, put his glasses back on his thin face and scratch his head. "Then I'll make sure you never get out of here."

He had a great way of making me feel like a worthwhile person even if I wasn't a worthwhile student.

Another great teacher was Mrs. Moncur. First of all, she was dang good-looking, but even more important was she making everyone feel great when they were around her, even those of us who were dumber than a box of rocks.

Mr. Coltrin, our English teacher, had been a fighter pilot who flew F-104s. He came to Declo during my sophomore year, bought a farm and then took up teaching to support it. On the second day of class I got caught talking.

"Rhoades," he said in perfect military sternness, "bring your desk up here next to mine, turn it around to face the class and sit."

I did, and for the next three years that is where I sat every day for English. After the first day or two I knew I didn't have to stay there, but I liked being the wingman for this fighter jock. It made me feel important to sit next to him. It was like we were a team working together to educate those other numb-numbs in English. Once again, he was able to separate my lack of academic diligence from who I really was.

Probably the most colorful teacher was the math teacher, Mr. Turner, a big, raw-boned farmer who rarely showed his anger. If a student screwed up really bad in his class, he calmly said with a smile, "All right, you have a choice. You can come up here and take a few whacks from the 'board of education,' or you can do two extra hours of homework tonight."

We never thought it was in our best interest to get over-educated, so we usually opted for the board of education. Funny, how we felt he cared because he whacked us. There were so many other teachers who cared for us: Coach Chugg, Coach Wilson, Mr. Martin, and Mrs. Chrisman. All of them just seemed to like kids, and teaching in general. Yes, I did like school, even though I was not academically gifted by any stretch of the imagination.

We were a small community, lying in the farming patchwork along the Snake River. I, with about a hundred other students, competed daily for the best back-row desks to sit in before leaving to milk the cows and do the other farm chores necessary to keep parents and employers happy. Our graduating class had 28 students, 20 boys and 8 girls. It was a good thing there were lots of girls in the other grades. If not, two or three boys would have to take the same girl to the prom.

The best job I could think of after graduation, if I graduated, was working in the potato-processing plants the rest of my life. I would get married and have a kid or two, buy a TV, a new hunting rifle, and get a big belly before I died. I knew there must be something out there better, but I didn't know what it was or how to get it. I felt vulnerable to outside influences and powerless to do anything about my life. My course was set, and I was sure nothing would change the obvious destiny of my life—that is, until I met Ur.

The Vietnam War was in full swing, and the Beatles, Beach Boys, and muscle cars were red-hot in Declo. Kids gathered nightly at

15

Minn's Café to drink iron-ports, cherry cokes, milkshakes and eat fries with homemade fry sauce while talking about whom or whatever. I was as average as a telephone pole, and like most guys I wanted the cool things: a nicer car, chicks noticing me, and Moose's hand intertwined with mine.

Today it seems simple, but back then it seemed harder than giving a cat a bath. I didn't seem to feel happy, I mean the in-control, peaceful happiness we all crave. My home wasn't perfect either. My mom was a single parent who struggled to make ends meet.

I guess I wanted what I saw on the TV: dinner served by perfect moms and dads who laughed when their sons messed up and always taught some moral solution to a problem. I wanted a "Leave It To Beaver" life, where everybody was happy and confident and no one was embarrassed of their mom and dad, or scared to bring friends home in fear that their brother might make crude sounds in his armpit at the dinner table. Everything on TV looked good to me, everything except the war in Vietnam. My brother Dean was in Vietnam, but he seemed a long way off, and I didn't feel very close to Fred, my other brother.

That night I had other things to worry about, like the cutest Moose in the world. She had scratched a message on notebook paper, ripped it out of the wire-spiral and stuffed it in my locker. (We didn't have locks on our lockers. We figured who in their right mind would steal schoolbooks? What were they going to do read them?) Scrawled between the light blue lines was a heart-stopping invitation for me to come over and watch *The Wizard of Oz* with her—tonight!

Her family just bought one of the first color televisions in Declo... Okay, let me backtrack here. Her real name wasn't Moose—it was Judy, but Moose is what everybody called her. The name Moose (I know what you're thinking) made no reference to her size, her nose or excessive facial hair; she was a cute little cheerleader. Of course, with so few girls in our school everyone was a cheerleader. Her big brother Kenny, one of my best friends, while teaching their little brother how to talk, told him Judy's name was Moose and after that it just stuck. Anyway, she had perfect hair, perfect teeth, and was cuter than a bug's ear as they say!

In those days, all we had were black and white TVs, so none of us had ever really seen what color the horse-of-a different-color was in the movie *The Wizard of Oz*. It was coming on TV and Moose invited me over to watch it with her. I was as excited as a birthday boy not only to see what color the horse really was, but even more so over the possibility of holding Moose's hand. She and I had dated a couple of times, but I was too scared to touch her. I always felt too big and goofy to ever hold her delicate little hand.

Because my car was nearly out of gas, I walked the mile to Mr. Johnson's farm where I worked every day before and after school. While I walked, I thought about Moose, the color TV, and her delicate hand. The birds seemed to be singing twice as loud, with chirps filled with double the usual happiness.

Mr. Johnson was in his early thirties, lean and well muscled. He stood 6'2" with dark hair circling an otherwise bald head. He had a wonderful blend of gentleness and a dynamic personality that commanded respect. His shy darting eyes always reminded me of Mayberry's Sheriff, Andy Griffith. He and his wife had a few young children, and both of them were active in the community and the schools. It was well known they had contributed heavily to every program needing money.

I felt lucky to have a job working for him. His wife had beauty that went all the way to the bone. She was a wonderful lady who always treated me with kindness by listening to me yap about my life, and by inviting me to eat supper with them. She cooked farm style with tons of meat and spuds, and every dinner ended with a dessert that tasted good for three days.

It was one of those smooth and wonderful fall late afternoons when the third cutting of alfalfa hay spread a sweet aroma all over the countryside and the stillness was so perfect you could hear a hammer strike an anvil three miles away.

Looking east and west from Declo, the country is so flat if you stand on your tippy-toes you can see the back of your head. To the south are the hills with Mount Harrison standing behind them like a sentinel. To the north in the blue distance, far across the desolate lava beds, rise the ragged razor peaks of the Sawtooth Mountains.

Walking west, I crossed one of the many canals where the fishy smell of the diverted Snake River wafted up to me; its quiet mass journeying toward the thirsty soil of many surrounding farms. I could see the gigantic cooperative grain elevator silhouetted against the golden evening horizon nine miles away in Burley. I loved this sight. It looked like a great packet ship sitting at anchor in the Snake River. The whole taste of the evening filled me with the rapture of hope. Yes, something was going to change in my life; something wonderful and good was going to happen to me…soon.

I couldn't think of anything that could possibly happen in Declo or especially to me except the wonderful possibility of holding Moose's hand.

Somewhere along the road I started humming. Soon my happiness was too big to be contained in a hum so seemingly without my permission I burst forth with singing *I Want to Hold Your Hand* by the Beatles. When all alone on a rural road in southern Idaho, you tend to think bigger and sing louder than you normally should. Without really even knowing it, I was singing at the top of my lungs and taking particular pleasure in the part where the Beatles hit that really high "Ooooooo."

As I got closer to the farm, I saw Mr. Johnson come running out of the shed as though he'd been stuck in his Dickies with a pitch fork. He saw me, stopped dead in his tracks, and stared.

"Wha-da-ya doin'?" he finally asked with profound curiosity.

I walked to where he stood riveted. I looked back at him with a face just as bewildered. "I'm sing…ing." My voice kind of trailed off at the end like a used-up whoopee-cushion. I realized I probably just said the stupidest thing I could possibly could say considering the circumstances surrounding the question.

Mr. Johnson continued to stare. I felt his shy, gray eyes search every part of me in disbelief. He was quiet a long time, so quiet I heard a cow cough up a cud in the corral and a humming bird zing by on flower poking duty somewhere. I felt weak and realized I wasn't breathing; the only thing moving was a young heart and an old heart both trying to figure out the other.

He finally said, "You were singing, huh? Thought someone had got himself caught in a hay baler. I think you'd better hold it down a little 'cause you might make the cows go dry."

Some old farmers thought that if cows heard something really loud or scary, they would stop giving milk. I tried to say I was sorry, but he abruptly shook his head in amazement, spun on his gumboots, and said over his shoulder, "Let's get to work."

My job was milking Mr. Johnson's cow by hand. It would have been a simple process if you didn't have to include the cow. Bessie (that was the cow's name), like every other girl (cows, dogs, humans or horses—it didn't much matter), was shy of me. That may sound strange, but it was true. Bessie would stand perfectly still in the pasture, ignoring me while I stealthily walked around behind her. She always waited patiently, lost in some cow dream, until I was almost in position, and then she tore off through the pasture like a Holstein dragster. She would run to the complete other side of the pasture, stop, turn around, and look all innocent like she didn't do anything. Now Mr. Johnson, he could go out and stand in the barn door and shout, "ca-Bess, ca-Bess, ca-Bess!" and the old girl would just come running, kicking her large udder from side to side.

On this day, probably because I was in a hurry, she was more impossible to get into the barn than ever before. When I walked up to her, she gave me a disappointed look like she had heard my singing too and kind of hoped I really was caught in a hay baler. Then faster than greased lightning, she bolted and I gave chase, yelling, "We'll see how fast you move on a hamburger bun, you old heifer!" By the time I finally got her into the barn with her head and neck locked between the sliding slats of the stanchion, I was really running late. Not only that, but because the recent rain had turned everything into sludge, she was extra messy. It took an extra 10 minutes to clean off her udder before I could start milking.

Mrs. Johnson had sweetly asked me three days in a row not to let Bessie ruin the milk. Yet, for the past three days, every time I was just about finished milking, Bessie would kick the bucket and send milk spraying everywhere, and no matter where I sat, I always got drenched. I would rage and kick the wall and scream things like "Rump roast," or "T-bone," or "double cheeseburger!" right into her ear. It didn't do any good, though; her passive cow face would hardly glance at me as she calmly continued to chew her grain.

Today I had to get milk to the Johnsons and I had to get home in time to change before going over to Moose's house. I put two sets of hobbles on her and tightened them down so tight her hooves turned blue.

"There, you filthy old hay burner, see if you can kick today!" I triumphantly yelled. I milked like a madman for 15 minutes while watching her hooves for any sign of attack. When I had almost filled the bucket to the top, I slowed to a daydream speed. In the rhythm of the splosh, splosh, splosh, I forgot everything about the killer cow. I slowly let my mind go back to thoughts of Moose and became lost in the potentiality of holding her hand. I even caught myself starting to hum again, and then a cold sweat of warning stopped me.

In this moment of weakness I let down my guard, and Bessie, with the instinct of a weasel, sensed it immediately. Just as the milk foam was about to reach the rim and I was once again about to make my move on Moose's hand, Bessie's left rear hoof jerked, and in a mighty leap it landed smack-dab in the middle of the bucket. The pure white milk swirled around the manure-crusted hoof like wind-blown trash.

Everything in the barn world froze as I stared at the green and brown floaties in the milk. It was only the steel cables of unparalleled discipline that kept me from hitting her with my 90 mile-per-hour whack, which would have been fatal (to whom I'm not sure). Finally, when the barn world thawed, I removed the hobbles and carefully grabbed her hoof with both hands and lifted it out of the bucket. Snatching the bucket, I sprinted to the closest beam of sunlight forcing itself through a dull, fly-specked window. The bucket was still mostly full, but a thin layer of floating manure, old hay, and mud skimmed the top. I had been saving a good tizzy to use on my brother Fred someday, but I decided to go ahead and use it on the cow. I set the bucket down and turned on Bessie. It was time for a showdown! It was going to be either the beef or me. It couldn't be both. Somebody had to be boss.

I looked her right in the eye, and then I looked in her other eye, since cow eyes are so far apart, and yelled in a voice quivering with righteous rage, "All right, Old Bessie, BRING IT ON!"

She stared right back and snorted. She had the confidence of Cassius Clay. She felt she could whip me with one tail tied behind her back. As I took an aggressive step toward her, she tossed her head from side to side in the stanchion and mooed so loud I almost wet my pants. I stumbled backward nearly kicking over the remaining milk before falling over my milking stool. Raging in blind, white-hot fury, I shouted, "I'm gonna make about 800 pounds of beef bouillon out of you!" I charged her, swinging with my right fist at her broad side.

Cows are really strange-looking creatures when you think about it. Just in front of the hind leg is the flank, a nice soft place to slug errant cows. In the fuzzy blur of wrath I intended to hit her in the nice soft place, but right above the flank is the hip bone, a big hard round bone about the size of a soccer ball. That is where my right-handed 90-mile-an-hour whack hit. Have you ever heard a cow laugh? Me neither, until that moment. I launched into more descriptions of dead cows and stood vigorously shaking my hand and blowing on my burning knuckles. Meanwhile, Bessie watched me with a look more pleased than a sunflower at sunrise.

I dejectedly turned to stare at the milk bucket and ponder my upcoming position as an unemployed cow fighter, when I saw the milk strainer. It sat atop the milk can in the corner where the sun was hitting it. There it shone like silver salvation to the damned. I figured if I ran the milk through the strainer pad twice, then maybe nobody would notice. I reasoned nobody actually tastes milk as they drink it anyway. It's not until it's down the hatch the taste arrives. They'd probably put it on cereal or use it in cooking. Thoughts did cross my mind that the children might get some bad cow disease or maybe some sickness from the corral, like what the chickens had that caused their feathers to fall off, but I quickly dismissed these as unnecessary details. Especially since the children didn't have feathers.

I believed in simplicity, and sickness was way too complicated for my mind, so I thought of happy thoughts, like keeping my job and having money to buy nice things for Moose. I thought of other nice things too, like gas for my car so Moose would hold my hand as we just drove around. Then I realized it was getting really late and I still needed to get changed before going to watch *The Wizard of Oz*. This was the deciding factor. I strained the milk twice, dabbed on the Bag Balm, let the cow out, and rushed the milk into the house.

The little Johnson kids were all at the dinner table. They looked at me the same way they always had. It is the look all little kids use when they gaze upon high school kids. It is a look of magnificent incomprehension. They see high school kids as free citizens who can go and come and do all of the really cool things, like, drive a car or go get a milkshake anytime they want. I was suddenly struck with a guilty feeling for the thing that I was doing to them. Tomorrow morning after the milk cooled, Mrs. Johnson would skim off the cream and give it to Mr. Johnson so he could put it on his hot mush. I thought it might be funny to see his expression if he ever found out what had been standing in his cream. I shook my head and thought, poor little kids. I wavered for a moment but then told myself, "No! I must focus on holding the beautiful little Moose hand."

THE PRISTINE AMERICAN DREAM

# CHAPTER 3

## I Have a Right to Laugh at Myself

W hile running home I took a short cut through Old Man Owen's garden. He didn't like kids running through his garden and was always threatening to call the cops on someone. Feeling reckless and since I didn't see him around I decided to go for it, but I didn't even get half-way through the pea patch before he appeared from between two rows of corn and yelled, "Hey, You!"

I froze. He took a direct line toward me while stepping carefully between the rows of peas and carrots, all the time yelling about calling the cops, which in Declo was an impossibility since we didn't have any. I decided I had two options. One, tell him that I had to go to the bathroom and that I really couldn't hold it so I cut across his garden to get home quicker. Two, tell him the truth; that I was late to see *The Wizard of Oz* on Moose's new color TV.

Since I had been anything but honest back at the Johnsons' and since Old Man Owen was once a young man himself, I opted for the latter and tried to tell him the truth. I got out the part about *The Wizard of Oz* just fine, but he cut me off when I mentioned the part about the color TV.

"Did you say you'll watch *The Wizard of Oz* in color?"

I replied, "I hope to, yes."

Rubbing his chin and staring at a cabbage ball near his boot, he said, "You know, I've always wondered what color that horse-of-a-different-color might be. I've always thought of it as kind of a mix between a nice, light peach and a teal myself, but my wife is convinced that it's more like a reddish-brown with a yellow mane. Or was that a green mane? Oh well, there she is. Let's ask her."

At this point his wife was stepping out the back door. He yelled over to her, "Hey, Gerti, what color did you say that horse-of-a-different-color is on the *Oz* show again?"

She yelled back, "It's a burgundy marble with an orange mane, I'm just sure of it."

About this time from over a sagging barbed-wire fence, their neighbor Julian Engstrom overheard her answer and yelled out as he pushed the top barbed-wire of the fence down with his shovel handle and swung a leg over, "Oh, no it's not!" He roared in pious defiance, his wild red hair struggling from under a faded red, sweat-stained I-H ball cap. "It's straw-colored with a purple tail."

"Good grief!" I thought. What ensued was a lengthy debate where I'm sure every color scheme known to man was mentioned twice. After about five minutes of trying to sneak away, I began wishing that Old Man Owen had in fact called the police. That way I could have been charged, hauled off to jail, done my time and maybe still made it to see the last five minutes of *The Wizard* in living color.

After what seemed like a year and a half, Old Man Owen stopped in mid-sentence and looked at me with a blank expression, as if there was something he had started to do but couldn't put his finger on it right then. Finally it came to him like an errant dog and he lit into me like 40 biting-sows about respecting other people's property and all of the other junk adults yell at kids when they can't think of anything new to lay at the little sinners' feet.

After five minutes of hard-core tongue lashing, he turned away and started talking to his wife and Julian about how kids just aren't like they used to be. I finally had my fill. I knew if I didn't break away then I never would. I ducked my head and made a break for it, expecting any minute to be called back, but no call ever came. In fact, I don't even think they missed me.

Flinging open the door at home I realized I was a good 15 minutes late already, and to make matters worse my brother Fred was in a chatty mood. He said, "Thought you were going to go see that color TV at Moose's house."

"I am," I mumbled.

"Better hurry, little brother, or you'll miss the horse part and..."

I just glared at him.

"What...you little twerp!" he snarled.

I walked to my room grabbing and sniffing shirts looking for a clean one. In a manic minute I was dress and charging out the back door to avoid Fred. I made the four block drive faster than cheetah while trying to groom my hair with a rat-tail comb.

At Moose's door I composed myself and tried to lift half of my face in a movie star grin, checked both pits just in case and knocked. Through the gauzy curtain her delicate features were silhouetted against the back-light of the living room. My heart started thumping slowly like a locomotive just starting out and gained momentum with every step she took, until it felt like a mile-long Union Pacific was running around inside of me blowing his whistle and ringing his bell. The door swung open and so did my mouth. The light from her living room seemed to cling to her, and her smile filled the entire doorframe. I blew a little air out and said, "Hi."

"Come on in, you're late. You've just about missed all the black and white part," she teased.

To be honest, at that point I could have cared less about any part. She had her hair all stacked on her head in a really far-out way with a pencil stuck through it. Turning she led the way to the color TV. I'd never really looked at the back of a girl's neck before, so I figured hers was a pretty good one to start with. It wasn't all hairy like Fred's. She walked ahead of me in bare feet with red toenails that glowed like hot coals against the brown carpet.

She led me into her living room and then went to get me a drink. *The Wizard of Oz* was on, but I found myself looking around the room instead. A standard assortment of family pictures were plastered on the wall—you know, the kind that you would die if anybody ever saw, but your mother loves, so she sticks you up on the wall as a one-year-old taking a bath, naked as a jaybird.

There were a few of Moose as a young girl riding her bike and another one of her camping and then a more recent one of her in her cheerleading outfit. I admired this one for a long time before noticing something out of the corner of my eye that froze me. Right above the mantle was a life-sized portrait of her father and mother. Her mother had a smile as pleasant as a sleeping cat, but her father had a glare that would freeze used motor oil on the Fourth of July. His eyes bore into me and seemed to say, "There'll be no hand holding tonight!" I tried to ignore him and look at other pictures, but his glare followed me all around the room like a bad cold. I finally stopped looking around, flopped myself onto the couch and tried to concentrate on the TV.

Moose startled me when she re-entered the room carrying something to drink. She put two glasses of punch on the mahogany coffee table and sat on the couch just far enough away to keep me guessing. The couch was one of those old davenport things from the 1950's. All the springs were blown out in the middle, probably from jumping on it, which made it so people just kind of slid together when they sat down. It was the kind of couch that was your worst nightmare during family reunions when you're forced to sit by Aunt Bertha or Uncle Lenny. I took a peek at her old man and was grateful I wasn't sitting by him.

I grinned when I thought of her dad and his football buddies trying to watch the Green Bay Packers on their new color TV while sitting on the couch. Four tons of football fanatics sweating and struggling to grab onto the armrests or whatever in an effort not to touch each other. What would have to be Hades for her dad was heaven for me.

Before the first commercial Moose and I were pleasantly supporting one another like two poles in a teepee. About this time a little flame of possibility sprung to life. Everything was present to make it possible to hold her hand. She had a hand and so did I and we were sitting close enough to make it happen. The possibility continued to expand like a hot air balloon in a Volkswagen until I could not think of anything else. I wanted to hold her hand and I wanted to hold it tonight

My brother Fred told me once while we were stacking hay exactly how hand holding was done.

"It's an art," he declared with air of a college professor. He went on to explained that there is an international sign used my men and women alike that signals, I want to hold your hand. I sat the hay bale down and wished I had brought something to take notes with.

I sucked in some air, tightened my jaw and got to work on some hand holding. I scratched my left thigh, pretending it itched, and then left my hand sitting there just like Fred said so that if Moose wanted to hold it, it would be available. After the next commercial she pretended her right thigh itched, and left her hand sitting within maybe four inches of my hand. The train, which had slowed down considerably after discovering her father's death stare, began to speed up again chanting encouragement, "I think I can, I think I can."

"Okay, big boy, this is it. Are you going to hold her hand or be a weak wus? It's inches away. Come on just grab it, just go for it." I thought about the Beatles' song; I thought about the cowardly lion; I thought about what the Lone Ranger, Roy Rogers or John Wayne would do. I decided to go for it. I cut a glance at her father and that reminded me of my own. He had been a professional hunter and if he taught me anything about hunting it was to sneak up on things lest they get away.

I gritted my teeth and began sneaking up on her hand. I quietly sent my little finger crabbing sideways in the general direction of her little finger. My eyes were frozen forward watching the lion cry because he had no courage. My heart was pumping me into a dizzy spell. After what seemed like three or four days, my little finger stretched far enough to touch her little finger right at the tip. I looked down at my hand, my little finger was locked in an awkward position; reaching out like an inch worm searching for something to hold on to. I couldn't move it. What's going on with my little finger? I'll bet she can't even feel it. Soon my hand started to cramp and spasm.

Just as I thought I couldn't hold it anymore, the most wonderful thing happened. Moose, who had tons of cool, just lifted her hand and wove her fingers in between my fingers and placed both of our hands on her lap. I stared at my hand like it wasn't my own and thought her hand in mine was the most beautiful thing I had ever felt. It was the happiest feeling I could ever remember. Was this love?

After three or four minutes of sensory overload, I finally started watching the movie again. It was at the part where they were entering the city, which meant that we would finally see what color the "horse of a different color" really was. In the moments before the horse appeared I noticed our hands started to perspire. I didn't know what to do. Should I say, "Hey your hand's sweatin' like a joggin' hog, wipe it off," or should I let go and wipe my hand on my pants? The last thing I wanted was Moose to think I didn't want to hold her hand.

While deliberating with myself Moose solved the problem. She pretended to have an itch on her nose. She released my hand and started to raise it to her nose just seconds before the horse emerged…

Looking back on this later I probably should have washed my hands after milking the cow. You could call it a lack of judgment, a mental lapse, maybe even an overlooked detail, but no matter how you say it, it all adds up to the conduct of an underachieving human.

You see, when you milk cows, you always get a little bit of what the cow sleeps in on your hands. Now cows sleep where they stand around all day. Do you know what I mean? It's like this. Where cows live, it is like there is only one room in their house. They don't have bedrooms, or kitchens, or bathrooms. It is all just one room. Needless to say, their one room is really untidy and filled with the perfume of a corral, which meant my hands smelled like used up hay. I knew this when I got home earlier. I also knew I should wash my hands really good, but have you ever done something stupid and you knew it was stupid but you did it anyway?

Moose started thrashing around, jumped up throwing her hand away from her nose and staring at it like it was a smashed worm. Then she yelled, "SICK! What's on your hand?"

When I'm caught off-guard I usually tell the truth so I blurted out, "Cow!"

She looked at her hand with a new perspective and carried it to the bathroom like a dead puppy. She was gone for a long time and I could hear water running in a bathroom. When she came back, she sat in a straight backed chair on the other side of the room. During the commotion I totally missed the horse, so I sat dejectedly all alone in the middle of the big fluffy couch with my big stinky hands on my lap for another full hour, too scared to touch anything.

I could relate to Dorothy…I wanted to go home too, and I figured Moose wanted me to go, but I couldn't come up with any excuse to leave. When the movie finally ended, she threw me a pitiful smile and showed me the door. Neither of us said anything as I sulked out the door.

I felt more discouraged than a fishing worm as I undressed for bed. I just wanted to go to sleep and try to forget about the whole rotten day.

Our small white frame house was comprised of one bedroom, a living room, a kitchen, and a bathroom. Fred and I shared the double bed. Every morning around 2:00, when Mom came home from cooking at Minn's Café, she made herself a bed on the couch. Fred and I never thought about her being uncomfortable. As you can tell, I didn't think much about anything ... except myself. Mom said she preferred to sleep in the same room as the TV. For some reason I never realized the television didn't have anything on that late except the test signal and a tone.

The house was always cluttered and I often wondered why Mom didn't clean it better. I was embarrassed when people came to visit, and usually felt angry at how our house looked. I never thought to clean it myself. It looked great on the outside—a small white cottage with green eaves. The yard was nice too, with a big crab-apple tree in the front and a white picket fence enclosing the small front yard.

I hated the bed Fred and I slept in. it was built in the dark ages and was used primarily to get information from the enemies of the king. This ancient rusted steel-pipe bed had a mattress that sagged within two inches of the floor. It was like sleeping in a giant half cantaloupe. Fred and I rarely went to bed at the same time. I guess it was because we would have to cling to the sides in order to avoid touching each other. Fred and I didn't hate each other, but we weren't best friends by a long shot. By morning we were in the middle of the bed all tangled together like worms in a bait can. Whoever awakened first shoved the other away and shouted, "Get over! Don't touch me!"

Tonight Fred was watching some late-night show on our black and white RCA TV.

Laying in bed I thought about all of the rotten things in my life. I felt messed up and without hope of ever being different. Everything in my life seemed to be average or below. At work, I probably poisoned the little farm kids. Their hair will probably fall out by Monday. Moose will probably tell everyone at school how my hands stink. I cringed and rolled over. Then the teasing would start, and I didn't handle teasing well.

The teachers all knew I was dumber than a bucket of apples, and at times I just wanted to drop out of school and get a better job and a better car. The year before last, I made a gallant effort to do better in geometry by working with another kid on our book of theorems. He got an *A*-grade while I got a *C*. I asked the teacher why and she said, "Jon, you're a *C* student."

I think I know now what she meant by that, but I didn't know then. It hurt. It felt like the time I was sliding off a haystack and in desperation grabbed at a string on a hay bale only to have the bale roll off with me, both of us tumbling all the way to the ground. I landed in a heap with the hay bale on my chest, knocking the wind out of me and pinning me to the ground.

That was another thing—I always seemed to get my feelings hurt too easily. Someone would say something off-hand and I would take it wrong. Like that time at work when Mr. Johnson said there was a lot of guys looking for milking jobs. I took it to mean that he wanted to hire someone else and was too nice to fire me. So I just up and quit. Mr. Johnson was shocked, and asked me why. When I told him the reason, he explained that he was just making conversation. I felt stupid and went back to work.

I rolled over again and begged for sleep to come and put me out of my misery. Soon Fred came in and we both started clutching the sides of the bed in a desperate effort to keep our legs from touching. In a moment he was "sounding" asleep.

I know people are always talking about loud snoring, but all other snoring is a whisper compared to Fred's. When he really gets revved up, I swear he can suck the paint right off the ceiling. At least I never had to put up with flies buzzing around in the room at night. He has a blue ribbon, grand-champion nose for snoring. When Fred lies down on his back, he looks like a ship had just raised its main-sail. I swear he could smoke a cigarette in the shower and not put it out. His friend, Nelson, was always teasing him about his nose. "Rhoades's nose, anything goes. Speak beak!"

With Fred asleep, I continued appraising my unsatisfactory and underachieving life. My clothes were ugly; never once in my whole life did I have really popular clothes, although Fred did. He always bought the best clothes, but they were too big for me to wear. I found that out the hard way with Fred's hip-huggers.

Fred was gone someplace out of town and had left his pants hanging over a chair. Even though they were the super tight hip-hugger style on him, they were still way too big for me, so I decided I would tie the front belt loops together with baling twine and wear my shirt tails out. (Baling twine is very strong string made out of the tiny strands of hemp and is used to hold baled hay together.) On my way out the door I noticed these particular pants had a problem with the zipper staying up. I could zip it up all the way, but after taking a few steps the zipper would start to slide down. That was all I needed—to hear barn door jokes all day. I thought, no problem, I will run some of the baling twine through the little hole in the zipper tab and tie that to the rest of the twine holding my pants up.

I went to school like this, feeling cooler than I had in years. Everything seemed to be working all right until fourth period.

I had put off going to the bathroom knowing that when the bell sounded I could just rush there—you know how your brain will kind of synchronize your getting to the bathroom with the last possible moment you can hold it. Well, my timing mechanism was working perfectly. The bell rang, and with my teeth clenched and my eyes fixed solidly on the men's room door, I juked and jived my way through the crowded hall. After hitting the door, everything intensified and my brain went into the final countdown mode.

When I felt the twine, my brain froze. I had forgotten about the twine. Once tied, baling twine is about as easy to untie as a spit-chewed-knot. A couple of guys giggled. Fleeing into a stall, I locked the door and started frantically untying the knot. It took all of two seconds to realize this knot was not going to untie. Even if it had been a warm, sunny afternoon with plenty of time and nothing else on my mind, I could not have untied that knot. Finding myself in a screaming, eye-watering, teeth-grinding situation, I panicked and started jerking and thrashing around in the stall like a hobbled hog.

I could hear muffled voices outside the stall, but at this point there was only one thing on my frenzied mind: Get relief. I didn't have a knife nor fingernail clippers, so I used the next sharpest thing: my teeth. I folded over like a clasp knife, biting like a horse reaching over a pole fence for the last blade of grass. As I was thrashing and snapping with my teeth, my weight shifted forward, throwing me hard against the door. This caused it to strain at the hinges, bulge and the lock to fail. The door flew open with the speed and violence of a mule kick causing me to stagger out, barely keeping my balance. Unfortunately, Lars Stutz was peeking through the crack trying to see what was going on in the stall.

The door caught Lars, who had never been faster than a fence post, between the eyes, nearly knocking him out. Sweat cascaded off my brow. I was frantic. Then the break bell rang. Like a wild animal I yelled, "Someone give me a knife!" Everyone checked their pockets, but all they produced were a couple of nickels. The only one with a knife was Lars, and he was nursing a disjointed nose and a red mark that went from his hairline to his chin. I was so desperate I was like a cornered badger that has nothing to lose. My eyes must have said, "You will die if I don't get that knife," because Lars used his free hand to dig into his pocket and quickly hand me the knife. Back in the stall the string was cut and the problem solved in a maniacal moment.

For the rest of the day I kept one eye out for anyone teasing me and the other on my fly to catch it the moment it started unzipping. After that I sullenly endured teasing for weeks.

Groaning at my humiliation, I turned over one more time. I felt so powerless to change anything. I was as helpless as a new born field mouse to change my situation.

Is this how life is? How do other kids make significant changes in their life? Maybe there isn't any way to change. Maybe I just have to go with the flow. But maybe I'm flowing down the wrong hill into a stagnant, bug-infested green pond. Maybe how things turn out in life is just a big chance. Maybe there isn't any way to direct how things turn out. Yet—I could have washed my hands before going over to see Moose. I could have worn my own pants instead of Fred's. I still felt powerless to get better grades or to rise above mediocrity in anything.

Oh well, who cares anyway? Maybe I should just ride through life and see what happens.

After a few more discouraging thoughts, sleep finally put me out of my misery. Little did I know the next day I would meet a strange old man who would become my best friend and help me turn my life completely around.

# CHAPTER 4

## I Have a Right to Expect Good Things in Life

At 6:00 my alarm sounded. I could barely hear it above Fred's snoring. Still groggy from last night's struggle, I got up, dressed and slipped out do the morning milking. The absence of stars told me it was overcast as I headed to Mr. Johnson's. Mrs. Johnson was up and skimming the cream from last night's milking. I knew I should say something, but once again, I felt powerless to tell the truth. Downcast, I went out to milk.

When I finished the morning battle with Bessie, I came back into the house and everyone looked at me in a funny way. Mr. Johnson asked, "Did everything go okay last night with milking?"

"Sure, why?" I said innocently.

He swirled some milk in his glass and said, "Milk tasted funny; that's all."

Leaving my face unreadable I said, "Oh," and left.

That night I after milking, Mrs. Johnson said she was going to start selling milk to Mrs. Wood, and would I mind dropping it off in the evening on my way home? She said Mrs. Wood's twin brother just moved in with her and he liked fresh milk and cream. This was good news for two reasons: first and most important, Mrs. Johnson said she would help with a little gas for my car, and second, I knew Mrs. Wood always had chocolate chip cookies at her house.

Mrs. Wood's husband had been killed many years earlier and she never remarried. I met this unusual lady on Halloween night three years earlier.

Halloween in Declo resembles a veggie war zone where every possible rotten vegetable is used as a weapon. After the trick or treaters go home then the big boys come out to play. Kenny and I were creeping along the shadows looking for Fred and his buddies with a sack of rotten tomatoes to throw, when I was hit in the back of the head with a tomato so hard it stung like the dickens. I whipped around just in time to see someone or something disappear through a hedge. Figuring that one of Fred's buddies had somehow got around behind us, I signaled to Kenny and we rushed with foolish abandonment through the hedge.

Just as we cleared the hedge we heard a blood curdling scream that would make Dracula wet himself. You know there are different kinds of scared. There is the kind of scared when you jump, and then there is the kind of scared from which break-dancing was invented. This was the second kind. Screaming, spinning and high stepping, we ran to the far end of the yard and saw that we were trapped. Turning around I could see a rather tall person coming toward us slowly, definitely not one of Fred's buddies. I could see that this person was thin and angular in shape.

Even though I could not recognize who it was, I thought, what the heck, and whipped out a tomato and hurled it. I rushed my shot and the tomato went wide. The stranger zipped two tomatoes at us so fast that we couldn't move, hitting Kenny and me center chest causing both of us to let a cuss slip out. Then in nothing flat five more come zinging at us each one stinging like all get out. I threw another tomato and this time I heard the sweet sound of plop and it struck home. It was a plop mind you not a zinging zap like the kind we were receiving. The stranger just tipped over and lay on the frosty yard apparently dead as a door nail. As we crept up, extra ammunition dripping through our fingers, I thought I heard giggling and then full blown woman-laughing. Needless to say you could have knocked me over with a piece of June grass as I looked down on Mrs. Wood! She was easily over 50 years old at the time.

"Are you all right?" I asked.

"Sure," she said, "That was fun."

She took us into the house to let us clean up and then fed us tons of good stuff.

"Where did you learn to throw like that?" Kenny mumbled, both cheeks resembling a squirrel as he plunged another chocolate chip cookie into a glass of milk.

"Oh, I used to coach, and I played ball in Burley's city league for years."

"Well, you sure enough can throw a mean tomato," I chimed in.

While walking home later, keeping a sharp eye peeled for an ambush from Fred and his buddies, I commented, "She's an old lady that doesn't seem to be that old. Know what I mean?"

"Yeah. That's the way I want to be," Kenny said.

"Me too…'cept I don't want to be an old lady." I observed.

Milking seemed to go better that night, and I looked forward to seeing Mrs. Wood again and maybe vacuuming a cookie platter or two when I delivered the milk. After milking I watched Mrs. Johnson fill an old gallon Mayonnaise jar with fresh milk, "You sure you don't mind dropping this off Jon?"

It was early evening and the night chill from the constant wind made me shiver as I knocked on the door. In southern Idaho, the wind always blows. The people there don't measure the wind with a wind velocity indicator; instead they use a logging chain tied to a post. Nobody worries about wind speed if the chain is hanging or even standing straight out from the post; they only worry when the wind starts snapping links off from the end of the chain.

Soon I heard the floor squeak as someone came to the back door. Mrs. Wood opened the door and her lively hazel eyes smiled at me, "Please come in."

Handing her the jug of milk I said, "I need to be getting home. Here's your milk."

"Why, there isn't anyone there except maybe Fred, and he won't have baked any fresh cookies, will he?"

She was right. Dad passed away eight years earlier and we were left almost destitute. Because Mom had a stroke before I or my two older brothers were born she couldn't read or write. But she could cook and show love. I guess if a mom can't do anything else, those are about the two best qualities for a boy's mom to have. She worked at Declo's small town café, Minn's, cooking on the swing shift for one dollar an hour. Sometimes I would go almost a whole week without talking to her at home. She would be asleep when I left for milking and school in the mornings, and then she was gone to work when I got home after school and football practice. I saw Fred a lot, and Mrs. Wood was right. He wouldn't have baked any cookies, at least not any edible ones.

My oldest brother Dean was in the army and stationed in Vietnam. He was a grunt, or a foot soldier. He only had five months to go and then he would be home. It upset Mom really bad to watch the news because it showed too much of the war. She was always worried about seeing a green army car drive into our lane with two stone-faced soldiers in uniform. She heard that is how you get told your son is missing or dead.

But by January 15, it would all be over and Dean would be home. Dean knew how much Mom worried, and he always told her he was working in a kitchen trying to be as good a cook as she. I believed that for six months, until a friend's brother came home from the war and told me he had seen Dean.

I asked, "Did he cook you anything?" He just stared at me as if to say, "You are without doubt the dumbest kid I have ever known."

"No, he didn't cook me anything. I was being dropped off in an LZ on a hilltop while he was being taken off with most of his dead patrol."

"Oh," I said, a tightness beginning in my throat. "I thought he was a cook or something."

"I don't think so" was all he would say. I never told Mom or Fred, but I'd had this uneasy feeling ever since.

Mrs. Wood's kitchen was all black and white. It had a black and white checkerboard tile floor, with wooden cupboards painted white. The oven and refrigerator were white with black handles and knobs. In the center of the kitchen floor sat a gray kitchen table and chairs, with chrome-piped legs and gray vinyl covering for the seats. It also had the best smell in the world: chocolate chip cookies with walnuts! How did she know those were my favorites? She sat me down and I started grazing through a big pile of cookies. We chatted about this and that, and I was surprised at how easy she was to talk to.

She asked with a smile, "Have you been practicing your throwing arm for Halloween night?"

I gulped some milk and told her, "I'm too old for that stuff. I'll probably just drive around with my buddies and watch the younger kids battle it out." She looked at me kind of funny, and I wondered if she thought I thought she was too old for that too.

Suddenly she said, "I want you to meet my brother."

I nearly choked on my eighth or ninth cookie when she brought her brother into the kitchen in a wheelchair. It was obvious he didn't have any legs below the thighs, but there was also something different about his eyes. They were blue, just like Mrs. Wood's, but his seemed to stare off someplace. His skin was white, almost transparent. My stomach tightened, and I started feeling real uncomfortable.

"This is my brother Ur," she said proudly.

"Hi," I stammered.

"He can't hear you," she said simply. "He can't see you either, but he can talk to you."

My discomfort was starting to increase with my curiosity, as Mrs. Wood explained that Ur lost his sight and hearing during World War II.

"How?" I asked, imagining all kinds of heroic things.

"Painfully." She went on to explain that because he had already acquired speech before his deafness, he still had a pretty good speaking voice.

She saw me glance down at his legs, or rather at his no-legs.

"He didn't lose those during the war. Because of his diabetes problem he had to have his legs amputated over the last six years."

She went on to explain that Ur just moved in with her from his home in Illinois two weeks earlier.

"Why?" I asked.

"Well," she explained. "his wife passed away about a month ago."

In my mind I was wondering who would marry a deaf and blind guy with no legs.

"How long was he married?" I asked as I glanced in his direction.

"His first marriage was 5 years and his second was 18 years."

"Wow," I said softly. "But who would … ah … I mean, what was his wife like?"

Mary smiled. "His first wife, Beth, and his second wife, Ellen, were two of the most angelic women I have ever known. Beth was delicate, beautiful, gentle and innocent. Ellen was well educated, like my brother, and she was also deaf."

I interrupted, "How could they get an education? I mean especially him."

"Well, someday maybe he will tell you."

I got up to leave and Mrs. Wood put her hand on my arm. "Don't leave without telling Ur goodbye."

"Oh," I said, dragging one side of my mouth down in uneasiness, "How do I do that?"

"There are three ways people can communicate with Ur. First, you take his hand and print into it using large block letters."

She demonstrated by printing on her hand. "Second, if you knew sign language, you could hold his hands and sign into them. This is how I communicate with him usually. And third is a technique rarely used."

I raised an eyebrow and leaned forward with interest. "It was used originally by two deaf-blind brothers from southern California. As fantastic as this may seem, Ur has mastered this mode of communication too."

"What is it?" I asked, full of curiosity.

As she started to speak, I could tell she had explained this a few times. Miming as she spoke, "He places his hand on your face and sets his thumb on your lips and his first and second fingers along your jaw with the last two fingers on your Adam's apple." She took both of his hands in hers and started to swish them around in strange little circles and bounces.

"What are you doing?" I asked.

"This is signing. This is how he and his wife used to communicate. I learned it over the years. I am still a little rusty, but it's coming along. If you want, you can just print in his palm."

So I printed, "H-I." Since I knew he couldn't see me, I watched his face intently. A wry smile started at his lips. It was the smile you see when a kind heart is once more required to engage in child-like conversation.

Then Ur said with a beautifully small, monotone voice, "How do you do?"

I had never heard a voice with such power and gentleness woven together. I felt drawn toward him, and totally captivated. After a moment of staring at him I printed, "F-I-N-E."

"What is your name?"

That voice, or something about him, seemed to radiate understanding. Since I became a teenager I hadn't seen much of that in adults. I spelled, "J-O-N."

"Good," he said, and then he took my hand and felt it all over. He touched my knuckles and carefully felt the big letter "D" in the middle of my high school ring.

I looked up at Mrs. Wood, questioning. "It's okay, he's just getting to know your hand. He likes to recognize people by their hands before they tell him their name."

"Cool," I muttered.

It was then I noticed a crude tattoo of light blue numbers on his forearm: "59331." That was weird, I thought. He must have been in the Navy or something.

I knew a guy who got a tattoo of a naked lady on his forearm when he was in the Navy. After the war he came home, married, and got religious. He could never wear short-sleeved shirts. I overheard him say once that he wished he had never gotten tattooed. He said that sometimes you can do foolish things when you're young and pay for it all your life.

As I slowly withdrew my hand he whispered, as if he had thought about this for a long time and had just now come to a decision, "Your hand is large, strong and smells like cows, but I think they are good hands that need a gift."

Reddening, I stood to leave, wondering what he meant about the gift. At the back door I turned and asked, "How much education does he have anyway?" In my mind I was thinking maybe high school at the most.

"She looked at me and said, "He has a doctorate degree from the University of Michigan in European History."

"Oh," I said casually, like I heard that every day. My mind was swimming as I started my old car and continued home. That deaf-blind guy has a doctorate from some university and I couldn't even pass Declo High School. I felt more depressed. I wondered how he could do so much with so little.

# CHAPTER 5

## I Have a Right to Choose a Good Attitude

I Stopped at Declo's newly built post office and stared at the 83323 embossed in blue metal letters on its front. This zip code identified our little village and gave Declo a place in America. Slipping out of my car I crossed to the other side of the street and passed an old garage where I stopped again and looked at a window pane which had been painted with white house paint. Andy Anderson had written with his finger in the wet paint, "Andy the Great." That simple signature had given Andy a place and an identity. I knew Andy. He did well in school and seemed to be a friend to everyone. If there had been another window with wet paint right then I probably would have written, "Jon the lesser." I squinted again at the lettering and let my thought go back to people I knew who had it rough.

There was this Down Syndrome man, Leonard, who had a steady job working for a farmer. Since his parents died he had continued to live in the house where he grew up. Every day he got himself up, dressed, and walked to work. This guy couldn't even read time, but he cooked and cleaned and drove the tractors. He put in a full day's work six days a week, and then the farmer picked him up for church on Sunday. I wondered what it was that made some people do more with what they had than others. Like Terry, for example.

Neither Terry's dad nor mom worked, so they lived in this old, unpainted house without electricity or indoor plumbing. His clothes always had an odor because they probably didn't have a washing machine. He studied by a kerosene lamp, while keeping a job to help pay the family expenses. Still, with all these problems he got really high grades and his homework was always finished on time. I wondered why there are some people like that and then there were people like me.

Granted, I didn't have the most ideal situation, but I was not as bad off as Terry, or Leonard, or Ur. I hated how I was; yet still I felt powerless to change. I felt like an old truck that was going along a slick rutted road and no matter how I steered I just seemed to continue in the same direction. How could I get out of the ruts? I know this sounds crazy, but in some ways I wished I was like Leonard, or Terry or Ur because it seemed like they had more control and potential in their lives than I did. Maybe if I had more problems, life would seem easier.

When I got home Fred said, "Sue called."

If anything good had come out of going to school, it was Sue. She first moved to Declo when I was in the fifth grade. At that time things weren't going well at our house. I felt like the village idiot. My clothes smelled strong of Mom's cigarette smoke, and I never did my homework. I didn't understand math or any other subject, and because of Mom's stroke she couldn't help me. I didn't have any real close friends at that time except Tom, who was Sue's cousin.

Sue was tall, pretty, and when she entered our school she immediately became popular. For some reason, in the seventh grade Sue started being friendly to me and we became friends—not as boy/girlfriend, just friends. Her boyfriend's name was Bryce, and he and I got along well. The best way to describe Bryce was a telephone pole with a great personality.

I could talk to Sue about everything. She was a great friend and always kept my secrets. She was Mrs. Johnson's babysitter, so sometimes when she babysat for them I could see her at milking time. I think it was her friendship that helped me want to clean up a little better. Like I said, we were not romantic, but we did kiss one time.

Since her parents were gone for the evening, she was tending her little brother and sister. She met me at the door, and I noticed her shoulder-length dark blond hair was tied back in a ponytail, revealing her flawless features and perfect skin. She was breathtaking, I thought, as we entered the family room. We played <u>Chutes and Ladders</u> with the kids for awhile, and then I helped her put them down for the night.

After the kids were sleeping, we lay sprawled on the living room floor in front of the fireplace facing each other, our chins propped in our hands, our elbows making tepees. The orange and yellow firelight was dancing on her pretty face. We talked about everything, including if my mother died that her family should adopt me and then we would be brother and sister. Finally it was late, and as I left through the mud room I turned back to say good-bye. She was right behind me, her deep blue eyes looking up into mine.

It was one of those experiences when I knew exactly what she was thinking and she knew what I was thinking. I knew she wanted to kiss me and I wanted to kiss her just to see what it would be like. Without either of us speaking, I reached out, putting my hands on her hips while she put her arms around my neck. Her sweet Wrigley spearmint breath relaxed me. We closed our eyes and leaned together; her lips were warm and soft, yielding to pleasant affection and a gentle kiss. Our lips parted and our eyes met for a moment, sparkling in excitement, then I turned and left without speaking. We never kissed again, but we never forgot it either.

"Hi, Sue, this is Jon. What's going on?"

"Do you want to double date with me and Bryce on Friday night? You can take my friend from Burley."

"I've always wanted to date a Burley woman, so I guess this is my chance," I chortled.

"Ha, ha," she scolded, "Very funny."

"Who is it?" I asked, hoping this wasn't a mercy date.

"Linda, a friend I know from Burley."

"Okay," I agreed, "What's the plan?"

"Oh, I don't know. Maybe we'll go to a movie and then go throw dirt clods at people making out."

"Far out!" I responded, "I'd like that."

There wasn't much to do in Declo, so we made up our own fun. Declo was ribboned with irrigation canals that all have a dirt road on the canal bank. Most of these roads were very secluded. During the winter when the canals were empty of water, we sneaked up on lovers who were parked. Collecting soft little dirt clods or small sticks, we tossed them onto the hood of their cars, held our breath and listened.

"What was that?" usually the girl's voice.

"Oh baby. It was nothing," boy's voice soothed. Then we would launch another round. *Thump!* The girls voice now a little shriller. "I know I heard something!" "Oh, baby, it is probably nothing," boy's voice, less sure. *Thump!* Girl's voice now filled with panic: "I heard a story about this. It's probably—the Hook!"

By then the passion of the moment was gone and they would be convinced that the infamous Hook was even at that moment reaching his polished silver hook for their door handle.

I know this sounds pretty dumb to most people, but to us it was loads of fun, and we felt we were doing our civic duty in keeping down teen misdemeanors.

On Friday I borrowed Mr. Johnson's red '64 Chevy farm pickup for the date. I felt Mr. Johnson was extra generous, since I accidentally shot a hole in the side of it the week before. After picking up Bryce and Sue, we headed to Burley to get Linda.

Linda was pretty, well put together, and I could tell right away by her grip that she had been raised on a farm. When I took her hand while helping her in and out of the truck it was like grabbing up a horse-hoof to clean it out. No, that doesn't sound right. I don't mean they looked alike, or that Linda had that much hair on her arms. I meant her hand felt solid.

Sue had told me earlier that Linda's dad had eight daughters and no sons, so all the daughters had to do the milking and farm work.

We went to a spy movie and then out to eat at the Arctic Circle drive-in. By then it was only 10:00 and nobody had to be home until midnight. While we were eating our hamburgers we tried to decide where the best place would be to find our victims.

Then Bryce and I had the same great idea at the same time. "Let's all go to Granny's Pad."

Linda asked, "What is that?"

Sue explained, "That's where lots of kids go to make out."

I could tell Linda was getting nervous so I said, "We don't go there to makeout. We go there to torment the ones who do." It was obvious that Linda was completely lost as to why this was such a fun activity. I explained about throwing soft little dirt clods at the cars and then watching the people leave. I don't know, I guess Burley kids have more to do or something because she still couldn't see the fun in it, but agreed to try it once.

Granny's Pad was two miles north of Declo. It was a small, shaded pasture surrounded by trees on one side and a serene little pond on the other. It was secluded and hard to drive to. The dirt road with its deep ruts wound back and forth down a small hill through a stand of poplar trees. You had to drive slow so as not to tear the bottom off the car, but we were in a farm pickup so it didn't matter. With the girls sitting between Bryce and me, it was more fun being slammed and rocked through the pot holes and ruts. As we cleared the grove of poplar trees and entered the pasture our headlights reflected off of a car to our left. Swinging the truck to the left we saw a little sky-blue Dodge Dart parked with its lights off. We kept turning and our headlights filled the interior of the Dodge. It appeared as if nobody was inside, and best of all it had Minidoka County license plates bolted to the front bumper.

Minidoka County is the county just across the Snake River from us. Even though we didn't know why, we felt animosity for kids from that county. At seeing the Minidoka County license plates, even Linda started getting excited about throwing dirt clods.

We drove back out through the trees and across 100 yards of flat space to park the truck just over a little rise in the road about a quarter of a mile from the Dodge Dart. It was a beautiful night. There were no clouds just stars that looked like tiny lights suspended on invisible wires. A nearly full moon robbed color and cast everything in gray tones. "This is perfect," I mused.

Linda and I took out ahead of Bryce and Sue. We were walking so close to each other I could smell her shampoo; our sneakers made a quiet scratching sound on the road. The Snake River and the Russian olive trees accented the heavy smell of the evening. Our hands bumped and for a moment I thought about holding her hand, but based on previous experience I decided to wait until I could sniff my hand. Soon we were descending on the road through the grove toward the parked car.

Picking our way carefully through the ruts, Linda and I emerged about 15 yards in front of the car. Scratching in the humus near the base of a poplar tree, I picked up a couple of little soft dirt clods and handed

45

one to Linda. We positioned ourselves directly in front of the blue car. Linda's eyes were bright with adrenaline as she watched me count with my lips.

"On three," I mouthed to her, "Counting, one–two–three." Our arms reached back and then came forward gently hurtling the small projectiles. Just as we were fully stretched out, weight forward, our arms extended in the follow-through, fingers open—the car lights came on in terrifying brilliance and fully illuminated us. I could see the clods arching toward the car.

In light of the unexpected circumstances, I suggested to Linda that we run for it! Before the clods plopped innocently on the windshield, we spun on our heels and attempted to set sprinting records.

Linda was pretty to be sure, and she was strong enough to break baling twine with her bare hands, but fast she was not. I grabbed her hand without a trial sniff and without worrying if she wanted me to. With Linda flagging along behind, her feet touching the ground only occasionally, we increased our speed up the rutted road. The slant six-cylinder engine roared to life in the little Dodge, and its rear tires peeled out just before its lights started bouncing after us. Lucky for us, the ruts and roughness of the road slowed the car so much that we started to out-distance it. We cleared the trees on a dead run, the smooth road lying open before us. The revving of the car's engine told me it would clear the top and easily make a road-pizza out of us long before we could drop over the small hill to the safety of the pickup. We were running flat out, our breath coming in gasps and our legs turning to jelly. Lights reflecting on some trees to the right of us told me we were definitely in serious trouble.

A pheasant exploded out of a shallow ditch to our left, scaring the be-jabbers out of us, but giving me an idea. A quick side glance revealed the shallow ditch running parallel with the road. Just before the car came out of the trees and its lights swung around to level on us, I shouted, "Hit the ditch!" Linda and I dove into the ditch and flattened ourselves against the gravel bottom. I quickly pulled a tumbleweed partially over us, its stickers making me itch. The car leaped over the summit, lit up the road, and slid to a stop.

I could feel the driver thinking, "They have to be here someplace. Where are they?"

We pressed ourselves deeper into the ditch and tried to pull the over-hanging grass over us, and waited. Above our haggard breathing, I heard the crunch of the car's tires as it rolled slowly along the road. The car stopped right above us and the window was rolled down. I could smell the driver's cigarette burning. Looking up through the tumbleweed, I heard the driver curse and felt Linda wince at his profanity. Then there appeared a tiny glowing globe arching toward the tumbleweed covering our faces. He had thrown the cigarette into this weed! There it hung, suspended in the tangled mass of stickers, a red ember beginning to ignite the tumbleweed over our faces.

Linda started to panic. I squeezed her hand tighter, and whispered, "Hold still!"

I smelled the smoke change from tobacco to tumbleweed. Finally, after what seemed like two years of school, the driver slowly turned the car in a wide arching turn through the field to let his lights sweep in a 360-degree circle. The lights crept over our heads as we tried to press ourselves into a gopher hole. Then the car slowly returned to Granny's Pad.

After throwing off the burning bush and stomping out its embers, I burst out laughing! This date had gone better than I could have imagined. Linda seemed quiet, but I figured that was because she was so spellbound with my creative dating technique and disappointed that the boys in her big city were so boring.

"Where are Bryce and Sue?" she asked in a quiet voice.

"I don't know, to tell you the truth. I haven't seen them since we got out of the truck," I explained as we cleared the rise and saw the truck below. To this day I still don't know how that guy got his Dodge Dart right behind us without us hearing him. But all of a sudden he hit his lights and we lit-up like two burning pine trees. I shouted, "Run!" I'll bet we were spinning our shoes like cartoon characters before they started getting traction. It's amazing how fast you can run with a car bumper pushing on your hip pockets.

We bounded down the rise and I jerked open the driver-side door and pushed Linda in first. You can imagine our surprise at seeing Bryce and Sue still in the truck. For a moment I wondered if maybe we would have been better off to stay and throw dirt clods at this truck instead. The little Dodge Dart slid up to a stop in a swirl of dust, and out stepped a man without his shirt.

The first thing I noticed was that he had muscles in places I didn't even have places. In two big strides he was at Bryce's side and placed his big hands on the truck's door handle and jerked. Lucky for us we had thought to lock the doors when we got in. I was frantically searching for the key.

My boss had just one key for the truck and I had set it on the floor before we got out. Most farm trucks have about six inches of dirt on the floor and this one was not an exception.

Bryce yelled, "What's going on?" The man outside was cussing and jerking at the door and threatening to make hog hash out of Bryce and me. I knew there were two of us and only one of him, but he seemed as mad as a teased bull, so I thought it was better to just drive away and let him cool off.

Now I was embarrassed by the language he was using, and thought maybe I should point out to him that there were decent ladies present, but at that moment a panicked thought crowded out all others. The key was gone! We must have dragged our feet on the floor while getting out of the door and the key fell outside in the sand.

"If you don't come out I'm going to tear this door off and come in and drag you out to meet your maker!" yelled the man, his muscles ripping like taut steel cables.

Bryce started yelling, "Get the key and let's go!"

"I don't know where it is!" I shouted back.

Something slammed hard against the window next to Bryce's head. We gaped at the spider-webbed window on Bryce's side. The man had hit the window with his fist. It didn't break out, but it cracked—I knew the next time he hit it, it would go.

It was at this time that Bryce and I threw away all resemblance to manhood and started begging this guy to leave us alone and that we were sorry. But the guy would not leave.

A terrifying realization crept into my brain. One of us needed to get out of the truck and find the key in the sand. I knew I wasn't getting out, and I wasn't sure if Linda could squeeze past between me and the steering wheel. Bryce didn't seem anxious to get out, and Sue wasn't budging.

The man said, "You got to the count of 10 and then I'm coming in."

Sue suggested that I look again on the floor. I turned on the dome light and started searching with great concentration. Can you imagine trying to look with eight legs filling the available space?

I was all bent over with my neck under the steering wheel thinking, I am sure putting a lot of dangerous pressure on my gut. To my surprise and relief I saw something shiny sticking out behind the gas pedal. It was the key!

"I found it!" I screamed, and jammed it into the ignition switch. The man was jerking like a lunatic at the door handle as the big V-8 roared to life.

Three things occurred to me at exactly the same time: First, the truck had big, deep-lug snow tires on the rear. Second, that guy was standing on a pea gravel road. Third, he did not have a shirt on. With these three important revelations on my mind I revved the truck engine to about 10 million RPMs and popped the clutch. Those big tires started spinning on the little pea gravel rocks and spitting them out the back of the truck like machine-gun fire.

Watching in the rearview mirrors, we saw the man make a very poor choice. As the truck slowly spun away from him, he stepped behind us to shake his fist and yell. It was then those little rocks swarmed over him like killer bees. He started twitching and jerking like guys do in the movies when they get machine-gunned.

Hoping to reclaim some much-depleted manhood, I rolled my window down and shouted, "Next time you better be careful who you're messing with, buddy!"

Linda seemed real quiet on the way home as we rehearsed again and again the details of our adventure. Sue later assured me that Linda had a good time, but I knew in my heart the truth. We never dated again. I figured those Burley women wouldn't know a good time when they had one.

At work the next day I had to tell Mr. Johnson how his truck's window got shattered.

I was all set to get fired or yelled at, but instead he just quietly said, "Things like that can be fixed, and that was an inexpensive lesson."

I wondered what he meant, and I also wondered why he didn't blow up at me. It seemed like the smallest things set me off. Was I just made this way and he his way, or was there some way to change? I could see all these things that I wanted to do or become, and yet I continually felt powerless to make any significant changes in myself. If this was supposed to be a free country, why couldn't I choose to be or do something else?

I continued to drop milk off at the Woods' house for the next few weeks. Everyday Mrs. Wood asked me to come in and graze her cookie platter to the roots. I loved the cookies, but Ur always made me a little uncomfortable. I wasn't sure why. Maybe it was his handicap, or maybe it was that he seemed to have a countenance full of serenity and joy. This bothered me because I couldn't for the life of me understand how someone who was blind, deaf, and legless could have anything to be happy about.

He couldn't watch TV or listen to rock-and-roll music. He had to read books without pictures with only bumps for letters. Granted, Declo wasn't the prettiest town in the world, but there were still lots of neat things to see, like the ol' smooth Snake River with patrols of carp silently gliding between the islands. There are also giant poplar trees and full-leafed sugar beets growing in straight green rows. If he didn't miss seeing all the trees and crops, then he must have missed seeing Moose. Of course, if he had never seen Moose then how could he miss seeing her?

Mrs. Wood was one the coolest ladies in town. She was tall, angular, silver-haired and without much natural beauty, yet she seemed to radiate some other beauty. I mean Marilyn Monroe was one good-looking woman, but to compare these two ladies would be like comparing a Corvette to a tractor. Still, I could not deny it; Mrs. Wood had her beauty, and it wasn't the kind she washed off at night with cold cream and put on again the next day with a paint kit.

# CHAPTER 6

## I Have a Right to Have Good Parents

Virginia, Minnesota, September 1, 1909

The summer seemed hotter than usual to the people of Virginia, Minnesota. On the first of September, this small town in the heart of the Iron Range had been hot and muggy since sun up. To the west, black and purple clouds were beginning to pile into vapor mountains, creating an ominous looking sky. All day long Anna Babiraski had suffered in the heat and sweat of her daily chores. Her back ached as she touched her bulbous stomach and wondered if she would burst from the great load she carried. How could there be a baby this big, she wondered. She was only five feet tall, and with all the added weight in front she had begun to walk leaning back to counterbalance her front. Soon Leo would be returning from work at the iron foundry, and he could rub her back and her feet.

Leo and Anna had met on an immigrant ship bound for America five years earlier. They were among the thousands of European immigrants flowing into America as a result of the reduced cost of travel. Inman and Cunard and other ship lines had slashed their steerage fares to $10 per person to cross the Atlantic.

Anna grew up in a large, poor family and could see little opportunity which her ambitious soul craved. So one day she announced

51

she was leaving for America. At barely 17, she hoped to escape the poverty of her Polish home by coming to America.

Leo and his father were traveling to Chicago where they hoped to earn enough money to send back so that their large family could join them in America.

At first she thought Leo was much older because he was so tall and masculine. At 18 he had a full beard and powerful shoulders that narrowed to his waist. She guessed he stood over six feet tall.

As soon as the massive ship left port and began its 25-day voyage across the great ocean, Anna quickly became seasick. Hour after hour she crouched at the back of the ship trying to conceal her throwing up. "Will this never end?" she groaned. Although many other passengers were also seasick, they seemed to have someone to help them. Without anyone to bring her water and because of her fear of passing out while walking to the other end of the ship to the water barrel, her situation became perilous.

By the afternoon of the second day she was suffering from dehydration. She knew she had to have water. All alone, and seemingly without anyone to notice her, she started to question her wisdom in leaving Poland at all. For the first time in her young life she started to despair.

A shadow crossed her in the early afternoon and she looked up. Leo stood with a cup in his hand. "Hello my little sister," he gently said, "How is it that you stay back here and do not eat with the people or talk with us?"

Anna was so taken aback at being called little sister that she sat straighter and avoided the question by saying, "I am fine, and I do not want for anything."

"Well, little sister, I have this cool cup of water. Are you sure you do not want to drink of it?" Leo had been watching her all day and he knew she had to be dying of thirst.

Her independence and pride had always been her strength—and weakness. Her mother had often said, "Pride is a ruthless taskmaster."

Quickly looking out at the blue, undulating ocean, she said, "No, I am just fine, and if you please, I want to be alone."

Ignoring this, Leo sat down beside her and stretched out his long legs. "I am Leo, little sister, and I think you do not have anyone to care for you. I think that you are here all alone and I think that you are getting sick from not eating, or drinking water." He reached the cup toward her hand.

"I am not sick! At least not from not eating or drinking," she retorted sharply, although green and trembling from her forced fasting. The roll of the ship had caused a little of the water to splash onto her hand. It felt very cool, and now she wanted a drink more than anything.

Leo saw her eyes and gently urged, "Come, little sister. Drink this water."

He held the cup to her, and she began to sip at it. It tasted wonderful. His large hands, bristling with black hair, seemed gentle and good.

When it was empty, she politely said, "Thank you, sir," and stared out again at the ocean.

"Little sister, where is your family?"

"Stop calling me little sister," she snapped, "Why do you keep calling me that?" For the first time she looked directly at him. His eyebrows jutted over his teasing dark eyes, and his nose seemed too large for his face. Dark unruly hair had been wrestled under a soft leather cap. His teeth were strong, white and partially hidden by gentle lips that twitched in the corner when he was nervous.

"Ah, that is because I am a big horse that does not know how to talk to girls," he smiled, "When I get to America, my father, that is him over there carving on that wood," he raised a callused hand and pointed toward an older version of himself sitting on a pile of coiled ropes with his back against the mainsail mast, "He says I should get married and raise my children in the promised land. I told him that I do not know how to get married, and he said you start by talking to girls and the next thing you know you are married. So I thought—I should start right away, you know to practice, and here you were."

Anna's small face turned toward him and she looked directly into his face. Looking into her eyes, Leo realized that she was not 12 or 14 years of age as he first supposed. She was older, and she was beautiful. Her delicate little round Polish face was determined, yet softened on the edges with kindness.

Shifting to see Leo more directly, Anna asked, "What is your name, Mr. Big Horse?"

"I am Leo Babiraski. I am 18 years, and I am from Warsaw."
"I am Anna Ziblinski. I am 17 years of age, and I am from
Wagroweic, Poland." She smiled a smile that radiated all the wonderful
and enchanting virtues of women.

Suddenly Leo felt a rush of shyness at knowing that this
wonderful young woman was so near his own age. He never called her
little sister again.

For the next several weeks as the ship plied its course toward the
land of promise, Leo and Anna became inseparable. The weather smiled
on the voyage, and on the young hearts. They talked about their past and
their dreams for the future.

Leo needed Anna to show him proper romantic protocol. She
taught him how to hold her hand and how to encircle her in his arms.
The night before they sailed into New York's harbor, the young couple
stood in the bow of the ship. The jib sail snapped taut above them, and
the gentle spray from the ocean breaking against the ship's bow was
whisked over and past them by the warm wind.

Leo lifted Anna and stood her on a block facing him so that their
eyes could be level with each other. With a nervous twitch teasing at the
corner of his mouth, he slid his arms around her small waist like she had
shown him and studied her face. Her breath was sweetened with cloves,
and the full moon cast a silver highlight to her hair. He leaned forward
and carefully kissed her yielding lips. Her eyes sparkled with love and
happiness.

Next morning they held hands on the foredeck while the great
ship passed the Statue of Liberty. Tears formed in Anna's eyes, and Leo
cleared his throat huskily and said, "Here we make our home, my little
Polish woman."

"Yes, my big horse."

"Anna, your big horse loves you. Please come to Chicago."

With Leo's father leading the way, they were processed through
Ellis Island and traveled by train to Chicago. They were married one
year later in a Chicago Catholic Church. For want of better work, they
moved shortly thereafter to Virginia, Minnesota, and joined a Polish
community to work in the iron foundry.

Eight months prior to their move, Anna had become pregnant.
Her violent morning sickness during the first three months had

frightened both of them. Watching his dear little Polish wife suffer during those months had caused Leo's love to deepen and mature. Sharing this difficult experience caused their lives to weave together with flaxen cords of understanding, respect and love.

One evening at 7:00, she saw Leo running toward their house. At first she was startled, fearing something was wrong, but then she could see he was trying to beat the storm. He was such a graceful man when he ran. In spite of the big hobnail boots he wore he had a smooth, powerful stride that could cover ground quickly. She could see his shirt was open, and his powerful chest, covered with coarse black hair, was thrust forward as he sprinted the last 25 yards before bursting through the door, gasping for breath. She marveled at the power of this good man's presence, and yet he was so gentle with her in speech and touch.

There was a childlike innocence about him which on occasion caused him to trust too quickly, sometimes causing financial errors. Like the car he bought for $50 not realizing it was only a down payment. From then on Anna handled the books and ran the household finances.

Quickly shutting the door, he breathlessly grabbed her and said, "How is my little round Polish flower?"

"I am hot, and I hurt in my back and feet, and I feel like I am big enough to harness up to a plow. Sometimes today I have bad pains ... " A clap of thunder overhead caused the baby to jump, and a sharp pain lanced Anna's waist.

"Oh, Leo!" she gasped, as she reached for a kitchen chair, "I think this is it."

Leo was struck with a sickening fear, like the fear you feel when you are on the verge of panic.

"Anna—What should I do?"

She had never seen Leo so shaken and befuddled. She laughed, "You big horse, go get Mrs. Kowalski. We will have a baby."

It was the longest night of Leo's life. The lightning, rolling thunder amidst the torrential rain plus Anna's cries were like a nightmare to him. Yet, the morning's brightness seemed like a beautiful new world. Standing before the four-poster bed, he looked down not at one large baby, but at two tiny children—a boy and a girl. Anna was exhausted and sleeping quietly.

Leo turned to Mrs. Kowalski and asked quietly, "May I hold them?"

Mrs. Kowalski put one child in each arm. Leo felt a surge of something new filling his heart. It seemed like his heart was expanding and constricting at the same time, and he felt a love so powerful and compelling that he stood with tears streaming down his cheeks and gathering in his beard. Soon his heart simply exploded out his mouth, "Ho, Ho! I am a father and I feel great love! Never before have I felt such love and such a need to live!"

Anna was startled awake, and seeing this great man bawling and shouting his love, her eyes filled with exultation too. She lay in the peaceful exhaustion of new motherhood admiring her magnificent husband, her face beaming in happiness.

Leo was surprised at his feelings. He thought that his love for Anna was the greatest love a human could feel, but now he felt a love so powerful and moving that he knew how God must feel. Now he knew the love of a parent.

The babies were named Mary and Ur Babiraski. Anna and Leo never explained where the name Ur came from, but many supposed it came from the Bible. A priest had once told them that Abraham came from the Mesopotamian city of Ur, which meant light.

Anna simply said, "We like sound of it."

And Leo teased, "It will be easy for the boy to spell."

Warsaw, Poland, August 16, 1936

Ur leaned on the kitchen table as he listened to the Olympic results of the day. A black man, Jessie Owens, was declared the world's fastest athlete at the World Olympiad in Berlin, Germany. He won gold in the 100- and 200-meter dashes and the running broad jump. He also was a member of the 400-meter relay.

"I'll bet Hitler is crying in his Bavarian beer tonight," Ur called to his wife Beth. "What an insult to the Aryan race," he continued, as he clicked off the radio.

Beth looked up from a game she was playing with Toby and Anna. "He makes me uncomfortable with all of this 'superior race' stuff. I wish there was more than just a thin border between us and his army."

"Ah, don't worry about the Nazis. There is no way they would try to enter Poland. If they tried that, the French and British would jump on them so fast they wouldn't know what happened!" He stood and walked to the window that looked out over Stawaki Street and closed it against the evening chill.

Ur had brought his young family to Poland to teach and study at Warsaw University on the Royal Route. With Polish as his native tongue and his excellent background at Michigan State University, he had no trouble getting a visiting professorship. His plan was to stay through the spring of 1940 and then return home to Michigan.

Even though Beth was at a loss with the language, she enjoyed the Polish culture and the city. Warsaw, with its brightly lit streets, stately homes, wonderful shops and coffee houses, had been a grand adventure to her. Ur's position at the University had given them enough means to travel and see much of Europe. Beth loved Saturday afternoon picnics in the park and walks along the Vistula River. Once they had taken a short trip south and even gone camping and hiking in the beautiful Carpathian Mountains. Movies from America had given her a twinge of home sickness from time to time, but she was so in love with Ur, their children, and life in general that she bounced back into the grand experience of living in a foreign land.

Ur instantly loved this historically rich land of his forefathers. He had even met some cousins and a few other relatives. The food, the music, and the way of life seemed like home to him. Back in Minnesota his parents had given him their native tongue and their culture. Many Polish immigrants had cut off all previous ties to their culture and heritage, but Anna and Leo Babiraski wanted their two children to love and respect their Polish heritage.

Anna would say, "How do you know who you are if you don't know who you are?" Recently Ur was starting to understand what she meant.

Growing up as a twin with his sister Mary, Ur had enjoyed all the joys and trials of youth. Sometimes he thought having Mary as a sister was a particular burden. Mary was so unusual. Ur had taken after his mother—short, sensible and studious. Mary had taken after her father— tall, gregarious and more apt to play than study.

As a child, Mary loved bugs and thought everybody else should love them too. She was constantly carrying them around in her "little bug box" to show them off. One time a June bug was smashed in the screen door, and when Mary saw it she cried, "Oh, no! My best friend is dead!"

She was also more apt to be found playing ball with the boys than dolls with the girls. By the time she was in high school she was a better baseball player than most boys, but was not allowed to play on the Roosevelt High School team because she was a girl.

Ur, on the other hand, liked all the normal boy things, but books were a world beckoning to be opened and explored. He hungered to read, and he loved reading about Poland. He had read about its sad and glorious history. He read about the time when Poland ruled an empire that stretched across most of central Europe. Later, foreign powers had conquered and divided Poland to bring it to its present size. In 1918 after World War I ended, Poland had become an independent republic.

Leo and Anna often wondered what would ever become of their totally different twins. Yet in spite of being so diverse, they were bonded in a sibling love that was both powerful and beautiful.

They often came to each other's aid in school. In the seventh grade after school, Rudyard, a bully 3 inches taller, and 20 pounds heavier, began tormenting Ur by calling him derogatory Polish names. Ur, normally amiable and easy going, bristled and turned to face the larger boy. Ur knew the fight would be over in a minute, but there was something in his heart that refused to yield to this kind of prejudice.

Mary was trailing along with her friends when she saw the dust start to rise in the street ahead. Always looking for some fun, she sprinted ahead, only to see Ur on his back with the larger boy on top pounding him. She rushed in and grabbed Rudyard by the hair. He came off Ur with a yelp. Screaming and trying to get to his feet, he bounced along scraping his knees and hands as she dragged him along. Finally, at about 10 yards Mary let him go and turned to face him.

She was large, strong, and full of fight. Her voice shook with rage, "If you ever touch my brother or even talk rudely to him again, I will drag you all over this flat country by your tongue!"

Rudyard was shocked and humiliated, and turning, stumbled to catch his balance as he ran down the street. Mary went back to Ur and dusted him off as they started walking home.

"Thanks, Mary, but I hate having you fight for me," he muttered, also somewhat humiliated.

"I know, but would you rather get pounded?" she retorted.

"Mary, why do you think people torment other people just because they are different? I mean, why do some people treat us differently because we are Polish, or Negro people because they are black, or handicapped people because of their problem?"

They plodded along in silence while Mary pondered.

"Ur," Mary started slowly, feeling her way through this very difficult subject, "I have noticed that people are usually tormented about things that they can't change, by those whose problems could be changed."

"Huh?" Ur grunted.

"Okay, most people get teased or persecuted because of the color of their skin, or their national birth, or if they are ugly or have some handicap, right?"

Ur picked up a stick and clattered it along the pickets of a fence while he thought on the question. "Yeah, I guess so," he said. As the fence ended, he tossed the stick into a ditch along the road.

Mary continued, warming to the subject. "Are these things they can change? Can a black man change his birth or a handicapped person change his problem? There are some who may not want to change. For example, we wouldn't want to change who we are. We are proud of our Polish ancestry, the same as a black man or anyone else. I'm not sure about handicapped people, I'll bet they would like to change. Anyway, these are things that people do not have any control over. Yet, those who give out the tormenting have their own problems—problems that are inside of them. Problems inside can usually be changed, can't they?"

Some birds were squabbling in an elm tree so Ur picked up a rock and threw it into the tree. The squabbling stopped.

"Remember last year when those boys were teasing Claire Lynn Morrison about being an ugly flea bag?"

Ur nodded.

"I don't know who decided what is pretty or ugly, but according to Hollywood's definition Claire Lynn isn't pretty. But can she change it? No! But those boys have an ugliness that is much deeper. It is inside of them and makes them feel so worthless that they have to try to hurt others to make themselves feel better, or superior."

Ur kicked a soup can ahead of them. "Go ahead, I'm listening," he said, surprised at how clearly Mary could explain things.

"Yet, I'll bet it would be easier for those boys to change their ugliness than it would be for Claire Lynn to change how she looks. I may be wrong, but usually those who can change torment those who can't."

Ur was impressed with her reasoning. She always seemed to be better at understanding and explaining things like this than he could.

*August 1, 1939*
*Warsaw, Poland*

*Dear Mary:*

*Well, how is everything back in the land of the gophers? Has the summer been hot and muggy? And how are you? Are you still loving teaching physical education at Roosevelt High? I'll bet all of the kids love you. You have such a great talent relating to young people.*

*I was glad to hear in your last letter that Mamma and Papa are doing well. We are so lucky to have dedicated parents who have always loved us.*

*I try to follow what is happening in the good ol' USA. I was very sad to hear that Lou Gehrig has been sick and is retiring after 17 years of baseball. In case you didn't see it (although I can't imagine you missing anything that has to do with baseball), I want to quote what "Big Lou" said at Yankee Stadium on July 4. You know he has that disease that is wasting his body away. He said, "I have been given a bad break, but I have an awful lot to live for; I consider myself the luckiest man on the face of the earth." Can you believe it? What a great man!*

*This is your happy birthday letter. In one month we will both be 30 years of age. Wow, that seems old to me! So much has happened to us in our 30 years. My life has been a dream come true for me.*

*I love my work here in Poland. I love the people and the culture. At age five, Toby and Anna speak Polish almost as well as the natives. Beth is even getting along pretty well now. She is a supportive and wonderful companion, and you should see what a great mother she is! I love her so much! She is full of life, yet she worries about Germany and everything that is happening around us. The Nazis overrunning Austria and Czechoslovakia has everyone here (including Anna) anxious and worried that they will blitz Poland too. I have tried to convince Anna that Poland has two strong allies in France and Britain, and therefore Germany would not dare cross the border. I promised Beth that we would leave this winter right after the fall semester ends in January.*

*So much for that gloomy thought. I wonder what the next 30 years will bring? Or even the next 30 days. Life is a grand adventure full of twists and turns, ups and downs. It is like that roller coaster we rode as children at the State Fair. Remember when we decided to ride it with our eyes closed? We couldn't see the corners or the dips. We thought it was more fun that way. Yet with all of life's uncertainty, I still love it. Give me what life has, I am ready for it! I hope my boasting isn't an invitation for life to test my arrogance.*

*I love you, Mary. You are the greatest sister! I could not have chosen a better twin if I had looked all around the world. Give Mom and Dad my love.*

*Your loving 30-year old brother,*
*Ur*

*August 30, 1939*
*Virginia, Minnesota*

*Dear Ur:*
*Thank you for your birthday letter. It is hard to believe that we are breaking into the 30's. That used to seem like such an old age. Now it doesn't seem old at all. You have done so much with your life. My life seems a little dull compared to yours, yet I have enjoyed what I have chosen to do. I love my work with the high school. And our women's softball team is undefeated.*

*We all are worried about you and your family's safety. The clouds of war are being driven ahead of evil men. I know what you say about the alliance Poland has with France and Britain, but Hitler has not exactly worried about those minor details, has he? Please come home before it is too late.*

*Mom and Dad are very worried, and want me to ask you for my birthday present to bring your family home to us.*

*I love you, my good and adventurous brother. I, too, would have chosen you to be my twin even if I had to search the universe.*
*Love, your single and searching twin big sister,*
*Mary*


Mary's letter was still sitting in the Virginia, Minnesota post office the next day when the Nazi war machine crossed the Polish border and cut a swath of death directly to Warsaw.

August 31, 1939

Ur was reading through some old documents in a small hotel room when the phone rang. The voice was obviously trying to imitate May West's husky and sensuous voice. "Hey, doll, why don't cha come up and see me sometime?"

Digging deep to find his tough-guy Humphry Bogart voice, he replied, "Sure, babe, maybe tomorrow." They both laughed and then got serious.

"My train leaves here at 1:00 P.M. tomorrow, and I get back to Warsaw at 4:00," said Ur.

"Ur, I love you, and when you get home we will have the best birthday dinner. I am going out tomorrow morning and buy all of your favorite things."

"Just seeing you and the kids will be birthday enough."

Ur had been doing some research for the past five days in a small town near Lodz. Beth hesitantly asked, "Honey, have you been following the news?"

Ur bristled slightly. Of course he knew what was happening, and even the latest reports had caused him some discomfort. He knew pride was a grueling taskmaster and cared little for reality, but this was an old argument.

"No, not really. I have been locked in an old monastery reading old documents," he quipped sarcastically.

Beth had been persistent lately about getting out of Poland, saying, "I just don't feel comfortable, I want us to leave!"

Every day she brought up some news report about the Nazis. Ur had become resentful of her constant prodding. Never before had anything in their marriage caused as much contention for both of them as this subject. Not wanting to spoil his birthday homecoming but unable to suppress her fears, she said, "Ur, the news says Germany is massing soldiers on the border of Poland—and I'm scared."

"Beth," Ur spoke with deliberation, "Germany will not invade Poland! How many times do I have to say that! Poland has two powerful armies as allies, France and Britain." His voice was rising so he calmed down and said more gently, "Come on, don't fret. I'll be home tomorrow, and in a few months we will be back in the good ol' U.S.A. How does that sound? I promise."

Quiet tears started to trickle down Beth's cheeks. With feigned peace of mind she answered, "Okay, you're right. Maybe I'm just tired. I'll see you tomorrow."

"I love you, Beth. Kiss the children for me."

"Okay, I will. Good-bye, Ur."

As Ur hung up the phone, there was a sinking feeling in the pit of his stomach. Something wasn't right.

Virginia, Minnesota, September 1, 1939

Waking was like trying to climb out of a deep tunnel. "Mary! Mary! Wake up! Hitler go into Poland! Warsaw bombed already!" Anna cried hysterically.

Instantly, Mary bolted upright, wide awake. "Mamma, when?"

"I don't know. You try call. I just hear on radio this morning."

All day they tried to call, and when that failed they tried to contact any government office to get the news. Finally they contacted the Red Cross who said they didn't have any information except what was on the news. Frustrated and reduced to tears, Anna and Mary held each other while Leo stroked their hair and stared out the kitchen window absently. An emptiness filled each of their hearts, a gnawing of sadness and worry that wouldn't leave or diminish.

Days stretched into weeks and weeks into months and finally into years without any word. Hope is always filled with happy possibilities, but as time passed their hope faded like the bright leaves of a Minnesota fall.

# CHAPTER 7

## I Have a Right to Care for Others

One blustery fall afternoon, Mrs. Wood had an extra big pile of cookies waiting for me when I dropped off the gallon of milk. This had become the highlight of my day—to stop by and chat with her. She had an uncanny way of getting me to open up and tell her everything that was happening in my life. I even told her about the hand-holding problem I had with Moose.

She laughed herself into tears and then said, "Awful things like that happen, and years later it will be funny to talk about."

"I don't see how that will ever be funny. I sure am glad Moose hasn't said anything to anyone, or I'd be getting teased to death," I said with a cookie filling one cheek and another poised in my hand.

"Moose sounds like a young lady with a lot of maturity, and I am sure she would not want to embarrass you," Mrs. Wood commented while pouring me another glass of cold raw milk.

I was amazed at how carefully I milked since I started drinking the same milk I coaxed out of old Bessie. It seemed after the last great battle when she had put her hoof into the bucket, we had drawn a truce. She stopped ruining the milk, and I stopped referring to her with names I had seen on a menu.

Ur wheeled himself into the kitchen and Mary went to sit near him on a straight-backed kitchen chair. She leaned over and started to sign into his hands. I was so used to this routine that I continued chowing down on the cookies and skimming the pictures in a *Look* magazine. There were a couple of pictures of Marilyn Monroe that gave me brain freeze, so I didn't hear Mrs. Wood when she said she needed to ask me something.

"Jon," she said again, glancing at what had caused my brain to high-center.

"Huh?" I looked up quickly embarrassed.

"Jon, I need to go out of town this next weekend," she said carefully, "I'll leave Friday afternoon about 3 and I won't be back until Sunday night about 9."

I shifted uncomfortably, afraid of what she was going to ask of me.

"Jon, Ur and I have discussed this, and we would like you to consider staying with Ur during that time."

"I have to milk!" I spouted a little too quickly.

"Well, Ur is very independent and you would not have to be here all of the time, just most of the time. Jon, I know this will be a little hard for you, and honestly I hate to ask, but there is just not anyone else I would feel comfortable leaving with Ur. And one more thing," she looked at me intently, "Ur says it is time to start giving you the gift."

There was that gift thing again, and how do you start giving a gift over a three-day period? You either give the gift or you don't.

"As you know," she continued, " this probably isn't enough, but I could give you $25 for the weekend."

Twenty-five bucks! Now I really had brain freeze. That was five tanks of gas, and more than I would make in a month at Mr. Johnson's farm.

She must have seen my eyes light up because she started to smile. "Will that be okay?"

I stammered, "Sure."

"Ur will explain his needs to you when you come over." She quickly swished a few signs to Ur, and I saw his face light up.

"Jon," Ur was speaking in that wonderfully quiet voice, "I promise you two things. First, you will enjoy this weekend; and second, you will never be the same again. That is the effect of the gift."

I lifted his hand to my cheek where he could read my speech. "What is the gift?" I said slowly and little too loudly.

His placid eyes seemed to twinkle. "You just wait."

Not that she would worry anyway, but I told Moose that I couldn't see her this weekend because I was baby-sitting a deaf-blind guy.

"Oh, that will be so rewarding," she cooed. Somehow I was sure she was not referring to the 25 bucks.

I also told Mr. Johnson I would have to have the weekend off. He said, "No problem. I'll bet Bessie will enjoy a change of hands." Then he enjoyed his own joke with a good laugh and slapped me on my back.

The Friday afternoon football game was pretty standard for me. I sat on the bench and jumped up every once in awhile to yell, "Good pass, Mike!" or "Way to catch, Bruce!" "Nice run Larry!" After the game, I dropped by Minn's Café for a chocolate shake with Kenny before going over to take care of Ur. I casually asked Kenny if Moose was all disappointed about me not being available this weekend.

"She hasn't said anything," Kenny said dryly, "How come you want to take care of some old deaf-blind guy?"

"It's rewarding," I said simply.

"How much?" Kenny asked.

Boys think alike, I thought. Bristling I said, "What makes you think I have to do it for money?"

"Forget it," Kenny snorted, "but I'll bet you're not doing it for free."

I put the 65 cents out for the milkshake plus a couple extra pennies as a tip and got up to leave. "See you next Monday, Kenny, and don't let your belt … loop."

Kenny grinned and shot back, "Okay, but don't let your … " Kenny thought for a moment, "eye … lash, or your ear … lobe!" Kenny and I always parted that way.

Popping my clutch, I caught a little rubber in my 1963 Plymouth as I shot across the only main intersection in town. I hoped someone noticed my car was hot enough to peel out.

Pulling up in front of Mrs. Wood's pretty white cottage just after dark, I noticed the lights were out. I was relieved to think that Ur had gone to bed. Grabbing my ditty-bag with some extra socks and Fruit of the Looms, I slipped out of the car. I noticed Mrs. Wood's car was gone and the house was totally dark. Since nobody in Declo locked their doors, I just clicked open the kitchen door and went in.

"Hi, Jon."

"Yikes!" I screamed as I nearly jumped out of my Converse All Stars. Sitting in his wheelchair facing the door was Ur. How did he know I was in the house? Catching my breath I smelled something great! You probably wonder how I could want any more food after dropping a chocolate shake in my gut. If the truth be known, I thought I had a hollow leg and that shake would only fill it to about my ankle.

"Come sit and eat." He spun his chair around and opened the oven. Using a hot pad, he slid out a tray of something. "These are Polish pasties."

It was hard to see them in the dark so I sat down and put my eyes down real close until my face started to burn. I did think about turning on the lights, but then I figured that the power must be off or a fuse blown. I was just grateful that the power hadn't gone off before he got through cooking. They looked like little pie turnovers. He popped the cap off a bottle of Hires rootbeer and poured it into a glass without spilling a drop.

My brain started twitching like it does when things are not fitting into the scheme of things. I mean, I could hardly see the cup myself. Yet Ur opened the old refrigerator, grabbed the bottle of rootbeer (he could have grabbed the Hunts Ketchup), picked up a glass from a low shelf and the bottle opener out of a drawer, popped the cap off, and poured a full glass without spilling a drop. I remind you, this in almost total darkness. Then he reached into the silverware drawer and picked out a knife and fork and slid them over to me.

"Go ahead and eat. I've made 10 of these; let's see if once and for all we can fill you up."

I didn't know what else to do so I reached out and touched his hand and then plowed in. These little folded pies were stuffed with spuds (an Idaho staple), carrots, sweet Walla Walla onions and several big chunks of deliciously seasoned beef. Between the 10 pasties and about a gallon of rootbeer, I was pretty much filled up in about 15 minutes.

"Are you ready for dessert?" Ur asked with a smile.

I touched his hand. He turned and opened the freezer part of the fridge. Stretching high, he retrieved a big dish of something and set it on the table in front of me. Leaning over and sniffing the big pile on the chilled plate, my heart and eyes lit up. Chocolate puddin' cake with homemade vanilla ice cream on top! With everything I had already eaten I was sure my belly button had already cauliflowered out; but what the heck, I didn't get puddin' cake every day. I threw it in on top of that milkshake and all those pasties, and for the first time since Thanksgiving dinner last year, I was full.

Ur sat quietly while I gorged myself. Finally he asked, "Are you finished?"

I touched his arm.

"Are you full?"

I touched his arm again.

"Let me show you something." He reached out and took my hand. Folding my fingers into a fist, he said, "Now let your fist nod up and down like your head when you nod yes." He kept his hand over mine and smiled when I nodded my hand. "Good, that is how to sign 'yes' and you can shake it from side to side to say 'no.' Do you understand me?"

After a moment, I nodded my hand and Ur smiled again.

"If you want to say more, put my hand to your face like I showed you before, okay?"

I nodded my hand again. He and I sat there for awhile and I felt a comfortable silence  come into the room. Finally, I reached out, took his hand and lifted it to my face. "How long has the power been off?"

"Power off?" he puzzled, "I didn't know the power was off. Are you sure?"

"Well, why are the lights all off?" I inquired.

A gentleness filled his voice and before he said three words I felt dumber than a thousand head of sheep. "Jon, I never know if the lights are on or not. My blindness is total."

For some reason I had never realized that for Ur the sun never rose, and darkness never came. It was always there. I knew I shouldn't ask, but I couldn't hold myself back.

"How did you lose your eyesight? I mean, if you don't want to answer it's okay, because it isn't any of my business," I added quickly.

Mildly he said, "I'm not sure I caught everything you just said, but I think you asked me how I lost my eyesight?"

I nodded my hand.

He touched a button on his watch and the glass part flipped open. Running his finger over the dial he said, "Tomorrow we will talk about the gift."

Did the gift have something to do with his blindness? If so, what?

He then closed the glass part on his watch and wheeled toward his bedroom. I followed him. He negotiated every turn and obstacle perfectly. He could see things in the dark house that I couldn't. I wasn't sure how that worked.

I followed him and busted my shins on a low table. Ur paused at his door. "Thank you for coming here to be with me. I promise you, I will make it worth your while."

Yeah, I thought, 25 bucks for two days is worth my while already.

"And I don't mean the $25 either." Did this old man read minds too?

"You can put your things in the guest room to your left and use the restroom across the hall."

I nodded my hand and then printed into his palm in big block letters, "T-H-A-N-K-S."

Again I felt a great gentle power come from his touch. I went to sleep wondering about the gift and feeling a strange anticipation. Maybe it was the feeling new recruits feel the night before they enter boot camp—a feeling that their lives will never be the same after tomorrow.

# CHAPTER 8

## I Have the Right to Give and Receive Good Gifts

I rose early with a bad case of bed-head. I dressed but trying to get my hair to lie down was harder than eating nails so I gave up and went to the kitchen. I cleaned up last night's dishes and put them away. About 7:00 I heard Ur moving around. I didn't know what to do or if he needed my help, but I figured that he would ask if he did.

When I heard the shower running I tried to imagine what that was like, to shower without any legs or what a life was like in total silence and darkness—jailed in solitary confinement for life. Yet Ur seemed to have a good attitude about himself, and I honestly had never met anyone more cheerful and optimistic, unless it was his twin sister.

I seemed to find myself getting depressed or giving up on things that didn't come easy. I just didn't seem to have any self discipline or stick-to-it-iveness. Like reading or math. I am sure if I stayed with it I would learn some of that stuff, but I just couldn't seem to concentrate on anything for more than two minutes except television. That was easy to concentrate on. I wish school was like the *I Love Lucy Show* or *F-Troop* or a movie, then I would get straight "A's."

Everything that was good for me seemed to be beyond my ability to get. I guess I could have done better if Mom had been able to read or write, or maybe that was just an excuse. Kenny said I had an excuse for everything and maybe I did. I'd say, "I can't do good in school because my parents aren't well educated," or "I don't excel in sports because it doesn't run in the family."

71

"You've got lots of excuses and not much action!" Kenny shouted at me one time when I didn't want to ride our bikes the eight miles to Albion.

I said, "I'm not sure my bike will make it." Yet in my heart, I was too lazy to try. But that is just how I was born and I figured I couldn't do much about it.

Ur wheeled into the kitchen about 30 minutes later. It looked like it took him longer to get ready than most men. Most men take about 30 seconds.

I don't know much about girls except Kenny said Moose takes about two hours to get herself all worked up into a presentable image. I had no idea why it would take her that long. I saw her once real early in the morning before she had "got ready." Her hair was all crazy and her face looked a little washed out, but she was still dang good looking. I didn't think she used much make-up; at least I couldn't tell if she did.

I'd like to have about an hour just to sit and study her face. Once in an assembly she sat right in front of me and I spent the whole time just looking at the back of her head thinking about her. It was the best assembly of the year and I didn't even know what it was about.

I held real still to see if Ur would know I was there.

"Good morning, Jon." He lifted his hand toward me.

I reached out and brought it to my face. "Good morning. I made some mush for breakfast. Do you want some?"

"Yes, that would be nice. Thank you."

"Do you want sugar, cinnamon and raisins in it or what?"

"No sugar please, and the rest doesn't matter; I like it either way."

After breakfast Ur and I cleaned up our dishes. I was still amazed at how he got around without bumping into things or spilling stuff. It was like he had this other sense.

"How do you get around without bumping into things?" I finally asked.

"I have memorized where things are and I see them in my mind. As long as everything stays in the same place I'm okay, but if something is moved," he blew out some breath, "I will hit it."

It didn't take long for me to prove him right. I moved a kitchen chair to sweep under the table and had not put it back. Soon, Ur came around the table and crashed into the chair, pinching his fingers between the chair and his wheel.

"Ouch! What is this?" he said, shaking his hand.

Taking his unhurt hand to my face, I apologized.

"Not to worry, I'm used to it. My sister Mary is always leaving things around. Sometimes it is like an obstacle course around here." Ur got a glass and filled it with water from the tap. He drank it and said, "Now if you will take me outside to the back lawn, I want to give you something."

Finally, the gift! I thought. I helped him out to the back lawn and he directed me to a post standing in the middle of the lawn. It was a gnarled old juniper post that had been there for many years. Folks in Declo called them cedar posts, but I heard they were really from a juniper tree. Regardless, it was a knotty, tough post, larger at the bottom than at the top.

Ur leaned forward and pushed on the post. "I think this was once an upright for a clothesline. The other post is gone. I bumped into this one day when I was exploring the back yard. I would like to give you this valuable post if you can get it out."

I just gawked at him. Holy Smoke! I thought. This guy's ears and eyes are not the only thing's busted. Not only couldn't he see, hear, or walk, but his whole concept of what was valuable was more screwed up than the governor's budget. Juniper posts were a dime a dozen, and what would I want with one anyway? But…I was being paid 25 big George Washingtons for this weekend, and even though I didn't know it involved hard physical labor, I guessed I could accommodate him.

And to tell you the truth, I was disappointed in the gift. I thought it would be something cool that I really needed like an old classic car he used to drive before the war or something like that. I told Kenny that Ur said he was going to give me a gift this weekend. Now what was I going to tell him? "Oh man, it was so cool! He gave me something I always wanted—a fence post!"

"Where's the shovel and pry bar?" I said coolly.

"Jon, I feel your disappointment," he whispered soothingly, "If you take this post out according to my instructions, it will be a treasure more valuable than you can imagine right now. If all the potatoes and sugar beets in this county were gold ingots and you owned them, it would not be as valuable as this post."

I shifted uncomfortably. This was not making sense to me. This guy was crazy, and I was beginning to think twenty-five dollars wasn't enough.

"Jon, you will need to take the post out with your hands and not with anything else. Not a shovel, not a pry bar or rope or anything." He let that sink in.

I scrunched one side of my face and stared off into the distance with the same look all teenagers use when adults are not making sense.

I noticed Ur's hand feel down the post searching for something until he found the right place. "Here, in this crevice you can see where I had Mary drill a small hole." I glanced down where his finger was pointing. "Rolled up and squeezed into that hole is a $1,000 bill."

I dropped to my knees like a chunk of lead and searched for the hole. I could barely see a tiny rolled thing way back in the crevice.

"When you get the post out, if you still don't think the post is more valuable than the money, you can have the money and I will say nothing. But you must think about the things I will teach you while you are removing the post. Take your time and be patient."

Dumbfounded by what he had told me, I reached out and pushed hard on the post. It was set like cement. I mean, if you run a mile-long Union Pacific freight train into that post, I'd bet it would have stood the train right on its nose. Without tools I had about as much chance of getting that post out as a worm crossing the highway on a sunny day.

Yet, we are talking about a $1,000. I could at least give it a try; and who knows, maybe Ur would see the uselessness of doing it without tools and say, "Hey, Jon, just go ahead and lay into it with a shovel and crow bar and you can still keep the money." Obviously, I didn't know Ur very well at the time, nor did I understand the value of the gift.

Ur looked directly at me, and speaking slowly with great sincerity, he said, "Jon, I know you can do this. You must realize that you cannot see all I want to give you at this point, and you must believe I can give you something of great worth. You only understand the post and the $1,000, but I understand the process, and I see what you can become. I really mean it when I say that the process of removing the post is more valuable than all the golden potatoes and beets in this

74

county. I don't expect you to comprehend this today, only to trust me. Jon," and he seemed to be looking right at me, "will you trust me?"

The question hung in the air like a hot air balloon, not going up and not going down. I looked at that question. I walked around it and studied it from all sides. I looked under it and on top of it. Somehow, I knew that if I said yes, it would change my life forever, and if I said no it would change my life forever. I knew yes meant doing something I had never done before. It meant a scary step along a dark path, along a path Ur said he could see. Could I trust a blind man to lead me down a dark path? He said if things stay constant, he can move in his world without danger. Who would be better able to lead in the dark than someone whose life is lived in darkness and yet sees? Maybe the truth was that my life was the darkness and his was the light. I certainly seemed to stumble along from day to day without any serious thought or direction in my life. He seemed to see more in life with his limited senses than I could with all of mine.

I stood and peeled a little bark from the post. I looked down at my hand. Why was it trembling? Did my heart sense the gravity of this decision better than my mind? I don't know how or why, but suddenly my entire being was filled with a new hope and confidence in Ur. I was like the drowning man who had a thin rope tossed to him. The rope appeared too thin to hold his weight, but because of his desperate circumstances he hoped with all his heart that it would be enough to save him. So even if I didn't understand how taking the post out could save me from the malignant mire of mediocrity that I was floundering in, this I did know—I trusted Ur! Never before had such hope stirred my young heart as I reached out my fist and nodded it into both of Ur's outstretched hands.

Looking into his eyes, I was surprised to see them glistening and a small tear coursing down his cheek. My throat got tight and my eyes started to burn. Who is this old man? And why did he care about me? Is this what it felt like to have a father?

With an emotional voice he said, "I have waited a long time to give this gift to a son. I don't have a son anymore, but I sense some kind of kinship with you. I sense your sincerity to accept this sacred gift from me. I know you will receive my gift."

He released my hands and rubbed his hand over his bald head as if searching for a thought. A hunting party of sea gulls passed overhead looking for something to bomb. Then he spoke again in a quiet guarded voice, "Yet, I must warn you. You are filled with conviction and determination right now, but real mettle is tempered by what you do after the emotion of the decision has passed. Jon, remove the post!"

I grabbed the post with both hands and tore into it like a D-9 Cat. I pushed forward and back, side to side. I tugged and pulled until my hands started to hurt and tear from the rough timber. Discouragement started to replace my enthusiasm; my breath started to come in gasps, and my lungs burned. The post had not moved even a fraction of an inch. Soon I dropped to the ground and rubbed my stinging hands. Ur leaned forward and put his hand on my sweating face.

"Talk to me," was all he said.

"I can't do it," I rasped.

"You have misunderstood and thought a great task was handled like a small task. A whim or fleeting thought does not move a mountain. Mountains are moved one shovel-full at a time. There is rarely ever an all-at-once in life; it is usually a long grind. You are seeing only the end as your source of happiness and satisfaction. Memorize this: "Happiness is cleverly nested in the process of attaining predetermined, worthwhile goals."

My eyes widened in confusion. "I don't even know what that all means."

"It means you must learn to recognize happiness while doing worthwhile things, not just in the end reward. Usually the greatest reward is in the process of attainment, not just in the finishing."

I got to my knees and knelt before him so we could talk more easily. "Is this what you mean when you say that removing the post will give me a greater reward than the $1,000?"

"Yes."

"How?"

"Because of what you will become when you do it. You change. It is like the weightlifter, who lifts weights to build strength. It is the doing that makes him strong."

My eyes stung with tears again. "Do you think I can ever make something of my life if I can get the post out?"

"I guarantee it!" and then he was quiet for a while before continuing in a mild voice. "But, you will have to be gentle with me and with yourself. I will teach you what I know as long as you are willing to learn. No one can ever be taught who does not want to learn. Nobody progresses against his will. It is impossible. Jon, I know you can if you will. Will you?"

With a determination I had never felt before, I nodded my hand again.

"Good, let's go back into the house. I want to tell you about the war."

I have the right to do good. I never have a right to do
bad...I only have the power to choose it.

# CHAPTER 9

## I Have a Right to Sleep Better When I Maintain My Inherent Rights

E ntering the kitchen I saw Ur open a drawer, pull out a giant bag of M&M's and pour them into a salad bowl. I guessed it was going to be a long conversation, but on a steady diet of M&M's I could listen a long time. Outside I heard the loud rhythmic hum of a hay baler in a field across the street. Larry Hurst was baling up his third crop of alfalfa. Occasional shouts of someone trying to give instructions across the same hay field were drowned out as the baler came closer to the house.

Ur positioned himself near me so he could reach out and touch my face whenever he wanted to understand what I was saying. With more self discipline than I have ever mustered, I ate the M&M's one at a time.

"Jon, you probably know by now that what I want to give you is not the cedar post, nor the $1,000 dollars for that matter." Ur smiled and I nodded into his hand. "What I really want to give you is The Pristine American Dream."

My eyebrows lifted in surprise.

"I want to emphasize that The Pristine American Dream is not wealth or power, although it may include both of them. Pristine means original, still pure, uncorrupted, unspoiled. When I talk about The Pristine American Dream, I am talking about how it was for the founding fathers of this nation. The Pristine American Dream is the maintaining of one's inherent rights to be and do good, and then going for the great and exciting privileges of life. Too many people go for the privileges of life without giving any serious thought to their inherent rights to be good."

I shook his hand to interrupt him. "What are privileges? I thought the privileged few were the wealthy?"

"Not always. I'll teach you more about privileges and how to receive them later. For now, just understand a privilege is a good thing you acquire by earning or qualifying for it. Life offers an infinite number of good things to receive. You will not live long enough to receive them all, but you can try for as many as you have the time.

"A few privileges are power through wealth, education, politics and parenthood. It is the honor of being a successful father, mother, doctor, teacher, and so on."

"I know a lot of people who seem to have wealth or power but aren't good," I challenged, trying to understand.

"Yes, so do I. Maintaining one's inherent rights is not required in order for someone to receive privileges, but it is required for the person to be safe with his privileges. Someone who does not maintain his inherent rights to be good is a threat to himself, his family and his community if he receives privileges. Especially powerful privileges, like political power, being a parent, or a teacher."

I swallowed some water to prepare my mouth for another onslaught of serious M&M eating when I thought to ask, "Why would they be a threat?"

"These people are dangerous because they hold powerful privileges and can influence other people toward their own unwholesome attitudes. If the person with the power is not good then the influence he naturally radiates is also not good; in fact it will be bad. If a parent is bad, he puts his children under a precarious influence, or when a teacher is a bad person, then he may exert an unwholesome influence on his students. We all know the corruption in politics and the havoc that is wreaked on societies when the leaders are bad. Take Hitler for example."

"I've never heard it explained this way before. Where did you learn this?" I interrupted with about a hundred M&M's in my mouth, having momentarily lost all of my control.

"Strange as it is, I learned this from an old Jewish man during World War II. Let me start from the beginning. Are you comfortable?"

"You bet. I'm as comfortable as a featherbed."

Ur paused for a second, trying to catch my meaning, then seemed to give up and began. Ur explained about growing up in Virginia, Minnesota, marrying Beth during his third year of undergraduate school, and the birth of their beautiful twins, Toby and Anna.

I thought at the time he was spending way too much time talking about his wife and kids. This part seemed a little boring to me, but with M&M's to hold my attention I figured I could stay with him until the exciting part started.

He told me that after he hung up the phone in Lodz on August 31, 1939, he had a sick, desperate feeling that he should call Beth and tell her to take the kids and get on the overnight train to Paris. "I knew what the right thing was for me to do, but I just couldn't bring myself to do it," he whispered in anguish, "Do you know what I mean?"

Man, did I know what he meant! I have felt that way ten thousand times—this week!

Ur continued, "Inside I knew I had made a mistake. You know that feeling? Inside you feel sick and trembling, your conscience is throbbing. Hindsight is 20/20 vision, right? I should have acted on my conscience and called Beth immediately."

"I tossed and turned until 3 in the morning and then fell into a fitful sleep. Something awakened me a little after 5:00. At first, I thought it was a fly buzzing in the room. The buzzing grew louder until it became the droning of a thousand Dorier bombers. I was instantly wide awake. Throwing off the covers, I ran onto the balcony and stood frozen with dread and loathing. The sky was full of Nazi bombers heading east towards Warsaw. Wave after wave roared by, until the sickness which started after hanging up the phone the night before spilled out over the railing into the flowerbed below.

"Running to the phone in the lobby, I tried to call Beth, but apparently the hotel operator had fled at the first sound of the bombers. For an hour I ran from hotel to hotel trying to call on the other phones in town, but there were not any lines open to Warsaw. By then there was wide spread panic and chaos throughout the entire town.

"Overloaded cars filled with heavily dressed families were struggling to leave Lodz in any direction possible. The train's engineers were refusing to move for fear of being bombed on open tracks. All of my options to get to Warsaw were closed except one, and that one option would give me plenty of time to think about my stubbornness and pride. I started walking toward Warsaw.

"By the time I cleared the city limits of Lodz, Nazi lorries were on the main roads, so I left the road and started across the fields. I was settled into a grim resolve to get to my family no matter what! I fought down the overwhelming panic I felt for my family's safety and tried to clear my mind. That which I loved the most in this world was still in Warsaw. Every step conjured up the terror-filled faces of Beth, Toby and Anna."

Ur stopped to consider how to tell the next part. I sat fixed in one position. Only then did I realize that the M&M in my hand was melted into pudding. Knowing Ur couldn't see me, I licked my hand clean and then wiped it on my sock.

I tried to imagine this man then, and the feelings he felt for his family. If it were Moose, I would have felt wretched. I would have cried all the way to Warsaw. I couldn't say much about how he felt for his kids, but I guessed it was strong.

Ur reached out, felt for my glass, and finding it, he whipped his wheelchair around to the sink and set his and my glass on the counter. He filled them with water and brought them back. I sipped the water as he started speaking again.

"That evening I stayed with a farmer and his wife in a small white cottage. We huddled around their radio to hear the reports. The Nazi army was moving quickly toward Warsaw, and Warsaw had already sustained severe damage from the bombers. The Polish army was putting up a valiant, yet useless defense. I waited with clenched hands to hear where destruction had happened in the city, but the report ended abruptly.

"That night I slept for an hour or two and then started out again, walking by the light of a quarter moon. After sun-up, I checked the knapsack I was carrying and discovered I had either lost my wallet with my money and identification papers, or I had left it at the hotel. My first thought was to retrace my steps over the fields and through the woods to search for my papers. Then I thought of my family and knew if they were dead I wouldn't care about living or my papers for that matter. And if they were living, well, I would just have to work that out later."

Ur suddenly addressed me, "Jon, what do you think scares your mom the most?"

"I don't know. I guess dying."

"No, it is <u>you</u> dying. That is what scares every good parent the most," he stated emphatically. "This is what was scaring me the most as I slogged along through the fields and the streams. I was distressed beyond words for the welfare of my wife and children.

"It took me five days to finally reach Warsaw. By this time the Nazis were in control, and because I had no identification papers I had to avoid the checkpoints. It took me another day to reach our neighborhood. Only the street sign told me I had found it. Smoke was still rising from the collapsed buildings and spreading a pall of death over the neighborhood. It was hard to tell where one building started and another stopped. Only the lighter gray stone finally identified our apartment house. It had taken a direct hit and only part of three walls still stood.

"I scrambled up the rubble crying out for my family. I tore at the wreckage until my hands were raw and bleeding, and a couple fingernails were ripped off. Exhaustion finally brought me to total collapse, shaking with sobs. I slept on the stones, with the nightmares of three faces filled with horror. I knew they were gone, yet I couldn't keep myself from looking for them. In the red haze of the morning's first light I saw a man, like me, sick with sorrow, pawing at rubble across the street. I asked him about survivors.

'Nobody got out. It was too quick, before they even awakened. The cowards just bombed them in their beds. I have lost my daughter and grandchildren,' he mourned.

"I sat on the rubble for another hour. Deep in my core a fiery hatred began to smolder into flame. It grew slowly, fed by the winds of guilt and injustice. I began to feel a hatred for the Nazis that seemed to consume my flesh. I wanted to die, but before I died, I wanted to let my hatred have its way. I wanted to kill, hate, and kill some more. Then I would die.

"At dawn, I erected three stone pillars from the rubble for my family and set out to kill and to die. Within a week I would have my wish."

# CHAPTER 10

## I Have a Right to Be Honest With Myself

I sat transfixed, unable to take my eyes off Ur. I had never heard a story like this before and wondered how much of it was true. Yet it seemed true. I mean, Ur seemed sincere. Ur shifted his weight and continued.

"I was a walking shadow of death. The guilt, hunger, and sleeplessness turned me into a miserable creature with sunken red eyes, wild with hopeless searching. A filthy and grizzled beard formed on my face, and my hair was matted and tangled. Everything was so chaotic. I wandered aimlessly for two more days.

"The stench of rotting corpses and burning buildings filled me with nausea. Someplace, I knew my little family was helping to fill the air with foulness. Without identification papers and money, I begged, scavenged and stole food.

"On the third or fourth day I saw two Nazi soldiers coming down a street toward me. From near a burned-out building I watched them as they split up, one going down a dead-end alley and the other one to confront me alone on the street. At the sight of the big black boots, heavy uniform, helmet, and the ugly red, white and black swastikas, I boiled over.

" 'Show me your papers,' he snarled.

"Jon, my life was a burden to me. I honestly didn't care if I lived or died. Even when I had legs, I was never very tall, but I was strong. I just attacked him. I threw myself at his legs like I had done with Mary so many times when we were growing up."

85

I tried to imagine Ur and Mary wrestling. It was an odd thought. "I guess I surprised him because he just collapsed, and his gun clattered to the ground. I swung my fist violently again and again at his face. Soon I heard feet running toward me. Good, I thought. It must be the other soldier coming. Fine, let him kill me now and end my misery. I continued to pummel the man under me. A strong hand jerked me away and I saw the bloodied unconscious face of the soldier, who now just seemed a boy. Swift hands were stripping him of grenades, ammunition and papers.

"An urgent voice whispered, 'Run, Mr. Fighterman! Run and you may fight again.' A young man smiled at me and then scrambled off, picking up the fallen machine gun as he darted away. I jumped up and started to run after him.

"'Hey, wait! Who are you?'

" 'One who lives to fight another day—Come join me!' he panted over his shoulder. We darted around a corner and headed down what appeared to be a dead-end street. High red brick walls closed in on us and panic seized me. I could hear whistles and shouts that announced the soldier had been found. Other soldiers would soon be swarming around the corner and this dead end would become my dead end.

"Sprinting for a pile of rubbish, the young man shifted his loot to one arm and with the other pulled aside an old mattress and a board, revealing a hole in the wall. After shoving the plunder through the wall he scrambled in and waved for me to follow. I squeezed through quickly. He reached out through the hole, pulled everything back in place to disguise his secret escape route, and watched through a crack. Nazi soldiers peered down the dead end street and then moved quickly on, searching for us in another place.

"Looking up at me, he introduced himself as Mordechai Anielewicz,[1] then stood, politely thanked me, and asked if I wanted to come with him and meet some others who were setting up an underground resistance.

"A short distance away we entered a basement and followed some kind of tunnel to another building. Climbing the stairs to the fourth floor we entered a room with about eight people. At first there

---

[1] In some places Mordechai's last name is Tannenbaum.

was a flurry of suspicion and angry questions about me being a Gestapo agent. After Mordechai explained how we met everyone seemed more at ease.

"Across the room sitting under a light was an old man who was introduced as Abraham. He was dressed in black, had a long white beard and wore small wire-frame glasses. I guess what stood out to me wasn't his age. It was his whole countenance. In the midst of all this death and destruction he had a peacefulness, almost a cheerfulness about him. This was such a sharp contrast to me that I almost loathed him at first sight. Trying to justify my own hatred, I thought, what could he know? If he had been through what I have been through, it would wipe that happiness right off his face.

"How did my world cave in so quickly? It amazed me to realize how fragile and unpredictable life could be. Only two weeks before, Beth, Toby, Anna and I had been picnicking in the cool of a shaded park, not a mile from where I then sat. People stopped and fussed over the twins. Now they were dead, and I was a hunted man in the middle of an ugly and savage war. If the Nazis found me I would be shot—that much I knew. Dying didn't scare me; living did. But before I died I wanted to deal revenge to as many Nazis as possible.

"Over the next several days the old bearded man tried to talk with me, but I ignored him. Mordechai was trying to set up some kind of organization that would protect the ghetto while attempting to evacuate the Jews and others from the Nazi persecution that assuredly would follow as soon as Poland was secure.

"It did not take long for the Nazis to begin their program of killing certain ethnic groups. Their focus was mainly on the Jews, but they also included Gypsies, some religious groups and the handicapped, especially the mentally handicapped. The mental hospitals were being emptied of the mentally ill, and all over German-occupied land people were mysteriously disappearing. You can imagine the uneasiness of the Jewish people I was associated with.

"Soon the 3 million Jews in Poland would be crowded into the ghettos of the larger cities. These were walled areas set aside for Jews, outside which they could not go. I was not Jewish but nobody knew the difference, or cared for that matter, so I was accepted into the resistance.

"For the first while our group did nothing except plan, try to gather arms, and keep communication open with the other ghettos. Mordechai's motto was 'We go not like lambs to the slaughter.' We really did not have much to fight with—a few guns, and some bottles and old light bulbs filled with acid. Later the group would become a force to be dealt with that inflicted great casualties on the Nazis.

"One morning Mordechai ordered everyone out scavenging for food and weapons except myself and the old man, Abraham Wiseman. I protested loudly to Mordechai and told him I didn't want to be locked up with that old coot.

"Mordechai bristled, and stated, 'You must learn something from Abraham. But this will never happen until you know him and are willing to listen.'

" 'What can I learn from that old man? Remember, I have a doctorate from a big American university,' I boasted.

" 'You are smart in your head, Ur, but you are not smart in your heart. You are not fighting the same enemy as we are. You are only fighting the same soldiers,' Mordechai said quietly.

"I sulked the rest of the day and grew restless toward evening. Abraham treated me with kindness, but I was so filled with hatred and anger that I could only respond with caustic remarks.

"As evening came on, out of boredom I finally asked, 'So, Mr. Wise-man Abraham, what am I supposed to learn from you?'

"With kindness I didn't deserve, he said, 'What would you like to learn?'

" 'Oh, that is it, huh?' I stood and walked to the window and looked out over the ghetto. People wrapped against the cold were hurrying here and there on unknown errands. I turned and faced the old man. 'We have to play some kind of word games, do we? All right. I am so bored I don't care. I want to know what Mordechai meant by, 'I am not fighting the same enemy as you Jews, only the same soldiers.'

"Abraham peeled off his wire-frame glasses and began polishing them with his handkerchief as he considered the right way to answer my question. 'The enemy you fight is hatred and anger. We fight the Nazi. We fight to protect and save our people. You fight to spew forth your hatred.'

"Stinging from the accusation, I struck out. 'What do you know, old man? If you had been through what I have been through, you would be filled with hatred too. I lost my wife and both of my children! And the Nazis did it! I want to kill as many as I can before I die.' The venom of my heart was erupting like a volcano. I could not stop it. 'This is not my war. I am not a Jew!... and I am not a citizen of Poland!' I shouted. My words echoed in the room as I stood rooted to the floor, glaring at Abraham.

"His eyes filled with compassion. 'My heart aches for your sad tragedy. You are not the only one who has suffered the loss of your loved ones. Yet, you are the only one in our group who rides your hatred to death.' He sat in our bare room, his back against the wall. A sadness filled his eyes as he rubbed the heel of his hand against his temple as if he was trying to massage some painful memory away. He took a deep breath and blew it out.

"Finally he looked up at me. 'I was in the outdoor privy behind my house when the Nazis' lorries rolled into our village. Before I knew it they were rounding up all the Jews in my village, including my family. From the parted door I watched as they were herded into the synagogue. They kept three men on the outside and locked everyone else—men, women and children—inside. One of the men kept outside was my son David. His young wife and three daughters were pushed with gun butts into the building. I watched from my hiding place as my son David and the other two were nailed to the door and the building set on fire. I listened to the screaming and pounding of my family and friends until the last scream was burned out of their throats.' He sat with his legs drawn up and his chin resting on his knees. 'Believe me when I say I know your pain and guilt.'

"Shocked, but pricked into more anger, I shouted, 'What guilt?'

" 'As you said, Ur, you are not Jewish. You are an American Christian. This is not your war. There was plenty of warning that Germany was going to invade. Why did you stay?' He asked directly.

"His question stabbed me like a hot piece of iron. It pierced me to the very center of my heart. Why did I stay? Maybe his question stung so badly because I knew the answer: my pride, my enslaving pride. I put the truth out of my mind and thought, is this old man placing the blame of what had happened to my family at my feet? Is he insinuating that I am responsible for the death of my family? I jumped to my feet and stood facing him, trembling with rage and hostility. 'What are you saying, you stupid old man? I'll kill you!' I shouted, and I started toward him. My mind was blind with fury.

"Abraham had not stirred, or made any attempt to defend himself. Halfway across the room, he calmly spoke one sentence that tore through the hard plate of pride and denial to pierce solidly into my heart and stopped me mid-step. In a voice full of love he simply said, 'The guilty person blows up at truth because it cuts to his very center.' He paused, 'Ur, you will never find peace until you are willing to be honest.'

"I stood immovable in the middle of the room. Every word he spoke sunk deep into my soul. I knew what he was saying was the truth.

"'Peace of mind comes when we exercise our right to be honest, especially with ourselves,' he said.

"In a defensive half-hearted tone I asked, 'How am I not honest?'

"He looked at me with placid eyes, and in a mild voice asked, 'Please, come sit.' He patted his old hand on the floor near him.

"I hesitated. Half of me wanted to go sit and be tutored, while the other half rebelled and wanted to strike out in anger.

"Seeing my indecisiveness, Abraham stated earnestly, 'Ur, never overlook the obvious solutions to your problems because usually they are the right ones, and the obvious solution to this problem is to come, sit and talk with me.'

"Sighing loudly I walked over to the window, grabbed a wooden chair, placed it in front of Abraham and sat down. I was tired, tired of hating, tired of fear, and war, and everything in Poland. Why did I sit down to listen to the old man? There was something in this old man that spoke peace to my mind and hope to my heart. How could this be possible in the middle of every man's worst nightmare? What wasn't I being honest about? The Nazis did kill my family, and isn't my hate justified and my desire to kill them the right response? Still, if these feelings are right, why don't I feel right about them?"

In Mrs. Wood's kitchen, Ur and I sat in quiet contemplation for awhile. A magpie had started up an argument in the tree out front while some kids were arguing about whose turn it was to mow their lawn. What I heard so far awed me to be sure. I didn't totally doubt Ur, but on the other hand he didn't seem quite the type to do much in a war either.

His near fisticuffs later that same afternoon with the meanest man in the whole county changed my mind about that.

One of the hardest things for people to grasp about unalienable rights is that they always are the right thing to do.

# CHAPTER 11

## I Am Born With Inherent Rights

"You see Jon," Ur concluded, "Maintaining our inherent rights is like maintaining a public highway. When properly maintained you travel faster, safer and with greater peace of mind through life."

I nodded my head. It was beginning to make sense. I noticed the watch on Ur's arm. I thought, that's the craziest thing I'd ever seen, a blind man with a watch on his arm. Ur was fumbling with some button on the watch's side and the crystal flipped up. With the tip of his forefinger he felt the dial. Moving closer, I could see that the watch wasn't like mine. His watch had bumps on the dial. He was reading the time by feeling the bumps.

"Jon, it's almost noon. Would you mind going with me down to Minn's Café for some lunch?"

"Sure," I said hesitantly, "but I want to hear the rest of this story."

"I promise you'll hear all that you need to, but right now I'm hungry for a cheeseburger and fries. How about you?"

"You know me, I'm always as hungry as a monk," I answered cheerfully.

Since Minn's was only a couple of blocks away, Ur asked me to push him. It was a rare and beautiful fall day. Some of the poplar trees were hinting of fall colors, and the little sticky yellow flowers were giving off pungent odors. The light wind was from the west and carried the comforting smell of Hurst's dairy barn. Looking toward the café I could see there were several late-harvest grain trucks parked across from it.

Minn's café was the only eatery in Declo, so it was the best. But I wouldn't have cared if there had been a thousand fancy-dancy big-city restaurants in Declo; Minn's would still be the best because my Mom worked there. She worked on the swing shift during the week and the noon shift on Saturday. Everybody agreed that she was the best hasher in the business. After my dad died, cooking was the only skill my mom had to support the family. She was grateful Minnie had given her a chance to work. She only earned a dollar an hour, but I guess she thought that was enough. Minnie and Chet owned and operated the café and the adjoining bar. The bar was creatively called Chet's Bar and the café was creatively called Minn's Café.

As I bumped Ur along the street near the post office, I started to become uncomfortable at the thought of someone seeing me with Ur. There were a lot of hard-drinking and hard-fighting farm hands that might think I was soft if they saw me with an old deaf-blind man. I couldn't completely understand my feelings just then, but my anxiety grew with each step.

When passing Gillette's grocery store I looked hard through the large plate glass window hoping to catch a peek at Christine, whose dad owned the store. I was shading my eyes against the glare of the window, when I heard a gravely voice shout, "You got a license to drive that thing? Ha, Ha."

In the reflection of Gillette's store window I saw Saul Bork. His big shaggy head had bushy eyebrows so thick it looked like two dead cats had been glued to his forehead. His head was screwed on a neck as thick as a fire hydrant. From his head down things, just got a lot bigger. Saul was an irreverent and mean-spirited man who took delight in embarrassing people and torturing any animal that got near him. Everybody was afraid of him. I don't think he had one friend in the whole town. Saul spit a long brown stream of tobacco juice onto the sidewalk and entered the café.

One time I heard he beat a man in front of Chet's Bar so bad that the man's eyeball just popped out. Saul didn't stop beating him even when the man begged him to stop. A friend of the beaten man tried to stop the slaughter, but Saul knocked that man down too. Saul lived alone out near Malta where he worked his sad little dry farm.

I guess of all of the humans in the world he was the last person I wanted to see in the café. I stopped pushing the wheelchair and tried to search through my mind for an excuse to tell Ur why we shouldn't go to the café.

Maybe I could say, "I'm sorry, Ur, there's a man in there that might embarrass me if we are seen together," Or, "Hey Ur, for the first time in the history of the world I'm not hungry and I'll bet you're not either." Everything I thought to say sounded stupid, and worst of all, it was a lie.

Ur looked back at me and asked, "Jon, are you talking to someone?"

I knelt down and put his hand to my face and said, "No, ah . . . just wondering about this man I saw go into the café. I'm afraid he'll make fun of you."

Ur chuckled, "I'll bet he'll get frustrated trying to get my goat since I can't see or hear him."

I tried to explain, "It's not you that he will get mad at— it's me. I don't handle teasing very good and sometimes I blow up."

"Is this man a bully?"

"Yes. He's big and he's mean."

"What is his name?"

"Saul," I said.

A mischievous smile appeared on Ur's face and I wondered, "What's up with that?"

"Jon, when we go into the café, no matter what happens, seat me as close to Saul as you can. Also, Jon, if Saul says anything bad about me, calmly say, 'This man is deaf and blind. To talk to him you will need to let him put his hand on your face.' Now, he probably will not like that so you just translate everything to me by repeating his words without voice into my hand."

"Okay," I said warily. It was a little awkward getting Ur through the front door of the café, and we did a lot of banging in the process. Finally, after wrestling his chair through the door we had made enough noise to scare a fence post out of line. Everyone in the café was watching us. I looked around and spied Saul sitting at a booth alone, mauling a triple-deck bacon cheeseburger and fries. One evil eye was looking at me, and a sinister grin started on his face as he chewed greedily.

"What you got there, Jonny boy, a new pet?" he roared with raucous amusement, blowing bits of fries and cheeseburger onto the table.

I swallowed a lump of fear and pushed Ur right toward him and parked the wheelchair on the end of the booth where Saul was sitting.

"Hey, what's this? Get it away from me. Now!"

I stared at Saul and said, "This man is deaf and blind. If you want to talk to him, you have to let him put his hand to your face like this." I showed him by putting Ur's hand to my face as I spoke.

"I ain't going to let that fishy-skinned, legless freak touch me. Get him out of here!" Saul growled menacingly.

While watching Saul out of the corner of my eye, I put Ur's hand to my face again and repeated everything Saul had said. Everybody—and I mean everybody in the entire café was staring at us. Even my mother and the old dishwasher, Greasy, had come out of the kitchen to see this strange little man confront Saul.

In a voice of authority that I had never heard Ur use before, he said loud enough for all to hear, "Saul, I am sure seeing a man like me must frighten you. Please understand that I will not harm you in anyway."

"I said, get that freak away from me!" Saul hissed in a voice that had fear and danger rising in it.

I repeated to Ur what Saul said. Then Ur did something that made all of us take in our breath; and for years after, when the story was repeated, people would say, "I don't believe it!"

Ur placed his hands on the tabletop and in an acrobatic move lifted his body out of the wheelchair, and letting his body hang along the table, he walked on his hands around the table and sat right next to Saul.

Saul was cussing and scrambling to get away, but he was trapped in the booth and, like a cornered rat, he turned to strike. A fist shot out from Saul straight toward Ur's nose, but faster than greased lightning Ur's hand came across his body and gently pushed Saul's powerful fist harmlessly to the side, missing Ur by three or four inches. Everyone watching jumped when Saul struck at Ur. Ur's hand closed over Saul's fist and with vice-like strength started pulling Saul's hand back. Ur's face was as calm and serene as a July morning.

I had never noticed the tremendous strength in Ur's shoulders and arms before. Saul seemed paralyzed, like a cat when you pick it up by the nape of its neck. His eyes showed he knew what was happening but he seemed powerless to stop it. Ur set Saul's filthy fist down on the table top and patted it like you would a baby's dimpled little hand. Saul's craggy head just stared at his hand in disbelief.

With that great gentle voice Ur said more quietly, "Saul, I think you have a great heart but it is a little overshadowed with worry about something." Turning back toward me he said, "Jon?"

"Huh?" I said, still stupefied at what I had just seen.

"I'm sure people are probably staring at us, so would you ask them to go back to their lunches so as not to embarrass Saul? And would you please order me a cheeseburger without onions, French fries and a large glass of water? You get whatever you want, I'm buying."

He turned back to Saul, who still hadn't said anything or even moved. Taking his hand off of Saul's, he said with wonderful sincerity, "Saul, how are you?"

It wasn't a "How are you" like you say to everyone without meaning it or even wanting to know the true answer. It was an "I really mean it, How are you?" Ur lifted his hand to Saul's face and said, "Just talk, I can understand."

Saul shied away at first and then mumbled, "I ain't never talked to someone like this before. Who are you?" Having said this he began to relax, so I headed back into the kitchen and all the farmers chuckled, shook their heads in disbelief, and went back to their hushed conversations. I found Mom in the kitchen and told her what we wanted to eat.

Since her stroke Mom had trouble expressing herself, so she just kept saying over and over, "Land sakes alive, did you see that? Land sakes alive, did you see that?"

I cut through the back room and visited the restroom before heading back to the booth.

As I approached the booth I could see that Ur and Saul were in a deep and private conversation. Not wanting to disturb them, I wandered over to the jukebox and dropped in a quarter. I punched up five of my favorites including four songs of the Supremes and one Beatles, *I Want to Hold Your Hand.* I sat down near the jukebox and opened an old copy of a *National Geographic* magazine and started looking at the pictures. After about 15 minutes I could see that Saul was getting ready to leave, so I walked back to the booth. Ur was hand-walking around the table to his wheelchair and Saul was scooting out of the booth.

Just before Saul stood up, he reached out and put Ur's hand to his face and said quietly, "I'm not sure I can do that."

"Yes, you can, Saul!" Ur emphasized.

Do what? I wondered.

Ur slid back into the booth and I slipped in next to him.

"Jon, tell me what Saul says."

After Saul had paid for his lunch, he started for the door then stopped and turned around. He stood there, head bowed, his great hulk seeming more like a child than a fearful giant. Turning his sweat-stained straw hat over in his hands, he raised his eyes and said to everyone, "I'm sorry I disrupted your lunch today, and please forgive me."

He stood there another moment and looked around. The room had turned so quiet that you could have heard a feather drop. He gave a little relieved smile, smashed his hat on his head, turned, and walked out. I stared at him like everyone else— all of us with our mouths hung open like a trunk lid on a rolled '57 Chevy. We all saw that a new spring was in his step as Saul crossed the road to his truck. He got in, started the truck, and craned his neck to see if the road was clear (usually not necessary in Declo), and pulled out.

"Land sakes alive, can you believe that?" finally broke the silence.

Now everyone turned his attention to Ur. He sat there innocently waiting for his lunch.

"Jon, has Saul left, and did he say anything?"

"Oops." I quickly took Ur's hand to my face and said, "He said he was sorry about disrupting everyone's lunch and would we forgive him."

"Good for him. I knew he could do it," Ur said with pride.

Our lunches came and we started eating. Everybody was talking about what just happened. I couldn't believe what I had just seen. Ur had manhandled the biggest and meanest man in the whole county and then got the man to apologize to everyone! After the shock had worn off, I started to almost bust open with pride. Imagine me sitting next to and being friends with a guy like Ur. No way! I thought.

As we were leaving, several of the farmers and farm hands called out, "Jon, you be sure to take good care of that guy" or "You take care, 'cause you sure got a great friend there." I was so proud I could hardly see straight.

Outside, Ur asked if I would take it slow since the sun felt so good. I stopped at our main intersection to let a large grain combine roar by. Ur must have felt the vibration.

"What was that?" he asked with a start.

"A grain combine," I answered simply.

"Tell me about it. I've never seen one. Is it like a threshing machine?"

"Oh boy," I sighed, "It's big and red and yellow and it has a sweeper on the front."

"Is the sweeper a man?"

Dang, … how to explain? I mused. How could I explain something as complicated as a combine to someone who only knew a threshing machine?

"It's like this great big bug, maybe 13 feet tall and 20 feet long and 16 feet wide. On the front is a paddle wheel like on a river boat, that's called the sweeper. It pulls the grain across the cutter bar and into the combine. Then the grain bounces around inside, and finally the straw and chaff are spit out the back and the grain is augured into a bin, where it's kept until the grain truck gets there to pick it up.

"Oh, I see," was all he said.

I wondered, What did he see? I realized that there is so much I didn't describe, like the big tires on the front and the little tires on the rear, or the driver's seat up on top, or the yellow umbrella-fan needed to keep the driver cool and shaded. He didn't see the dust that covered the faded body of this huge machine like sifted flour. I didn't tell him about the roaring engine.

I tried to imagine what I would be seeing if all I had to go by was my description. I would have a pretty incomplete and baffling picture.

As I started to push him across the intersection, I had a couple of heartfelt and bothersome questions come to me, 'Did he see the gift as clearly as I saw the combine? Is he trying to get me to see the gift like he does?' I guess I needed to understand that there was probably more to the gift than I could see or than he could explain. Was he trying to show me a combine and I only knew a threshing machine? Maybe that was the part where I must discover the gift myself, in myself. What was it he said this morning? "You only understand the post and the thousand dollars, but I understand the process, and I see the potential of what you can become."

I vowed to be patient with myself and force my mind to open, ask, and see more than just the obvious possibilities. Much later I would recognize just how important this decision was to me.

After I maneuvered Ur back into the house, he thought he had better rest. I stood at the kitchen door looking into the backyard at the cedar post beginning to cast a stubby shadow to the east. I went out to wiggle the post. I had never thought about deep or life-changing things before. It was like I was being drawn toward some destiny or event which would alter the course of my life forever.

"Take your time and be patient. The strongest trees don't grow in a day," I remember him saying. The fragrance of Mary's sweet-pea vines surrounded me. Looking around the yard to make sure I was alone, I knelt down and tried to see the $1,000 bill deep in the crevice. A greedy feeling tingled deep inside of me. It was still there!

I gently pushed the post back and forth, back and forth, my mind wandering to Ur's experience in the war. It was hard to imagine him fighting or hating. The grief he felt for the loss of his family would have been overwhelming. How would I handle that kind of grief?

I wondered what Abraham meant about the right to be honest. How could honesty help Ur? Back and forth I swayed, and pondered on things too heavy for my mind. Back and forth, letting my weight do the pushing and tugging— a mindless swaying and day-dreaming on a warm afternoon until . . . I woke up under the shady overhang of a nearby poplar tree. I didn't even remember walking over to lie down.

Ur was calling me. "Jon, are you out here?"

I got up, shaking the cobwebs out of my mind. A warm lazy breeze came springing up from the west, causing the poplar leaves to applaud. I jogged over to him. Taking his hand to my face I said, "I've been pushing on the post and I fell asleep under a tree."

"That's good. Let's go sit in the shade of that tree and talk, okay?"

"Sure," I answered and wheeled him over under the tree.

After reaching down and locking the wheel brakes, Ur swung himself to the ground with the grace and ease of a chimpanzee. I positioned myself so we could talk easily. Again the breeze rattled the broad leaves of the old poplar tree above us.

"Jon, do you remember what Abraham was trying to give me that day when we were left alone?"

"I think he was trying to get you to stop hating. But I don't understand that. I would think in war it is important to hate, because then it's easier to do all of the fighting and killing."

Ur reached out, patted the grass, and went on. "Hating hurts the hater the most. Hating is not a salve for the wounded soul; it is an abrasive that keeps the soul wounded and raw and oversensitive. I still had to fight, but I had to fight the same enemy as Mordechai and the rest of the underground. Before Abraham talked to me, I was fighting the war of hate."

"I hate a few people," I interrupted with candor, "I especially hate one man who used to hurt me when my mom wasn't home. I'm going to hate him the rest of my life." I couldn't believe I just said that. I had never told that to another living soul.

Ur's eyes hardened for a moment as he thought of what that man had done to me. Then he nodded his acceptance that I had told him something private and honest. Searching for the right way to teach me, Ur took his time before he started.

"Abraham said, 'Every good change we make in our lives follows a pattern. If we can know the pattern we can make the needed changes and take control of what we do with our lives.' Jon, I want to teach you this pattern and show you how to find real success during your life. Do you want to learn it?"

Sensing where this might be going, I asked, "Will I have to stop hating that man?"

"You don't have to, but you will. Jon, don't worry about that now." Ur looked worried for a second, and then just as quickly the worried look faded. "Tell me the one thing you want to do or have more than anything else in the world."

My answer came a little too quickly. "I want Moose to be my girlfriend and I want to hold her hand."

"Moose!" he exclaimed, and then busted up into a real belly laugh.

I just sat there feeling totally stupid. "Why are you laughing at me?" I challenged.

"Oh Jon, please forgive me. You caught me totally off-guard. I've never heard of a girl being called Moose. What does she look like?" he laughed.

Now I was smiling at this blind man's imagination. In my mind I was trying to see what he must have envisioned. I quickly explained that Moose was her nickname and that she was dang good looking.

He smiled knowingly and then said, "Improvements for the inside of you are acquired a little differently than wanting something that someone else has to help you get. You see, you can do all the right things for this girl to hold your hand, but if she doesn't want to hold your hand, she doesn't have to. Everyone has agency or choice. We should never try to force that agency or choice— instead we should try to convince people through truth to see things our way. If you try to force or to persuade through lies, you infringe on inherent rights. I know— I've lost you, but stay with me— it will all become clear."

"Boy, you can say that again!"

"Okay, for now just keep these two things in mind. You don't force, and you don't use dishonesty or manipulation to get what you want."

"Okay," I said, still pretty fuzzy on the whole subject, "In my family if someone wanted something from someone he would yell or complain until he got it, or if he got mad he would slug the other person."

"Jon, most of the things that make people happy do not come from others, but from someplace inside you. These things are called inherent rights, and if you maintain them you are happy and enjoy peace of mind."

A tree root was gouging me in my rear pocket. "Just a second. I need to move to a more comfortable position," I said as I shifted my weight and moved over a few inches, plucked a piece of grass and sniffed it before biting off the end.

"You know already about the rights that the government gives you, such as the right to remain silent or the right to a speedy trial. Yet, in the Declaration of Independence it says:

*We hold these truths to be self-evident, that all men are created equal, that they are endowed by their Creator with certain unalienable Rights, that among these are Life, Liberty and the pursuit of Happiness.*

What this means is that all people are born with certain unalienable or inherent rights which are not given by the government, but are born with us.

"Ur?" I interrupted, "I don't mean to sound dumber than my fence post, but what is the big deal about rights?"

"Okay," he paused and waved off a fly that searching his head. "I'll go over this carefully because I want you to understand why rights and maintaining them are so critical to peace of mind, happiness and true success. Really, the maintaining of our inherent rights is a solid foundation for peace of mind, happiness and success  for ourselves, our families and our nation. Rights protect us and provide a secure feeling."

"Think of it this way. Imagine an ancient city in the jungles of South America. This city is filled with people who are doing things like working, learning, playing, falling in love and raising families. These people are free to follow all of their good dreams.

"Then one day an enemy army is discovered near the borders of the city. The army isn't attacking, but seems poised and ready to strike. What happens to the people of the city?"

"I guess they get all nervous and worry about getting killed," I said weakly, not sure what this had to do with rights.

"Yes, they lose peace of mind. In fact, they worry so much that it interferes with nearly every aspect of their lives. The threat inherently weakens everything they do. The threat hanging over their heads distracts them and they have a hard time focusing on work, study, shopping, and falling in love. Families become more uptight because of the constant threat, and squabbling breaks out in the homes.  What once was a happy peaceful city has become unstable and is filled with people who are anxious and short tempered.

"Now Jon, what do you think would help this city feel less threatened? For the sake of the story, let's say getting rid of the army isn't one of the choices."

After thinking for a moment I said, "I guess put up some kind of defense around the city."

"That is just what this city did. They built a gigantic wall around the entire city and posted guards to warn them if the enemy came near. What did the wall and guards buy for the people in the city?"

"Well, they didn't have to worry about getting killed."

"Right! It bought for all of the citizens peace of mind. It gave them the freedom to go back to the peaceful happy way they lived before the enemy was seen. Even though the wall surrounded them, they again enjoyed the freedom to follow their dreams. For us, each inherent right is part of the wall that protects us and gives us the peace of mind to live our lives in true freedom, and to be happy."

Ur stopped as if waiting for me to respond. I heard a car pull into the Simpsons' driveway next door. Mrs. Simpson waved through the fence as she got out of her car but didn't speak.

I lifted Ur's hand to my face and said, "I understand the story, but I still don't know what inherent rights are."

Shifting his weight and stretching his powerful arms over his head, he sucked in good Idaho air and blew it out. "What is that smell on the wind?"

I had not noticed anything on the air, but I flared my nostrils to the wind and sniffed. "Third cutting of alfalfa."

"It has a fresh, sweet smell, doesn't it?"

"Yeah, I guess so," I said unenthusiastically.

Ur thought for a second. "Why is it called third cutting?"

"It's the third crop of alfalfa cut this season. We get three cuttings between the last frost of spring and the first frost of fall—if we're lucky."

Ur considered this for a moment. "I will tell you more specifically in a minute what inherent rights are, but the important thing I want you to understand now, Jon, is this: When people today do not maintain their inherent rights, they feel the same distracting vulnerability as the ancient people in that city would feel when they let their protecting wall crumble. To feel true happiness and peace of mind, we must maintain our own inherent rights."

He rubbed his arms. "I'm getting a little chilly. Would you mind if we finished our discussion in the house?"

"No problem," I said cheerfully, "I never liked sitting on the ground. I guess I don't bend right."

Sitting more comfortably in the kitchen, Ur continued. "Okay, the Declaration of Independence listed three inherent rights, but there are many more. It says: " ... *endowed by their Creator with certain unalienable Rights, that among these are Life, Liberty and the Pursuit of Happiness.* These three may be considered the basis of all rights. Let's break these down."

"I'm sorry," I interrupted, "What does 'unalienable' mean?"

"Good question. Unalienable means absolute, unchallengeable, inherent, essential, inborn, God-given. A government can't take them away from you. You won them by virtue of your birth."

"Okay, I got that part. Go ahead."

Ur began to speak from the depth of his soul on his favorite subject.

All unalienable rights are defined by that miraculous moral compass that is present in all of us at birth. That is the law we received at birth to help us make right choices. Most of us recognize that compass and base our lives on its gentle influence.

# CHAPTER 12

## I Have the Right to Protect the Health of My Body

Ur began, "Most people do not recognize the rights they were born with, yet if they maintain them, they will be happier, less burdened, and feel more peace of mind to live their lives in freedom. Let me demonstrate this principle with a question."

He paused, and then asked, "If you are walking along the road and a car swerves toward you, what do you do?"

"Man, if a car swerved toward me all he would hit would be my shadow—'cause I'd be gone!" I joked.

"Why?"

"Why what?"

"Why do you avoid the car?"

"Gees, I don't know, instinct, I guess."

"Why do you have the instinct to get out of the way?"

"I don't know, I just do."

"You have that instinct because you have that inherent right." Ur paused, letting that sink in. "That example is clear and easy to understand, but our way of life has clouded the need for maintaining this inherent right, and for some people it has even dulled their need to protect it. Remember this: all rights are like that wall which protects and insures peace of mind. Think of the things some kids feel pressured to do which are harmful to their bodies."

It only took a second to see where this was going. Although I had never used drugs, cigarettes or alcohol, I was giving it serious consideration because it seemed like, "everyone was doing it." If I were honest, I'd have to say those things looked pretty fun at times.

It never occurred to me that not drinking was protecting an inherent right. One of my friends, Lonni—I swear she was already an alcoholic at 15—all she did was look for another party. Once she even came to school drunk.

Sometimes her eyes seem scared like Fred's eyes did when his bicycle brakes got wet going down a steep hill. He was more out of control than a blind Brahma! Maybe that's what Ur meant when he said, "If you maintain the right to protect your health, you don't have to worry about addiction or having an addiction get out of control."

Take smoking cigarettes for example. One kid, David, looked real cool when he smoked. He knew just how to flick the end of the cigarette to knock off the ash, and how to squint his eyes as he dragged on the cigarette and blew the smoke through clenched teeth. When he lit it up it looked real cool too. He tapped the cigarette on the back of his wrist and then struck the match on his pants. All of that seemed neat, but I just never wanted to pay that much money to be cool. I'd rather spend my money on a pair of hip huggers that have a dependable zipper.

From what Ur was saying, I had been unknowingly maintaining at least one of my rights by not using drugs, tobacco and alcohol. I guess I did have more peace of mind. I didn't have to worry about where my next drink was coming from, or where I'd get a cigarette. My mom smoked real heavy. Sometimes she awoke in the middle of the night to have a smoke so she could sleep through to morning. One time when we were living on the farm, right after Dad died, she ran out of cigarettes. Normally she would just drive to town and get some more smokes, but Dean had the car. She about went nuts! In desperation, she sent us the half-mile through the fields to a neighbor's house to borrow a few to get her by till morning.

The rest of the afternoon slipped by as Ur and I talked about why protecting the health of my body was one of my most sacred rights. "When we have good health we then can enjoy so many things. You're young now and your body is naturally fit, but the day will come that you will only dream of running or climbing." I looked at him in his chair and wondered what he dreamed about. "I'm not talking about avoiding risky things, like rock climbing, skiing or other challenging things. Those things are fun and thrilling and provide the spice of life for some people. But other things—like Russian Roulette, fighting, or playing chicken with cars—are just plain stupid."

"Wait a minute," I interrupted, "You almost got into a fight with Saul today, and although you handled him today, under other circumstances he might have killed you. By the way, how did you know he was even punching at you, let alone where it was coming from?"

Ur looked misunderstood. "I wasn't pushing him into a fight so I could hurt him. I was pushing him so I could help him. I would never try to violate another person's rights."

"Okay," I said, "but how did you know where to block the punch?"

Ur smiled sheepishly, "I sensed his anxiety and felt he would strike out. You remember, in the booth I was sitting on the same soft bench as he was. When he loaded up his punch, he shifted his weight. I felt movement in the bench that indicated he was coming with his right fist. I waited until I felt that little bounce in the bench that told me he had let it go. A deaf-blind person's other senses are more acute than yours because he depends on them more. The rest was just pure luck."

I stared at him, trying to comprehend what he was saying.

"Please remember, Jon, I never did that to hurt or embarrass Saul, but to help him. And that is the basic rule of life: help others in the same way you would want them to help you."

Ur flipped open the crystal of his watch, fingered the dial and quipped, "I thought I was hungry. What do you say we order some pizza for supper?"

I know this won't sound very profound, but as I was looking up the phone number of the pizza place, I suddenly realized that the reason Ur and Mary were always doing these nice things for me was that they really lived that basic rule of life. They didn't do it to impress me; they did it because it was a well-cultivated instinct within them.

Listening to Ur teach was like feeling a flow of soothing water moving lightly over my soul. It was gentle, yet I sensed there was great power behind it. Even with the little bit he had already taught me I was feeling my confidence increase in my ability to make some significant changes in my life. What those changes would be I could not even imagine.

That afternoon, he said people need to base their lives on time-tested and proven true principles. "Principles," he said, "are solid truths on which you can base your life. A principle can have general application to many things in your life. For example, live by the principle of protecting the health of your body and you have already made many related decisions. Deciding this means you don't have to decide again and again about drugs, alcohol or tobacco."

I needed to develop what he called an instinct to always protect my health, and the instinct must be based on a true principle. He said that was what was so cool (my word) about the Bill of Rights of the United States. It is a time-tested document that we can depend on and feel good about adapting into our lives.

The word "instinct" threw me for a second. I had always thought that instincts were inborn, but he said not all are. A cat may have an instinct to chase things, but the mother cat helps its young to learn and develop the skill of catching mice or birds.

I knew this was true. I remember watching this old one-eyed broken-tailed mama cat at Mr. Johnson's farm bring dead or half-dead mice to its litter and teach the little kittens how to eat mice steaks. The only thing more amazing than her tutoring of mice cuisine was her finding any husbands because she was as ugly as road-rash.

We ordered up some heart attack pizza from Maxie's in Burley. I asked Ur if he wanted to ride along into Burley to pick it up. He thanked me and said, "I'd love to ride and catch the evening smells."

I wheeled Ur out and loaded him into Fred's green and white 1957 Pontiac Chieftan. As the big 389 V-8 roared into life, I glanced over at Ur and wondered what it would be like to be deaf and blind.

The highway to Burley runs nine miles straight west out of Declo along the old Oregon Trail route. It is sandwiched between the wide, slow Snake River on the north and a spur of the Union Pacific Railroad to the south. Then it undulates along a high bench for about five miles before passing through Unity and dropping onto the flood plain where Burley nestles; Not only is it a beautiful drive, but the musty smell of the river always takes me back to my childhood.

Up until my dad died when I was eight years old, we lived on 140 acres of sand that bordered on the Snake River. Often on summer evenings after the farm work was finished, Dad loaded the family on the hay wagon and pulled us down to the river with our gray and red Ford 9N tractor.

We would pile our fishing gear and a couple of old kitchen chairs on the wagon to use when we got to the river. Mom would sit on one of the kitchen chairs supervising her domain like the Queen of Sheba. I loved riding on the tail end of the wagon. Dean, Fred and I dragged our heels on the sandy road making squiggly lines that zigzagged and figured-eighted behind us. Sometimes Dean pushed Fred or me off, and then the war was on as we tried to catch up to the wagon and get back on.

The road wove through a thick sweet-smelling stand of tall sagebrush with an occasional jack rabbit darting away from us, or the screeching of a bright-colored ring-necked pheasant breaking from cover for a short flight with hooded wings. As we bounced and rattled along, the mossy smell of the river would build until it filled our world. In the early summer, the Russian olive trees bloomed and sweetened the air with their unusual fragrance.

It was wonderful and it was scary at the same time. From my earliest childhood I heard stories about people drowning in the river. Fred told me, "When someone drowns in the river, the Sheriff pulls this big Jackson-fork through the water behind his boat to hook the body and float it to the surface. The bodies," he continued with relish, "are all wrinkly, like when you stay in the tub too long, and the fish eat the eyes out!"

Dad was a good fisherman, but we boys mostly caught suckers, chubs and carp. None of these were very good to eat, but the carp could get as big as 30 pounds. The carp is a lazy fish that lies in the shallows eating off the bottom. He is so lazy that he doesn't even put up much fight when he's caught. Fishermen hate to hook carp because they get so bored trying to reel them in most of them take a nap.

Every time I smell the river or the Russian olive trees, I get this warm, cuddly feeling like I used to when Dad would fish holding me against his wool Pendleton shirt. He smoked his handmade cigarettes and cast his worm-laden hooks into that old smooth river, and talked quietly to the fish as the summer silk of evening enveloped us. The smell of the river took me right back to those happy memories.

We took the frontage road out of Declo until it crossed the tracks and intersected the Burley/Declo highway. I turned left and stomped the gas pedal to the floor. I heard as well as felt the deep, throaty 'waaaan' of the carburetor as it sucked in air to mix with the gas and rocket the car forward. Ur was flung back against the seat, and I saw a grin creep across his face. When the speedometer ribbon hit 70, I let off and backed it down to 60. Ur said, almost reverently, "I liked that!" The road dipped unexpectedly several times as it followed the contours of the bench. With the first dip Ur cried out in mock terror, finally saying, "The only thing more terrifying than this is riding with Mary at slow speeds."

I slowed to 55 as we entered Springdale and let the big sedan cruise. I glanced at Ur again and felt an unusual affection for him. True, I hardly knew him, but I was drawn to him. When I was around him, I felt loved, cared for, and filled with hope. He was so gentle, so good, so powerful, and yet he was fun! I never heard a critical statement come from him about anyone or anything. He focused on building me and giving me light to see my life better. I was proud he was my friend.

Our pizza was ready in a big flat box sitting under heat lamps. I bought a Hires root beer for myself and a Fresca for Ur and got back in the car. "Mmmm, that smells delicious," Ur said. "Where should we go to eat it?"

We decided to go across the river, near Heyburn, into some sand hills that formed the north bank of the Snake River. The teenagers in the area called this place the Boon-docks after a popular song. The Pontiac swayed and bounced as I maneuvered it along a sandy road to the river's edge. Even though it was chilly, Ur rolled his window down and let in the fresh air while we sat in the twilight eating pizza. We didn't talk for a long time, we just sat munching pizza and drinking in the river smells.

Across the river I could see the Burley Golf Course with a few die-hard golfers trying to chase down their balls in the growing darkness. A couple of magpies were squabbling in a Russian olive tree near the bank, and once or twice I heard the whistling of ducks gliding in for a landing on the river.

Ur was a steady eater when it came to pizza. I thought I was leaning into the pizza-eating pretty good, but Ur started to pull ahead of me, and then abruptly he stopped, wiped his mouth and chin and pushed the last two pieces toward me.

"Here, Jon, polish this off." He laid his head back on the seat and relaxed, basking in the cool evening. After a moment he turned toward me and said, "Jon, what is your opinion about what I have told you so far?"

Sliding his hand to my pizza-lubed face, I said, "Well, I'm sure I don't understand everything you are trying to tell me, but I know I trust you, and I hope I have enough brains to pick it up."

"Whether you have enough brains or not isn't my worry or my question. Do you have enough desire to pay the price for it?"

Someone who has never felt like a big zero can ever fully understand how quickly and intensely hope for something better ignites the soul. It's like a drowning man who finally sees the surface above him. He will do everything in his power to claw his way up to suck in the life-giving air. I felt like I was forced under the waters of mediocrity and was suffocating in the mud of nothing. I was so afraid of dying— and even worse, living in this condition—that I would have lunged for anything hopeful. Now Ur was asking me if I had enough desire to pay the price for it? How much would someone pay for air if they were suffocating?

The burning was back again. I did desire it, and I knew I would pay any price! I wanted to be something in life. I didn't want to see my life squander away in insignificance. I didn't care what I did in life; I just wanted to do it well and for it to be significant.

"Ur, I don't know how much desire is needed…but I'll give you all I can muster! I have always desired to do better. I have just never known how to do it."

"Success in life is not like a firecracker, Jon. It is like a tree. A firecracker explodes with a burst of light and a puff of smoke and is gone, but it takes a lifetime to grow a tree, and real success takes a lifetime to achieve."

I thought about that and then asked, "You mean by the time I die I'll have success?"

Ur laughed, "No, I didn't mean that, exactly. You must find small personal victories to be sure. Still you shouldn't look at success as a one-time event. It is a process that takes our whole life, and in the process we will enjoy the fruits of success. Real success and real enjoyment in life relates to the kind of person you are, not what you possess when you die."

"Are you talking about inherent rights again?"

"Yes I am."

"Gees, I hope I'm not too dumb to get this."

"You're not!" Ur said with force and then continued more gently, "I promise you this: Nobody is too dumb to benefit from understanding and living by their inherent rights."

"Well, I'm not very good in school."

"You are plenty good enough, and the conduit through which success flows will expand as you go along. How does that sound?"

"Sounds better than a call to supper."

Ur got a question on his face and then caught my meaning. "You'll have to excuse me; sometimes you throw me off with your colorful language. Don't get me wrong—I like it. Most people talk in a stilted way to me. I miss hearing the old colorful way people speak." Speaking with earnestness, Ur continued, "Jon, do you know what the word 'harrow' means?"

"Yeah, I think so. We harrow the fields after we've plowed and disked them. Is that what you mean?"

"What does the harrow look like?"

"Well, it's a square flat rack with hardwood crossbars. Each crossbar has 8-inch spikes sticking out the bottom. We pull it around the field and it tears into the ground and breaks the clods of dirt into littler pieces and puts air into the soil."

"That's right. It is almost the same thing I am thinking about, Jon. I won't explain it tonight because you won't sleep, but tomorrow I will tell you some things about the war and my involvement that may harrow your soul and be painful to hear. I will not tell you everything, but just enough to help you understand the inherent rights of man. Tonight I want to tell you a happy thing."

# CHAPTER 13

## I Have the Right to Maintain My Inherent Rights in Any Circumstance

U r settled back, took a deep breath of summer evening air, and began.

"From 1939 until 1942 I stayed with the Resistance in Warsaw. I'm happy to say that we did a lot of good in getting many innocent people out of Poland. The Judenrat (the Jewish government in the ghetto) came under increasing pressure to bring people to the trains for departure to work camps. We were certain that these camps were actually extermination places. We heard this from several who had escaped.

"It was the most heart-breaking work you can imagine. If Judenrat did not comply with the Nazi demands, there would be mass murder in our streets, and worse, starvation. Yet, complying put these men in the unhappy position of deciding who lived and who died. We all hoped that the war would end before the ghetto was emptied. Nearly every day, men, women and children were herded into cattle cars to be shipped off to a death camp. We set up a false medical infirmary to pull some people out of the lines because of trumped-up illnesses and thus saved their lives. Eventually the Nazis caught on and the medical staff was ordered onto the trains as well.

"In 1942, Mordecai assigned me to the town of Lodz to help with the Resistance there. You will remember this was the same town I was in when the war began. I traveled at night with false papers in case the Nazis stopped me. While traveling I began to hope I would have another assignment with less violence. I was tired of the violence that accompanied my work with the Resistance.

"Since my talk with Abraham about inherent rights and the peace of mind that comes into one's life when they are maintained, I had sensed some things changing. I found myself cherishing my inherent right to forgive. With so much hatred being demonstrated toward the Jews, I could clearly see that hatred was like a canker that festered and grew inside. I wasn't a stranger to this kind of feeling, and I pressed myself to change my attitude. Abraham had explained that forgiving people did not mean that we lie down and let others trample our rights. He said we have an inherent right to protect the health of our bodies and that means defending ourselves.

"That was the difference between us and the Nazis. They killed because they hated, and when we did, it was to maintain our right to protect ourselves. It is hard for me to explain the change that came over me with this new perspective. Slowly, over the months, peace of mind came. The hardest part for me was forgiving myself for staying in Poland too long and bringing on the death of my wife and children. I don't want my story to bog down in the details of all the suffering and tears I passed through before peace came to me, so let me just say that peace did come to me eventually.

"There was a flood of emotion as I traveled back on almost the same route I had taken three years earlier. I even walked past the same small farm where I stayed that first night. Now the place was deserted and all the animals gone. The once pleasant farm cottage stood like a giant skull in the moonlight, ragged curtains blowing gently in and out of the eye-like windows.

"In the hours of quiet night-time walking, I was filled with loneliness for my family. I would have given my life if I could have held my darling Beth and my little twins once again. There were many hours of wracking sobs as I mourned the loss of my family.

"I entered the Lodz ghetto and made contact with a tall, skinny man named Nathan who worked with the Underground. He asked me what my strengths were and what kind of work I wanted to do.

"'I was a teacher before the war, but in Warsaw I worked mostly falsifying documents ... and throwing bombs,' I answered carefully.

"'We don't need documents here, nor do we need to throw bombs,' he smiled. 'There are not any routes out of this place, and lucky for us the Nazis are not bothering us very much right now. It is true we are starving slowly, but we can hang on for quite awhile still. What we need is someone to work in the orphanage.'

"'No, I am not very good with that sort of thing,' I answered, painfully remembering my own twins. They would be eight by now.

"'Come on,' Nathan pressed me. 'That is where we need you.'

"'Ur, please give it a try,' Nathan's wife begged as she bustled into the room and gave me some strange tea to drink. A cheery woman in her forties, she continued, 'You would be wonderful for the children, and I think they would be good for you too.'

"Nathan put his hand on my shoulder, 'Our little orphans are from all over Poland. They mostly came here right after the war began. Come, at least visit the orphanage, and then you can decide.'

"The orphanage was several blocks away in an old red brick warehouse. We entered through a side door. There must have been two or three hundred children ranging in age from toddlers to teens. They were all gathered in one room singing some children's songs. Their little faces were a sea of youthful hope. My heart melted and filled with love for these poor little innocent victims, all alone in the world. I knew I would find further healing in their service. Nathan was watching me with a side glance.

"'I will do it!' I whispered. 'Thank you for asking me.'

"After the singing ended, Nathan touched my elbow and we walked around to the front of the audience.

"'Excuse me,' Nathan said with gentleness to the teacher, 'I would like to introduce a new teacher, Mr. Babiraski. Please, Ur, tell them something about yourself.'

"Staring out at the blur of children, I shifted uncomfortably. 'I...really don't know where to start. I was born in America.' Some excited whispering started. 'I guess you know about America. Well, I came here with my family in 1936 . . . six years ago . . . ' I was nearly overwhelmed at how much had happened to me in the last six years and lonely tears started to sting my eyes. 'I was here in Lodz when my family was killed in the bombing of Warsaw. I miss my Beth, Toby and Anna very much. So much has happened since . . . '

117

"There was a disturbance about halfway back among the children as a girl cautiously stood. The back light from the rear windows made it hard for me to see what was happening. Squinting against the light, I shaded my eyes with my hand. I saw a frail little girl with short-cut hair standing, and tugging at a little boy's hand, trying to get him to stand. The back-lit features seemed familiar.

"'Daddy?' came the girl's small voice. My mind froze I knew that voice.

"'Daddy!'

"I let out a startled cry, 'Anna!' The little boy stood. I shifted my focus to him. 'Toby?'

"'Daddy!' The little boy cried.

"The two children started forward, walking at first and then running, weaving and tripping through the seated children.

"I stood dumbfounded, rooted to the floor. 'Oh my Dear God! I thank you, I thank you!' I choked, as I dropped to one knee to receive them.

"Tears of joy coursed down my cheeks as my children rushed into my arms, and I stood and twirled them around and around, sobbing. Toby and Anna, not dead, but alive, and in my arms again! They felt so light and fragile. Could these little ragamuffins really be mine? I put them down and then held them at arm's length. My tears made them look blurry, but they were mine, and they were alive!"

Tears were stinging in my eyes as I heard Ur tell about his happy reunion. There were times when I dreamed that my father's death had been a big mistake, and one day I would see him again, crawl on his lap, and get whisker rubs.

Ur coughed to clear his husky throat. "My children and I kissed and hugged, and then I pleaded, 'Where is Beth? Where is your mother?' I looked around anxiously for Beth.

"Now their tears of joy waxed into agonized sobs of sorrow. Anna, always the first to speak, said, 'We don't know. Mamma took us to a friend's house to sleep because she didn't want us in the way while she worked late preparing for your birthday. In the morning there were the bombs, and the friends told us Mamma was gone and we needed to go to Lodz to be safe. We thought we would find you here.

"Such bittersweet emotions cannot be imagined. The wonderful sweetness of holding my children and the bitter sure knowledge that my Beth was gone. The pain of missing her grew again and wracked my soul. Looking around, most of the children were crying with us. I guess it renewed their hopes of seeing their parents again, or reminded them of what they had lost.

"It took awhile to finally realize I had my children back. As it dawned on me that I had been given another chance to save my children, I knew I had to get myself and my children out of Poland as quickly as possible. Yet, with all of my connections in the Underground I knew it would still take a long time, if ever. Underground escape routes through Holland, Denmark, Sweden and Finland were nearly closed. It would take time to get the papers and arrange for the passage.

"Six months later we were still in Poland. The tide of the war had shifted, and now Germany was backing up. The escape routes were all but closed, and I knew we were stuck in the Lodz ghetto. We had to make the best of it.

"Food was very scarce, so we were always hungry; everybody was starved down to bones. At night Toby and Anna would ask me to tell them about Thanksgiving dinner in America. To us a sliver of bread seemed like a banquet, so you can imagine how Thanksgiving dinner seemed to the children. Somehow we got by until the summer of 1944. Anna, Toby and I suffered a great deal during those two years, but our suffering was tempered with our love and togetherness. Nobody can know how important families can be until they are separated as we had been. All three of us shed many tears over our loss of Beth.

"I had one picture of Beth that I carried in my shirt pocket, so it wasn't lost with my papers. Of all of the pictures that have ever been taken of Beth, this is the one I am glad I was able to preserve. I took the picture on the tower of St. Stephen's Cathedral in Vienna, Austria, while we were visiting there in 1936. Beth was standing with her back to the beautiful red-steepled roofs of Vienna. Beth was tiny, just barely five feet tall. Her flowered dress was blowing against her delicate form. She had her head tipped toward her shoulder, and her lips and eyes had that provocative smile she used when teasing me. I still have that picture. Wait a minute." Ur dug into his shirt pocket and pulled out a small leather wallet like the kind a businessman would carry his business cards. He opened it and slid out a small picture.

"Here, I'm pretty sure this is it. I like holding it sometimes. It's about the only thing I have from the pre-war years."

I looked at the picture and tilted it to catch the dome light better. It was as Ur described, only the picture was scratched, stained and tattered so badly that I could hardly make it out. What I could see confirmed that Beth really was cute. I handed the picture back to Ur. He carefully put it back into the little holder, explaining, "This way I always know where it is when I want to hold it and remember.

"Oh, how I loved her and missed her. Toby and Anna found it hard to remember much about their mother, so in the evenings, I told them stories by the hours. As I said, these were hard days, but our lives were filled with much joy too.

"We grew very close to the other orphans. When one died, and many did because of our conditions, we mourned. Toby and Anna appeared to get used to saying good-bye to their friends. My heart grieved to see them grow up fast.

"My Toby and Anna were bright and eager to help. By then they were almost nine and could teach and entertain the younger children. I can still see in my mind the wondering eyes of those children. It seemed like their eyes said, 'So this is life. It is not as great as I hoped it would be.' Most of the children could not remember anything except war, hunger, and the fear of black-booted Nazis. So many of the children became like the Mussulman."

"What's that?" I interrupted.

"The Mussulman was a term camp people used to describe the men, women and children who were as thin as skeletons. They were half-dead people with little strength or will to live. They sadly waited for death to mercifully close their eyes."

"Why didn't they just commit suicide if they were so miserable?" I asked before thinking.

Ur swung his head toward me and stared in blank incomprehension for a minute. The tone of his voice took on a new intensity. "Some did. Jon, I want to tell you something very important. In fact, it may be the most important thing I will ever tell you."

Sensing the seriousness of the moment I suppressed saying, "I'm like Dumbo, all ears." Instead I said, "Okay, I'm listening."

"Your life is among the most precious gifts you have. It is more valuable than nearly any other thing on this earth. The right to life is a cherished inherent right. Remember, I have the right to protect the health of my body. Sometimes life deals out some pretty painful stuff. You can count on it. Most people will not go through what I and millions of others went through in World War II, but to them their problems may seem just as great. It is a lot like playing golf in the jungle."

"Huh?" I grunted.

"A man told me this story once and I think it best illustrates what I want to say." He got himself a drink of Fresca and asked, "Would you like some drink before I start this story?"

I reached over and shook my closed hand in his hand.

"Okay. The basic rule of golf is you must play the ball where it lands, right?"

"Right."

"In the jungle the rules are the same except that in the jungle you not only play the ball where it lands, but you also must play the ball where the monkey throws it."

"I'm lost," I confessed.

"Okay. In the jungle there are monkeys, and monkeys like to play with things. A monkey may see the ball land nearby and swing down, pick up the ball and toss it before the golfer can get there. Is that good or bad for the golfer?"

"Bad," I shot back. "No wait a minute. It could be good if the monkey throws the ball to a better place, say near the hole."

"Good thinking. Whatever life deals out to us is a little like the monkey—unpredictable. I can do all I can to get the ball into the cup, yet a monkey may toss it some other direction. It's not my fault; it's just life. I can cuss, jump up and down, throw my golf club into the pond or even quit, but that won't finish the game. I must finish the game to gain the prize. All finishers are winners. Let me emphasize again: I must finish the course come what may, no matter how frustrating it may become. I also must recognize that the monkey will probably, in the long run, help me about as much as he hinders me."

He paused for a moment and then plunged on. "My point is that we must maintain our right to live with the tenacity of a cat. We say cats have nine lives, right?"

"Sure," I interjected, "I have seen lots of times when cats have cheated death."

"It's not because they cheat death," Ur said firmly. "It is because they choose to live no matter how bad off they are."

I looked at Ur's missing legs, blind eyes and deaf ears. I spoke quietly. "Ur, has the monkey helped you as much as he has hurt you?"

Taking in a deep breath, Ur blew it out slowly while rubbing the back of his neck as if he was reviewing sixty-some years of living. "To be honest, there have been times when I thought the monkey was picking on me. Yet, I cannot deny how wonderful my life has been as a whole. The more you get to know me, you will see that I am not an object to be pitied, I am a man to be envied. Most of my problems I have brought upon myself because I did not maintain my inherent rights.

"Remember, inherent rights are like a wall that protects us and gives us peace of mind. My family and I suffered beyond description during the war, and most of that suffering occurred because I did not maintain my right to a soft heart. Pride, defensiveness, and stubbornness for my own way kept us in Poland long after we should have left. A hard heart is not able to change easily; it is set in its own way. When our hearts are hard, we do not open our minds to see other possibilities in our relationships or in our careers.

"I was determined to stay until spring. I refused to see any other possibilities even though Beth, my family, and probably every other human being could plainly see the danger. As a result of my hard heart, Beth and many others have suffered, including me." Ur sat quietly for a moment, then interlaced his fingers and pushed his hands away from him, stretching. "Let's start for home. It must be dark by now."

I put his hand to my face. "One more thing," I said, "What good places do you want the monkey to throw the ball?"

"You mean now?"

"Yes."

He smiled, "Well, one thing is fishing. Jon, I want to catch a fish before I die."

I stared in disbelief. "You mean you've never caught a fish?"

"No, never."

"Ur, I'll make sure you catch a fish," I stated with conviction. Little did I know how hard and painful this was going to be. On the way back to Declo, Ur was quiet. I knew talking about the war conjured up some painful stuff for him. I sat full of amazement at this little man's life and what he said about the right to a soft heart. I never heard anything like that before. I could see how keeping your mind open to all of the possibilities would be difficult, but I could also see how much more power that would give someone to succeed.

I wanted to see Ur catch a fish. I wanted that more than anything, including holding Moose's hand. In fact, tonight holding Moose's hand seemed pretty insignificant when compared to what I had been told, and what I felt and learned.

When we arrived back at his house, I got the wheelchair out of the back and helped him into it. He seemed really tired, like he was carrying about 40 years of "I-was-responsible."

Inside the house he took my hand gently and said, "Thank you Jon, for wanting to learn these things. And thank you for being my friend."

Then he wheeled off to his room. Later, I heard him crying. What an overwhelming affection I felt for this little old man!

A strange melancholy crept over me and I found myself crying too. I was crying for all of the lonely years that I didn't have a father and for all the years that my mom didn't have a companion to share her troubles. I felt sad for her loneliness and for my own.

All unalienable rights are just common sense. That is why when we see someone waive this right or that right we stare in disbelief. To us it is so obvious what they are doing is destructive to their peace of mind and happiness. Then we are lead to say, "They just don't have any common sense!"

# CHAPTER 14

## I Have a Right to Support Governments That Protect My Inherent Rights

Neither Ur nor I felt much like a heavy breakfast after bloating ourselves like three-day-old road kill on pizza the night before, so we just had some fruit and a bowl of Cheerios. A fall storm had arrived during the night, and a cold wind was driving heavy rain into the side of the house in gusts of rhythmic tattoos. I built a warm fire in the fireplace, and the room became cheery as the blaze grew.

"Thank you for the fire," Ur said. "You know the feeling of a fire most resembles what it looks like."

I closed my eyes and discovered that he was right. I seated myself so I could comfortably talk with Ur. Half of me was excited to hear the harrowing part, yet the other half was worried about what I would learn. I cared for this old man, and to hear more about his pain would tear at my soul.

Ur began, "For reasons I didn't understand, the Nazis left the Lodz ghetto until last to be emptied. Eventually the inhabitants were transported to the death camps to be killed, or assigned to work details, or used for human experimentation.

"In August of 1944, the Judenrat was ordered by the Nazis to bring 1500 men, women and children to the train station the next day for deportation to a work camp. These long-faced and sad men of the Judenrat worked all night making life and death decisions. At 5:00 in the morning Nathan knocked on our door. His expression was stricken and his eyes were red and worried.

"'Ur, I'm sorry, but the Judenrat has ordered our orphanage to the train.'

"I looked at him with sorrowful eyes and then at my children who were sleeping on a makeshift bed under a window. 'When?'

"'Seven this morning. I'm sorry Ur. I argued with them, but I also understand that they can do nothing. I'm sure it is a nice camp.' His sad eyes flickered to the right as he told the lie.

"A few of the children had been smuggled out of the country through the Underground via Denmark, Sweden, Switzerland, Spain and other countries, but mostly they had died of sickness and sadness. So by the time we were ordered onto the train, we only had about 100 children left in our orphanage. Most of the adults knew we were not going to a work camp, but the optimistic part of us wanted to believe that we would be okay.

"Due to my work in the Underground, I was able to better prepare our little ones for the trip. Afraid of this day, I had been collecting cans and bottles for our little troop. With these we were able to bring water and a little crust of bread in each of our pockets. Even though we had been ordered to be at the train station at 7:00 a.m. the train didn't arrive until 2:00 that afternoon. By then the water bottles we had carefully brought were mostly used up, and the children had eaten their bread. I asked a guard repetitively to allow us to at least fill our water bottles before the train arrived. He laughed and said, 'This kind of *kindergarten* (child-garden) does not need water.' It makes me sick to think that he meant within 48 hours these little children would be gassed, cremated, and their precious ashes scattered on the ground.

"By 2:00 p.m. the hungry and thirsty children were whining and crying when the locomotive finally arrived pulling a long line of cattle cars. Each car was boarded up solid so you could not look out except through a little barbed-wire slot at the very top. The loading ramps were dropped and our little orphanage was herded and beaten into one car. There was not even enough room to sit down. The children were crying and calling out, '*Wasser Bitte?*' before the door was even shut. There were three of us adults to shepherd these children. I kept Toby and Anna close to me in the cattle car.

"The train sat there for three hours before it started to move. As the heat rose in the hot August afternoon, the children started to pass out. I pounded on the walls and shouted that the children must have water, but these shouts were ignored, except for an occasional guard who hit the car's side with his stick and shouted for us to be quiet or he would shoot into the side of the car. I cannot begin to describe the agony of those three hours.

"The first to die was Little Lenny. He was small and frail for his age, and the heat was just too much for his feeble little body.

"At last the train began moving. The late afternoon wind blowing through the slits brought us some relief. We all hoped that the ride would be just a few hours. Toby and Anna were holding up pretty well, partially because I had not drunk my water so I had some I could give them. To see these precious little children suffer was beyond what I thought I could endure. When children passed out they would slump but not be able to lie down, and I couldn't wade through the packed mass to help them.

"Because of the damage done to the railroads by Allied bombers we had frequent stops. What should have taken a few hours at most— took twenty-four, and twenty-four of our children died—about one per hour, although most died during the last six hours. Most of the children died, I guess, from dehydration or suffocation. There are not the words to describe what it was like. I loved all of the children and knew them all by name. I picked Toby and Anna up and held them for hours and whispered my love for them and their mother. I was sure we would all be together again soon.

"Finally the train clanked to a stop at a platform. Through the slot I saw the sign, AUSCHWITZ. When the doors fell open, some of the little ones literally tumbled out and flopped partially down the ramp. Only about half of the 75 living children were able to walk. We tried to get them up, but the SS guards kept shouting and beating us, '*Schnell, schnell!* Hurry, hurry! Leave them, we will send nurses to help them. Move quickly so you can shower and clean up for supper.'

"The first thing we all noticed was the terrible, nauseating, sweet smell and the blood-red sky. The next thing we noticed was the grayness of everything—the ground, the buildings, the fences, the prisoners' clothing and worst of all, their faces. All of this contrasted to the scarlet sky of human smoke. We were formed into a line and walked toward a very nice-looking and impeccably dressed SS major. He rested his right elbow in his left hand and pointed casually with his index finger to the right or to the left. Now I know, the right meant life, and the left meant death within the hour. Mostly he pointed to the left. This was the first selection.

"About 20 yards ahead of us a woman started screaming as she was sent to the right and her children to the left. Struggling to get back to her children, she broke from her friends who were trying to restrain her. The handsome major, with the most tranquil expression, snapped his fingers and an SS soldier clubbed the woman to the ground, and in a roar of violence she was shot dead. The whole line jerked in terror and surged away from the convulsing and twitching corpse.

"When our small herd of children got to the major, he stopped the line and told them how cute they were and how happy he was to see them. He put us all at ease as he talked about the very special *kindergarten* he had prepared for the children. With a gentle smile and sinister eyes, he pointed left. We gathered the children like a chicken gathering her flock and moved toward the left. Ahead of us, towering high in the sky, were the chimneys spewing forth red smoke.

"'Sir,' I heard the SS major call after me. I turned around to face the man I would later know as Dr. Josef Mengele[2]. 'Are there any twins in your little flock?' he asked with a bright smile.

"I stared numbly at him. All I had just seen and been through caused me such shock that I could not even hear his question.

"'What did you say?'

"'Are there any twins in your little flock?' he asked, staring intently at me.

---

[2] Josef Mengele, (Beppo) was born March 16, 1911, in Gunzburg, Germany. His father, Karl, owned a farm equipment manufacturing factory. In his early years he was an average student with a sweet, innocent personality. He was well loved by the people in his father's manufacturing plant and in his community. He eventually graduated from University of Munich with a doctorate in Philosophy and later with a doctorate in Medicine from the University at Frankfurt, Germany. He had a lust for research, which later led him to his work at Auschwitz. After the war, he fled to Brazil, and there it is believed he died. The Last Nazi, Gerald Astor, Donald I. Fine, Inc. New York.

"Was it good or bad to be a twin? I could not tell. Were the twins killed more quickly because they were unusual? I had heard that the Nazi super-race did not have room for anybody abnormal. I looked back down the corridor that faced us. At the end I could see the smoke stacks. Finally, I whispered, 'Yes.'

"Taking a step toward me he demanded, 'Excuse me, what did you say?'

"'I said yes. I am a twin and my son Toby and daughter Anna are twins.'

"'You and your children are twins?' he asked incredulously. 'Where is your twin?'

"'She lives in Virginia, Minnesota, in the United States.'

"He studied me for a long moment as my little flock of orphans continued walking down the long corridor to the left. 'When did she leave Poland?'

"'She didn't, she was born there.' I said quietly, and waited to let it sink in that I was an American. I studied his face to try to understand what it would mean to me and my children.

"'Are you Jewish?'

"Straightening, I said, 'Only in my heart.'

"He stepped forward again, put a gentle hand on my shoulder and said brightly, 'You are courageous, and I am interested in you and your twin children. I will ask a soldier to take you to my special barracks and you can help me with my research on twins.'

"Jon, I was stupid not to see that the research he wished to conduct would be on us, not with us. For a second time, I had led my children into a frightening and painful trap.

"We were escorted through a fence and along the outside of the corridor where the sad people were walking toward a building with a sign, "Showers." I stretched my neck and tried to see the little children one more time, but they had been swallowed up by the mass of humanity.

"A hot breeze brought the stench of death to us. To our right there were ivory-colored bodies with the skin across their faces stretched tight, causing them all to look like they were smiling horribly. Hollow eyes stared into the crimson sky. They were stacked like cord wood along the fence near one of the ovens. They were stacked closely together, their feet and heads jutting tightly from the stack. The corpses were waiting for their turn in the ovens. I turned Anna's and Toby's heads away. The soldier laughed derisively.

"'Where are the orphans going?' I asked.

"His smile was cold when he said, 'To the *kindergarten*, of course.'

"Near the ovens and in plain sight of what was happening were the Twins Barracks. In the barracks we saw several sets of twins, different ages, from two years old to a pair of girls about 20. There were boys and girls, fraternal and identical sets. Some looked healthier than others. Some had bright countenances with more hope in their eyes than some, who were like the Mussulmans.

"After the guard left, the children swarmed around, asking us all sorts of questions about where we were from, what was happening with the war, etc. When we said we were from Lodz, several children, hungry for any information about their families, asked about aunts and uncles. They seemed to brighten when we knew their relatives. I couldn't bring myself to tell them that their aunts and uncles were starving to death and a few I had just seen sent to the left.

"I learned that it was unusual for the boys and girls to be together here in these barracks; the girls were housed a few yards away in another set of barracks nearer to the Gypsies' family camp. I learned that in another barracks were housed the midgets and dwarfs.

"That evening Mengele came to visit with a beautiful assistant named Angela. Mengele gave Toby and Anna a piece of candy when they cried as the tattooed numbers were burned into their thin little arms. Then Angela took the girls back to their barracks. Mengele stayed behind and talked casually with the boys. Everything seemed friendly and safe. Mengele asked if I would accompany him out of the barracks.

"'Where are the orphans?' I asked directly as soon as we were outside.

"'In the *kindergarten*,' he answered pleasantly.

"'And where is that?' I pressed.

"'Well, it is everywhere. It is on the ground and in the air. But right now your Jewish orphans are there.' He pointed to the red smoke belching from the chimneys. I choked down a rush of bile in my throat."

Mary's kitchen seemed to swim before me. I stared at Ur in disbelief. "The children! Why . . .? How could the children hurt the Nazis?" Still staring, I thought of the little children at the elementary school. Although I would never admit it to my buddies, I had often thought they were cute and fun to watch. How could anyone willingly hurt them? I imagined the little first graders marching off to be gassed and burned. A deep sickness started to settle someplace near my heart. "Don't they have a right to life?" I challenged.

Speaking patiently, Ur said, "We must do all that we can to protect and maintain our rights, but that will not stop some bad people from infringing on all or part of our rights. Bad people infringe on other people's inherent rights. A civilized society is one that honors and respects each other's rights. Do you realize, Jon, that there is very little, if any, conflict between people who maintain their inherent rights?"

"During the war the Nazis decided what civil rights people could exercise or not exercise. Governments may differ in what civil rights they secure for their citizens; however there are other rights—what I call unalienable or inherent rights—which governments do not have the power to give or take away. Yet the government has the duty to protect its citizens and to encourage them to maintain their civil and inherent rights.

"In the United States our Bill of Rights lists some of the civil rights guaranteed by our government, such as: freedom of speech, freedom of religion, right to remain silent, etc. But Article IX states:

*'The enumeration in the constitution of certain rights shall not be construed to deny or disparage others retained by the people.'*

"In other words Jon, there are many other rights that we as free people must maintain to feel truly free. These are called inherent rights.

"For the Jews and many others their civil rights or their freedoms were slowly taken away. In the early years the Nazis took away their rights to own and operate businesses, to teach, or to have government jobs. Later they started to infringe on their inherent rights, but inherent rights are impossible to take away; they can only be infringed upon or surrendered willingly."

"Whoa," I interrupted, "How can that be? What about all of those walking into the gas chambers to die? Weren't their rights to protect the health of their bodies taken away?"

"No."

I stared at Ur for a moment. He said "no" like that answered all of the questions, but it didn't.

"Jon, you are seeing civil rights and inherent rights as existing only if one can exercise them. Inherent rights are given you at birth by the very fact that you are human and are born. These are sacred and belong to you as long as you maintain them and hold them to be sacred. Because human nature is good, most people maintain most of their inherent rights. The more inherent rights we know about, protect, and live by, the more independent we are, and the more freedom we enjoy. In the United States of America we are a people who govern ourselves. Do you see that the very nature of our Constitution requires its constituents to maintain their inherent rights?"

Ur took a breath and then spoke solemnly. "If the time ever comes that the people of this nation waive their inherent rights, we will not be able to safely govern ourselves anymore. Our Constitution will hang by a thread and we will be ripe to fall. We will be like the Romans and the Greeks were just before they collapsed into anarchy."

"What's anarchy?"

A sadness came into Ur's face. "The police are no longer able to enforce the laws of the land, lawlessness reigns, and eventually our society caves in on itself. In anarchy you are only safe if you have the biggest gun or strongest gang. Neither you nor your family is safe to walk to the store or to ever be out alone. And everything you own is in danger of being taken from you if you can't protect it."

"Have you ever seen anarchy?" I asked.

"Yes."

We were quiet for a long moment as I stared at the rain through the blurry window. I felt like the blind man trying to comprehend a grain combine. I closed my eyes and sat back into the soft chair and tried to fit all this into a picture of something that would be clearer to me. My head felt like it was stuffed with cotton. I once was told that if you massage the nerve in the webbing between the index finger and the thumb it helps to clear the head. I started massaging this nerve and it hurt like Bessie standing on my tongue, but my mind did seem to clear a little.

I noticed the room had become chilled, so I dropped four or five pieces of quaking aspen onto the fire, then stirred and blew on the embers. I continued to blow until billows of white smoke started slowly rising into the chimney. The smoke grew thicker and thicker until it burst into bright, warm flames. Sitting back into the chair, I realized that my mind was like the fire. Ur had just dumped a load of thought onto my mind and my pondering was like blowing the embers. Even though right now my mind was full of smoke, if I continued pondering it might burst into bright understanding. Ur seemed to understand my sudden quiet mood, and sat quietly himself enjoying the warmth of the flames.

I started thinking about freedom of speech.

Does the person who lacks the ability to speak and write have the right of freedom of speech? I thought about this for a few minutes and decided, Yes! If a person cannot talk or write he still has the right of free speech even though he can't exercise it. He still owns it with the eventual hope something will change and he will be able to speak, thus fully exercising the right.

I placed Ur's hand on my face and spoke. "I guess even though the children did not have the power to prevent their dying in the gas chambers, they still could keep peace of mind by not going willingly."

A slight, wry smile twitched at his mouth, "Well, I doubt if peace of mind are the right words, but they did keep intact their integrity.

"When the Nazis invaded Russia, Poland, and other countries, they executed hundreds of thousands of Jews by firing squad. Men, women and children were stripped of clothing and jewelry, walked to a forest, told to lie face down and were shot. Others were walked into pits and told to lie down on the corpses of their friends and family and then shot. Many people wondered two things about these incidents. First, why didn't they resist more vigorously? And second, how could they go to their deaths with such calmness?[3]

---

[3] In a forest near Jozefow, Poland, 1500 Jews were mass murdered on Friday, July 12, 1942 by a Nazi military police battalion. Later, in an interview, one policeman remembered, "When the first salvo was heard from the woods, a terrible cry swept the marketplace as the collected Jews realized their fate.

"I may not have the entire answer, but I believe, to answer the first question, that it was obvious there was not anything they could do. They were hopelessly outnumbered and outgunned. Some people did escape. That is a matter of record. Most did not. They were not cowards. That is obvious from the films that were made of these executions. They were just trapped."

I asked, "How could they face death with such calmness?"

"I am sure the whole answer is not this simple, but I believe they maintained their inherent rights even when they could not exercise them. I saw this thousands of times in Auschwitz. I will tell you more about that later.

"Jon, I have told you about only a couple of your inherent rights. There are many more you must learn about.

"Do you understand about the inherent right to protect the health of your body?"

"Yeah, I think so. It means that I will be careful about what I drink or eat, and I will not give up on life and commit suicide. Am I close?"

Ur smiled, "You're close enough. Will you do all you can to maintain your right to life by protecting the health of your body?"

"Sure, why not?" I committed casually. To be honest, I wasn't sure I would keep my commitment. After all, what if my buddies were all drinking or smoking. I knew I would feel pressure to do it too. In fact it would be hard not to. A commitment like this was easy to make to an old man who can't see or hear. I mean, how would he know if I didn't keep it? And we all know just as soon as we decide to do something hard it seems like all kinds of opposition gets thrown into our face.

Like last year during wrestling season. To make weight I had to diet from 138 lb. to 130 lb. Just as soon as I knew I had to lose weight, everybody and his dog was bringing cookies and junk to school to share with me. I would go up to the café and Mom would offer me a free milkshake. Mrs. Johnson would say, "Hey, Jon, why don't you stay and

---

Thereafter, however, a quiet composure—indeed, … an unbelievable and astonishing composure—settled over the Jews." Ordinary Men, Reserve Police Battalion 101 and the Final Solution in Poland, Christopher R. Browning, Aaron Asher Books, Harper Collins Publisher, 1992.

have some lasagna and a triple-sized dessert?" Get the point? The harder you commit the greater the opposition to keep the commitment. So maybe it's better to not make any commitment, and then you don't have any problems. Hmm, somehow that didn't sound right either.

"Not good enough!" Ur shot back, his voice full of emotion. "Not nearly good enough! You sound like you just decided to have a chocolate shake instead of a vanilla one. Don't answer now, I can tell something is frightening you away from a full commitment. Go push on the post until it moves and then let's talk again about what frightens you."

I felt a little miffed at being dismissed into the rain to push on a stupid post while trying to decide what I already decided, kind of.

"What the heck," I sighed, as I got up to go outside.

"Jon," Ur's voice was gentle again, " Is it still raining?"

I bent down, pulled the curtain aside, peeked out the blurry kitchen window, walked back and took his hand to my face. "Yeah, and blowing too," I said, hoping for a reprieve from post pushing.

"Good," was all he said.

I pulled on a gray sweatshirt, tossed the hood on my head and started out the door. My attitude began to sour as the cold wind whipped the hood off and the rain soaked in.

"I hate this cold Idaho rain. Why can't we ever have warm rain like in the Amazon? I don't need this today!" I grumbled in my mind.

Walking to the post I almost decided that Ur was a little kooky. The water squished around my black low-cut Converse sneakers, my Adler socks getting soaked as I crossed the grass. I stood facing the twisted old cedar post. It looked as solid as ever. My hands were still raw from the previous attempts to move it, so I pulled my sweatshirt's sleeves over my hands for makeshift gloves.

I shuddered at the cold and thought I would probably die from hypothermia before this dumb post moved. Checking the change in my pocket I almost decided to just go to Minn's and have a hot chocolate and then come back later and tell Ur the post moved. It wouldn't be a big lie, and heaven knew I had told bigger ones to my mom.

Then I thought about that grain combine and my promise to trust Ur and do what he asked, so I gingerly started pushing on the post. I don't know which I realized first, the post giving a little or the sound of water squishing around the base of the post. Nevertheless, it moved! I was so excited I gave it a couple more big tugs, squatted down to make sure the $1,000 bill was still there, and then sprinted for the door. When I threw open the door I saw Ur sitting in the living room facing me.

"What took you so long?" he asked with a smile even before I closed the door.

How did he always know when I entered the house? Kicking off my wet shoes and peeling the sweatshirt over my head, I went to Ur. "How did you know the post would move?"

"You said it was raining, and I thought it would weaken the hold Mother Earth has on the post. Most of all, Jon, I wanted you to know that opposition can be your friend. Opposition can be the fire that tempers the better sword, as well as the ice that cools a fiery temper. Don't ever run from it, learn from it!"

"You probably saw the rain as your foe," he said as I glanced out at the rain, "when really it was your friend. You probably see my disability as a foe. I wish I could tell you how deeply I have come to love and respect my opposition. Opposition helps us discover greater qualities about ourselves if we have the right attitude, but I am not ready to teach you about the right of attitude just yet. Remember, attitude is the key that unlocks all of the good as well as the bad things of life."

Ur talked for a long time about the camp, how it functioned and what life was like for the "lucky ones" who were in work details. He said that the worst things for most prisoners were the selections.

"Nobody knew when his or her time would come for extermination. When a *Kapo* (a prisoner with status and power over other prisoners) or a guard yelled out, '*Blocksperre*,' the prisoners' blood ran cold. This was an inspection with all of your clothes off. If you were too skinny or sick your number was written down and you were called out for death the next day.

"Other times when on a work detail, a guard might grab the cap from a prisoner's head and throw it down the road. Then he would order the prisoner 'to go get it, quick!' As soon as the prisoner started running after his cap, the guard shot him for trying to escape. Later the guard would get a congratulation and a few days' vacation for preventing the escape."

Ur sat looking exhausted, "Jon, I hope I haven't harrowed you up too much. How are you feeling?"

I was stunned, shocked and a little sickened by what I had heard. It was hard to imagine that part of Ur's life while sitting in Declo, Idaho, where about the worst disaster to ever hit our town was when Marsh Creek overflowed its banks last December. "I'm okay," I said quietly, "Is there more?"

"Yes, I'm afraid to say, there is much more. Would you rather not hear it?"

I wouldn't want my wrestling buddies to know this, but I had had enough. Yet I looked at Ur and said, "It's very interesting. Go ahead, I'm listening."

He clicked open his watch and said, "It's almost lunch time. Let's have some lunch and a nap."

"Sure," I said, thankful for some time to digest what I had heard.

We do not need to invent new moral standards when we allow the rational part of us to be our guide. The laws which define our unalienable rights are called the Laws of Common Sense. Jefferson sometimes refers to them as the laws of nature. Regardless of semantics they are the same thing. Any nation that can successfully govern itself must be allowed and encouraged to follow the Laws of Common Sense.

# CHAPTER 15

## I Have a Right to Be Positive

After lunch Ur headed off for a nap and I flipped on the TV to watch the Green Bay Packers pound on the Chicago Bears. The front window was a wavy blur of rain water. Every time someone drove by I looked up to see who it was. Our town was so small that we not only knew all the residents and their problems, but we knew their cars by the color and the sound they made.

When Pea Lye Gibson came to town in his old blue Chevy pickup, I knew it was him without looking because he had a pinion bearing going out that made a whining sound. Greasy Park's old Nash had a bubble on the right front tire that thumped when he drove it, while Clovis Osterhout's '52 Studebaker pickup was missing a muffler and tail- pipe. People said you could hear Clovis coming clear from Burley nine miles away.

Leonard Moffet said it was Clovis's thundering truck that caused his chickens to lose their feathers last winter and freeze to death. He said he knew it was Clovis's truck that caused his fowl problem because he heard Clovis go by about midnight and the next morning his chickens were naked and dead. Clovis defended himself by saying that Leonard's chickens were so full of fleas that the foxes wouldn't even chase them; that they probably died because they were tired of living as Moffet's chickens and hoped chicken heaven was a better option.

Far off down the road coming from the east was the unmistakable sound of Moose's dad's truck. He had an old '39 Ford

139

pickup he had painted with a brush. It was baby blue and had two Volkswagen front seats in it. There were two reasons I knew it was his truck. First, I could hear his flat-head V-8 engine purring along. A flat head V-8 sounds different than overhead valve engines and there just weren't that many still on the road. But the real reason I knew it was him was because he didn't have fourth gear anymore. He drove in third and that meant his engine was revved up to about 8,000 RPMs and took on a high pitch scream that could kill dogs.

I dashed to the kitchen and slapped on my wet sneakers and then I headed for the front door at a dead run, hoping to catch a glimpse of Moose riding with her dad. I jerked the doorknob so hard that I almost dislocated my arm. The front door hadn't been opened for about 20 years and wouldn't budge today. I turned and bolted out the kitchen door. Immediately the pounding rain soused me. Ignoring this, I ran full blast around the house and slid to a squishy stop on the grass in the front yard. I shielded my eyes against the driving rain and searched down the road. Yes, about 50 yards away was the blue truck headed my way with a haze of road spray surrounding it. It lurched from one lane to the other as it hydro-foiled down the road, its vacuum-powered windshield wipers barely moving. From the silhouette of her high-piled hair I knew the passenger was either Moose, or her dad was carrying a load of beehives in the front seat with him. It suddenly occurred to me how stupid I must look standing in the front yard in the cold deluge without a coat, hat or umbrella casually waving, "How do you do?" I would look dumber than a bent steel post.

Her dad would say, "Look at that kid! He ain't got brains enough to come in out of the rain. Don't ever date him, ya hear? Why I'd have grandkids so stupid they would put their underwear on backwards."

It was too late to run and hide so I started pretending to look up into the big poplar tree, hoping it appeared like I was looking for a lost cat or something. They splashed by and Moose stared at me in astonishment. Our eyes locked for a moment and I gave her a man-nod while my face flushed redder than a Pontiac potato. I rushed back into the house arriving wetter than an otter. Slipping off my shoes I sloshed into the living room where I tugged off my wet socks and hung them on the fireplace screen to dry. I leaned back into a soft chair and put my feet up in front of the fire. I had a lot to think about.

Listening to Ur's story made me remember what a man said once when he first saw the Grand Canyon. "I could see it, but I was sure I couldn't comprehend it."

About all I knew of World War II was what I had seen on TV or in the movies. There was a TV show called *Combat*, where the GI's were always winning battles. Another called *Hogan's Heroes* was about silly men who were in a prisoner of war camp. The Nazis were stupid and, incompetent, and nobody ever got hurt.

From what Ur was saying, the Nazis were anything but stupid and incompetent. Instead they were serious about killing everyone who disagreed with Hitler. They were also anxious to kill everyone who was different from themselves in skin color or religious beliefs. Yet, I knew Ur wasn't trying to teach me a history lesson about World War II; he was trying to teach me something much greater, something that would make my life easier and more worthwhile. That was the hard part. Like the Grand Canyon, I could see it but I just couldn't comprehend what he was trying to teach me.

I thought I had figured out that inherent rights are born with us and that they protect us. I thought I understood that they gave us peace of mind when we—what did he say— maintain them. I was pretty sure I understood the word maintain. The county maintains the roads, which means they keep them in good condition so it is safe and comfortable to drive on them. They put new oil on once in awhile and fill in the potholes once a year. So, if I maintain my right to be honest, I don't have to keep wondering what lies I have told or who is going to catch me. And if I don't use addicting things then I don't have to worry about getting hooked. In other words, I guess, I am freer to do fun stuff.

I thought maybe this would be a good time to go work over the post and take advantage of the rain-soaked ground. I stood at the kitchen door and looked out into the wind and cold rain descending on the glistening post. I almost had my nerve up to go out and give it a try when the back door jerked open and a soddened woman slammed into me. If I had never lost my bejabbers before, I sure had them scared out of me then. I went jumping and high-stepping backwards while squealing like a squashed cat just as Mrs. Wood grabbed me and said, "Sorry, Jon." Rain water had splattered on her glasses, and her hair was matted down like she had been wearing a helmet. She was soaked!

"What happened?" I stammered wild eyed, trying to get my heart to slow down.

"Well, I hit a big puddle in front of Lynches' gas station and got my engine all wet. My car coughed and sputtered up the hill but died just this side of the tracks. So, I got out and ran. I've never seen it rain so hard before. I have got to get a better car." Then looking at me more closely, "What are you doing at the door, and how's Ur?"

"Ur is fine. He's taking a nap. I was about to go outside and I...(I wasn't sure if I should tell her about the post or not)...was going out to look around," I said weakly.

"Look around! Are you nuts? It's raining hard enough to drown frogs."

I glanced dumbly out the window.

"It will let up in a bit and maybe you can help me go get my car running," she added brightly.

"Sure," I nodded. "How come you're home so early? I thought you wouldn't come back 'til tonight."

"Gees, I got bored in the big city, so I came home. What did you and Ur do?"

"Oh . . . just talked." How much could I tell her?

"About what?" she ask casually as she tugged at her wet sweater.

How could I explain everything, like Ur whipping Saul or the ride to Burley or the incredible things that happened to him in the war? "How much do you know about Ur during the war?"

She shook out her wet hair and looked at me. "Well, I think about everything except what happened to his children and how he lost his eyesight and hearing. He doesn't talk about that, to me or anyone." She studied me with seriousness. "Did he talk to you about his life?"

I nodded.

"What did you think about what he told you?"

"I don't know. I guess it's true."

"Jon, it is true. That much I do know. Let me get out of these wet clothes and then I will make us some hot cocoa."

We sat at the table sipping the best cocoa I had ever tasted. She didn't just mix cocoa and milk with some sugar; she mixed a little cinnamon, some real cream, and a dab of butter with it. It was fantastic.

As I was slurping the hot cocoa, Mary explained more about Ur. "After Ur left with Beth and the children to teach and do research in Poland, world tension started to heat up. Mamma, Papa and I kept writing and encouraging him to bring his family back to the States. I guess Ur was too much into his career at the time to see what was going to happen."

I must have looked at her with a funny expression.

"I am not being critical, just telling you what happened," she smiled. "Things are not that different today. I have known lots of kids over the years whose parents were more into their careers than into their families. Some of those parents couldn't see down the road any farther than the end of their nose. Later they wondered why their kids hardly knew them and seldom wanted to come home. Anyway that is another thing all together.

"Ur was just too focused on his career. He kept saying things weren't that bad yet and he would leave as soon as he felt in danger. He waited too long and has suffered greatly for it.

"I will never forget our birthday on August 31, 1939. I was living with my parents in Minnesota at the time. We heard over the radio that Germany had invaded Poland. We tried to find him and his family through the Red Cross and the State Department. It was as if they had vanished from the face of the earth. My parents never recovered from their grief.

Later, after the U.S. entered the war, I joined the Women's Army Auxiliary Corps and flew bombers from the factories in America to England's air bases. The men were needed for the war, so we girls got to fly the new bombers to them."

"You were a bomber pilot?" I asked incredulously.

"Yes, it was pretty exciting. We never flew combat missions, but we had a great time. While I was in England delivering a plane, I met my husband. He was from Declo and worked as a ground crew chief. After the war we moved here where he became a police officer in Burley and I taught school. For some reason children never came."

She got up and poured me some more hot cocoa, cut a thick slice of homemade bread and decorated it with wad of butter. I could hear the rain was letting up.

She sat down and said, "Anyway back to Ur. I continued to make inquiries to the Red Cross after the war, but there wasn't any information about Ur or his family.

"About six months after the war ended in January of 1946, my parents received a telegram from the Red Cross saying their son, Ur Babiraski ,would be arriving in Virginia, Minnesota, on Wednesday, January 30, 1946.

"There are not words to describe how much joy we felt. Yet, we worried that the telegram said nothing about Beth or his children. Nor can we describe our shock and horror when we first saw him at the train station.

"I took a train from Rupert out to Virginia, Minnesota to be there when he arrived home.

"He was helped off the train by a Red Cross volunteer, who noticed our sign, 'Welcome home! Ur Babiraski family.' He looked like a little old man. Mamma exploded into a silent cry, pressed her knuckles to her mouth and turned herself away. Papa just stood cemented to the ground, staring at his son. The volunteer wrote something into Ur's hand with her finger and started walking him toward us."

"Whoa," I interrupted, "He could walk?"

"Oh, sure. He never lost his legs until about 10 years ago, due to his diabetes. I am sure I told you this before, didn't I? "

"Oh, probably, I don't remember." I said quietly. "I thought he lost them during the war, that was all."

"I can see how you could misunderstand. No, he could walk, kinda. Even though he was only 36 years old, most of his hair was gone, and what he had was white. The most shocking thing was his eyes. It was obvious that his eyes were not seeing, and yet his eyes did not seem dead. Do you know what I mean? They had life and peace like they do now. There was something serene and loving in them—not fear, not hate, just kindness."

I nodded.

"We had no idea that he was handicapped until then. We had not been told. Somehow that was left out. I ran to him and hugged him. He whispered, 'Who are you?' My tears were already flowing, but I looked to the volunteer for help.

"'He is deaf as well as blind,' she said gently. 'Take his hand and print into it with big block letters.'

"Wiping my tear-stained hands on my pants, I took Ur's pale hand and printed M-A-R-Y. For a moment I thought he didn't understand, but then he coughed and said with a husky voice, 'My sister, I love you!'

"And he grabbed me for a hug. 'Where are my Mamma and Papa?' I led him to my parents who had not moved, my mother still racked with sobs of grief and happiness mixed. I printed M-A-M-M-A and then my mother held her arms out waiting for him to walk into her embrace. Ur mouthed 'mamma,' but just stood there not knowing what he should do or even where she was standing. It was awkward, but I nudged him in the back and he stepped forward into his grieving mother's arms. They stood there for a long time clutching, both afraid to let loose that they might not find each other again.

"My father stood there looking older than I had ever seen him. He had always been big, raw-boned and ruddy. His strength and vitality were legendary in our town. He had a big roaring laugh and everyone loved to be around him. Up until last year, he was still joining in the Founders Day celebration foot races. Now his shoulders were rounded and slumped, and his gray face was stricken in pain like I had never seen before. His wrinkles were etched like deep cuts in granite. Even his smile wrinkles in the corners of his eyes were drooping in sadness and grief. I always knew my papa was great, but this day I saw his greatness as I had never seen before. I saw his jaw start to grind, as it always did just before he made a big decision, his eyes flashed understanding, and then I heard his booming voice shout with joy, 'Ur, my son, my son, you are home and I love you!' In one stride he had wrapped his massive arms around Mamma, Ur, and me.

"With his Polish accent he shouted to the whole world, 'Ho! We just one big family again. I have all family here again!'

"He clutched us tighter and tighter. Soon Mamma was laughing and saying, 'Leo, you big horse, you want that you should kill us with your big arms?'

"'Oh Mamma,' Papa teased, 'where are your piano ribs that I can play them and hear your music?' Then his stout fingers started to search down Mamma's abundant side looking for her ticklish ribs.

Mamma was out of control when she was being tickled. Soon there were peals and shrieks of laughter, all of us gasping, laughing, and crying at the same time except Ur. Soon we noticed that Ur stood there with quiet tears flowing down his face, with us yet not included like he was before the war. Things would never quite be the same again. That was 21 years ago."

"But you don't know what happened to his children or how he became deaf and blind?" I asked.

"I've asked him, but he said he doesn't remember. One time I said, 'You don't remember? How could you not remember something like that? These were your kids and your hearing and eyesight. What do you mean you can't remember?' He said to me in that gentle and patient voice of his, 'Mary, I am afraid to remember right now. I think my mind is protecting me. It may be better not to probe just yet.'"

# CHAPTER 16

## I Have a Right to Do Good for My Children

Oakley, Idaho, 1949

Joy Reynolds was born during Idaho's worst winter in a hundred years. The snow began falling in late November and continued steadily for two months. The incessant wind had piled snowdrifts 16 feet high in some places and sent the wind chill to below –40 degrees. Some outlying country roads were closed for weeks before heavy equipment could get to them and push the snow off. Then the wind began blowing again and the roads drifted closed before the next day. Cattle could not be contained in fences because the fences had long ago been buried. Nobody worried about the cattle wandering off because the only source of food was near the haystacks. However, there was plenty of worry about providing shelter for the stock. Hundreds of heads of livestock died from the constant exposure to the cold and wind.

Dairy farmers resorted to milking their herds of Holstein cows and pouring the milk to the hogs or out into the snow, as there was no way of getting it to the creamery. In some places the drifts were high enough to cause mothers to warn their children not to play near the power lines for fear they would touch a hot wire and be electrocuted. After two weeks of this kind of weather, people began to adjust. Farmers hooked up large sleighs to old teams of dray horses and drove them as-the-bird-flies to wherever they wanted to go. For the first time in over 100 years there were no roads or fences to restrict their direction of

147

travel. The drifts became so hard that the heavy sleighs pulled with horses could move easily over the undulating expanse of white with barely a mark to show where they crossed. They used groves of trees or neighbors' barns to guide their journey.

All the people in the small, hilly community of Oakley, Idaho, pulled together, sharing what they had while hoping for an early spring. Sometimes a week passed before the 21 miles of main road north to Burley would open. When it did, several farmers who had large trucks, caravaned to Burley to bring back a load of lump coal or 55 gallon barrels of fuel oil. These old trucks rarely had adequate heaters if any at all. The trip usually required scraping the gauzy fingers of frost on the inside of the windshield. Accompanying these caravans were always several cars filled with families hoping to see the doctor or restock their dwindling supplies.

On Sunday, January 9, 1949, the wind started to moan up Birch Creek at six in the morning. It slid over the rounded hills, picking up snow from the windward side of the hills and dropping it on the lee side. A sturdy log house stood in a cove on the banks of Birch Creek. Chester Reynolds had homesteaded there around the turn of the century. Years later he passed it into the hands of his only son by the same name.

Young Chet married Evelyn Anderson, a beautiful red-headed girl of local stock. Children were hard to come by, but in 1938, they were blessed with a daughter whom they named Sandra. They hoped for more children, but every pregnancy until this one had ended in disappointment. Now Evelyn was due at any time.

They talked about moving her into town with her parents for the delivery, but each time they got ready to leave they were either snowed in or a storm was threatening. The seven-mile drive over unpredictable roads seemed too big a risk to take. Now there weren't any choices. The baby would be born there on the farm, and Chet felt it would be soon. He shuddered at the thought, but a lifetime of living in that harsh land and three years fighting the Japanese as a Marine had taught him one thing— prepare as best you can and take life as it comes.

In addition to the uncertainty of the delivery was the fact that Evelyn had been sick with the German measles during the first three months of this pregnancy. Dr. Trehune said there might be complications with the baby.

"What kind of complications?" they asked.

Concern darkened the white-haired doctor's features for a moment. "Sometimes when the mother contracts German measles during the first trimester of her pregnancy, the child may be born with some defects, such as mental retardation, blindness, deafness or cerebral palsy."

Looking out the window Chet saw the snow whip around the corners of the log barn his father had built. It also blew in curling plumes off the roof of the house. Chet Reynolds knew the drill. He had to get the stock fed while he could. He had tied a long strand of strong baling twine between the house and the barn to guide him during the white-outs.

During the first white-out, last November, he became disoriented between the barn and the 50 yards to the house. He wandered around for almost 45 minutes before bumping into the well-house and finally getting his bearings. The experience had frightened him enough that the next day, when it cleared up, he rigged up the line.

First he must stoke the fire. Throwing on his coat and jamming his hat over his ears, he grabbed a five-gallon bucket and pulled open the door. A frigid blast of winter pierced him and made him catch his breath. The entire yard was whited out from blowing snow. He knew that giant drifts were piled up on the lee side of the house, even though he couldn't see them.

Moving along the house under the veranda, he slid his hand along the outside wall feeling for the latch that would open the coal shed. Finding it, he turned the latch, kicked the frozen door open and stepped in. He caught his breath and looked around. He felt a satisfaction at seeing the 15 tons of lump coal he had laboriously hauled from Burley last summer, one ton at a time. At the time he had nearly talked himself out of it, thinking, he could get some more coal during winter if they ran out. The reasoning seemed good in 90 degree summer weather. Now he knew the satisfaction of being prepared.

After stoking the fire, he turned and headed out again to do the feeding. "I'll be back in a few minutes," he shouted over his shoulder to Evelyn as he went out the door. From the porch he climbed the six-foot snowdrift and felt the full blast of the raging wind. He searched along the eves of the house until he found the twine running to the barn. The first leg of the twine took him to the big poplar tree near the front gate. Following the twine through the yard, he could see the odd distorted shapes of the yard. The tire swing was buried, and all he could see was the chain descending into the snow. The second leg took him to the Farmall M tractor Chet had parked in the middle of the yard. The twine was tied to a steel post Chet had wired to the steering wheel. The lee side of the tractor was almost buried in a hard drift. The last leg ran straight to the barn door. Stopping abruptly near the barn, he squinted through the blizzard and swore softly at the sight of the open door.

Stumbling forward he slid down the drift to the open door. As he peered into the barn his worst fears were realized. Amiga, his wife's pride and joy, was missing. Probably got out before the storm got up so bad, Chet thought. The gray quarter horse had been Evelyn's since she was a teenager. To lose this horse would nearly kill her. Without thinking of the consequences, Chet rushed out the door and up on the drift. Blinded by the stinging snow, he strained his ears through the roar of the storm for any sound that might help him. At first only the fierce, howling wind could be heard; then he thought he could hear snatches of . . . a whinny. He ran toward it and then stopped hoping to hear it again. There it was again. He started running hard in that direction, finally stopping as his lungs began to burn with the effect of the frozen air. There it was again—only this time it was to the north or was that west, he wondered. A panicky feeling started to penetrate his almost frozen mind. He was lost! He knew he would have to get a grip on himself or he would never survive. Getting down on his hands and knees, he tried to follow his invisible tracks. Soon he gave up. He knew his hands were freezing and his face was numb. He had to get out of the cold. He had to find some kind of shelter until the wind slowed down.

Moving into a crevice of snow, he dug a small snow cave to get out of the wind and think. Slipping back into the cave, he immediately started to feel warmer. He tried to identify all of his options. He couldn't really be that far from the house and barn. Yet to go the wrong way— even five feet was certain death. He finally decided to try to wait until the storm let up.

Shortly after Chet left the house, Evelyn suddenly felt a rush of warm water—the water which surrounds the baby had burst. The baby was coming, soon. Evelyn looked at the door for a moment and then walked directly to it. Opening the door she shielded her face from the slashing snow and shouted, "Chet!" The wind ripped the words from her lips, shredded them into a million pieces of snow and blew them away. It was useless to shout again, and it was too dangerous for her or Sandra to go get him. She would just have to wait. She put water on to heat and got out all the clean towels and several extra sheets. As she was reaching for the sheets, the first labor pain started.

"Where is your dad?" Evelyn said with more fear in her voice than she intended. Sandra, already aware that her father had been gone longer than normal, shook her head.

The hours drug on, and with the contractions becoming more violent and closer together, Evelyn went to the window and looked out at the whiteness. Finally she went to the bed and lay down. Sandra had come quickly with only four hours of labor. Evelyn shuttered at the thought of giving birth without Chet's help.

"Sandra, honey, you're going to need to help me," Evelyn said with gentleness and pleading.

Trembling slightly, Sandra came to the bedside and held her mother's hand. Neither of them wanted to state the obvious. Chet had been gone over three hours now. Something must have happened to him. Even now he could be hurt and slowly freezing to death. Yet, there was not anything they could do. Fighting down the panic, Evelyn knew she must concentrate on this baby's delivery. She could hear Chet's well-worn maxim: "Prepare as best you can and take it as it comes."

By late afternoon, little had changed except the closeness and violence of Evelyn's contractions and the dwindling of her strength. Chet still wasn't home, and with the long and fervent labor Evelyn knew she was in trouble.

Chet had become sleepy in the afternoon, but was afraid of going to sleep. He knew that hypothermia caused people to become sleepy just before they froze to death.

The storm had not let up; in fact, it had strengthened. Since his experience in the war Chet had always been a praying man, and he found himself praying now with more fervor than he had in years for anything that would help his situation. He kept having the feeling that Evelyn was in trouble and needed him. Another hour had gone by and now it was getting dark. He had to do something, but what? Take a chance? What were his choices now? Slithering out of the snow cave, he jogged in place to get the circulation moving again. Suddenly he was knocked off his feet and pitched hard into the snow.

With Evelyn in a semiconscious condition Sandra made a decision. Throwing on her coat, she headed out the door. How hard can it be to find the barn? she reasoned. I have been to it a thousand times.

Sandra had never tried it in a blizzard. The wind tore at her face, stole her breath and numbed her hands almost immediately. She stumbled up the drift and searched for the baling twine to guide her. The wind had sent the wind chill to -40 degrees. Before she reached the tree, she was crying from the pain in her exposed legs and hands. Her uncovered head had a sharp pain like the kind she got in the summer when she ate ice cream too fast. Wrapping her arm around the twine, she shoved her hands into her pockets, closed her eyes against the stinging snow and pressed on. By the time she reached the tractor, she was completely exhausted. Too tired and cold to go on or return to the house she slumped down near the tractor. In a moment she felt peaceful, sleepy and warm.

Scrambling to his feet, Chet made out the shadowy form of Amiga. "Oh, you cursed animal. You got me into this fix!" he shouted. Then he remembered something his father had told him when he was lost over in the City of Rocks. He spent most of a day trying to find his way out of the miles of giant boulders before he finally hit on the right trail. When he explained why he was late, his father chided him saying, "You could've given your horse his head and he would've brought you home. He's got a better compass than you do."

Chet wondered if this old hay burner could find her way home. If she could, why hadn't she? Or had she? For the first time Chet noticed that her gray coat wasn't covered with frozen snow as it should have been if she had been in the blizzard all day.

Moving to her rump he took her tail and tapped her gently; she began to move. For almost 10 minutes she plodded along with Chet finding it increasingly hard to keep up. Just as he was about to collapse, Amiga dipped sharply, and Chet lost his footing and slid into the barn.

"Thank you, thank you!" he whispered as relief swept him. "Oh, thank you!"

Chet stood and began jogging in place and slapping his arms around his body to stir his circulation. He knew there would not be a second chance if he collapsed between the house and the barn.

Chet hurried along the twine as fast as he could. Reaching the tractor, he paused for a moment with his back to the storm to catch his breath, then started to the house. His first step away from the tractor felt different, soft and… reaching down Chet's numb hands fumbled with the object. Blinded by the snow, he had a hard time trying to figure out what it was and almost decided to hurry on when he realized that something about the object felt familiar. Grabbing whatever it was, he pulled it out of the whiteness and lifted it to his face.

"Oh, no!" he cried when he saw it was Sandra. Her long hair was frozen solid, and her face and clothes were covered with snow and ice. Chet wasn't sure she was still alive. Gathering her under one arm, he hurried along the line. Finally he reached the house and slid down the drift. Still clinging to Sandra, he stumbled along the veranda and pushed open the door.

He laid Sandra near the stove. His numb hands fumbled as he peeled off his frozen clothes. His body began to shake as it let the cold out and struggled to bring its temperature up to normal. Checking Sandra he could tell she was still breathing. Then he bolted to the bedroom calling his wife's name.

Evelyn's eyes fluttered open and he could see the tears of relief start to flow. She whispered, "Something must be wrong because the baby ain't come. Where's Sandra?"

Taking things as they came, Chet threw a quilt over the stove then stripped off Sandra's frozen clothes. Wrapping the warm blanket around her he laid her again near the stove. He knew he had to get the house warmer.

Grasping the coal bucket, he headed outside again. Soon he was back in the house where he stoked the fire to red hot. Then he turned his attention to Evelyn.

Feeling around her stomach, Chet felt sure the baby must be coming breach. Evelyn whimpered as another contraction wracked her weakened body.

Chet knew he would lose his wife unless he did something. "Take it as it comes," he mumbled. "Take it as it comes."

Sandra had awakened and was crying softly from the pain of warming up. She was trembling as her body warmed up and there was a little frostbite on her nose. Reaching outside, Chet got some snow and rubbed it on Sandra's nose to relieve the frostbite.

Throwing some leftover soup on the fire to warm up, he decided on a plan. While feeding Sandra some hot soup, he explained what he wanted her to do. "Sandra," Chet asked, "you remember last spring when the hog had trouble farrowing?"

"Yes," she said.

"Remember how I asked you to reach your small hand inside and move the piglet that was blocking the birth canal?"

She nodded, "Is that what is wrong with Mom?"

"Yes, I need you to do the same. Will you do that?"

Weak as Sandra was she nodded, and 45 minutes later Chet was drying off an 8-pound 3-ounce baby girl who had the most beautiful red hair and blue eyes they had ever seen. While Evelyn slept soundly, Chet and Sandra cried great tears of joy. Kissing the infant's forehead Chet breathed, "Out of our pain, sorrow and fear has been born pure Joy."

The spring thaw, much to everyone's relief, came early, and in spite of the mountains of snow, the melting caused very little damage along Birch Creek. By April 1, Evelyn had recovered fully from the ordeal of delivery. Sandra had little opportunity for school, partly because of the harsh weather and partly because of Evelyn's poor health.

A year later, Joy had entered the cute stage and kept the family entertained with her smiles and laughs during the long winter nights. Yet, there was something different about Joy that no one could put their finger on. Joy's eyes never searched for who was speaking to her.

While Joy was prattling on in the middle of April, Evelyn slipped behind her and whispered her name. No response. Then she clapped her hands. Still no response. Finally she stomped on the floor, and Joy looked around to see her concerned mother.

Evelyn and Chet quietly discussed that the next time they went to Burley they would take Joy to have Dr. Trehune give her a good looking over.

Their fears were confirmed when Dr. Trehune said, "There is a high probability that Joy is profoundly deaf. But the only way you can really know is to take her to the audiologist in Twin."

Chet and Sandra sat stunned while trying to digest what all of this meant as Dr. Trehune scribbled down the telephone number of a Dr. Ross Cleaver. Two weeks later on a blustery and rainy morning Chet, Evelyn and Joy made the 60-mile trip along U.S. Highway 30 to Twin Falls in their dark green 1942 Chevrolet pickup. While the pickup splashed along with the vacuum windshield wipers stalling on the upgrades and then beating furiously on the slope, Chet and Evelyn sat in sad silence pondering what it would mean to have a deaf child. To them deafness was like farming pineapples– not in their life experience– just something they had never thought about.

At the Magic Valley Hearing Clinic on Blue Lakes Boulevard, Dr. Ross Cleaver confirmed that Joy had a profound hearing loss in both ears. He recommended that since they were this close they should visit the Idaho State School for the Deaf and Blind (ISDB), 40 miles farther north in Gooding. Chet was reluctant, but Evelyn was adamant to go there today. Dr. Cleaver called the school and made an appointment for them to meet with Dr. Clarence Smith, the school superintendent.

"Don't over look the obvious solutions to your problems because they are probably the right ones."

# CHAPTER 17

## I Have the Right to Make the Best Decisions I Can for My Small Children

Evelyn's heart weighed heavier with each passing mile. All she could think about was how sad her little daughter's life would be without sound—no singing birds chattering in the early spring trees—no gurgling of Birch Creek as it passed the house. A tear started to slide down her cheek as she hugged Joy a little tighter and thought no mother's lullaby, Christmas carols or church hymns. How could she call her if there was danger? She would have to stay with her 24 hours a day.

Chet also was in his own silent garden of anguish. Would the government require her to be institutionalized? I won't stand for that! he thought. Surely she could never marry, so children would be out of the question. How could she hear them cry for help? He sucked air in sharply as he thought about how people would treat his deaf daughter. He would not let that happen. She would not become an object of scorn, ridicule or pity. She would live on the ranch with Evelyn and him until . . . then what? Sandra would take care of her. Was that fair to Sandra? Chet suddenly felt a great tearing in his chest, a panic of being cornered by circumstances. He pounded the wheel in frustration and shouted, "I hate this—not being able to do something! Joy just can't be deaf . . . she can't!"

Evelyn jumped at his explosion and Joy started to cry.

"If you wouldn't have got sick, Joy wouldn't have got this problem!" he shouted.

"I beg your pardon!" she fought back, her own frustration and sadness letting go. "If you wouldn't have stupidly wandered off and got lost that day when I really needed you, you could have helped sooner with the delivery. Have you stopped to think that maybe it was the strain of the delivery that caused her deafness? Remember, you were the one who procrastinated moving me into Oakley with my family." Now she was crying and Joy was screaming as she sensed the hostility in the truck. "How dare you accuse me of causing Joy's deafness!" She yelled over all of the commotion. Chet gripped the steering wheel harder and glared out at the miserable weather.

Turning north at Wendell, they traveled in sullen silence over green, rolling hills with black lava rock jutting up here and there like the cracked backs of partially buried prehistoric creatures. Soon they entered Gooding, so named for the man who donated the land for the State School for the Deaf and Blind as well as the tuberculosis hospital. As these institutions were built, a small community grew up around them. This community had a larger-than-normal number of professionals. Teachers, administrators, doctors and nurses moved into the small, barren community. Chet eased the dripping truck up to a curb near a large red brick building. Chet and Evelyn stared up at an ominous building through the blurry side window.

Chet reached out a hard, weathered hand and wrapped it around Evelyn's and said, "I'm sorry about what I said. I know it's not your fault. I'd rather have my foot hung up in a stirrup of a run away mustang than to face this school today."

Evelyn lifted Chet's hand and kissed it gently. Then putting it to her cheek she whispered, "I'm sorry too. I spoke out of my own guilt. I worry that I'm responsible for her deafness." Her eyes glistened again.

"No Evelyn! Don't say that! It just happened, that's all! We'll face it together all right. We've done all we can. Let's just take this as it comes."

Inside they met with Dr. Clarence Smith, a nervous man in his forties. His oily black hair was parted just above his right ear and thrown over the top in a futile effort to cover his pale scalp. His short, pudgy body had been shoehorned into a black suit with a vest full of buttons that threatened to machine-gun someone if he took a deep breath. Nodding with a patronizing smile, he reached out a clammy, bread-soft hand to shake with Chet. Chet looked at Dr. Smith's overloaded vanity wall of diplomas and certificates and then sized up the man in his own mind as someone as clammy and bread-soft as his hand shake. Dr. Smith invited his head teacher, Miss Brandish, to join them. She was in complete contrast to Dr. Smith. She was tall, trim and very charming with a professional air about her. Her kind eyes smiled as she greeted them.

When everyone was seated, Dr. Smith began, "So you have a deaf child. I am so sorry to hear that." His voice dripped with condescension. "And what do you think caused the child's deafness?"

Evelyn dropped her eyes to her fidgeting hands wrapped around Joy as she slept on her lap. Chet's voice took on the hardness of flint. "Why's that important?"

"Oh, well, perhaps it is not," he retreated. "Does she have any other handicaps, such as mental retardation or visual impairing?"

"No," Chet said defensively.

"Good. Now I don't have a lot of time to spend with you so let me be brief. When your child is ready to start school—say around four or five— you bring her here and we will teach her how to speak and read lips..."

"What're you talking about? Bring'er here! That's a three-hour drive, each way," Chet interrupted.

There was that condescending smile again. "This is a residential school, Mr. Reynolds. That means the children live here in dorms and..."

"Joy's not going to live in a dorm. She's going to live at home," Chet broke in.

Dr. Smith sighed indulgently. "I don't have time to explain all of this to you now. Miss Brandish will," he grinned at Chet. "Let me just say you have these choices. One, send your child here, two, drive here every day, or three, move here."

Chet flared, "How about the fourth choice? She stays home with her own family!"

"If you do that," Dr. Smith was standing, looking up at Chet and speaking like a parent to an errant child, "then your precious Joy will grow up stupid and unable to communicate. I have a doctorate in Special Education. I know what I am talking about!"

Chet stood, trembling with rage and frustration, clenching and unclenching his giant fists. He towered over Dr. Smith by six inches.

Miss Brandish spoke quietly, "Mr. Reynolds, would you and your wife like to see the school before you leave, please?"

Evelyn reached up and tugged at Chet's sleeve, "Come on, Chet. We just as well look around this place before we leave."

Glaring again at Dr. Smith, Chet turned to follow Evelyn and Miss Brandish into the hall. As he did so, Dr. Smith's parting comment was, "Remember, if you want your daughter to grow up normal, don't let her ever sign. Make her vocalize." He raised an index finger into the air as if to accentuate his point.

Chet waited just outside the door as Evelyn politely thanked Dr. Smith, then joined him in the hall. While he waited, he had to admit that the last statement of Dr. Smith's did make sense. Miss Brandish guided them down the hall and out a side door into another red brick building.

"We were just in Old Main, our administration building and this is our elementary classroom building and dormitory," she said as she ushered them into another long hall smelling of varnish and oil. Here the children are taught lip reading and speech as well as some other subjects."

"Are you saying," Evelyn started with hopefulness, "that Joy can be taught to read lips and speak so she can communicate as well as hearing people?" Chet, having cooled off, looked hopefully to Miss Brandish for her answer.

Miss Brandish shot a look toward the administration building and then lowered her voice. "There are two schools of thought on this subject. One says that you only teach lip-reading and speech to a deaf child. The ideal is lofty and the objective appears good."

"If that's possible then naturally that's what we want for Joy and nothing less," Chet determined.

Miss Brandish stopped near a white porcelain drinking fountain and offered Chet and Evelyn a drink. They shook their heads. Loud slow speaking was coming through the walls of a nearby oral classroom. She continued, "Only 50 percent of the sounds are visible on the lips. That means if someone could read lips perfectly he would still only get 50 percent of a conversation. And usually, hearing people don't give the deaf perfect lips to read. They mumble, have moustaches, put their hands over their mouths, speak too fast or too slow, or turn away. In my opinion lip- reading is a gift, like the gift a musician has. He may enhance his gift by training, but without the gift the perfecting of the talent is nearly impossible. Speech is equally difficult to acquire in a vacuum where there is not yet any language."

"This sounds a little discouraging," Evelyn interjected.

"Dr. Smith is of the opinion that Oralism—lipreading and speech—is the only viable way to teach the deaf. He is also of the opinion that deafness is so horrible that the deaf must be pitied and cared for all their lives. That opinion is not necessarily shared by everyone," she stated with caution.

Evelyn put Joy down so that she could crawl and said, "Is that opinion shared by you?"

"Let me show you the school and then I'll answer your question. Okay?"

Chet and Evelyn were amazed at how many deaf children there were in the school. They were told that the school was segregated into four groups of disabilities: the oral deaf, the signing deaf, the blind and the deaf-blind. They noticed that the oral deaf had to sit on their hands in one class. When they asked Miss Brandish why, she said the teacher must have caught them signing. Chet decided that even though he couldn't understand the oral students they were not as wild and grotesque in their facial expressions and gestures as the signing students. And besides he thought, "You can't talk to most hearing people with signs." One of the things that most amazed them was that one of the teachers was deaf. The school was orderly, and for the most part, pleasant. Chet started to relax.

After they had seated themselves in Miss Brandish's office, she closed the door. "What did you think?"

Chet began, "I won't institutionalize my daughter."

Sidestepping his challenge, Miss Brandish said, "I understand that and totally respect your feelings and decision, but what questions do you have about what you saw today?"

Feeling less threatened, Chet said, "I like the idea of Oralism because the deaf are more like normal people."

"Evelyn, what are your feelings?"

Evelyn glanced at Chet and said, "The signers seemed more involved in communicating with each other and the teacher. I want whatever will be best for Joy."

Chet interrupted, "You don't want her looking like some animal, do you?" He stared hard at Evelyn.

"Mr. Reynolds, sometimes when someone sees a signing deaf person for the first time it looks a little . . . strong. Let me assure you that every gesture—every facial expression, tilt of the head, movement of the mouth, widening or squinting of the eyes—is a beautiful symphony of language and, most important, communication."

Evelyn asked, "You said you would tell us your opinion about Oralism versus signing. Is this a good time?"

"Yes, I am glad you brought it up. Both of my parents are deaf."

Chet and Evelyn looked at each other then back to Miss Brandish. "Do you mean the deaf can marry?"

"Of course," she smiled, "and get driver's licenses and do almost anything hearing people can do if it doesn't require total hearing. For example, the deaf can't be telephone operators or policemen, but nearly everything else is open. My parents both have college degrees from Gallaudet College in Washington, D.C. My mother is a full-time mom and volunteers at the Riverside School for the Deaf in Riverside, California, and my father is an accountant. My parents have six children. I am the oldest. Neither of my parents has a good speaking voice, and both depend on signing to communicate except when they interact with hearing people; then they have to write. My parents are happy, well-adjusted people who have a great marriage and are heavily involved in their children's lives."

Evelyn interrupted, "How did your parents communicate with their children? I mean, before you could read and write?"

Miss Brandish smiled cheerfully. "We all signed long before we talked. Sign language is my first tongue, so to speak."

Evelyn persisted, "Well, yes, I can see that, but Dr. Smith said if Joy learns signing first she will never learn to speak. How did you learn to speak?"

"Without being too disrespectful, I must say Dr. Smith doesn't know everything." Miss Brandish glanced nervously at the door. I know what people say about Oralism because it is currently the prevailing philosophy in deaf education. But honestly, since 1880 when the decision was made by hearing educators of the deaf in Versailles, France, to move all deaf education away from signing to Oralism, I think deaf education has declined in effectiveness. There are significantly fewer deaf professionals now than before 1880. The deaf—and I mean the signing deaf—have a very strong sense of community. They live their lives almost like a subculture to the hearing culture. Their lives are as fulfilled and happy as any hearing person.

For the next four years, Chet and Evelyn discussed how Joy should be educated without ever coming to a decision. They had even talked about the possibility of selling the ranch and moving to Gooding. Chet and Evelyn both knew that option was not possible. What kind of work would Chet do? He didn't know anything but ranching, and his roots and his ancestors' roots were too deep in the ranch. So what did that leave?

When Joy was three years old, Evelyn gave birth to Chester Joseph Reynolds, and someday the ranch would fall into his hands.

"What is true of every member of the society, individually, is true of them all collectively; since the rights of the whole can be no more than the sum of the rights of the individuals." --Thomas Jefferson to James Madison, 1789. ME 7:455, Papers 15:393

# CHAPTER 18

## I Have a Right to Sacrifice for My Children

Joy lived up to her name. She was spoiled with love and attention, and she had a knack for showing affection. Regardless of her deafness, she was required to work along with Sandra. Communication had always been superficial with homemade signs and gestures. Evelyn longed to have a deeper conversation with her deaf daughter. Early on, Evelyn had been too protective, always following Joy around or sending Sandra to be with her. Because Joy was so active, following her around had nearly worn the entire family to exhaustion.

At three, Joy had terrified the family one day by slipping away and making the two-hour walk to Grandma's house in Oakley. Evelyn imagined her meeting a rattlesnake and not hearing its warning. Everyone was frantic with worry and Chet and Evelyn nearly had a nervous breakdown while searching for her in the surrounding hills before Grandma's red Studebaker bounded into the yard with Joy's beautiful smiling face staring out the side window. Chet and Evelyn both cried with relief when they saw her. Both hugged and kissed her, but she just kicked and scrambled down to go play. Chet and Evelyn knew then, if they had not known before, Joy had an independent spirit.

In the summer of 1954, Chet and Evelyn had to make a decision; and even though they didn't want to admit it, they both knew what the decision would have to be.

The first week of June, Chet and Evelyn drove to Gooding and met with Dr. Ron L. Jacobs, the new school superintendent. He was a

165

man of medium height, whose baby-faced countenance illuminated happiness and enthusiasm for his work. He was also deaf and did not use his voice. Miss Brandish, now married and going by Mrs. Martin, interpreted the meeting. Chet immediately liked Dr. Jacobs. He said since he became the superintendent, he had encouraged more students to learn by the use of sign. The school still had a good speech and lip-reading program, but the emphasis was to get language into children as soon as possible through sign language and then to supplement their education with speech training.

"A deaf educator named George Verditz said in 1913, 'Sign language is the noblest gift God has given to the Deaf.' I believe it and that is my philosophy and my passion," said Dr. Jacobs.

Changing the subject, Evelyn asked hesitantly, "How often can we see Joy?"

"As often as you wish outside of school hours, and that only because it would disrupt the classes," Dr. Jacobs explained. "The children are encouraged to go home on the weekends. A bus drops off in Burley . . . Mrs. Martin hand me that schedule please . . . thank you. Okay, on Friday evenings at 5:30 in front of the Oregon Trail Café. The bus picks up again Sunday evening same time, same place—that's easy. We have excellent dorm moms who love the children and take good care of them. Our dorm moms are all deaf."

"Is that safe?" Evelyn asked, suddenly alarmed. "I mean, what would happen if there was a fire? How could she hear the alarm?"

Dr. Jacobs smiled, "I understand your concerns. All of our buildings have very loud clangors and bright flashing lights when an alarm goes off." Evelyn relaxed a little and settled back into her chair.

They discussed the particulars of registration and what she would need to bring. They talked about activities and school breaks. Finally Chet and Evelyn were satisfied that Joy should attend school in Gooding, but they had one more question.

"Dr. Jacobs, how do we explain to Joy that we are leaving her for just a short time at school and not abandoning her?"

Sadness clouded his eyes as he signed, "I don't know."

"What did your parents do with you?" Evelyn pressed.

"I don't remember." He patted the desktop with both hands, as if trying to get up the courage to say something and then finally said, " To be totally honest, dropping Joy off will be the hardest thing you have ever done, but it will be one of the 'rightest' things you ever do also," he said sincerely. "Without your ability to explain to her what is happening, she will be on her own to learn by experience, and that may take a few weeks until she realizes that she goes home on weekends. The first three weeks of each school year are always hard on the new students, staff and especially the parents. I wish it were different."

The rest of the summer flew by. Never had Joy been so cute and so fun to have at home. Her incredibly beautiful natural curly red hair and deep blue eyes were enthralling. She had become a jokester. She was always hiding things—her mother's kitchen utensils, her dad's tools. Then when they looked for them she would stare at them with an impish smile and wait until they looked her way. Then they would move their mouths and shake their heads and chase her. She would run squealing with delight. The family became used to her squeals. They were different sounding from other children, but they were just as joyful.

August 26, 1954, the whole family, including grandparents, gathered to have a party before Chet and Evelyn took Joy to the Idaho State School for the Deaf and Blind (ISDB) to begin school. The family tried not to think about the actual leaving of this small child. It frustrated and frightened them to know that there wasn't a way to explain what was going on. Their conversation with Joy was always superficial. Eat, drink, sleep, play were all they really could talk about. Of course, there was much nonverbal communication that showed love, anger, happiness, approval, disapproval, etc. But as far as they knew Joy had no real concept of time other than day and night. When they walked away from her at school, it would seem like they had just abandoned her; so no one tried to think about it. It would break her little five-year-old heart, and for her parents there would not be any language to describe their sorrow.

On Sunday morning, right after church, Chet and Evelyn loaded Joy's small luggage into a 1950 De Soto sedan borrowed from Evelyn's parents. Loading Sandra, Joseph and Joy, they began their drive to Gooding. Everyone was as downcast. Everyone, that is, except Joy. She bounded around hugging and waving. To her, this was a great adventurous trip. She wondered why the family had sad faces.

Joy loved riding in the De Soto. The pickup was always crowded and she never got to sit near a window, except when she and her father went some place alone. The De Soto had a window for everyone except little Joseph. The pickup was too noisy—not in sound but in bumps and vibrations. The De Soto was smooth like the Snake River on summer evenings. With her window down she put her arm outside and flew her hand up and down in the wind like an airplane, then she put her face outside the window. She loved to feel the invisible soft pummeling of the wind against her skin. She wondered what that thing was that slapped at her face and whipped her red hair while stealing her breath away.

When riding at this speed, the smells changed so quickly. One moment a field of hay lay curing, sending a profusion of sweet alfalfa smell, which was soon replaced by the musty smell of an irrigation canal. There was the dry smell of harvested grain fields and the penetrating smell of sagebrush. Such ecstasy and adventure! Yet, the car had a somber feeling.

Best of all, she loved the cities. In Burley they passed colorful storefronts and wonderful smells from hamburger joints. The car turned off Overland Avenue west onto U.S. Highway 30. The highway followed closely the old Oregon Trail route through several small towns, until they turned north on a narrow farm road. The road went a short distance until it seemed to Joy that the earth fell away into a giant chasm with purplish-black walls that dropped hundreds of feet. Dad stopped the car and they all got out to look. Far below Joy could see the Snake River as it crashed through Hell's Canyon. It took her breath away to be so near the edge. Dad held her close as the family stood there watching the seagulls and other birds ride the currents below them. After awhile the family all piled back into the De Soto and the trip resumed.

Further down the road Chet turned at a sign with an arrow. The words said SHOSHONE FALLS. Again the car proceeded toward that great crack in the earth. It terrified Joy at first because she couldn't see over the big car hood, and she thought they were going to tumble head first over the edge. Grabbing onto Sandra, she closed her eyes and prepared for the crash. But instead, the car smoothly went over the edge and glided down the long winding road into a park. Scrambling to be the first out of the car, she flung the door open and ran toward some playground equipment. To her surprise no one was following her. They all stood on the other side of the car staring at something.

Rushing back, she was astounded to see the massive river thundering 200 feet over a ledge into the boiling white river. Chet took her hand and they walked to an observation platform. The wind and spray buffeted her. Joy was sure she had never seen or felt anything so powerful in her whole life. The unbridled majesty of the massive waterfall was astonishing. It flowed green and smooth as it cut over the brink to disappear into the swirling white mist exploding from the river. The experience filled her from her head to her toes with awe and wonder. It entered under her skin and muscle into her bones and started them pulsating. So moved and yet so immovable, she stared with her arms out and her fingers spread like miniature antennas to capture the vibrations. The spray and plumes of the water coupled with the vibration gave her a sensation she had never before felt—she felt sound for the first time. Not just sound, but the roaring, raging, bellowing, reverberating, thundering and blasting of sound. She tilted her tiny head back and laughed and blasted her own tiny voice into the all-encompassing din. For the rest of her life whenever she was near Shoshone Falls, she would come to this platform and immerse herself again into this cacophony.

At about 1:30 they stopped in Jerome for lunch.

The American Café was a strange name for a Chinese restaurant. Joy had never been to a restaurant before, and she was amazed at the strange looking food. Her eyes widened as she pointed and laughed at her father when he started eating with what looked like two pencils. Chet tried to show her how to use them, but she found it easier to stab the sweet and sour pork rather than pinch it. The crowning surprise was the strange shaped cookie with a slip of paper folded inside.

Sandra reached over and picked up her paper while she ate the cookie. After she read it she passed it on to Evelyn. Chet leaned over and read it with his wife. "Endure today for the rewards of tomorrow" They looked at each other without speaking, then Chet folded the paper and slipped it in his wallet. Bouncing out to the car, Joy felt this was one of the most interesting and exciting days of her life.

The car droned on in the August heat, and soon Joy fell asleep. She dreamed of the falls. She was in the water above the falls riding an inner tube as she had done with the family in a canal near Oakley. The only difference was she was now all alone. The river perpetually moved her toward the falls. She wasn't afraid because she didn't know how powerful and dominating the water could be. She was swept over the edge and fell into the plumes of pummeling sound. All around her the white mist swirled, yet there was nothing to hold onto. While falling, the mist buffeted her, tossing her one way and then another. She held tight to her inner tube, knowing that in the end it would float her to the top. She felt strength come into her as she realized that the plumes of sound could flick and pitch her around but they couldn't hurt her. She awoke with a start, her eyes bright with confidence. No fear, just innocent confidence.

At 4:08 the car entered Gooding and stopped in front of a large red-brick building. Chet reached over and squeezed Evelyn's hand and, without speaking, opened the door. Joy's door flew open and out she sprang. Bouncing up the sidewalk ahead of the family, she was ready for the next adventure. She pulled on the handle of the large door, but it was too heavy for her small hand to open. Chet soon opened it and she found herself in a large hall with the strong smell of varnish and oil used on the floor. She held Mom's hand and felt it trembling slightly.

Looking up, she studied her mom's expression. Hmmm, she thought, what did that face mean? It was sad and maybe frightened. It is the face she had when her horse lay down last year and didn't get up. Dad dragged it off someplace with the tractor. It was a sad, scared face. For the first time that day, Joy was worried.

Entering a room Joy saw a tall, pretty lady looking out the window, who turned and smiled as they entered.

"Hello, Mr. and Mrs. Reynolds. How are you?" Mrs. Martin cheerfully asked.

"As well as can be expected, I guess," Evelyn said evenly.

"And who is this tall, pretty girl?" she asked, taking Sandra by the hand.

"This is our 15-year-old daughter, Sandra."

"My, look how much Joy has grown. Come everyone sit down." The family maneuvered around a table in the middle of the room. Chet sat looking straight ahead, his face locked in firm resolve. Evelyn set little Joseph down and folded her nervous hands on the table, an emotion tugging the corners of her mouth down. Sandra flounced her long hair and then chewed on her Black Jack nervously.

Mrs. Martin started, "Okay, I will not pretend to understand how difficult this is for all of you. Someday when I have children I will be able to understand better. All I can do is assure you that this happens every year, and so far it hasn't seem to scar them for life."

Chet spoke, "There must be some easy way to do this without upsetting Joy."

"I am afraid that, at this time, there isn't," Mrs. Martin softly answered.

Chet straightened to the task ahead and so did Evelyn. "Okay, what do we do?" Chet asked determinedly.

"We have some fun activities that will keep Joy involved while you go."

"Wait," Evelyn pleaded, panic starting to rise, "don't you think we should take her clothes and help her put them into her dresser? Then she will know that she is staying."

"We have tried to do this every way possible. We used to let parents do that; but when some of the children realized that they were staying, they would hold onto the parents' legs crying. When we try to pull them free, hysteria would begin. There is just no easy way. She will be okay, and when she sees you come next week she will know everything is all right. I'm terribly sorry but I have some other parents coming in a few minutes. Can I show you the activity room?"

Joy noticed the mouths moving and the concerned glances her way. She started feeling uneasy and if she had done something wrong and these people would punish her. Why was Mom crying, and why did Dad have such a stern look on his face? Even Sandra's eyes were frightened. Dad stood and took her bag. She had seen her mom pack her clothes into her suitcase, but where were their bags? Clinging to mom's skirt and sucking her finger for the first time in two years, she left the room with them. Now Joy could see there were other children in the building with their parents. They followed Mrs. Martin down the hall and entered the most exciting room Joy had ever seen.

There was a clown who was making funny shapes out of balloons and  there were other children playing different games. Bright-colored streamers and good smells of candy and cakes filled the air. Everybody was smiling. Joy noticed most of the people were not moving their mouths; instead they moved their hands and faces. Their faces were easier to read than her family's faces. These faces were full of energy and communication.

Her mom knelt and kissed her and so did her dad and Sandra. Then she was drawn into a fun game while her family quietly slipped out the door.

Sandra and Evelyn were crying as they hurried to the car. Chet was carrying Joseph and clearing his throat huskily. He started the car and drove away quickly. No one noticed the red sunset glowing over the western horizon of the Magic Valley.

Evelyn was imagining Joy's little face, frightened and crying. She could see her running and beating on the door, strong arms pulling her away and someone shaking her, shouting, "Stop it, you're staying here!"

"Chet, I can't do this!" She cried. Turn back, please."

Chet's neck was an iron sinew, and his mind was set with a deeper bite than any plow he had ever submerged in a field. He wished he could say something to comfort Evelyn and Sandra, but his own emotions were locked in a great battle like the horns of two mighty elk in the throes of death. He remembered Joy's heartrending sobs, like the time her best-friend-cat Cleo, had been killed. Her alien and endearing cries had rent his heart like a bolt of lightning splitting a juniper tree. Without words to explain death to her, all he could do was hold her and rock while speaking his comfort into a void. Finally Chet reached over and took Evelyn's hand.

The car sped forward into the gathering darkness. Steering with one hand, Chet thumbed a slip of paper out of his wallet and turned on the dome light.

"Read this out loud one more time," he said with heaviness in his voice, and handed the paper to Evelyn.

Between sobs she read, *'Endure today for the rewards of tomorrow.'*

"We've done what's right; now we'll take things as they come." Then Chet blew out a large breath of pain and stared out at the undulating highway passing beneath the De Soto.

Joy was absorbed in a game where a blindfolded child swung a stick at a colorful paper animal hanging on a string. Soon it was Joy's turn. This was something she was good at. She had walked behind the old milk cow many times and swatted her rump with a stick to make her move faster. While gripping the stick, gentle hands began to turn her in circles. She thought how big her family's smile would be when she hit the thing. That will make them happy.

On the very first blow the stick connected and the paper animal exploded in a shower of hard candy. She pulled off her blindfold and saw the floor covered with candy and children diving in to get a handful. She grabbed some and ran bright faced to where her family had been. They weren't there. She started looking for them. A lady kept guiding her to this game or that, but she pulled away, and now more frantic she continued her search for her family. Bawling and near panic, she found the door and tried to open it. Someone was kneeling next to her and a gentle arm was around her waist, not pulling, not demanding, just there, full of warmth and understanding. Through blurry blue eyes, Joy looked into the kind and understanding face of Faith Wilkie, her dorm mom.

Faith did understand, because she had been through this same experience 20 years ago, when she was five years old. Only back then she had spent the next 12 years trying to orally understand and talk about the experience before she was moved into a signing program. Joy would be communicating in a week. Within three weeks she would be expressing her feelings about tonight.

Faith was grateful Dr. Jacobs had become school superintendent and brought deaf understanding and deaf sense to deaf education.

Her heart was bursting with compassion for this feisty little redhead. She wanted to hold her and with a magic wand sweep away her fear and confusion. To Faith Wilkie, this was like the polio shots all the children had to have—painful at first but in the long run worth it. Soon Joy collapsed into Faith's arms and sobbed.

By 8:00 the parents were all gone, and Faith gathered her five new and shaken little girls into their dormitory. After writing their names in the lining of each of their clothes, she showed them how to stow them in the drawers. By 9:00 they were all exhausted and in bed. Their lonely, frightened sobs echoed in the dormitory room—unheard.

"This week has gone slower than cold tar running up hill in January," Chet mused to the family at supper on Thursday night. Looking at Evelyn he saw the dark shadows laced under her eyes from lack of sleep and she had lost weight also. "I asked your parents to come with us tomorrow," Chet spoke between bites of steak and potatoes. "We'll leave about noon." Evelyn brightened.

Evelyn had gone to her parents' house and called to the school every day to check on Joy. She was assured that Joy was fine and she had made a good friend.

On Friday the whole family rolled into Gooding about 2:30, and while Sandra played with little Joseph in the park, the grownups engaged in idle talk while riveting their minds on the clock.

At 3:30 the family was hurrying up the sidewalk to Old Main. Entering the building, Evelyn shuttered. Then and ever after the smell of oil and varnish used on the floors would stir feelings of dread from leaving Joy a week earlier. A host directed them and several other families into the gymnasium where they nervously took seats in the lower bleachers. Soon there was a commotion in the end of the gym as Joy's teacher, Virginia Hunt, held a door open and Joy's class entered in a line with their arms folded.

"She's beaming!" Evelyn cried. "Look, Chet, she's beaming! She's okay!"

Mrs. Hunt signed something and the little students burst from their line and dissolved into their family's hungry arms.

After giving everyone much needed hugs, Joy started pulling Chet by the hand toward the door and signing something. Not knowing what she wanted to show them, but realizing she wanted them to follow, they padded along after her out of the gym. Catching them just outside the door, the librarian, Mrs. Link, told them that Joy wanted to show them her classroom. Barely keeping up she explained that the children had done finger painting and some other projects. They entered the brightly colored room where the family found other parents inspecting their children's achievements. As they looked at Joy's work, Mrs. Link interpreted what she said. Chet and Evelyn were pleased with her painting, but what impressed them even more was her ability to communicate. They were amazed at her enthusiasm and the brightness of her eyes as she talked about her classroom. Soon a little dark-haired girl with large black eyes and brown skin came near. She waved her hand at Joy, and when she had Joy's attention she signed to her. Mrs. Link said, "This is Joy's friend Angela. Angela's parents are both deaf, and her father owns a printing business in Rupert, down in Minidoka County.

174

Part of the reason Joy is signing so well this soon is because she has had Angela to talk with. Joy has taken to signing like a duck to water. It is natural for her and easy to learn." Mrs. Link asked something of Angela and Angela nodded. "Because her parents are deaf, she has always signed. It is her first language. She is also the brightest in her class and already helps with the other students. It will take Joy awhile to learn the vocabulary and understand the expressions, but she is bright and she likes it. I'm sure she will continue to progress quickly.

A well-dressed, nice looking couple came over, smiled and then signed to Angela. Angela signed something to Joy, hugged her and then took her mom by the hand and skipped away.

Mrs. Link excused herself and left them alone. An awkward feeling settled on Joy and her family. A moment before, there was life, contact, nearness. That had been replaced with distance, loss and void.

"I will learn this language!" Evelyn whispered emphatically to Chet.

Mrs. Hunt approached and spoke with them. As she spoke she also signed. "Joy has done very well. Have you noticed how well she communicates?" Everyone looked at Joy and she was beaming again.

"Is there a book or something that I can learn signs from?" Evelyn asked hopefully.

"Well, yes, I will loan you one. A minister back in Iowa, who taught the deaf, wrote it. I must warn you that learning to sign from a book is pretty difficult. Signing is not one dimensional—it is three dimensional, and it involves more than just the hands." She turned and signed something without voice to Joy. Her face beamed as she nodded. "I just asked Joy if she would help the family learn to sign on the weekends. She said, 'Yes.'"

By the time they left Gooding, the sweet smells of the rolling Idaho grasslands started to rise with the coming on of evening. The windows were down and the air temperature was perfect. Joy was snuggled between her grandma and grandpa in the back seat. She thought about all of the new things in her life—school, a best friend, and best of all signs. A black curtain was opening, and a whole new world of communication was beginning to illuminate her soul. She couldn't wait for her family to learn signs so she could see into their hearts and they see into hers. Everything in her life seemed perfect.

Any policy, law or procedure that is antifamily is anti-humanity and <u>always</u> goes cross grain to our unalienable rights.

# CHAPTER 19

## I Have a Right to Learn From My Mistakes

On November 30, 1967, I was slowly being rolled over. The pressure was being applied down the back of my neck and up under my armpit. The half-nelson, the oldest and most often used pinning combination in wrestling, was being successfully employed to pin me!

By the middle of November football season had ended and wrestling had begun. I was pretty lackluster in football, but in wrestling I had some potential in the 141-pound weight class.

My opponent was Greg Land from Valley High School. With me flat on my stomach, he worked his hand and arm under my armpit and over the back of my neck and was levering me onto my back for the pin. My ears were searching the thunderous roar from the home crowd for Moose's yell. She was a cheerleader, and I think she had the best yell of everyone. In a moment I was on my back with his unshorn armpit in my face, but I wasn't worried. I had never been pinned with a half-nelson in my life, and it wasn't going to happen that night.

I was gifted with a neck made of spring steel and a back strong as a mule. I made a human bridge from my head to my heels. Bowing my back, I lifted my opponent and my shoulders far from the mat. In practice I had another wrestler sit on my chest while I did bridging exercises. I could do 20.

I wormed my way around so I could see the J.R. Simplot Company scoreboard and clock when I looked left and Moose cheering when I looked right. There were 45 seconds left in the round. Plenty of time to tease the crowd, I thought. I slowly lowered my back toward the mat. The referee scrambled around and flattened himself to the mat to better see the pin when it happened. The volume of the crowd increased as I lowered my back. I was watching Moose through squinting eyes. Her hands flew to her lips in a gasp, and then she started jumping up and down and shouting "No! No! No!" while she flailed her arms like a wounded duck. Smiling inwardly I raised my shoulders higher, and she screamed, "Yeah!" and jumped and kicked like cheerleaders do.

After about the fourth time the fans started to point and laugh as everyone figured out I was just playing for the crowd reaction. Then Moose stood with her tiny fists planted on her tiny hips and stared at me with that, "Oh, you! I'm going to kill you!" look.

There were two snapshots of me in the yearbook that year—both were wrestling pictures. One was taken this night, the other two weeks later when I wrestled a deaf-blind boy from the Idaho State School for the Deaf and Blind. This one I was proud of while the other still makes me cringe when I see it.

I noticed Burl Okelberry, the yearbook staff photographer screwing in a flash bulb. When he aimed the camera at me, I smiled as casual as a cow in a pasture. Then the first round was over. In the second round I pinned Greg Land with my own half-nelson.

After the match, which we won, I strutted into Minn's Café where a crowd always gathered after school events. Someone had the juke-box playing a medley of Beach Boys' hits. I was wearing my bright orange school sweater with four white rings displayed on my sleeve. Each ring represented a school year in which I had received a varsity letter. Not many kids had four rings so I was particularly proud to be seen in my sweater.

"Way to go, Strangler. Man, you sure can bridge!" Skinny Matthews hollered from a booth where he sat with his wife. Skinny always called me Strangler. I was never quite sure why, but it always sounded tough so I didn't mind. Several others slapped me on the big Hornet scribed across the back of my sweater. I nodded and smiled like an idiot and said, "It was nothing—just an easy match." Mom was back in the kitchen waving at me through the order-window to come back and see her. She never came to the matches because she said, "They . . . make . . . me too nervous."

Passing through the crowd, I approached the booth where Moose was sitting with some of her cheerleader friends—Sandy, Trish and Vicki. She still had on her cheerleading outfit. She was extra cute in the little orange and white pleated skirt with the orange sweater top and a big Declo scribed across the front in orange, black and white. She patted the seat next to her as she slid over. She was looking at me with the brightest and shiniest eyes I have ever seen. They were full of admiration and invitation. Pleased to have her attention, I slid into the booth next to her. It was breathtaking to feel her warmth so close to me. Then I remembered my mother had called me. Promising to return, I excused myself and went to the back into the kitchen.

Mom had the grill full of everything from burgers to steaks, and the deep fat fryer was boiling about a hundred pounds of fries. While she shuffled food on plates she stuttered out, "Howd cha do?" It took about two seconds to tell the story of my win because I left out the part about teasing the crowd. I felt a little bad about giving her such an abbreviated version of my match, but I knew she wouldn't complain. I kissed her and bolted back to take up my warm spot next to Moose.

I stopped just behind the booth, frozen by what I saw. Sitting next to Moose with his big hairy arm lying gently across the back of the booth behind Moose was Elton Greasefark.

Elton Greasefark stood six feet and weighed about 190 pounds. He was gifted with a great build, but he never participated in sports. He drove a nice Mustang and was always bragging about his sleazy success with girls from other towns. I knew he had a drinking problem and had been arrested for stealing gasoline from a farmer out in Raft River. I knew it wasn't because his family didn't have the money. His dad owned a big dry farm up in Albion, but I heard Elton never worked on it.

To see Elton sitting that close to Moose with his defiled arm all but around her nauseated me. Moose didn't seem to be bothered at all; in fact, she seemed to be enjoying his attention. An ugliness started to grow deep inside me. It was like a grotesque volcano intensifying into an uncontrollable explosion. I knew what was going to happen and it frightened me. I stood with clenched fist and saw in my mind what would happen next. I would step to the table and tell Elton to get his filthy arm out from around Moose and his raunchy body out of the booth or I would personally throw him out. Then he would say something smart and I would explode and hit him. Then the victory celebration in Minn's Café would be over for everyone.

I felt sick about what I was going to do, but I couldn't stop it. It was like some force driving me along that I was powerless to stop. My jaw was set, my eyes were set and my mind was set. I started forward. I didn't think how it would embarrass Moose or my mother or how it would affect my fans, nor did I care. Next thing I knew I was at the table, fury and hate filling my eyes and my jaw clenched and set to spit out the words that would send me hurdling down this one-way street.

Then a small wheel cut across my foot and parked on my big toe. The pain in my foot caused me to cry out and wrestle my toe from under Ur's wheelchair. Mary stood behind him, her eyes pleading.

Ur spoke, "Jon, introduce me to your friends."

The adrenaline was still pumping and needed to be released, but not with fighting, not in front of Mary and Ur. I blew out a long breath and knelt next to Ur's chair both to speak with Ur and to conceal my shaking, which started as the adrenalin began to burn off. If Ur noticed my trembling, he didn't say anything as he put his hand to my face.

Then I heard Elton say, " Okay, Moose, I better go find my date. Tell your dad thanks for the help and give him the check." Elton pushed past us with a brief, "Excuse me."

My ears started to burn with embarrassment. I closed my eyes against the pain of what I almost did. Glancing up at Mary, I saw her wink and smile. Relaxing a little I said, "I would like all of you to meet two," my voice got husky for a second, "of my best friends Ur Babiraski and I think you all know his sister Mary." With Ur's hand to my face I said, "These are some of my friends—Trish, Sandy, Vicki and Moose." I noticed Ur smiled a little when I introduced Moose.

"Nice to meet all of you pretty young ladies," Ur said. "Please excuse me for not standing," he smiled.

At first the girls didn't know what to think until Mary slapped his shoulder and said, "Ur, stop teasing." Then everyone relaxed and laughed.

Moose quirked, "Well, don't worry about that. You're still doing better than Jon when he was wrestling. He was flat on his back."

Everyone laughed while I put a mock expression of hurt on my face and repeated it to Ur. Ur laughed.

Mary broke in, "It is so nice to meet all of you. Jon has been a wonderful friend to Ur and me."

"I didn't know you were there tonight," I spoke into Ur's hand.

"Mary gave me a flop-by-flop account, so to speak, but you scared me when your opponent put you on your back. Then Mary told me you were just playing with the crowd. You must really be a good wrestler to be able to play with your opponent."

I reddened a little at the compliment and then grinned sheepishly, "Well, I just liked watching Moose squeal like a run-over cat."

Moose slugged me and threatened, "See if I ever cheer for you again!"

Ur reached out and put a five dollar bill on the table. "I am proud of you, Jon, and I want to buy the drinks…or whatever you are having."

I said, "Thanks."

"We have to leave now, but we will see you tomorrow."

"Thank you both so much for being here," I said with deep gratitude, thinking how different my evening would have been if they had not interrupted me.

"Wow, they are so cool!" Trish said, and everyone agreed.

I sat there quiet for a moment, folding and refolding the five-dollar bill while I thought about inherent rights. Which one had I almost violated that led me into near social suicide? My eyes burned for a moment as I thought of how much I loved Ur and Mary.

Suddenly Moose grabbed the five-dollar bill and we had a tug of war over who would get it. After a moment of struggling, I had both of her hands in mine and we were facing each other, smiling and laughing. I had the greatest feeling surge through me—love, puppy love, infatuation, affection or just great friendship, I didn't know; I just knew it felt great!

Soon the restaurant started to clear out as farmers and their chore boys headed home. In Declo people tended to go to bed early because milking started before sunrise. Moose began gathering her coat to leave.

"Would you like some protection on your way home?" I offered.

"From what?" she countered.

"Ah… I don't know. The cold air," I said weakly.

181

"Okay," she smiled.

She only lived a block from the café, but a sweeter block I have never walked before. "Is your hand cold?" I asked awkwardly. "Because if it is, I'm available to warm it up."

"Milked any cows today?" she teased and reached for my hand and put both of our hands in her coat pocket. I started walking slower to make the time stretch out. The air was crisp, and under the street light our breath was like blue smoke. Some wrestlers drove by and rolled their window down to yell, "Yahoo for you two!"

I didn't know what to do, but Moose yelled back, "You guys better watch it or I'll cheer for the other guy next time." They squealed around the corner and were gone with a short chirp from the rear tires as the driver grabbed second gear.

"Tell me about Ur?" Moose asked.

I didn't know what to tell her. His life seemed almost too fantastic to believe, even to me. If I told her and she didn't believe me, I knew I would be offended. Besides, Ur had not told me I could talk about his personal life to others. It was like his life was a sacred story that needed to be shared, but in a special way when it could be believed and accepted. I decided I could tell her about inherent rights, so I plunged in, and about five minutes later I could see a glazed look come over her eyes.

"Listen, Jon," she interrupted, "I'm getting a little cold."

Stung by the interruption, I guided her toward her front door. All of the romance of the evening had fizzled like a wet firecracker.

At the door I released her hand and quietly said, "Thanks for letting me walk you home. See you on Monday." I turned and walked away. She stood there for a moment, staring after me, and then slipped inside and closed the door.

My mood had suddenly turned quiet. Why did it bother me that she couldn't appreciate the importance of inherent rights? I tried to remember how I felt when Ur first explained it to me. For the first time I realized how important my inherent rights had become to me.

Since the weekend that Ur and I spent together, almost two months ago, I had focused on maintaining my inherent rights. I had to admit that my life was tons sweeter. My personal confidence level was way up, yet I had not become arrogant like the other times I had experienced confidence. I hope—I can say this without seeming too boastful—I had actually started becoming popular. I didn't know what else to attribute this to except the maintaining of my inherent rights.

I had become more honest, caring, responsible and careful to protect the health of my body than ever before. With the increase in popularity, I had more opportunities to go "party." At first I would make some excuse like "I am in training," or "the coach will kill me." Then I began to say, "No thanks. I don't do that." I started feeling the mightiness Ur had told me about. He had said, "Mightiness is the offspring of maintaining one's inherent rights, and mightiness is the father of peace. Mightiness," he said, "is safe, powerful confidence, the kind of confidence that draws people to you." I determined then to be mighty.

I finally began feeling that what he said was true. It took about a month before I finally notice things were changing. The change was not fast, but it was steady. I was becoming more confident and more disciplined. Negative peer pressure was not the problem it had been. I actually felt I was gaining power to do something with my life, if I only knew what to do. Ur promised me that when I understood and maintained my inherent rights, he would teach me how to get the privileges of life.

He said, "Only the person who has the mightiness to maintain his inherent rights can be safely trusted with the privileges of life. Privileges are the sweet things of life. It is not only the nicer cars, houses, vacations, and social power, but more importantly the opportunity to serve our fellow beings. It is dangerous to give weak people the secret of gaining privileges. The weak person is the opposite of the mighty person. These people are selfish and arrogant. Their riches and power corrupt their lives and bring misery. They become hedonistic, self-centered and cruel. Remember, Jon," Ur said, "the only path to happiness is not in the gaining of wealth and power; it is in the maintaining of your inherent rights. I will teach you how to receive the privileges of life when I know you will be safe with this power because a person who maintains his inherent rights will do good with his privileges. So, when I feel you are ready, I will teach you."

All unalienable rights build, strengthen and edify individuals, families, communities and nations. And this nation will stand stronger as, we the people, maintain our unalienable rights.

# CHAPTER 20

## I Have a Right Not to Be Offended

The first week of December, the old wrestling bus approached the turnoff from Interstate 86 onto the Gooding Highway. In the back of the bus, the 183-pounder had just slugged the130-pounder for opening a can of sardines. The 130-pounder said he wrestled better with bad breath. The 183-pounder said he wouldn't have any breath at all if he didn't throw the stinking can out the window.

Coach Chugg stood and started up the isle. Coach Chugg was a great coach even though he didn't have a lot of wrestling experience. He was built like a gorilla and had about as much hair. Our 121-pounder said once, "I'll bet he has to use a weed whacker to shave in the morning." We all liked him and respected what he said. When he got to the middle of the bus he asked the bus driver, Mic Darrington, to turn on the interior lights.

"I have two things to discuss with you men tonight," his voice rasped like a bad set of truck brakes. "First, please don't bring sardines on the wrestling bus anymore. The smell makes me and all of you, except Nathan, sick. Second, we're wrestling, as you know, the Idaho State School for the Deaf and Blind. Some of you are wrestling deaf guys and some of you are wrestling blind guys. Jon, you are wrestling a deaf-blind guy. You men go easy on these boys and make them feel good about the match, but don't get sloppy and lose." Everyone laughed with easy condescending confidence.

The bus squeaked to a stop in front of a large red-brick building and we filed off carrying our diddy bags stuffed with our wrestling gear. Passing up the sidewalk, we entered into the building and were struck by the strong smell of varnish and oil. It reminded me of the elementary school I attended in Declo. Moving directly through this building we stepped outside and entered the gym. We stopped, as wrestlers tend to do, and analyzed the wrestling mat before moving into the dressing room to weigh-in.

ISDB was already getting on the scales. Some were guiding their blind team members to the scales. Other wrestlers' wild hand gestures and facial expressions made us stare. One of their team members saw us gawking and showed us a hand sign we were familiar with. I looked away in embarrassment and started getting ready to weigh-in.

While I was warming up out in the gym, like most wrestlers, I started checking out the cheerleaders. For the most part they all looked pretty good, but then girls always looked pretty good in cheerleading uniforms. I thought, since it was a deaf school, that it would be real quiet and peaceful. I was amazed at the noise! These kids are just like us, I thought. Then just before the matches began, another cheerleader ran in and took her place in the line of squealing, kicking, arm-flapping cheerleaders. I only caught a glimpse of her back, but I could see that she had beautiful, curly, long red hair.

Refocusing on the match, I decided to put the cheerleaders out of mind until after I wrestled.

Our first wrestler was Champ Anthon, our 98-pounder. He struggled against a deaf wrestler, but finally won by decision for scoring more points. We lost the next two matches. Then Brian Matthews and Jimmy T. Kidd won their matches. I was up next.

I had already identified my opponent as a quiet guy sitting in the middle of the bench. He looked like he was asleep except when one of his team members would tell him who won. I would have really felt sorry for this guy if I had not known Ur. I felt I could handle him without much trouble, and decided to go easy on him so that he would feel good about himself.

Their coach led my opponent on the mat and gave me his hand. I frowned and looked at our hands clasped like we were going on a date. I waited anxiously for the referee to start the match, but he went to the scorer's table to straighten out some problem. While he was gone, I was left in the middle of the mat holding hands with this guy and feeling foolish.

I thought, why not, so I spelled into his hand, "I AM JON. NICE TO MEET YOU. GOOD LUCK."

He spelled, "I AM LUTHER AND YOU ARE DOG MEAT."

I heard a girl, who had seen what he spelled into my hand, giggle. I looked around. The redhead was looking at me with a beautiful teasing smile and spellbinding bright blue eyes. I smiled at her and spelled, "WATCH ME." She raised her eyebrows in disbelief. I smiled.

The referee returned and made us hold hands again so the guy could find me. That canceled most of my strategy. Then he signaled the match to begin.

Like I said earlier, there were two wrestling snapshots of me in the yearbook. The second picture was about to be taken. As the beginning whistle sounded the referee touched Luther to let him know the match had begun. While I glanced up at my team with a silly smile of confidence, this deaf-blind guy threw a fireman's carry on me so hard my shoes nearly came off. He picked me up on his shoulders and started to stagger around the mat. It was then the picture was snapped. My expression of confidence had changed to one of horror as I was carried helplessly around the mat on a deaf-blind guy's shoulders. The team was in stitches and the crowd roared. Then with a grunt he whipped me off his shoulders and folded me up like a wallet. He squeezed me so tight I thought mayonnaise was squirting out of my skin. I struggled to breathe as he slammed my back on the mat for the pin.

I was dumbfounded and shocked as I stumbled to my feet gasping for air and shaking my head to clear it. While the referee raised Luther's hand in victory, I glanced over at the redheaded cheerleader. She was looking directly at me, and then she winked one of those magnificent blue eyes and did a cute little wrinkle of her nose. Half of my face raised in a movie star smile, and I gave her the slightest man-nod and walked back to our sobered team bench.

The bus was silent as we rode back to Declo in defeat. We had underestimated the deaf-blind school. We thought since they were missing one or more senses it would affect their athletic ability and their desire to be winners. It was a mistake we wouldn't make again.

If there was a silver lining in the cloud, she was dressed in a red and white ISDB cheerleading uniform. I lost myself in my own thoughts for the two-hour drive home. I took the most beautiful spring time stroll with Little Miss Redhead through the pasture of my imagination. She was so beautiful in face and form. Little Miss Redhead's name was scrolled across her sweater, but I couldn't read it. I knew it was a short name, maybe with only three letters. I wished I had walked past her and looked. Yet, without the name I still didn't have any trouble envisioning her. She was about 5 feet 2 inches tall, oval face with pure smooth skin framed in a halo of exquisite dark, curly, red hair. I tried to envision her eyes in my mind. From a distance, they looked like the pure deep blue eyes of a baby doll.

She used signing, not just finger spelling. I determined to ask Ur to teach me signing so next time I saw her, I could communicate faster.

The next day I was the talk of the school. I had to endure tons of good natured teasing as wrestlers told and retold the story of my match. Six months ago the teasing would have made me mad, but somehow since my confidence had increased from maintaining my inherent rights, it didn't bother me. In fact, I joined in, adding some funny detail or thought about my match. It sure felt good to be able to laugh with people instead of getting uptight. Maybe that was part of the freedom Ur talked about.

"You are only really free when you maintain your inherent rights," he told me.

"In what way?" I had asked.

"You lose your Divine freedom when you trample your inherent rights underfoot."

Now I was beginning to understand that freedom and it felt great!

Ur began teaching me signing right away. He emphasized not only learning the signs, but also insisted that I learn about grammar and the way of the deaf. He taught me about deaf history and deaf manners. He said that during the 1800's the deaf had better schools because there were more deaf teachers and administrators, and most of all signing was more prevalent.

"After 1880, Oralism started to spread more quickly in the school systems, and signing was slowly being eliminated. Some have called this the dark ages for the Deaf. Now there are people who are fighting back and the Deaf are striving to reclaim their schools. More and more deaf people were getting higher education degrees from places like Gallaudet College in Washington, D.C., and San Fernando Valley State College (SFVSC) in Los Angeles. Gallaudet College is a college dedicated specifically for the deaf. Its charter was established during the turbulent years of the Civil War. President Lincoln signed the legislation for Gallaudet College along with their first college degrees.

"San Fernando Valley State College is a regular college for hearing people, but it also has an integrated program to assist deaf students. Dr. Ray L. Jones is a good friend of mine," Ur said, "He directs the National Center on Deafness at SFVSC. Along with earning regular college degrees, some deaf students enter into the National Leadership Training Program for the Deaf. I know this may seem a little boring to you, Jon, but you must understand that we are sitting on the threshold of a whole new era for the Deaf."

I patiently endured these long lectures on Deaf history hoping they would, in some way, help me the next time I met Little Miss Redhead.

About the middle of December, Ur said he needed to ask me a favor.

"Sure, anything," I signed. Since I asked Ur to teach me signs, we had talked almost exclusively in sign. He put his hands on mine to feel the signs. At first it was slow, but recently it had improved, and our communication was getting faster.

"I don't know if you can help me, and please say so if you can't or don't have an interest, but I have been asked to give a series of lectures at the Idaho State School for the Deaf and Blind. They are to begin right after the new year and will be once a week on Friday evenings. I know you have wrestling, but I think your matches are always on Tuesday or Thursday. I will need a driver and an assistant to interpret for me when people ask questions. The school is willing to pay $25 an evening for my assistant. Are you interested?" Ur smiled, knowing the answer.

Ur and Mary had often heard me talk about Little Miss Redhead. I hesitated, speechless with joy.

While laying a plate of dynamite cookies in front of me, Mary offered, "Jon, it's okay if you aren't interested. I will be glad to go."

"Well," I said with mock nonchalance, "if you really need me, I guess I can do it," and then I sat there beaming as they laughed at me.

Seeing through the smoky glass of the future allows us to enjoy present happiness without worry. Had I known the tragedy that awaited me the next week, I could not have enjoyed this moment with Ur and Mary.

Every human has a handful of experiences that are so poignant, so powerful, and so memorable they remember them for the rest of their lives. They remember where they were and what they were doing when that experience happened. For example, when I heard President John F. Kennedy had been assassinated, I was playing football during the lunch hour on the east end of the school.

On Tuesday, December 20th, at 2:25 p.m., I had another of those experiences, but this time it was on a more personal level.

# CHAPTER 21

## I Have a Right to Mourn

I was sitting in Mr. Black's American Government class preparing a spit-wad to be blasted through the empty barrel of my Bic pen at a kid named Garth when my world began its slow tumble. Mrs. Turner, the school secretary, opened the door and motioned for Mr. Black to come to the door. Right away we all knew that something was wrong because Mrs. Turner's normally cheerful countenance was pasty white with dread. While she whispered something to Mr. Black, he glanced at me. I started getting a feeling deep inside that told me Christmas was ruined.

"Jon, would you please meet with Mrs. Turner in the hall and... bring your books."

"Okay," I said. My heart started a deep steady thumping as I gathered my books and shuffled down the row of desks. Every student was staring at me with curiosity, anxiety etched on their faces. A year ago I doubt they would have even given my difficulty any more than a passing thought. Today, I felt genuine concern and affection from my classmates. It was truly amazing how different my life had become in such a short time.

I murmured something about never getting a decent nap in U.S. Government without being interrupted. A few friends let out a nervous laugh.

Passing into the hall Mrs. Turner said, "Jon, you need to go home right away."

"How come?" I asked a little too loud.

Just then Fred came around the corner and said, "Come on little brother, Mom needs us." I stuffed my books into my locker and we started running.

Our house was only about 200 yards from the school across a community park. "What's going on, Fred?" I shouted as we sprinted across the park. He didn't answer.

As we got to the house Edith, a big lady who was Mom's best friend, was holding the door open. "Thank goodness you boys are home. Your mamma needs you now."

"What's going on?" I asked in exasperation.

"Dean's dead, Jon, and your mamma ain't taking it too good," she whispered.

The two men in the green army car had finally come and Mamma's nightmare ended only to be replaced by a reality more painful and monstrous than any dream. She had fretted over that green car coming ever since Dean shipped out for overseas. When a car was heard driving to our house I often saw her stand and look out the window with anxiety. Any color but green brought relief and then she would mutter, "It's not green."

Now the green car had come. It came when she was all alone. She was so shocked and devastated by the appearance of the green car that she could not get her limited speech to work. She stood at the door, her mouth open and her eyes wide with fright, as the two men in crisp dignified uniforms stood ramrod straight and inquired, "Are you the mother of Dean Rhoades?"

She nodded, her face starting to buckle under impending sorrow then the tears of realization began.

"On behalf of the people of the United States, we are sorry to inform you that your son has been killed as a result of hostile action by an enemy in Vietnam. The people of the United States extend their deepest condolences." He extended a hand with the official letter for Mom.

Edith had seen the green car from her kitchen window and immediately started lumbering toward our house. It was she who snatched the letter from the soldier's hand, thanked the officers and guided Mom back into the house. There she called the school to have me sent home immediately.

Mom sat on the couch, a cigarette dangling from her lips, while she held a picture of Dean in her hands and rocked back and forth. It was the picture of him in his uniform sitting in front of an American flag.

"He just . . . c-cooks," she kept muttering. "Why kill a... c-cook? He's . . . good b-boy." Fred and I sat on each side of her with our arms around her. Edith sat quietly, absorbed in her own sorrowful memories of her son, who was killed in Korea.

I held in my grief. Mom needed me now to be strong. I put my hand on Fred's arm across Mom's back and felt comfort and strength from touching him.

"Anyone that you want me to call?" Edith finally asked.

Fred answered, "No, we're alone for the most part. Thanks, Edith, for being here."

The word spread like wildfire through our small community. The phone rang incessantly. Edith handled all the calls and gave what few details we knew of Dean's death.

As I suspected, Dean had not been a cook. He was just a regular soldier who went out on patrols and tried to kill before he was killed. On December 15th, one month before he was to come home, he was killed by an American hand grenade that the Viet Cong had booby trapped on the trail. No other details were available.

We all sat there absorbed in our shared grief. We held onto each other for more than an hour. Edith took the phone off the hook and said, "I'm going to get you something to drink and call the café to let them know you won't be in tonight. Anything else you want me to do?"

"No, thank you, Edith. It's going to be a long night," Fred said.

We sat there for what seemed like forever. I kept looking at Dean's picture which was now sitting on a knickknack shelf. I finally rose and stood in front of it, staring at Dean. The picture held him and time...motionless. It captured Dean in a moment of happiness and life. I looked into his eyes. They could not see today, as I see it. Now his eyes were dead, his face, arms, hands, feet and brain were all dead. My big brother, who had sheltered me when Dad died, was dead. He, who had tried to naively talk me through death then, now understood it perfectly. If what he told me was correct, he was with Dad, I guess.

I went back to the couch and sat down again and put my arm around Mom like I had done before. The three of us sat there holding onto each other for a long time. I never before felt our family so all alone and small. I had never met any of my aunts or uncles. They were all back East someplace. My grandparents died before I was born. I had never thought much about being alone until now. A shutter of fear came over me. I felt like we were shrinking and becoming more alone and more insignificant with each passing minute. I glanced at Edith and I was glad she was there.

My eyes studied our living room, the torn plastic curtains, smoke- dulled walls and two nondescript landscape pictures hanging crooked on the wall. The two worn-down couches drew everyone's attention to the television. The television, for my mother, who couldn't read, was her window to the world. The TV brought the Vietnam War into her living room with deadly violence, but the men in the green car brought the violence of war into her heart and devastated it.

At sundown a knock at the door brought me out of my numbed trance. Edith rocked herself off the couch, struggled to her feet and looked out the window. "It's Mary Wood."

Mary entered juggling a casserole on one hand and a chocolate cake on the other. Edith helped her with the cake as Mary said, "Delma, I heard about what happened to Dean. Ur and I feel the greatest sorrow. Everyone does. We all love your family and want you to know that we are here to help you through this hard time. We knew you wouldn't feel like cooking, Delma, so Mrs. Johnson and I will make arrangements for meals to be brought in until after the funeral." She took Mom's hand and with eyes full of compassion asked, "How are you folks making it?"

I felt my heart start to burst with love. Love for these good people who maintained their inherent rights and just lived humane lives filled with vigorous virtue and active love. I realized for the first time the people I most admired and felt the greatest security with, were the people who maintained their inherent rights by living good lives. The smallness and all-aloneness started to thaw with the realization that none of us are lone-posts, but each are connected to someone else.

Mary turned to me, "Ur's out in the car, Jon. Why don't you run out and say hi to him?"

I stood and Mary hugged me and whispered, "It will be all right, Jon. Time heals all wounds, as they say."

I nodded and went out the door. The jolt of the cold evening wind cleared my head and I picked up my pace and trotted toward Mary's car. Opening the door, I slid in next to Ur.

He turned to me and said, "Jon, I am so sorry this sad event has come into your life. Are you handling this all right?"

Taking his hand to my face I said a little too stiffly, "Sure."

"I sense that to be the least enthusiastic and convincing 'Sure' I have heard in a long time. Does that mean, 'Sure, I am handling this okay.' or does it mean, 'Sure, I am being strong for my mom's sake, but inside I am bursting with sorrow'?"

I felt myself starting to collapse emotionally into Ur's strength. Starting to cry, I said, "Dean was always there for me. When I had trouble handling my dad's death, it was his shoulder I cried on."

I don't know why I started talking about Dad's death, but I couldn't seem to hold it back. "When my father died, Fred and I were staying on the ranch of a family friend. I remember Fred and I were riding horses with the daughter of the people who owned the ranch. A much older and distant cousin drove up to us and got out of his car. He looked up and simply said, 'Boys, your father has passed away.'

"Fred and I looked at each other and shrugged because we didn't know what that phrase 'passed away' meant. The cousin left and I said to Fred, 'Does that mean Dad's dead?' and Fred said, 'I don't know, but I suppose so.'

"The next day we were taken back home. Our house was filled with neighbors and a few friends all talking in low tones. I went into a bedroom, which was just off the living room, and laid down for a nap."

Ur interrupted, "I have forgotten. How old were you when your father died?"

"I was eight, or almost eight. My birthday was the next day. I guess everyone felt sorry for me because I got my only birthday party ever that year.

"Anyway, as I was saying, I laid down on the bed for a nap. About an hour later I awoke with my whole body racking in great sobs. Dean came in—I guess he was about 14 at the time—and held me. He didn't say anything, he just held me. That night Dean asked me to sleep with him in his bed. He rubbed my back and talked to me about Dad. He told me lots of stories about him I had never heard.

"The more he talked the more I felt my dad was real and still with me, only in a different way. Dean said my father loved the woods more than any other place, and if I ever really got lonely I should go to the woods and remember all that he had told me about Dad.

"I have done that many times," I started to cry again. "But losing Dean is somehow different, maybe because I am older. But I don't see how I can go on without my big brother. I know I have to because Mom will need me and Fred to help her. I don't understand death or why it has to happen to good people like Dean."

My tears and grief flowed over onto Ur's hand; he didn't wipe it off.

As Ur exhaled a long breath, I realize what I had been saying had harrowed up some distant and painful memories.

"Jon," he said, his voice filled with compassion and sadness, "I am not sure any of us really understand death until we pass those sacred thresholds ourselves. During the war I sat with scores of friends while they yielded their last breath, and last year I sat holding my dear wife's hand as she passed on. There is much I don't know about death, but this much I do know. If you have lived a good life and have endured to the end, you die in peace. I have a strong personal opinion, that I can't prove in court, yet I believe to be true, that human existence doesn't end with death. I have had some experiences in my quiet darkness with passed on loved ones that seem too tangible and genuine to be imagined."

"Have you had this experience with your first wife and twin children?" I asked innocently.

"No, not with my children, only with my Beth. I feel she is in a place of safety and peace. There was never a better person than Beth." Ur shifted uncomfortably. Changing the subject, he asked, "Jon, how is your mother holding up?"

"As well as can be expected under the circumstances. Mary is talking with her."

"Oh yes, Mary. She will comfort your mother."

"What do we do now?" I asked. "I mean, how do we arrange a funeral and how do we get Dean's body home? Will someone need to go over and bring it back or will they bury him there? I don't want that. I want Dean resting here in our Declo cemetery where I can visit him often."

Some snow started to whip past the headlights as we sat in silence, each of us stirring a blend of melancholy and happy thoughts of past loved ones. The wind hissed through the crab apple tree in our front yard and the power lines began their mournful song.

"Don't worry about that. Mary will be there to help your mother with the arrangements." The car rocked as the wind gusted.

"What is that?" Ur asked suddenly.

"It's the wind. Looks like it's gettin' up a storm."

"Maybe Mary and I should leave before it gets too bad."

"Okay," I paused and took a deep breath. "Thanks Ur for talking to me. I feel lots better. I know it will just take time. If we can get through the next week or so I'm sure everything will get better."

As I opened the door the wind caught it and almost pulled me out. I knew Mary would need help getting Ur back into their house. Entering the house I saw Mary was sitting next to Mom, talking quietly. Mom looked much more relieved. Fred had gone to bed.

"Ur thinks maybe you ought to go home before the storm gets worse."

"Ur is right," Mary said brightly.

"Mom, I'm going to follow them home and help Mary get Ur back into the house."

"Okay, but careful," she said with a bit of worry in her voice.

Because the ground and roadways were already frozen the snow started to stick immediately. The roads were getting slick and the road signs were plastered white. The stoplight swung violently from its cable in the wind. We only passed one car inching its way home through the driving snow. I quickly helped Ur and Mary into their house and returned to my car.

The pitch of the storm unsettled me even more, so I decided to drive around the mile square before heading home.

In rural America everything was and is laid out in one mile squares. One square mile contained 640 acres, enough land in the days of horse and plow for four families to farm. Nowadays with newer and bigger tractors and equipment, farmers could handle much more than 180 acres.

Small drifts had started their white fingers across the north-south roads. I knew by morning these drifts would be much larger. Passing

Wes Penrod's place, I noticed several cows along the road. They seemed confused and stood with their tails to the storm. Knowing it would be certain death for them to be out during the storm without westward shelter, I turned into Penrod's yard to tell him.

Wes Penrod was nearly 70 years old, and cataracts had faded his vision. I knocked on the door and Wes opened it.

"Come on in before that hurricane claws you right off the porch," he drawled.

I explained why I had come. He grunted understanding and turned to go get his coat and boots. I looked around the room. It was obvious that when Mrs. Penrod was alive she had a knack for decorating. Trouble was she had been dead for 15 years. Some say Wes had not changed a thing since the day his wife died, that her clothes still hung in her closet and her shoes were still sitting in the same place she had left them. It certainly didn't look like anything had changed in the room for a mighty long time. There were lots of old pictures scattered around the room like a memorial to youth. One of the pictures caught my attention. It was of two soldiers standing arm in arm in front of a bombed-out building. One had his rifle slung over his shoulder while the other had his resting at his side; both were wearing their helmets.

Wes came back dressed in a heavy canvas dairyman's coat with a heavy winter cap, ear flaps pulled down, and rubber galoshes covering his leather boots.

When he saw how I was dressed he said, "Look at you! You ain't got brains to duck. You'll freeze your nubs off dressed like that. Follow me," he ordered.

"I thought I was just going around the mile. I didn't know I would have to stop and chase cows for you," I said loudly as I followed him into his mud room on the back porch. He threw me a sweat shirt and some coveralls. While I got dressed he searched for a flashlight.

As it turned out, it was blowing snow so hard Wes's near blindness didn't seem to give him much disadvantage over me. The cows seemed to recognize Wes and were pretty easy to get back into shelter. I helped Wes put out some extra straw to give the cows a little more warm bedding. By now it had been over an hour since I left Mom, and I was anxious to get back. I asked Wes if I could call home.

"Sure, if the line's not broke," he chortled.

The line was still up even though the wind continued to gain intensity.

Mom sounded relieved to hear from me. She said that she was getting worried and thought I should be careful driving home. I told Wes I needed to leave and took off his borrowed clothes. As we walked through the living room again I asked, "Who's that in the picture?" pointing to the picture of the two soldiers.

"That's me and my brother Ernie in Italy during World War II," Wes said as he picked up the picture and tried to focus on it. "He and I met over there when our units were close. He was killed the next week," Wes said directly. "It was a rough time for me. He and I were pretty close."

"We heard this afternoon that my brother Dean was killed in Vietnam . . ." I choked and cleared my throat.

He shifted his gaze from the picture to me, understanding etched in his face. "Sorry to hear that. Dean was a good boy." He stepped close and put an arm around me. "How's your mom handling it?"

"It's been pretty rough for her." I sucked in air. "People have been good to us. Edith's been there all afternoon, and Mary Wood came over and brought supper," I said.

Wes fumbled to put the picture back on the shelf. "I didn't think I would ever get over it. Same when my wife passed away, but I did. Time heals all things, they say. You'll get over it in time."

Wes walked to the front window and looked between the curtains. "A funny thing about drifting snow is you can learn a lot about life by just watching it."

"What do you mean?"

"Snow always drifts to the downwind side of an object, it piles the snow in one place while it is bare in another. It doesn't always pile the snow in the same place either. If the wind comes a little more to the north it will build the drift more to the south. What's important to remember is it doesn't always pile on the same place every time. It may seem that your family is getting piled on right now, but the wind will shift."

He reached for the doorknob. "Well, you better skedaddle before the storm makes you stay the night and I have to feed you. Be careful going home."

In spite of the storm, the drive home was pretty uneventful. The drifts had pushed halfway across the road in some places. I swerved my car to cut my front tire into the trailing end of the drifts just for the fun of it. A couple of times I cut a little too deep and the snow would grab the front wheel and try to pull me into the ditch. I loved to see the snow burst over the front of the car and explode in my headlights.

It was almost 10:00 by the time I got home. Mom seemed to be doing better so I offered to drive Edith the block to her home. She gratefully accepted. She hugged Mom and said, "You'll be okay, honey. Just give it time and get your rest. Don't worry about the funeral none. Mary and I will be here to help you with it."

After she settled herself into the front seat of my car, Edith said, "Your mamma will be okay. I thought I would die when my Artie was killed in Korea. In fact, I wanted to die too. His dad was long gone living in Florida and Artie was my only baby. I hated everything for awhile— the army, the war, the Koreans, and even found myself at odds with my religion. We all deal with grief differently. Some do it better than others. I didn't do it very good. Your mamma will be okay. A lot of people around here love her. She's a beautiful human, treats everyone good. She don't ask much, just tries to give."

I started the car and drove the short distance to her small house. "There's a whole lot of people would like to give back. You be there for her, Jon. She's lucky to have you boys there to stay with her. I didn't have no one, but that don't matter now; it's all in the past. Life's for the living—I've heard that and I believe it. We do what we do here and the dead do whatever it is that the dead do. I guess what is important is that we make the best of wherever we are, be us dead or alive." She shook her head as she laughed at her own humor.

Edith struggled as she got out of my car in the wind and snow, but finally I was walking her up to her house. After I made sure she was safely into her house, I turned back to my car.

Suddenly the wind just stopped and snow started falling straight down. The snow made the light from the street lamp look like an inverted funnel. The air grew a little warmer and the flakes became about the size of half-dollars. It was so quiet, not only because the wind stopped, but also because the huge flakes absorbed the sound. The world became muffled and at peace.

Edith was right; people did want to pay Mom back for all of the good things she had done. Because of some kind of hitch in the army, it was two weeks before we could hold a funeral for Dean. During that time someone different brought over a meal each evening.

"Snow always drifts to the downwind side of an object, it piles the snow in one place while it is bare in another. It doesn't always pile the snow in the same place either. If the wind comes a little more to the north it will build the drift more to the south. What's important to remember is it doesn't always pile on the same place every time. It may seem that your family is getting piled on right now, but the wind will shift."

# CHAPTER 22

## I Have a Right to Sacrifice, Even Give My Life for Others

I was wrong about Christmas being ruined. The snow that fell on the day we heard about Dean continued the whole next day. It piled up almost two feet on the cars, lawns, roofs, and rail fences. The amazing thing was the wind didn't blow again until January 15<sup>th</sup>, which is probably a world record for the wind not blowing in Idaho.

Since it was so close to Christmas, school let out early for the holidays. I think the only ones disappointed were the little kids who had practiced a Christmas program and wanted to perform it. Yet, even with the bad weather, the dinners still came.

Christmas was great, mostly because my family had never felt so loved. Minn gave Mom a week off with pay, and people kept calling by and cheering her up. I guess that is what communities are for—to mourn with those that mourn and comfort those that need comfort.

On Christmas Eve a little Christmas miracle happened to us. Dean always made Christmas special for our family by buying things that we seemed to really need or want. He seemed to be there for us after Dad died. He had the ability to anticipate our needs.

Mr. Gillette, our slightly stooped and balding postmaster, came down to our house after he closed the post office to deliver two packages and a letter. One package looked official, and the other package had Dean's handwriting on it.

"These were special delivered this afternoon out of Burley's main post office," he said. "I guess the folks in there knew they were important." His gaze was steady but compassionate. "Hope you're doing all right, Delma. We're sure sorry about what happened to Dean. War's a terrible thing." He shifted uncomfortably and finally said, "Well, I better be going or I'll have a hot cook and cold supper waiting for me when I get home." He stopped and turned before he closed the door and called out, "Merry Christmas!"

Mom smiled and said, "Thanks...Merry Christmas."

The official-looking package had Dean's dress uniform and personal effects inside. Mom began crying as she pulled out his clothes and the knickknacks he had collected in Vietnam. The clothes had a strange musty smell not common in Idaho except in root cellars. In the bottom of the box was an audio tape. Someone had tried to wipe a delicate smear of blood from the label.

Fred got out the tape recorder. Since Mom couldn't write or read very well, she communicated with Dean using a tape player. Fred took the cassette from Mom and slipped it into the tape player and pushed play.

Dean's voice came into our living room, just like he was sitting in the old green chair near the window. *"I'm in the barracks now and we are getting ready to go out into the field. Oh, I forgot to tell you it's December 13, 1966, and I am in...oops, I can't tell you where I am, but I am having a great time!"*

Two days before he died. He sounded so full of life and fun. The sounds of the barracks surrounded him and at times drowned him out.

*"I'm going outside where I can concentrate...*click. *Okay, this is better. As I said, we're going out into the field this afternoon and I wanted to start a tape and take you along with me as I use this battery tape recorder. I know how much you worry, Mom, so I thought I would just pack you along for the next week."*

The tape went on for about 20 minutes of a travelogue as he flew in a noisy helicopter and sloshed through the jungle. Everything seemed like a vacation without anything to bring concern. His last entry on the tape was just after noon on December 15, 1966.

*"I'm cooking up some spaghetti C-ration for lunch. We all like what I cook, don't we?"* There was a chatter of laughter from the other

men. *"I need to tell you that I am a cook, but I mostly cook for myself in the field. I know that I had misled you about what I do. I don't know why I'm telling you this now. I guess I've been feeling a little guilty about lying to you. I don't want Fred and Jon to follow my bad example. Besides, I'll probably be home by the time you receive this tape.*

*"There's so much lying that goes on in war and maybe especially this war. I've had my fill of it."* There was a crunching sound from his feet as he moved away from the others. *"So, I want to come clean. And there is something else I wanted to say to you guys. Maybe we will get pulled out of here sooner than planned and I can get this tape to you before Christmas. I sent a Christmas package just before we went into the field. They say a letter will travel faster so I'll mail this as soon as we are pulled out and hope you get it before Christmas. Oh, yeah, I was saying, Jon and Fred, get yourselves an education in something to support yourselves. War isn't all it is cracked up to be. Mostly it is just boring, and when guys have a lot of time on their hands they do things they will regret later.*

*"I love our country. I love the freedom that we enjoy and the peace of our lives in Declo. I don't understand the politics of it sometimes, and sometimes I think the politicians are more interested in getting re-elected than in doing what's right."*

Someone yelled something to Dean. *"Okay, that was the lieutenant saying we are moving out in 10 minutes. So, I will wrap it up for now and say, Mom, I love you. You have been the best mom a boy could have. You were always light on criticism and heavy on love. You just seemed to know how much to trust me and let me have my head to do things. You taught me a lot about what it means to care for people. I know you have a hard time expressing yourself in words, but I always knew you loved me. I see how war affects people. For some people it makes them better and some people become the lowest kind of human. I can't judge them. I can only say that knowing I am loved at home has helped me get along better, I think.*

*"Well, the guys are grabbing their stuff so I better sign off for now. In a month I will be walking the streets of Declo again and grazing in Minn's Cafe. That seems like a whole different world to me. I love you all!*

That was the end of the tape. We sat in silence, the tape player still humming. We were trying to imagine the words that would have been said next had he lived. I tried to imagine his whole life of coming home, going to college, marrying and raising children, but his words were stopped and the tape player clicked off.

What words he said had filled our little home with peace for Christmas. Next we opened his Christmas package. The presents consisted of trinkets and stuff typical of Vietnam. I knew we would treasure these things all of our lives. I was carrying a big load of wrapping papers to the garbage can when a letter fell on the floor. It was the letter that had come with the packages. It had an army address on it in San Francisco. Mom opened it and handed the letter to Fred to read.

*December 18, 1966*
*Chu Lai, Vietnam*

*Dear Mrs. Rhoades:*
*I had the pleasure of commanding Dean for the last six months and was with him when he was killed by a booby trap a few days ago. I wanted to personally write you and express to you my feelings concerning Dean.*

*Your son was a fine soldier and a very good man. Many of us are indebted to him for his bravery and good humor. During the hard times we could always depend on him to find something funny about our situation. He is missed by all of us.*

*I want to thank you for raising such a fine son. He often spoke of you and his brothers. He loved you all very much. Sometimes this war doesn't make much sense to us, especially when young men like Dean die, while others with so much less to give are still living.*

*Someday I hope to meet you and your sons and share all of the great things Dean did here. You have my deepest condolences.*

*Sincerely,*
*Lt. Ronald D. Lummar*

*P.S. Enclosed is a letter to your son, Dean, which I would appreciate you putting in his coat before he is buried. If you want, please go ahead and read it. The medic who attended your son in the field wrote it. He was a close friend of Dean and is having a hard time dealing with his death.*

Fred handed me an unsealed envelope with Dean's name written on the outside. I turned it over and on the back side was written, "I'll never forget you, my brother." I slipped the letter out of the envelope and unfolded it. I let my eyes gloss over the letter until Mom gently said, "Read..it to...me...please."

*December 17, 1966*

*Dear Dean:*

*I can't seem to get any peace of mind since you died, so I am writing this letter in hopes it can be put in your pocket before your funeral or at least laid on your grave and I can get on with this war.*

*I remember when I was trying to heat a can of C-ration spaghetti, same as your last meal. It was hot that mid-day. I saw your patrol step out of the perimeter and seconds later I heard the blast and the screams, "Medic! Medic!" I grabbed my bag and was on my way so fast the black puff of smoke was still dissipating over you. When I got there, you tried to wave me by. You insisted someone up ahead must be hurt worse. But I took one look at you and the left pant leg was already saturated with blood. I knew this is where I was needed.*

*I stopped the artery spurting at your thigh. Someone else discovered the sucking chest wound under your T-shirt. You panicked then. But you calmed down with a lot of fast talking from our head medic. "I'll be all right," you told us as the company RTO popped smoke for the dust off. We thought so too. But when we hit our night position that evening they told us you were DOA at the 27th MASH in Chu Lai. I will wonder all my life if it would be different had I seen the sucking chest wound first. But mostly, I wonder if I'll ever measure up to you. The rest of the squad told your story that night in the perimeter. The point man snagged the trip wire and cried the warning. The guy you were trying to wave me forward for, the Cuban kid, froze as the rigged U.S. grenade dangled beside him.*

*You could have hit the ground. But you piled onto the Cuban kid instead. It worked. He lived. He lost his foot. You lost much more as the blast tossed you backward. I have often wondered if, faced with the choice of saving my life or a friend, I could, on reflex alone, choose the friend.*

*I may never get that choice. But I have always hoped I could sacrifice at least my comfort and leisure in service of someone else. I try. I've succeeded sometimes. Probably the best thing I've done is to promise myself to tell your story to my kids. I hope it does some good with them.*

*My time in 'Nam is full of heroes and villains. But you will always be my personal hero. Take care and God rest your spirit.*

*Doc,*
*C. 1/46th*[4]

On Christmas day Moose and her mom came down to see us, and when it was time to go, Moose asked if I would walk her the four blocks back to her house. That was one of the sweetest walks I have ever had. Neither of us had any gloves and the air was biting cold, but as soon as we were out the door in the bright sunshine Moose grabbed my hand, interlaced her fingers in mine and put our hands into her coat pocket. We scuffed along in the new snow letting our boots submarine along under the white blanket. We tossed snowballs at her mother when she drove by later, and in the park we laughed as we made angels in the snow, even though the snow was too deep and fluffy to make good ones.

It took about an hour to walk those four blocks. We talked like friends talk, easy talk, not strained or striving like young infatuates do, but a gentle flow of concern and guardianship of a precious relationship. That walk changed my relationship with Moose forever from a wrestling

---

[4] This letter was adapted from a letter written in 1996 by a man identified only as Doc. It was written to a Frank, from Mississippi. The letter was found stuck to a fence in Missoula, Montana. It is the author's hope that the sacrifice of Frank from Mississippi may never be forgotten and that he may be remembered as a hero who maintained his inherent right to give his life to the most worthy of causes, his friend.

for romantic favors to a beautiful and soul satisfying kindredship. I knew that was what I wanted in a marriage, regardless of who I married. I wanted a beautiful, soul-satisfying kindredship.

On January 3rd we held Dean's funeral. The chapel was packed with old school buddies as well as the whole community of Declo. There were even two soldiers who knew Dean in Vietnam. They spoke with Mom and hugged her, both fighting to control their emotions. "Dean loved his family," was all they said.

I think the longest part for me was the slow drive in the black Cadillac from the chapel down the slope over the railroad tracks and the Burley-Declo highway, across Marsh Creek and up the small cemetery hill that overlooks the town. How many other sorrowing people have made this same aggrieved journey? This is life and we will, eventually, all make the same unknown passage through the portals of death. I mused, Why should it be so scary if so many others have made it successfully? I smiled at my private humor.

I took my mother's hand. She sat looking out at the white landscape, skeleton trees jutting up on the horizon. Her other hand was placed at her mouth with her index finger quivering slightly on her lips, like she always did when she was nervous.

She looked at me with the woeful, watery eyes of a mother who has lost her son and doesn't know where to look to find him. She said quietly, "It is ... so cold ... to.. day." Fred and I supported her as the final words were said over Dean's grave and some soldiers fired their guns. Mom flinched at the sound of the rifle fire. How ironic that the same sounds of war which brought us to this sad day were used to salute him good-bye.

Two soldiers folded the American flag that covered Dean's casket and handed it to Mom. She took the flag with the same tired old hands that had raised Dean. She stared silently at the flag with an anguished expression, but said nothing.

Unless this nation re-discovers the unalienable rights our
Creator endowed us with we will make many  foolish
decisions by the voice of the people.

THE PRISTINE AMERICAN DREAM

# CHAPTER 23

## I Have a Right to Be Attracted to Beautiful People

I never tire of the Magic Valley sunsets. The quiet evenings gathered darkness in beautiful shades of yellow, crimson, and purple spreading along the uninterrupted western horizon.

It was on a frozen January evening like this that I sped with Ur to his first lecture at the ISDB. We were driving Mary's new 1966 Plymouth Fury III Sport Coupe. The beautiful red interior smelled new and clean. The steering wheel felt light in my hands as we quietly floated through the stark frozen terrain.

Mary had insisted that we take her car saying, "That's why I bought it. And Jon, it's broken in so stomp on it a couple of times because you know how much Ur likes it."

When I told Mary I might wreck it she laughed and said, "I trust you with my brother, don't I? And he is far more valuable than a brand new car."

Coming north out of Declo we had passed the quarter-mile drag marks painted on the highway and I floor-boarded it. Ur smiled brightly as his head snapped back and I quickly accelerated to the speed limit.

"Wow," he said, "This car really goes!"

KBAR radio in Burley was playing some mellow music so I turned it off and asked Ur what he was speaking on. At first it was a little awkward speaking to him while driving. Then I figured out how to reach over to spell and sign my questions and comments with one hand.

"They asked me to speak about deaf education. Do you want to hear a little about it?"

"Sure," I said.

Ur opened a big folder with a bunch of brown stiff papers inside. His notes were all in Braille. Feeling along with the tips of his fingers, Ur filled me in on deaf education over the past 100 years—the struggle between hearing people, many well meaning, and the deaf. He said that some hearing had suppressed the deaf by controlling education and dictating how the deaf should be taught. They also tried to make the deaf into hearing people without giving thought to the fact that the deaf may be happy in their deafness.

"Wait," I said. "Do you mean that the Deaf are satisfied being deaf and don't want to hear?"

"I mean there are many deaf persons who don't have anymore desire to become hearing than you do of becoming deaf," he said.

With surprise I asked, "Why? Don't they know what they are missing?"

"An equal question would be, 'Jon, don't you know what you are missing by being hearing?' You are trying to interpret everyone's life from your perspective when there are as many perspectives of life as there are people. There are the laws of inherent rights, a universal code of conduct which applies to everyone. Yet for the most part, a person's satisfaction comes from living his own unique life while maintaining his inherent rights, not from having or not having some physical attribute or mental gift. Jon, do you think I am happy and satisfied with who I am?"

"You are about the happiest person I've ever known," I said sincerely.

"Well, thank you. I have come to know that happiness is a perspective as well as a commitment to maintain our inherent rights. I really am very happy. Knowing you makes me happy. I am glad you came into my life."

I blushed with joy. How could someone as great and important as Ur think I was anything special, I wondered.

He droned on about deaf education and its development since 1880 and what he called the hundred year war between Oralist and Manualist. I wasn't really interested so I let my mind wander to something I had wondered about ever since Ur invited me to accompany him to ISDB. Would Little Miss Redhead be there? The possibility made me smile.

There was a bad crash between a large truck and a train on the railroad tracks at the Wendell cutoff. The sight of the mangled truck haunted me because of a phobia I had with trains. The road would be closed for hours. That forced us to drive almost to Bliss and then cut back to Gooding, making us 15 minutes late. I saw Ur flip open the crystal of his Braille watch several times, but he never showed any anxiousness or told me to hurry.

Arriving in front of Old Main, the administration building, I helped Ur into his wheelchair and hurried up the sidewalk. Dr. Jacobs greeted us at the door and said he understood there had been an accident in Wendell and knew we would be a little late. He asked us to excuse him for a minute so he could go get Joy Reynolds, the student body president, who would be introducing Ur.

The strong odor of varnish and oil in the hallway brought back a flood of humiliating memories from the wrestling match little over a month earlier. Soon we heard the clacking of high heels approaching us from around the corner.

I had expected to see Little Miss Redhead in the audience, but seeing her now without proper mental preparation wobbled me a little. I thought there was a flicker of surprise and recognition in her eyes before she showered Ur's unseeing face with a beautiful smile. Taking his hands she signed quickly.

"It is such an honor to meet you. I have read much of your writings and especially your articles on deaf education. You bring honor to our school and community by being here."

Ur asked, "What is your name?"

My eyes focused on her beautiful hands as I never wanted to forget her name.

"Oops. I forgot to tell you. My name is Joy Reynolds."

"Joy Reynolds," Ur spelled slowly with his hand and then felt her hands carefully. "Joy, you have beautiful, graceful hands that indicate a joyous heart like your name."

Joy smiled. Her smile wasn't just a regular smile like you see every day. It lighted up her face, the entire hallway, and especially my heart. Her eyes danced and her countenance sparkled.

Ur spoke. "Joy, this is Jon. He is one of my best friends, and for tonight he is my professional assistant."

I lifted my head and took on a professional look, although I wasn't sure what that look was supposed to be. Joy painted my face with one of her great smiles, then she signed to Ur, "I haven't met Jon before, but I have seen him wrestle."

I could see the wheels turning in Ur's head for a moment. Then with a sly smile he asked, "Is your hair red?"

I busted out with an embarrassed laugh and looked away. Joy looked confused for a moment and then smiled with understanding, cut a look my way and then signed, "Yes."

"Oh," Ur said while slowly nodding his head. "Then I have heard quite a bit about you."

Joy glanced up at me again with a curious look as I stood there grinning and looking stupid. Joy asked Ur a few questions to add to her introduction.

There were about 100 people at the lecture and I was astounded by Joy's introduction of Ur. I had no idea that he was so famous and important. He had sat on the U.S. President's Council for the Handicapped. He had traveled the world as an expert on both deafness and blindness. He had met with Prime Minister Ghandi in India as well as Queen Elizabeth of England. He had written four books, two of which were books on his philosophy of deaf-blind education. He was the previous president of the Hadley School for the Blind in Illinois. Even with all of these important credentials, he still called me his friend.

I played a major part in the evening as Ur's "professional assistant." I relayed all of the questions and comments from the audience to Ur while Ur signed and voiced for himself. I could tell that Joy was impressed.

After the presentation there was a short reception for Ur. While I was busy assisting Ur, I kept looking for Joy so I could talk to her. Towards the end of the reception Ur asked me to assist him to the restroom. I had not seen Joy since the meeting ended and had given up trying to get to know her better. As we exited the restroom, Dr. Jacobs met us and asked if we would mind dropping off a student in Burley, as her parents were coming from Oakley to pick her up there.

"We would love to," Ur agreed. "Who is it?"

"Joy Reynolds."

Ur's and my face exploded in happiness. "That would be wonderful! Is she here or should we pick her up at her dorm?" I said, a little too enthusiastically.

"If you don't mind, she is waiting at her dorm. She missed the bus to Burley tonight because she wanted to be here to introduce Ur. She wants to spend time with her family on weekends as often as possible."

Dr. Jacobs gave us directions to the dorm. While driving over Ur said, "Jon, this is your lucky day."

I thought I had died and gone fishing as I loaded Joy's bags into the trunk of Mary's car. Ur insisted on riding in the back seat pretending he was tired and wanted to lie down.

We sailed out of Gooding toward Wendell, hoping the road would be open by now. All of a sudden shyness overwhelmed me, and all of the imagined bravado melted like snow before a Chinook wind. I looked straight ahead without even a friendly glance toward Joy. I sensed her looking at me and appraising me with those remarkable blue eyes. She was wearing some fragrance that was light and captivating. I didn't know what it was called, but I had smelled it on other classy girls. I wanted to say something really cool, but nothing seemed to feel right so I sat in silence.

The atmosphere seemed to thicken as we drove the 30 minutes to Wendell. The tracks were clear so I stopped at a Texaco service station to top off the tank. Joy got out of the car and wandered into the station and bought an Orange Crush. Ur didn't want anything so I bought a Pepsi and a bag of Planter Peanuts. I popped the cap off the Pepsi, took a swig, tore the top off the peanut bag and, using my cupped hand as a funnel, poured the whole bag of peanuts into the bottle. It fizzed for a second so I put my mouth over the top to prevent it from spilling over. Joy looked at me in disbelief.

"What are you doing?" she asked, her signs and slightly high pitched voice easy to understand.

"What? Oh, you mean the peanuts. Everyone at my school puts peanuts in their Pepsi."

"Yuck, doesn't it make your breath smell all peanutty?"

I froze. She was right, and the car would start to smell like peanuts. I tried to cover quickly. "Well, we don't eat the peanuts, we just let them flavor the Pepsi," I explained weakly.

She looked at me with a look that said this was probably something that hearing do and that the deaf cannot possibly understand.

Heading east on I-84, Joy turned around in the seat and asked Ur to tell us some poems. Ur agreed saying that one of his favorite poets was another deaf-blind man named Dr. Richard Kinney, the current president of the Hadley School for the Blind in Illinois.

"I have tried to memorize some of his poems. They seem to reach down inside me," he said with a soft melancholy tone in his voice.

I turned on the dome light so Joy could see Ur signing, but I thought to myself "Poetry, what a boring thing to do."

Ur signed and spoke at the same time.

> *No pitted toad behind a stone*
> *But hoards some secret grace;*
> *The meanest slug with midnight gone*
> *Has left a silver trace.*

> *No dullest eyes to beauty blind,*
> *Uplifted to the beast,*
> *But prove some kin with angel kind,*
> *Though lowliest and least.*
> *Dr. Richard Kinney*

Joy said, "Those are words of hope and beauty. How about another one?"

> *To feel the thought within the breast*
> *Mount to the lips and sing,*
> *As some shy bird within the nest*
> *Should serenade the Spring;*

> *To feel the small words, silver-bright,*
> *Trill up and cool the tongue;*
> *No fountain, leaping to the light,*

*More joyously has sung.*

*For there's a yearning in the dust,*
*The rich warm dust of man,*
*That will be silenced if it must,*
*But music if it can.*
*Dr. Richard Kinney*

I glanced at Joy and her eyes were moist with tears of understanding. I saw her in the rearview mirror sign "thank you" and then squeeze Ur's hand.

As she turned around and sat facing forward again I felt an explosion of affection for her. Nothing was said, but I reached my hand out and took hers. She placed my hand on her lap and opening my palm she wrote with her fingertip while voicing, "THANK YOU FOR TRYING TO UNDERSTAND." Then squeezing my hand she placed it on the seat between us.

I wasn't sure what that meant, but I knew I liked her and hoped we would become good friends. I asked her to tell me about her school and she took off chattering about a mile a minute. I had a little difficulty understanding some of her speech, but I got the jest of what she was saying.

"You know that boy that beat you in wrestling when you came to ISDB last month?"

"Yeah, sure, how could I forget him? He pounded me."

"Well, he has bragged all over the school about what a great wrestler he is and how nobody can beat him. He moved here from someplace back East and I guess he was a state champion there and has not lost a match in all three years of high school. I know I shouldn't feel this way, but I just wish someone would beat him once," she emphasized.

"Don't you kind of feel sorry for him, you know being deaf and blind and all?"

She stared at me. "Why should I? He doesn't want my pity and he doesn't want yours. Do you feel sorry for me? Because if you do I'll knock your block off!" Then she smiled.

I didn't know what to say. So I said, "Help me to understand."

"I don't want anybody's pity. I like being deaf. Last month at the FHA state convention in Pocatello, I met someone who didn't know I was deaf. When she found out I was deaf, she said, 'Oh, I'm sorry. I didn't know you were handicapped.' I said, 'I'm not. I'm Deaf!'

"Sure there are some things that I am curious about, like what the wind sounds like or the cooing of a baby. I am curious to know why the hearing like music so much. I wonder what rain or streams sound like or frying bacon. These are things that I am curious about, but I like being deaf. I have never been kept awake by a barking dog or been distracted by some noise when I am reading. Most of all, I like me. The wrestler likes himself too—in fact, maybe a little too much. I'll bet you beat him next time. When do you wrestle him again?"

I was starting to pick up her speech better now as I got used to it, and I tried to catch her signing out of the corner of my eye. "I'm not sure. I think about a month before the state tournament, but I doubt if I will ever beat him. He is way out of my class." She didn't say anything, but looked at me a little weird, or was it with disappointment?

I turned off at the first Burley exit and passed the Ponderosa Motel and Golf Course. It was still covered with snow. I drove down Overland Avenue amidst scores of honking teenagers dragging "Main", which was really Overland Avenue. Everyone was showcasing their best pick-up skills in farm pickups and heavy cars. I secretly hoped that someone from Declo would see me in a beautiful red car with a beautiful redhead next to me.

I turned left at Main Street and slipped the car into a parking place about a half block from the Oregon Trail Café. I got Joy's bags and carried them back to the café. As I wrestled them through the door, I saw a big weathered cowboy get up and come toward us. Ignoring the customers, Joy ran to him and gave him a big hug.

He was dressed in a faded blue denim shirt with a Bull Durham tag hanging out of one pocket. His jeans were Levi's 501s, and his boots exhibited a lot of hard wear. "Jon, this is my father, Chet Reynolds." A hand hard as clam shells collapsed over mine.

"Thanks for dropping Joy off. I sure do appreciate it," he drawled. His big hands clumsily signed to Joy as he picked up her bags and started for the door.

"Thanks, Jon. Will you be coming up with Ur for the other three lectures?"

"You bet-cha!"

"Good, then maybe you can give me a ride back?" she asked with a wink.

"My ... pleasure," I stammered as I stared at Joy catching up to her father and heading out the door. One thing I knew for sure—Joy Reynolds was made of the stuff that could stir my chili!

Everyone has inner impressions to help the needy, or return a lost item to its owner, or tell the truth. God bless all of those who do what is right because they know in their heart it is right...an unalienable right.

# CHAPTER 24

## I Have a Right to Try to Earn Privileges

All the next day my mind was buzzing with thoughts of Joy. I kept seeing her magnificent red hair and baby-doll blue eyes, her perfect features and form. I was sure she would be there next Friday and I could drive her home again. I even took a drive to Oakley, looked up her address in the telephone book and tried to drive past her house. The only problem was I couldn't find her house since the address simply said RFD # 1, Birch Creek Road. I drove Birch Creek Road several times hoping I would see her.

Saturday night Declo played Murtaugh in basketball. The game was a screamer and all of the wrestlers sat together and backed up the Pep Club. Sometimes there was tension between the wrestlers and the basketball players. We called them round-ballers and they called us arm-pit-smellers. After our workouts we usually ran our laps together in our small gym. It wasn't unusual for cutting remarks to be made between the two squads and occasional pushing with veiled threats. But at the games all of this was forgotten because we all knew we were fighting for our school pride and the traditions of the mighty Hornets.

In our small community most of the people came out to support the school events. It seemed like the gym was filled with just about every person in and around Declo, including those who didn't have kids in school. Like I said, our gym was small with bleachers along one wall and a stage on the end. Opposite the bleachers on the other wall was the large painted letters DECLO HORNETS with a giant, fierce-looking hornet painted between the words. I guess it was put there to terrify the opposition, even though I never did see any of them looking at it and being scared.

The score seesawed back and forth until the last 20 seconds when the game came down with a buzzer beating shot from mid-court by Kay Schrenk, and the Hornets won 71-70.

After the screaming, jumping and back pounding was over, I stood up and stretched with the other wrestlers (hoping the girls would notice my muscles bulging and snapping like leaf springs on a two-ton truck) and watched Moose. She and the other cheerleaders were on the floor taking care of the messy job of patting the ball players on their sweaty backs while being ignored.

That's a funny thing. Cheerleaders work their guts out practicing difficult and sometimes dangerous cheers to help the athletes perform better, yet when the game is over the athletes rarely ever thank them or even give them an appreciative glance. But the cheerleaders don't seem to mind because they just keep patting sweaty backs and being ignored. I wondered what would happen if they all went on strike.

I strutted up to Moose with my hands in my pockets and told her I thought she had done good. "Why don't you cheerleaders think up some trick cheers to throw off the opponent's cheerleaders and maybe that will give our guys an advantage?" I asked innocently.

She slugged me and ignored the question. Ever since that day when I walked her home in the snow after Dean's death, our relationship had evolved into a beautiful friendship. I felt such warmth and tenderness for her, so different from the superficial counterfeit love we had before. Some people probably thought we were in love, but most of our friends knew we were simply best friends. It was really cool because it was common for her to put her arm in mine or to hold my hand or to run up to me at school and take both of my hands in hers, look into my eyes and bubble out some happy news. She dated others and knew I dated others also. I knew she had a crush on Jerry. She was always asking me what she should do to get his attention. Tonight I wanted to share my feelings with her about Joy.

After the ritual at Minn's Café, we invited Gary (star basketball player) and Sandy (beautiful cheerleader) for a drive. "Where to?" they asked.

Declo is pretty small; less that 300 people live there. But it does have train tracks—a spur off from the Union Pacific line in Burley. It was intended to go much further but ended just east of Declo. Someone said the money ran out.

There had never been a car-train wreck in Declo that I was aware of, but those tracks held some kind of fear for me. I silently dreaded them, yet their long arms seemed to draw me to them. They offered adventure and seemed to say, "We dare you!" I heard stories in the news of cars torn in half and bloodied, broken bodies scattered along the tracks after wrecks. The tracks gave Declo importance because such a tragedy could happen there.

Perhaps part of my phobia for trains came because my face carried a patchwork of paper-thin scars, resulting from a near collision with a train in Rupert when I was a small child. The driver had not seen the train coming and slammed on the brakes, propelling me into the open glove box and deeply cutting my face.

One night after a wrestling match with Raft River High School, I had some wrestlers with me. We carefully drove my car parallel onto the tracks in a quiet intersection (they are all usually quiet). I aligned the tires perfectly on the rails. In crazy youthful glee we started driving the car on the tracks toward Burley. The car glided smoothly on the slick rails. I turned loose of the steering wheel and let the tires guide themselves silently on the rails between the spud cellars, past the city limits and out towards Burley. Picking up speed, we were screaming with fear and pleasure. The rails left the flat ground and continued onto a high rail bed above a fenced pasture on both sides. On either side of the rail bed was about six feet of loose gravel, and then it sloped steeply down to the pasture. Kicking on the radio we were pounding on everything as "Mony, Mony" rumbled through the car.

In our monkey-like jumping and pounding to the music, I accidentally stomped on the gas pedal. The rear tires spun causing the car to lurch forward and slightly sideways, skidding the tires off the rails and slamming the axles down hard on the iron tracks. We all laughed and punched each other as we tumbled out to see our predicament. The tracks were too high to drive the car back onto the rails, so we tried to jack the car up and set the wheels back on the tracks. It was while we were doing this that we saw one bright light approaching from Burley about two miles up the tracks. Clyde saw it first and screamed, "Train's coming!"

We stared at the iron monster sweeping around the bend in the pitch dark. After the initial brain freeze, I jerked into action and screamed, "Help me get this thing off the tracks and onto the side bed!"

I slammed the jack under the car, and furiously lifted the car and then they helped pushed it off the jack to the side. It moved about a foot. Lowering the jack and rushing it to the front of the car, we repeated the process moving the car crab-like. Then to the back and again to the front. Now all we had to do was get the tires over the rails. The bright beam was closing fast. I crammed the jack under the back bumper and jacked with all my might until the jack reached its limit. We pushed on the side of the car, but nothing happened. I dropped to my knees and could see that the tires were still a good four inches lower than the rails. The jack was not tall enough. It couldn't lift the car high enough to clear the tracks. I tried to lift on the car while shouting, "Lift!" Everyone stared at me for a second and then scattered like a flock of startled chickens as the light started covering the last half mile. I felt sick watching the bright beam approach to mutilate my car. I stepped off to the side of the tracks.

It was then I noticed something I had not noticed before. U.S. Highway 30 parallels the railroad tracks all the way from Burley. There couldn't be more than 25 yards that separates them. That bright light looked a little too far to the right to be on the tracks. "Yes!" I screamed, "It's a padittle-car with the lights on bright!"

Soon the one-eyed car whisked past us and continued toward the yellow blinking light in the Declo intersection. With a reprieve I started to shake in relief and my "friends" returned to finish removing the car. We piled up some short boards and placed the jack on them to give it more height, and soon we had the car onto the side bed. Backing the car carefully along the side bed to the intersection ,I slugged Sam when he said, "Come on, let's do it again."

That was then and this was now, and once again I was in my car—this time with Moose, Gary and Sandy. We turned down a street to drive between the potato cellars which lined the railroad tracks. It was the same street that the funeral procession used when we took Dean's body to the cemetery.

The potato cellars lay along the tracks like giant loaves of bread. A potato cellar was made by digging a long deep pit and then overlaying the wide hole with timber, netting wire, straw and finally a covering of about two feet of dirt. Add a couple of large double doors on either end and you have a place to store spuds for the winter, or until the train comes to pick them up. These cellars were laid end to end close to the tracks. I always thought they looked like squashed loaves of bread.

Maybe it was our excitement from winning the game or just silly kid's stuff, but we had not given a thought to a train passing at that moment. I was glancing the other way when Moose, Gary and Sandy all screamed at the same time, "Train!"

It was too late. The car was already straddling the tracks when I hit the brakes and killed the motor. Too late. The enormous headlight was towering above us and the great iron hitch was less than four feet from impacting my door. It reached out ahead of the train like a monster's fist ready to tear through the metal door, rip our bodies into bloody pieces and scatter us along the tracks.

The news would spread fast! The headlines in the Burley Herald would say: "Four teenagers were plucked out of innocence and cast into eternity by the iron fist of the great train." Declo would be as famous as its spuds.

Everything was in slow motion. I heard once that when you are just about to be killed everything turns into slow motion. This was slow motion so I knew I was going be killed! I could see Moose in the intense light of the train—her features bleached, her eyes wide, her hands clamped to her head in total terror with her mouth open in a death scream.

Sandy and Gary were holding onto each other with their heads buried. They didn't want to see the final moment just before impact when the iron fist would drive into their bodies and force life from them.

I could hear the roaring of the diesel engine, that mighty diesel engine driving the cold iron fist into our warm soft bodies while crushing our dreams and ambitions out of us. The ripple of our deaths would shake the school and the community. The picture of my mother flashed into my mind. How could my mother survive another death? Hot tears sprang into my eyes as I thought of the pain I would cause my mother.

Above the roar of the engine I heard laughter. Hysterical laughter, joyous laughter! I wondered who was laughing, the angels or the devils, or both. Then I felt the first splintering of pain in my right shoulder as the iron fist began its work of death.

I closed my eyes against the pain as it struck again and again . . . What was going on? How could this train keep backing up and keep hitting me again and again? And it is hitting me on the right shoulder. The train was on the left. Then I heard Moose's voice above the roar of the diesel engine as she slugged me again. "Jon, you idiot! The train is stopped. It's parked there! Let's go before it starts up and runs over us."

I snapped my head back to look. Sure enough it was parked there—right by our car! Probably loading some spuds. We weren't going to die. I pounded the steering wheel and shouted, "Out of sight!"

Sandy and Gary both slapped my head, "Hurry up, Meathead, before we get squashed."

For the next three Fridays I accompanied Ur to Gooding. It was during these trips that Ur began to teach me about receiving the privileges of life. He said the time had come when he felt that I could both understand this and more importantly, be safe with the knowledge. But, to be honest, this knowledge didn't sink in until I needed to beat Luther.

The next Friday we hummed along in Mary's Fury III as Ur began explaining about the Privileges of Life.

"Remember, The Pristine American Dream is the result of maintaining inherent rights and receiving privileges. Many of the good things in life are called privileges. They are the nice things which we have to earn. Do you remember what rights are?"

"Sure," I answered. "They are guaranteed to us. Like the right to remain silent or the right to bear arms. Our government guarantees them to its citizens. You said that there are other rights called inherent rights or *unalienbull* or something rights. These are guaranteed to all humans at birth—like the right to be honest, or the right to forgive, or to protect the health of my body."

"unalienable you mean."

"Oh, yeah, unalienable. That's hard for me to say."

Ur smiled, "Getting the post out and collecting the thousand dollars is a privilege. You have to earn it. By the way, how is that going?"

"Are you kidding? That ground is frozen harder than Fred's head. I couldn't get that post out now with a jack-hammer and the Osterhout brothers combined."

"Who?"

"The Osterhout brothers. They are these brothers who are all huge and strong as horses. They're famous in two counties for their strength."

For a moment I thought of that cedar post and how it had become an intimate friend. Even though I had given up getting the post out this winter, I had not stopped visiting it and leaning on it. No matter how rushed I was, I made a habit of touching it every time I entered the back-yard. There was a smooth place of darker wood where my hands naturally reached. I often felt a peace and strength come from it. Like Ur and Mary, it was a secure thing in my life, something I could depend on to be there.

Ur thought for a moment and then continued. "Okay, privileges are easier to get at during certain times of our lives, so I guess posts can come out easier at some times than at others." Ur checked his watch and then continued, "The government makes available certain privileges. For example, a driver's license is a privilege. You have to qualify for it. A totally blind person like me, cannot get a driver's license. I can't go to the driver's license division and demand to have one, claiming it is my right! It is not a right. It is a privilege."

"Oh yeah," I interrupted. "I remember that from drivers education. A driver can lose his driver's license for drunk driving and too many speeding tickets. Stuff like that, right?"

Ur spoke while counting on his fingers, "It is a privilege to join the army or serve on a jury. It is not a right. You have to qualify for it. Those are government privileges, but there are many other privileges that are available to you by virtue of the fact that you were born in America. It is a privilege to have good grades or to enjoy earned wealth. It is a privilege to enjoy success in sports. It is a privilege to be liked by your peers. If you want to enjoy the privileges of life, you have to be prepared to earn them. Nothing in this life—and I mean nothing—that is valued is achieved without work…sually hard work. If you want the privileges of life, you have got to learn to enjoy hard work. You've got to…"

"I enjoy *some* hard work," I interrupted. "I can throw hay bales all day and not really mind, but I can't study 10 minutes without getting more restless than trees in a breeze."

Ur stared at me for a moment then continued, "Some work is easier than other work. That is true, but if you want the privileges associated with education you must learn to enjoy studying. The first rule is you must learn to enjoy meaningful work."

I tried to digest what he had said and then I asked, "How do you learn to like something if you don't like it already?"

"That is a good question. It took me a long time to figure that out myself. The first thing you must do is change your mind. You must come to *believe* you like it,"

"Huh? I'm lost already."

Ur continued patiently, "Okay, Jon, do you remember when I told you that if you were to make real changes in your life, you would have to follow a pattern of *hope, belief* and *knowledge*? Do you remember me saying that?"

"Umm, not really," I said while maneuvering the big car around a slow-moving black and white Shaw semi-truck.

"You must understand how *belief* and *hope* work together, like headlights and a steering wheel, to keep us on track with our goals. For most people, setting goals is not the problem. Actually, for many people the biggest problem is staying with the goal after the emotion of the decision has past.

"Yeah, that's me all the way. I get all pumped about doing something and brag it all over the school that I am going to do this or that, and then I just fizzle like a wet firecracker and let it drop after awhile. I'm sure nobody believes me anymore."

"Jon, from now on keep your goals private and only share them with someone who is really close, whom you can trust."

"Like Moose?"

"Yes, like Moose. Okay, follow me carefully."

I moved the car into the right lane and slowed to 65 so I could better concentrate on what Ur was telling me.

"Suppose I had a handful of diamonds of different sizes. Some are worth $200,000 while others are only worth maybe $500 to $10,000. Now suppose I take this handful of diamonds to a school assembly and offer them to the student body free of charge. Do you think they would be interested?"

"Gees, you wouldn't stand a chance of even getting out of the school. They'd be at you like starving chickens. I know how much Moose loves diamonds. She would put a stick in your spokes before you could even get turned around," I laughed.

Ur chuckled and continued, "Well, let's suppose I tell everyone to wait while I went out and scattered the diamonds on the football field. Then I returned and told the student body to go out and look for the diamonds if they wanted to. How do you think the students would respond?"

I pondered for a moment. "I guess my first thought is everyone would rush out and look for diamonds. Yet, I guess some wouldn't *believe* you had any diamonds, and others wouldn't *believe* you actually scattered them on the football field. So, I figure there would be different reactions from different students."

"You are probably right. Some students would completely *believe* in me and *hope* they could get a 'piece of the action', so to speak. They would *hope* they would be able to find a diamond. First they would have to *believe* in me—that I actually put the diamonds there. In other words they would have to *believe* I made it possible for them to actually find some diamonds.  And second, they would have to have *hope* they personally could find a diamond. They must have *belief* it is possible and *hope* they can get one. Could they *hope* they could find a diamond if they did not have a *belief* I actually put diamonds on the football field?"

"No, that's impossible," I said with conviction as I started to catch on.

"Would, they go looking for diamonds if they felt no *hope* in finding one?"

"Nope, not a chance," I was rolling with this now.

"Maybe they *believed* I actually put them on the football field, but for some reason they didn't have any *hope* of finding one themselves. Would they go looking?"

I thought for a moment. "Well, probably not, except maybe some would kinda *hope* so they would go out just to glance around."

"Oh, Excellent!" Ur exclaimed. Ur seemed to take on some kind of golden glow when he taught and I understood. "You are really catching on. Yes, there are different degrees of *belief* and *hope*. Watch. Some of the students would rush out and fall to their knees and start searching with great enthusiasm. Others would go out and maybe casually walk around the football field with casual *hope* of finding a diamond. Still others might stand along the sideline and mock those searching.

Ur shifted his weight and stretched his arms for a moment. "Suppose they looked for two hours without anyone finding a diamond. What happens to everybody's *belief* I actually put the diamonds there?"

"It would start to deflate like a ruptured tire."

"And what would happen to everyone's *hope* in finding a diamond?"

"Same thing. Pttttffff," I sprayed like the air leaving a balloon. "Sorry," I said as Ur wiped his hand.

"Do you provide towels with your conversations?" he smiled. "Okay, do you see how *belief* and *hope* are inseparable? If *belief* goes down, so does *hope*. This is important to remember. Most people fail because they only *hope* for change or *hope* to achieve the goal. You must *believe* in the goal to generate mobilizing and enabling power.

I will come back to how *belief* is generated, but for now think about this. Suppose after two hours of searching with no one finding a diamond and enthusiasm starting to slacken, Kenny Turner finds a diamond and he jumps up and shouts, "Hey, everyone! I found a diamond! It's true! Ur really did put diamonds out here, I know because I found one. Keep looking!" What would that do to everyone's *belief* that I really put diamonds there and their *hope* they could find one?"

"It would be like a kick in the pants for everyone. Their *belief* and *hope* would skyrocket."

Ur paused for a moment. "Skyrocket? Just from one testimony?"

"Sure, because they had a real witness, a… Something you could hang your hat on," I answered with confidence.

We rode along in silence for a few minutes quickly approaching the Wendell turnoff. Finally, Ur spoke in a voice of quiet conviction.

"Jon, I want to share a diamond with you. Is this a good time?"

"Sure, let me make this corner first."

After I turned the car onto the road through Wendell, I said, "Go ahead, I'm listening."

"I know the United States of America provides the opportunity for you to realize your greatest dreams, your Pristine American Dreams," he paused. "It is all here, the privileges of life are all available to you, if you want to go for them. We are the freest people of any nation in the world or in the history of the world; a free place where anyone can achieve the great privileges of life if they will. Your legal rights and inherent rights are both protected under our inspired Constitution by the most powerful army ever assembled on the face of the earth. That army is assembled not to suppress you, but to protect your rights and give you real freedom...the freedom to go for all of the privileges, if you are willing.

I love this great nation, Jon. I never knew what it meant to be free until the war. I went along like a door turning on its hinges without any thought of what it meant to have my rights and privileges protected by the Constitution. How blessed we are to live here, and to know how to truly be free! Even a deaf-blind man like me can enjoy tremendous privileges. Think of that! Think that even mentally handicapped persons enjoy great privileges in this nation. *Believe* you can achieve wonderful privileges in your life for you and your family."

"I guess we all don't enjoy exactly the same privileges, do we?" I observed.

"No, we don't enjoy the same privileges, but we can enjoy all of the privileges we are capable and willing to receive."

I squeezed Ur's hand to signal I needed a moment to digest what he had just told me. To be honest, I couldn't ever remember thinking how neat it was to be an American. Like a swinging door, I had always just taken it for granted. But the more I thought about the Pristine American Dream, the more I thought it was pretty cool to be an American.

I knew this was one of those grain combine experiences where I was not seeing the whole picture, yet I was seeing enough to start getting excited. "Okay, tell me about *knowledge*. You said *belief, hope* and *knowledge* were needed. So tell me about *knowledge*."

"All right. Remember, these three things keep you going for the privileges of life. Let me help you understand how *belief* and *knowledge* work together. Are you with me?"

"Sure, put it on me like house paint."

"What? Oh, well never mind. You do throw me sometimes with your language," Ur chuckled. "Okay, Jon, do you *believe* in Lake of the Clouds, Michigan?"

"Ah . . . I don't know, I guess so," I said without conviction.

Ur smiled and shot back, "You do?"

"Well, I don't know. I've never heard of it before."

"So do you *believe* in it or not, yes or no?" he pressed.

I thought for a moment, "I guess not."

"You are right. You don't *believe* in it. Stop me when you *do* start believing in it, okay?"

"Sure."

"Lake of the Clouds is a beautiful, long, narrow lake situated in Porcupine State Park in upper Michigan. This region has some of the highest mountains in the whole area. This is a beautiful wooded area with high cliffs along part of the lake. Fishing is excellent, although the water is a little chilly for swimming."

"Stop," I interrupted, "I *believe*."

"You *believe* now?"

"Yeah."

"What changed?" Ur probed.

"What do you mean, what changed? You told me a bunch of stuff and now I *believe* you."

"Yes, but what changed?" Ur asked again.

I was stumped.

"There is only one thing that changed. You went from dis*belief* to *belief*. What changed?"

I hit the brakes to slow behind a two-ton truck carrying a couple of cold horses and about five sheep crammed in with the horses. This bought me some time to think of what changed.

"Come on, Jon, What changed?" Ur persisted.

"Okay, okay," I said a little testily. "I guess my mind."

Ur beamed, "Oh, excellent! You are right." Ur tried playfully to slug me but miscalculated the distance and missed me a mile. "The only thing changed was your mind. How did you do that?"

"I don't know, you told me a bunch of stuff and I just decided to *believe* it."

"Very good. *Belief* is a decision. You weighed the evidence and my credibility and made the decision to *believe*. Once you decided to *believe*, you gained power. You have authorized yourself to gain knowledge. What do you need to do to know if Lake of the Clouds is true?"

Whoa, here we go again, I thought. "I guess go there and look at it."

"Yes, experience it. As you experience it, you will no longer *believe* in it, you will know. So, if you want to get the privileges out of life you must follow a similar pattern. You must *believe* it is possible to get it (that means decide). You must *hope* you personally can get it, and you must do it to gain the power of *knowledge. Belief, hope,* and *knowledge* form the pattern for getting all the great privileges of life and making significant changes in ourselves. Are you still following me?"

"Yeah, I'm following you, but this stuff is new to me."

"Let me tell you about someone I read about once. This man had earned great wealth by building a business selling garden tools; but when the Great Depression hit, he lost all of his wealth overnight. Nobody wanted to buy garden tools with what little cash they had left. He had all of his money invested, and when the banks closed and the stock market crashed he lost everything. He survived the lean years of the Depression, but when it ended he immediately began to amass great wealth again. How did he do it?"

I could see Gooding up ahead and knew we would have to postpone this conversation pretty soon, but I didn't want to postpone it. I was catching onto what he was saying and I was seeing the potential from this simple pattern. It made perfect sense. I was deciding to *believe*, and I *hoped* with all my heart I could change. I had plenty of reasons to change. To start with I could help out my mother. I wanted to change so my future wife and children would have better opportunities. I wanted to change so maybe someday I could help other kids raised in poor or neglected homes find peace though inherent rights and enjoy the privileges of life.

Ur shook my hand. "Oh, sorry," I said, "I was thinking about what you said. The wealthy man could do it again because he already knew the pattern. It was like he had been to Lake of the Clouds and he not only knew it existed, but he also knew how to get there."

"Jon, do you *believe* you can change whatever is necessary so you can start receiving the privileges of life?" Ur asked me with calm intensity.

I took Ur's hand from my face so I could think for a minute. He understood and sat quietly. All my life I wanted to do something noteworthy. I always wanted my name to stand out a little bolder. Not bolder than someone else's, but just bolder. I've always been average and below. I felt Ur was telling the truth, and the truths he was teaching me were true principles. In fact, I *believed* they were true. Ur told me about a man, Dr. Ray L. Jones, who was the head of some deaf program in California. When he believed in some new idea or plan, he would say, "Why Not!" Ur said there are two kinds of people in the world: the Why's and the Why Nots. The ones who move mountains are the Why Nots. The ones who stop mountain moving are the ones who say Why. I wanted to be a Why-Not-person. I wanted to move mountains in my life, not just sit around and tell people why they couldn't be moved.

As we entered the outskirts of Gooding I took Ur's hand to my face again and said, "I *believe* in the process you have been teaching me, and I *hope* with all of my heart I will change, but I don't know how to do it." Then I quickly added, "I guess, once I walk that path it will be easier the second time."

# CHAPTER 25

## I Have a Right to Feel Pure Affection

We arrived about 30 minutes early. I parked the car in the usual parking place and started to get out.

"Jon," Ur spoke with a calm, sincere voice, "before we go in, I want to tell you I am proud of you. I have a lot of confidence in you, not only as my assistant, but also as my friend."

I looked at Ur's pale eyes and a lump caught in my throat. "Thanks, Ur. I've never had a friend like you before. I don't remember my father very well so I guess I don't know where to put you. I don't know if you fit in the father figure category or the best-friend category; but I know this for sure—you are one or the other."

"My father was both," he said quietly, "and I think I was both to my children also."

I squeezed his hand in appreciation and got out of the car. As I walked around the car, I realized that was a new thought for me. I had never considered  a parent could be a best friend. I smiled at the happy thought and hoped someday to be a best friend to my children. Then I smiled brighter as I saw a pretty red-headed girl showcased in the window of Old Main's front door.

Joy swung the front door open as we approached.

"Hi, Joy, you smell good!" Ur signed.

Taking his hand to her beautiful face she said, "Ur, are you flirting with me? And how did you know it was me?" Joy teased.

Ur smiled. "I am just trying to show Jon how to do it. He is a little awkward in that part of his social development." Joy peeked up at me. "And I knew it was you because you wore Tabu perfume last week and you seem to always chew spearmint gum, and you wash your hair with Prell shampoo. Same as me."

Joy glanced at his bald head and her eyes twinkled. "Well, with that kind of nose I am glad I took a bath."

"Me too." Ur replied with a chuckle.

I immediately became self conscious of my pits, but restrained myself from lifting an arm for a quick sniff. I decided to let the crack go about my social development. Joy looked up at me with those baby-blue eyes and winked to let me know she knew Ur was teasing.

I noticed for the first time a light shadowing of freckles that veiled her perfect features in a golden blush. Joy's high, unusual voice filled with playfulness, and lilted like a meadowlark on a breathtaking spring morning. She was wearing a navy-blue skirt and a white blouse that played around her firm shape.

That is something I have noticed about girls who were raised working on farms and ranches. They had this attractive firmness in their bodies. Their neck, shoulders and arms were—I don't know how to say it— shaped, and firm. I've seen some girls who don't do physical work or exercise, and I swear their arms would flap in a wind. I don't mean they should have arms like rippling steel, but a little firmness is great.

That reminded me about when I went on a blind double date once. I was sitting in the backseat holding hands with my date. My mind was dancing around the pleasant thought that she had solid hands. I gave her hand a little love squeeze and she gave me a squeeze back harder. I thought, well all right, I can work with this. I gave her a harder squeeze and she retaliated with a good squeeze.

Now, I have big hands, and over the years of milking cows by hand I have developed pretty good hand strength. You can imagine my surprise, after I gave her a good healthy squeeze, when she laid into m y hand and folded it hand up like a wallet. She squeezed my hand so hard that I swear peanut butter was oozing out from under my fingernails. It hurt so bad that it brought tears to my eyes and made me pull in my toes. When she turned loose, I determined to be more careful about whose hands I squeezed in the future.

I stood there privately admiring Joy's hands as she signed into Ur's hands. They were delicate and still strong. Her fingernails were perfect, not too short and definitely not too long. Her hands were also shadowed in a light scattering of freckles like gentle rain on summer soil. Her signs were precise, but not hard like a man's signs. She had a feminine grace and movement. I noticed that girls signed differently than men, and Joy certainly signed like a girl.

She stood and looked at me over the top of Ur. "Jon, I am happy to see you again. I saw you drive slowly past my house last Saturday, twice. Why didn't you stop in? Did you want to see me?"

That is another thing about the deaf I had learned. They always got to the point. At first it bugged me, but now their directness was refreshing. There was not the beating-around-the-bush that accompanied hearing people's sensitive conversations. Yet, I still blushed at getting caught.

"Yes, I wanted to see you," I answered while looking into her eyes and trying to be as direct as she was.

"What about?"

I faltered and looked shyly away and shrugged my shoulders. "I don't know. Just wanted to see you again." I glanced back to see her eyes frolicking in playfulness.

"Next time stop in and well go horseback riding. Can you ride a horse?"

"Heck yes! My middle name is Trigger." She did the sign for a gun trigger. From that point on she always referred to me with that sign. Her mouth would say Jon, but her hands signed Trigger. I later learned that deaf people, or hearing people who associate with the deaf, often have a name sign. It is given by a deaf person for some deed or characteristic.

Ur's lecture was on language acquisition for deaf children. I was lost faster than a blowout at 90 miles an hour. He was talking about cognitive dimensions of language acquisition, syntactic and semantic development. It was when he began talking about metalinguistic awareness that my eyes really started to glaze over.

I resorted to memorizing every feature of Joy to help me stay alert. Her face and eyes were so full of expression. It was obvious she was comprehending a lot more of what was being said. Every once in awhile she would turn to a friend nearby and sign something. Her signing was always so fast that I couldn't catch it. Once she looked directly at me.

I have the ability to raise half of my upper lip in a real cool "come-on" gesture. With a face of stone while staring directly at Joy, I raised half of my upper lip. She stared at me for a moment uncomprehending, and then I saw her eyes start to frolic again. I loved that expression. She tilted her head up a little and closed her eyes into slits like Marilyn Monroe would do and then kissed the air with the most tantalizing kiss I had ever seen. Then her whole countenance seemed to burst into the most joyous expression. That is when I really knew for the first time that Joy Reynolds...liked...me. I started beaming like the headlight on a Union Pacific freight train. I got so tickly inside that I could hardly hold still. Inside my chest was a little happy monster who was running around, jumping up and down, honking horns and ringing bells. The happiness radiating from me started to distract some people in the audience. I noticed them signing to each other, "What wrong with him?" Joy, realizing suddenly what her kiss in the air had done, glanced over her shoulder and turned redder than a Hereford cow. I delighted in watching her try to compose herself while I tried to take on an innocent air.

I was happy to hear Ur wrap up his lecture and reach out his hand for me to wheel him back. "What's going on?" Ur whispered as he sat down.

How did he know?

"Tell you later," I spelled quickly.

While Ur was talking to Dr. Jacobs, I noticed someone tell Joy she had a telephone call. Worrying that something might be wrong, I followed her into the principal's office where the secretary interpreted for Joy.

With the phone pinched between her shoulder and neck she signed, "It's your dad. He says the truck is broken down and he can't pick you up in Burley." Joy's countenance dropped as she glanced at me standing there. I knew she hated staying at the school on weekends when everyone else was gone.

"I'll take you up to Oakley," I said hopefully. "If it's all right with your dad."

"Are you sure?" she said. "I don't want to put you out. Are you sure you don't mind?"

"Heck no!" I signed. "I'd like that almost as much as hot chocolate." I slurred my signing and she only caught the hot chocolate part."

"Tell Dad that Jon will bring me home if we will give him some hot chocolate," she told the secretary.

I started to correct her and then gave up in embarrassment. I'll bet her dad thinks I'm an ignoramus.

While Joy was changing her clothes and getting her things together, I explained the problem to Ur. His eyes glinted for a moment and then he said, "I'm pretty tired. You might need to drop me off in Declo before you take her to Oakley. I know that will make your trip about 30 minutes longer I hope you won't mind." Then Ur smiled his teasing smile.

"I can switch cars in Declo and use mine," I explained.

"Mary won't mind. You use the Fury and drop it off tomorrow morning."

On the ride back to Declo, Joy took my hand and set it on her lap while she chattered away about the week of school. Then she stopped abruptly and asked, "Jon, can you understand my voice if I don't sign? Tell me the truth. It won't hurt my feelings."

"Pretty good, but the signing helps."

"Do you think my voice sounds funny?"

I glanced at her. "I love the sound of your voice. It's like you're totally unique."

"What does that mean uniq...whatever that word was?"

"It means you are different...ah... one of a kind...ah... unusual." None of that sounded right.

I glanced again and could see that I had hurt her feelings. Steering the car with my knee I signed, "Joy, I'm sorry. That didn't come out right. It isn't your deafness or your voice that is so unusual. It is your goodness and happiness. It is your beauty and smartness. I love to hear your voice because it doesn't sound like all of the other girls' voices. It's you!

"I stopped seeing you as deaf when I got to know you the same as I stopped seeing Ur as deaf-blind and legless when I got to know him.

The more you know someone, the more their differences disappear. I just think you are really cool and I am glad you are my friend."

She smiled, took my hand again and tried to bite, it which caused the car to swerve back for a moment as I fought to get free. I noticed the car behind me speed up and begin following close. Glancing back again, I saw a red light blinking in my rear view mirror. Joy clasped her hands to her face, turned and looked out the back window and shouted, "Oh no, I'll bet you get hauled off to jail!"

As I pulled the car off to the side of the interstate highway Joy quickly signed to Ur what was happening. The officer approached my window and I rolled it down, letting cold air rush in. That seemed to be Ur's cue.

"Officer," Ur said with a loud voice, "I think the driver has been drinking."

"Don't listen to him, officer," I said too quickly. " He is deaf-blind and legless. How would he know? Joy, tell Ur to be quiet," I signed to Joy. But she was laughing too hard to help.

"I'm frightened!" Ur called out again.

"Hey, what are you doing with your hands?" the officer shouted as he crouched and unsnapped his duty pistol, his flashlight in my eyes.

Putting my hands on the steering wheel, I said, "Nothing! She is deaf too. I was just signing."

"Step out of the car and keep your hands where I can see them."

As I stepped out of the car, the black uniformed Idaho State Policeman kept his flashlight in my eyes.

"Step to the trunk of the car and put your hands on the trunk lid and spread your legs."

I hesitated.

"Do it now!" he commanded.

I quickly obeyed. While I stared through the back window at Joy, her hands over her mouth and her eyes large in anxiety, the officer came to me and did a quick search of my pockets. Finding nothing more harmful than a half stick of Doublemint gum, he relaxed.

"Okay," he started using his commanding and matter-of-fact-cop-voice. "I first observed that you appeared to lose control of your vehicle about a mile back. It looked like you could possibly be drinking. May I see your driver's license?"

"Officer, I can explain." My hands were shaking as I opened my wallet and started fishing for my driver's license. "This deaf girl," I pointed to Joy, "tried to bite my hand a second ago and that is when I swerved."

He stared at me, "What were you doing that she needed to bite your hand?"

"Nothing, I swear it!"

"Reckless driving is willful and wanton disregard for human life and property. You might fit that definition."

"I'm sorry," I said humbly as the cold wind started making my eyes burn and my face go numb.

Handing me my drivers license he said, "Okay, I'll let you off with just a warning, but be careful. I'd hate to hafta scrape you and your friends off the road tonight." My eyes widened.

When I got back into the car, both Ur and Joy were watching to see if I was angry. I put on a hard face and pulled back on the interstate highway. Then I couldn't hold it in anymore and busted up laughing. Joy grabbed Ur's hand and signed something into it and we all had a good laugh.

After I helped Ur into his wheelchair, Joy gave him a hug and a kiss on his cheek. Ur beamed and told Joy not to bite my hand while I was driving, unless he was present. We all laughed again.

We rode along in comfortable silence until I made the Oakley turn off just past Test Hill. Finally Joy asked, "When do you wrestle Luther again?"

Inside I shuttered at the thought of wrestling Luther again. I figured I didn't have a snail's chance crossing the salt flats of beating him and to lose to him was humiliating. "Oh, I don't know," I tried to sound casual, "ISDB comes to Declo next week. Why?"

"Luther has been trying to pick up on me all year. He is such an obnoxious braggart that I can't stand to be around him. Last week, his friend Louis told him that you have been taking me home on weekends. I guess he is pretty jealous and has said a few bad things about you and me. He also threatened to hurt and make sure you are not able to do anything for awhile."

"What did he say about us?" Feelings of anger starting to burn with the thought that Luther could say anything unkind about Joy.

"I am not going to tell you. I know how boys are . . . all macho. Can he hurt you in wrestling?"

" Sure he could, but I doubt he would do something just to get back at me for taking you home. I am sure he is just running his mouth...or hands."

Joy smiled with a puzzled look at my play on signs. "I think, he can be real dangerous. I wish someone could beat him . . . just once. Do I sound bad?"

"No, of course not. Besides, I'll do the best I can," I promised weakly. I knew I didn't have a hog's chance in an Oklahoma slaughterhouse of beating Luther.

We got into Oakley about 11:15 and I turned up Birch Creek Road. About eight miles up Birch Creek, Joy told me to turn on a lane near a Farmer's Cooperative sign. A well-worn gravel lane crossed a cattle-guard and descended through a pasture toward Birch Creek. Nestled among the poplar and aspen trees was her home. It was a typical ranch house, one that had started out as logs years before but had been added to several times. A couple of split logs served as steps leading onto a porch and a screen door at the main entrance. Between the door and the kitchen window sat two willow rockers. A couple of dingo cow dogs announced our arrival, and I could see a light on in the kitchen.

Chet met us at the door and collapsed my hand in his. A plain lady with smiling eyes and willowy form introduced herself as Evelyn, Joy's mother.

"Come sit," Chet commanded. "Hot chocolate's almost done."

The kitchen was clean and had a woodsy smell about it. The adjoining living room had some rough furniture and a TV. On top of the T.V. was a picture of Joy as a little girl, maybe five years old. The picture had originally been a brown tone, but later enhanced with color. Joy stood with her head tilted to the side in a dark-blue sailor dress carefully holding a yellow rose, an impish smile playing on her lips. "That's my favorite picture of Joy," Evelyn said.

Evelyn turned to the stove, stirred a silver pan a couple of times and brought the steaming hot chocolate to the table while Chet set out some cups and a plate of homemade bread toasted up perfect with a big dish of fresh home-churned butter.

"Dig in. We don't want to keep you up late." We surrounded the round kitchen table and started buttering our toast, dipping it into our hot chocolate and slurping it to our mouths. We must have looked like a bunch of slobs to some people, but I couldn't think of another way to enjoy thick heavy slices of homemade bread baked in a wood-burning stove. A wood-burning stove always gives the bread a thick crust that just screamed out to be dipped in hot chocolate. Sitting around the table, we talked about lots of things—Joy's school, Ur's speech, the cattle and some of the embarrassing things Joy did while growing up. For about an hour I heard about the joys and sorrows of living on Birch Creek. Chet laughed till tears came as Joy told about me getting stopped by the State Policeman and what Ur did to me.

"You'll have to bring Ur over when it warms up and take the horses up toward the city," Chet invited.

"The city?" I asked.

"Yeah, the City of Rocks. You ever been there?"

"Nope, I can't say that I have."

"Come spring you guys take some horses and ride over. It's only about five or six miles east of here."

"Okay, I agreed."

After glancing at the wall clock, Evelyn said, "My goodness, look at what time it's got and we've been yakking away here like it was Sunday afternoon. Jon needs to get home before his mother skins all of us alive."

"It's okay," I said. "She doesn't get home until after two and as long as I am there before she gets there I'm okay. But I better be heading home now anyway."

After our good-byes and thanks, Joy threw on a light Levi jacket and walked me out to my car. The air had turned warm like it always did just before a storm rolled in. We walked in silence holding hands until we reached my car. We both smiled as someone turned on the yard light. Joy dropped my hand and turned to face me.

"Thank you for bringing me home and introducing me to Ur. I feel such . . . I don't know, I guess comfortable," she signed.

"Yeah, me too. You know, you have a great family. I feel so much love in your home. Do you guys ever fight?"

She laughed, "Sure, we're normal, but we do love each other and are happy being together." She looked around the yard for a moment and then glanced at the house. "My parents like you and so do I."

There was that directness again. I loved the pure direct way she talked—honest and unashamed of her feelings. I didn't know how to express my feelings to her so I opened my arms and my coat and she snuggled in comfortably as I wrapped my coat around her. We stood there for several minutes in the quiet ecstasy of a pure human embrace. She laid her head on my chest.

"I can't hear your heart. Are you dead?" She voiced.

Then we both busted up laughing.

"You are worse than Ur. How would you know if my heart is beating? You're deaf."

"Ooo, smart boy, but I can feel it with my ear on your chest."

Not knowing what to say I asked, "Is your heart beating?"

She pulled back and stared at me in shock. "Sure, but I am not going to let you put your ear on my chest to hear it."

My face exploded in a red that would make a fire truck seem pale as I realized what she had misunderstood as my intention. "Oh, gees! I didn't mean that."

She snuggled back in again. "I hope not! That stuff is sacred and must be saved for marriage. Do you agree? She pulled back and searched my eyes."

"Of course," I tried to sound like that had always been my desire too.

To be honest, I had not quite decided about the sequence of sex and marriage yet. I heard a lot of talk in the locker room, but holding hands and hugging was all I had experienced. I had the desires like all of the guys. Sometimes I seemed to burn with desire, but I had not sought any opportunities with the girls who were known to be willing. Now hearing Joy state so clearly that it was sacred and needed to be saved for marriage seemed to engrave the same standard on my heart. There was a lot about this subject I knew I did not understand, but I knew one thing for sure—I would never try to violate Joy's sacredness and I would be willing to give my life protecting it, even from myself. Yet I had to admit that it was definitely a warm fuzzy feeling having Joy so close. I had never been hugged by a girl this way before. It was neat and for sure a better hug than I ever got from Aunt Veda. I wished I had a dad that I could talk with about girls and the desire that burned inside of me. I thought I would talk to Ur about it if the opportunity ever came up.

Too soon Joy backed up, closed my coat. "Time for you to go home," she smiled. "Be careful driving back to Declo."

"Will I see you next Thursday at the wrestling match?" I asked. She got a worried expression and then said, "Yes."

"And on Friday at Ur's last lecture, if I am still alive," I teased. She smiled, "Yes. Can I ride home with you?"

"Sure. Tell your dad not to worry 'cause I'll bring you all the way back to Oakley. Okay?"

"Okay," she smiled with happy eyes.

On the way back to Declo my mind was fired up like a great boiler in a locomotive. I had just been hugged by one of the most beautiful and enchanting girls I had ever met. Not only that, but she said she liked me. Did I tell her I liked her? Well, not in words, but I think she got my message.

The next day when I dropped off Mary's car, I decided to talk to Ur about Luther.

"Well, try not to get hurt," was all that Ur said. It seemed like he hadn't understood my situation very well. However, I was sure part of the problem was that I didn't communicate clearly the situation to Ur or he would have been more concerned.

...sometimes you must walk into the cold, biting wind to get where you want to go. If you always walk with the wind to your back, you might feel more comfortable, but you are not free to go where you want to go.

# CHAPTER 26

## I Have a Right to Overcome the Effects of Another's Offense

On Thursday night we wrestled ISDB. The gym was packed even more than usual, partly because the crowd wanted to see the incredible deaf-blind guy thrash the home-towner, and partly because Declo was wrestling country. Ur, Mary and Mr. Johnson were seated on the lowest part of the bleachers. Chet and Evelyn even came over to watch Joy cheer and me wrestle. I wanted to do well, but the last time I wrestled Luther he did everything but stack me on my head.

Before the match my nerves turned my mouth into cotton. I wasn't just scared to death, but had already died, had my funeral, and been put into the ground with flowers growing on top of me. As we shook hands, I was glad he was blind because he would have read fear in my eyes. He turned his back to the ISDB crowd so they couldn't see and spelled, "LOOK, DOG MEAT, LEAVE JOY ALONE. SHE IS MINE!"

I glanced up at Joy and felt disgusted at the thought of this guy touching her.

The whistle blew and for the next three rounds I was made out to be a fool. He played with me like a cat plays with a mouse. He sought every chance to inflict pain. He used a deep waist ride that robbed me of my wind while clawing and pinching my belly where the referee couldn't see. He got me into the guillotine, a painful pinning combination, and then just before the referee would have slapped the mat, he let me up to stagger for a moment, only to take me down again and screw me up into some other pinning combination.

I looked like an idiot. I was embarrassed and scared. In the third round the entire gym became quiet. Even the ISDB crowd, who knew me from Joy and my association with Ur, was disgusted and shocked by how foolish I was being made to look. Finally, just before the end of the match he pinned me.

"LEAVE JOY ALONE OR NEXT TIME I'LL BEAT YOU WORSE!" he spelled in quick jabbing signs.

There was complete silence, a humiliating, painful silence which Luther neither saw nor heard as his hand was raised in victory. He slugged the air in triumph. With my face flushed, and before the next match, I went straight to the dressing room, dressed quickly and left without showering. Avoiding the crowd, I used a side door and walked home. The house was empty so I flipped on the TV and tried to bury my shame in a special on the Stock Market. Sitting there in the dark, I hated myself, my impotence, and most of all I hated Luther. I hated him and wanted to knock him into a thousand years. My teeth ground as I fantasized grinding his head into the gravel. Yet, I couldn't. I was powerless to legally do anything to him. For a moment I thought about catching him alone and wasting him with a baseball bat. I knew I wouldn't do that, so I let my thoughts drift to the people who watched me get humiliated. How could I ever face them? I cringed and sunk lower into my chair. How could I face Moose or anyone from Declo again? What did Chet and Evelyn think of me now? I'll bet Joy was ashamed and embarrassed of me. Luther would tell everyone how weak and lousy I was as a wrestler. Actually, he wouldn't have to say a thing. They'd already know.

A car approaching our small house at the end of our street interrupted my thoughts. It was probably Fred. If he said one word, I'd bust him so hard . . . a knock at the door. I sat there refusing to answer it. I reached over and turned the TV off and returned to my chair without even looking to see who was out there. The car left and I felt worse. Then there was a knock again. Who was out there? Why didn't they just go away? I sat there for 10 minutes. I hoped they were freezing. Then a louder knock.

"All right, I shouted," and went to the door. I whipped the door open and saw Ur sitting in his wheelchair in a light jacket. Immediately I was contrite for treating this dear man that way. I grabbed his wheelchair and pulled him up the step and into the house. He didn't say anything about how sorry he was for what had happened or Luther's un-sportsman like actions. All he said was, "So how do you plan to help him?"

"Help him?" I asked incredulously. "I want to kick his butt. Help him? I'll help him into an early grave," I raged.

"Is that how you plan to help him?" Ur asked in seriousness.

"I'm lost," I confessed in frustration. "What do you mean?"

Knowing I was exasperated, Ur began slowly, feeling for the right words while I turned on the lights. "You have the right to do the right thing. What is the right thing?"

I thought for a minute and then said, "I honestly don't know. Except getting my neck broke ain't the right thing. You already told me I have a right to protect the health of my body. So at least I know I don't have to lie down and let Luther pound me. Right?"

"Right."

I stared at Ur, trying to read his mind. To me it seemed simple— give it all I had and hope to win. That was what I always did and it paid off for me so far . . . 'kinda.

"Ur, I want to beat Luther more than any person I have ever wrestled."

"Why?"

"Why what? You know what he did to me tonight. He could have pinned me in 20 seconds and it would have been over, but instead he did everything he could to hurt and embarrass me. It should be obvious!" I knew I was getting defensive, but I didn't care.

"Why is it so much more important to beat Luther than some other opponent? Is it because Luther likes Joy, or is it because Luther is rude, mean-spirited, and generally appears to have a bad attitude?"

"Yes! Yes to all the above!"

"Is there anything else?"

"Anything else?" I whispered, my eyes sweeping the small living room as if searching for the answer.

What else could there be and what was the big deal about this match anyway, other than Luther wanted to hurt me, and I knew I wanted to hurt him too? That was the difference. In all of the other matches I never wanted to hurt anyone. In fact one time I accidentally dislocated another wrestler's arm. I felt real bad about it because it has never been my nature to hurt people—but, there was a difference with Luther. I hated him and even though hate was not a stranger to me, I had never felt it in sports, only for one of my mother's boyfriends.

"I hate him, Ur. I hate him with all the energy of my being and I want revenge!" I didn't intend to say hate and revenge, but when they came out of my mouth, for some reason, it felt good to say it.

"Jon, I want you to be totally honest with yourself and with me for a few minutes. Will you do that?"

"I'll try."

"Do you remember when I told you about my experience with the resistance army in Poland?"

"Yeah."

"Do you remember me telling you about Abraham Wiseman?"

"It is a little fuzzy. But what does this have to do . . ."

"Stay with me. You promised to be honest."

"Okay."

"Abraham was the old man dressed in black who had a long white beard."

"Yeah, yeah, I remember now."

Ur continued, "Something stood out to me and it wasn't his age. It was his whole countenance. In the midst of all this death and destruction he had a peacefulness, almost a cheerfulness, about him. This was such a sharp contrast to me that I almost loathed him for it at first sight. I thought, he couldn't understand what I had suffered? If he had experienced what I had it would wipe his happy face right off."

"Didn't he help you in some way?" I was calming down some.

"Yes. Remember that one morning when Mordechai ordered everyone out scavenging for food and weapons except me and the old man, Abraham. Mordechai said, 'You must learn something from Abraham, and this will never happen until you know him and are willing to listen. You are smart in your head, Ur, but you are not smart in your heart. You are not fighting the same enemy as we are—you are only fighting the same soldiers.'

"I sulked the rest of the day and then grew restless toward evening. Abraham treated me with kindness, but I was so filled with hatred and anger that I could only respond to everything he said with caustic remarks.

"Finally, with kindness I didn't deserve, he said, 'What would you like to learn?'

I want to know what Mordechai meant when he said I am not fighting the same enemy as you Jews, only the same soldiers.'

"'The enemy you fight is hatred and anger, my friend. We fight the Nazi to protect and save ourselves and our people. You fight to spew forth your hatred.'

"I felt accused. I told him I was justified in my hatred because I lost my family and I wasn't even a Pole or a Jew. Then he told me how he lost his family in the burning synagogue. Can you imagine how this made me feel, Jon?"

Listening to Ur, I realized I was not the only person who had suffered this feeling of helplessness and hate. I took Ur's hand to my face, feeling a bit more humble, and asked, "How can I forgive? I can't just say, no problem, you're forgiven, and it is done. Right now, to be honest, I am not sure I even want to forgive."

Though he was blind, I could feel Ur looking directly into my soul then he taught me from his great heart. "You forgive by overcoming the effects of their offense. And you find a way to put yourself back into the same or better position than you were before they offended you. Jon, you have to beat Luther. You have to become a better wrestler than he is, and you have to out wrestle him in a fair match. You don't have to humiliate him in the same way. You only have to get yourself in the same or better position than you were before you met Luther."

I stared at Ur. "I can't beat Luther. He is too good. He played with me like a cat plays with a half-dead mouse."

Ur's face was totally serious and he was slowly nodding his head when he said, "Jon, you can win! *Hope, belief* and *knowledge* will earn you that . . . privilege. I stared at Ur as he added, "Let's go back and watch the end of the matches."

In agony I whined, "Why tonight? Why not let it go tonight? I'll see people tomorrow." I wondered if Ur could feel my pleading and fear through his hand.

"I'm sure you feel embarrassed and going back is difficult, but sometimes you must walk into the cold, biting wind to get where you want to go. If you always walk with the wind to your back, you might feel more comfortable, but you are not free to go where you want to go. In life we don't avoid pain—we learn from it. We don't seek it out. Pain will find us often enough, but if we run from it or suppress it inside, it will begin to control our lives. The people you don't respect—like liars, thieves, cowards, and rapists—run from pain. Once they start running, it is hard for them to stop."

Ur put his hand on my arm and spoke with gentle determination, "I know that going back to the gym will be hard for you. It will be painful, but you must face it and walk through it so you will know that it is a wall of paper, not cement. It is the first step to forgiving Luther. If you see Luther, you will go up to him and congratulate him on his wrestling skills, and apologize for any difficulties you have caused him."

"What?" I shouted full of disbelief, "There is no way on this green earth I am going to apologize to him. He's at fault, not me!" I stood up and stomped around our small living room while Ur sat patiently waiting for my rage to burn itself out.

"Yes, he is, but part of the healing process for you is to make sure you have asked him to forgive you for any offense you may have done to him."

I returned to Ur. "He won't accept it," I stated flatly.

"He probably won't, but he will know at that moment that you are a greater man than he, and he will be uncomfortable in your presence until he resolves his own insults. He has the right to forgive too. Explain to him that the next time you two meet it will be your pleasure to give him a better match."

Ur turned his wheelchair around and faced the door, waiting for me to assist him out of the house. I felt a little lightheaded at the thought of seeing people, but Ur's face was set like flint and I knew with dread starting to fill me that I was headed back to the gym. While I hated more than anything going back, I knew I had to. Inside me I could feel it was the right thing to do—even though it wasn't the thing I wanted to do.

# CHAPTER 27

### I Have a Right to Face My Problems

We entered the gym as our 183-pounder began wrestling. I glanced at the score. So far we had lost one match— mine. I moved off to the side, hoping no one would see me. I didn't have any idea what to do next so I glanced around to see where Luther was sitting. He was sitting on the team bench, head down and cocked slightly to the side. No one was interpreting for him or even paying him any attention. He was totally lost and isolated from the events occurring just a few feet from him. His aloneness must be a constant wool blanket on raw flesh, I thought.

I could see that to him wrestling was his way of saying, "Hello world. I exist. I am here. My life has meaning." Had the pain of aloneness caused him to be like he was, or had it been something else? Was the difference between him and Ur just age and maturity, or had Ur channeled his pain so he could grow and learn from it? Had Luther's reaction to his problems caused a canker on his soul? Would his life be different if he knew and accepted his inherent rights? I knew the answer to the last question was without doubt-- yes.

Compared to Luther, Ur's life appeared to be tons more difficult, and also, Ur had suffered longer than Luther. It all had to do with perspective. Ur said once and then made me memorize this maxim from someplace: "A very large ship is greatly benefited by a very small helm in the time of a storm, by being kept workways with the wind and the waves. Therefore, let us cheerfully do all things that lie in our power; and then may we stand still, with the utmost assurance, to see the salvation of God, and for his arm to be revealed."

He said, "The little helm not only controls the ship in fair weather, but gives it the control it needs during the hard and dangerous times. The storm is not in our control, but the helm is. It is something we have the power to control, and when we work the helm right we can sail through the storms of life unscathed. Jon, the helm is our attitude."

The 183-pounder just pinned his opponent, and the Declo fans were going crazy. The last match was the heavyweight and since ISDB didn't have a heavyweight, they forfeited. With that new understanding of Luther, compassion sprouted. I started walking toward him when someone in the stands noticed me, and word spread through the crowd like wildfire. I guess my beeline and determined walk was misunderstood to mean that I was going to blind-side this deaf guy. When I neared Luther, some of his teammates stepped in front of me to block my approach. I quickly signed, "I just want to congratulate him." They looked at each other, shrugged, and let me pass.

When I tapped Luther on the shoulder, he turned and put his hands up for me to sign into them. When I identified myself to him, he slapped my hands away and signed, "Don't bug me, Dog Meat. You're not worth talking to." His coach started toward us shouting and signing, "Hey you, get away from him!"

Grabbing his hands I signed, "I just want to congratulate you on your good wrestling skills and ask you to forgive me." The coach saw what I signed and stopped to stare.

"Good," Luther signed. "Now you know I can hurt you. You better leave Joy alone or remember, I will beat you worse next time."

My ire started to get up at this statement. So I grabbed his hands again and signed, "Next time we meet, you're road-kill!" It wasn't exactly what Ur had said, '*It will be my pleasure to give you a better match,*' but it meant the same and I think he understood it. I turned and saw my team in an open huddle waiting for me to join them. It was then I noticed that everyone was watching me, not with sad, disappointed eyes that said I was the only loss of the evening, but with eyes of pride.

"You'll get him next time, Jon!" someone shouted and the Declo crowd cheered.

My eyes started to burn as I ran toward my team where we embraced and shouted, "HORNETS!" It was over. The humiliation was gone, and I knew this little community accepted me even when I lost. It seemed like everyone wanted to shake my hand and ask what I said to Luther.

Joy saw what I signed to Luther and was telling her parents as I approached. Chet stuck out his hand and said, "I'm proud of you, Jon. Next time I hope you kick his butt good!"

"Chet! Don't say things like that," Evelyn scolded with a smile.

Chet laughed and said, "I can't wait to see the next match. When is it?"

"Well, we're in different districts so I won't meet him at the District tournament. I guess the next possible time is at the State Tournament. The State Wrestling Tournament's in Twin Falls so it won't be a long drive."

"We'll be there," Chet said. "By the way, Jon, I never was a wrestler, but I learned a few things when I was in the Marines."

"I don't want to kill him, just beat him," I teased.

Chet laughed, "I can probably show you a couple of moves that will help without killing him or even wounding him, except maybe for his pride. If you have a minute I can show you right now."

"Chet," Evelyn chided "Not now. It's late and I am sure Jon is anxious to get home."

"It will only take a minute. Are you game, Jon?"

"Sure, why not."

Most of the people had already left except for a few old-timers standing around discussing their glory days. Chet kicked off his boots, removed his big belt, and walked out on the mat. I took off my letterman's sweater and joined him.

"I noticed he likes to ride you from the back, and each time you stood he started to try and gather you up. What was he doing?"

"He was trying to do the soufflé. That's why I kept dropping back to the mat."

"What's that?"

"It's kind of a circus throw…a little dangerous." I explained.

"Okay, let me show you something. You get behind me like you're going to throw the soufflé on me"

As I wrapped my arms around him and began to gather him up, his rear end slid sideways, and faster than you can say "slop the hogs," my feet were sailing up over my head and I was headed to my back.

"What was that?" I asked as I stood up shaking my head.

"Let me show it to you again a little slower. Grab me again."

Very carefully Chet showed me how to rotate my hips and slide my inside foot behind his and then straighten up while driving with my elbow into his chest. The move was really very simple, but effective. After that he showed me a couple of other things that had to do mostly with using my balance and weight to gain the advantage.

I thanked Chet and felt amazed at his interest in me. After confirming I was bringing Joy home tomorrow night, they left. I headed to Ur's house, hoping to see him and Mary before they went to bed.

# CHAPTER 28

## I Have a Right to Learn From Pain

The light was on, so I knocked.
"Jon, we were hoping you would come by," by," Mary said as she hugged me. "Do you want a cookie a cookie and some milk?"

"Sure, thanks." I sat at the table near Ur as Mary dug out some cookies and a cold glass of raw milk from the Johnsons' farm.

Ur was looking my direction. I spoke into his hand, "Thank you for what you did for me tonight. I can only imagine what I would be feeling if I'd not gone back. You saved me again."

Ur smiled, "Don't give me too much credit. You are the one with the courage to go back and face the dragon. Ur's countenance darkened for a moment, as if there was a dragon in his life he had not faced yet. Then just as quickly, it was gone. "What is your plan to win next time?"

"Well, I will just work my guts out and…"

"That will not be enough," he stated flatly. "You will have to work smarter, too, and decide to *believe* you will win. You will have to think differently. You must use your imagination and visualize yourself beating him and standing on the highest platform wearing the state champion medal. I am not a wrestler, but I understand the principles you will need to win next time. You need four perfectly executed moves that you can do in your sleep. Don't try to perfect all of them at once. Work on them one at a time. Perfect a takedown, reversal, escape and pinning combination."

"Whoa," I interrupted. "I can't remember all of this."

Mary stepped in, "Ur, you're going too fast. Slow down."

Ur smiled, "Okay. Mary has written it all down. If you are willing, we will help you win the state championship. Are you willing?"

I looked from Ur to Mary and then I stood, walked to the window and looked out into blackness. I could tell this was going to take a serious commitment on my part. Ur said once, "Only things big enough can motivate us." Was this big enough? I knew it was. I always dreamed of a state championship, but in reality I never really *believed* I could attain it. Now I knew if Ur said it could be done, it would be done. But did I have enough inside of me to stay with it? State was four weeks away. That was a long time for me to stay focused on something. But, if I did it, maybe I could become something different, and I knew I wasn't just talking about the state championship.

I turned around and hugged Mary and then Ur and said, "I am willing, but I don't know how to do it. I will have to trust you on that." Mary hugged me and Ur beamed. "You said, 'We will help you.' Who do you mean 'we'? Do you mean you and Mary?"

Mary refilled my glass with milk while Ur explained, "Yes, but I also mean everyone who cares about you. Mary talked to your mom tonight and she has agreed to let you take your breakfast and lunch with us. We are going to put you on a diet that will help you increase strength and stamina. I'm afraid you have eaten your last cookie for awhile. Tomorrow morning meet me here at 5:30 and you will get to push me around the mile square."

"You're kidding, that's four miles!"

"And bring a scarf to cover your mouth. It is cold and I don't want you to frost-burn your lungs. Then Mary will give you a good breakfast and you can go milk the cows for Mr. Johnson."

"Wow!" I thought. "This is going to be tough."

"You have to think differently. You must think greater thoughts. It is a fact that your mind limits or empowers what you do. If you want to do more you must begin to think bigger, and I am not just talking about thinking on the surface. The *belief* has to go deep into the roots of your soul. This isn't about the "I think I can train." There has to occur a fundamental change in the fibers of your thought. We will show you how to do it. If you yield yourself, it will forever change the pattern of your life."

I sat nibbling my last cookie and thought, this is what I have been hoping for—a challenge that would allow Ur to teach me how to receive the privileges of life. I can gut it out for a month. I can do anything for a month!

"Jon, remember when I first showed you the cedar post?"

"Yes."

"Remember how you threw all of your energy into the post for a short time without success?"

"Yes," remembering how I nearly tore the skin off my hands trying to remove the post and get the thousand dollars. "You said, 'There is rarely ever an "all-at-once" in life. It's usually a long grind,' or something like that. Oh yeah, and you said that I'd get happiness while getting the post out.

Ur smiled, "Ah…close, Jon. Happiness is cleverly nested in the process of attaining predetermined, worthwhile goals. In other words, enjoy the journey for the next month. Keep your mind positive and under control. Optimism is the sunshine that melts the impossible and gives growth to the dream. Feed your hopes, Jon, not your fears."

I got ready to stand and then said, "Thanks, Ur and Mary. You folks are great! I better go now—it 's almost 10:30. I'll see you in the morning. Oh, by the way, what time do you want to leave tomorrow for Gooding?"

"Four o'clock will be fine."

"I'll have the car all gassed up and ready to go," Mary added, "and, Jon, make sure you use my car when you take Joy home."

"Thanks, Mary. See you tomorrow."

The old Big Ben alarm clock rattled me to life at 5:15. Fred pushed me out of bed with the heel of his foot and then collapsed into a still life of a beached whale. I pulled on some sweats and a hooded sweatshirt, then rummaged in the chest of drawers until I found heavy wool socks to pull over my hands. I wrapped a towel around my neck because I couldn't find a scarf. I slipped out the kitchen door so as not to awaken Mom and started jogging toward Ur's house. The cold bit at my face. In my heart I hoped Ur had overslept. He hadn't. He was sitting outside the kitchen door, bundled up and waiting in his wheelchair.

I rattled his chair and he smiled. "Let's go," he said cheerfully.

I had to balance Ur's chair on the back wheels because the front wheels tended to slap back and forth on the paved road as I ran. The harvest was over and the morning shift at Simplot's, Ore-Ida and U&I Sugar factory was over, so we pretty much had the road to ourselves as we headed east. Once in awhile someone headed for an early shift passed, but for the most part, we ran along under the stars on a clear, moonless night. The air was crisp, and as we past farmhouses the yard lights illuminated my breath.

By the first mile I was starting to hurt, and as far as I could tell Ur must have been asleep. He had not said anything. Then rounding the corner for the second mile, Ur began talking about his experiences in the Underground during the war. I was so caught up in his story, I forgot my tiredness; and before I realized it, we were at the end of the third mile. Rounding the last corner to begin the fourth mile, Ur lapsed into silence again. Because I couldn't sign to him while I was pushing, I just trudged on. The last mile was hard, and I struggled to keep my mind locked on running. Then something seemed to snap in my mind and I slowed to a walk. Ur understood what had happened. He spoke, "Get the thought back in your mind and lock it."

I stopped the chair and faced Ur, "Why don't you keep telling me stories to get my mind off the pain?"

"I want you to feel the pain. Unless you feel the pain and learn how to deal with it, it will beat you when you least expect it. Pain makes cowards of everyone who does not know how to deal with it. Pain is a fleeting friend." I smiled at his small humor, shook my head to clear out the negative thoughts, focused on the pain and started running again.

It wasn't long until I was helping Ur through the kitchen door. A rush of heavenly smells flooded the brightly lit kitchen. Mary was listening to KBAR while putting the final touches on a great breakfast of homemade bran muffins, clover honey, orange juice, eggs, hash browns and a small steak. "Take those vitamins I put on your plate," Mary said. "You are going to need all the help you can get for this next month." I dutifully popped in a One-a-Day.

When I arrived at Mr. Johnson's farm, he was up and wanted to show me something. I looked at him curiously as he led me down into his basement.

"Mary called last night." He opened a door and we went into the fruit room, "She said you were going for the state championship. She wanted to know if there was anything I could do to help. Mr. Johnson flipped on the light and walked over to the side and threw back a green tarp. Underneath was a complete weight set of dumbbells, a curl bar and a disassembled bench set.

"You may not think it now, but at one time I was quite a weightlifter. I did it all through college and won a few awards. Weightlifters are not bodybuilders. We didn't try to bulk up into masses of hard body muscle. That would have only put weight on us, and like wrestlers we competed in weight divisions. So we always tried to get more strength without putting on much weight. I want to see you get that championship, Jon. What happened to you last night wasn't right, but what you did afterwards—I mean coming back to the gym and meeting that jerk again—showed your real mettle. You come here almost every morning to milk. It takes you about an hour to do all of the chores. You keep coming and I'll do the chores for a month. I'll also have a workout schedule tacked up here on the wall for you to follow."

I stared in disbelief. My throat caught when I started to talk. I cleared it. "I don't know what to say. You don't have to do this for me."

"Maybe not, and yet maybe I do." He walked over and picked up a 50-pound dumbbell and curled it like it was a Twinkie. "When I was a kid I got myself into trouble with the law. The police officer who arrested me took an interest in me and invited me over to his house to put on some muscle. I went over thinking if I put on some muscle I'd be a better fighter."

I just couldn't imagine Mr. Johnson in trouble with the police, especially in trouble for fighting.

"That policeman taught me more than just weightlifting; he taught me how to like myself and respect others. I went to his house for about a year before he was killed in the line of duty one night." His face darkened at the painful memory. "His wife gave me his weight set. She said he would have wanted me to have it." His voice grew husky and he coughed. "That lady who gave me the weight set is Ur's sister, Mary."

I looked away to save him embarrassment. Kneeling down I touched the metal while he got control of his emotions.

"You're not the first kid to eat cookies at Mary's table. I've eaten quite a few there myself."

"Mary and Ur are sure finer than frog fuzz," I said honestly. "We don't have any weights at the high school. Could you show me how to use these?"

"You bet. I know you're going with Ur tonight up to Gooding, so after chores on Saturday I'll get you set up and lifting, okay?"

"Okay!"

"One more thing, Jon. You're going to have to lean into the harness pretty hard to get ready for state."

"What do you mean?"

"Well, when we used to plow with a horse, to get more done the horse had to lean pretty hard into the harness to pull harder on the plow. I ain't never seen a field plowed by the plow pushing the horse around the field. I can't be the one pushing you and neither can the weights. You're going to have to lean into it yourself."

# CHAPTER 29

## I Have a Right to Visualize Good Things

All during Ur's lecture I had a hard time staying awake. One time when I drifted off I awoke to see Joy staring at me, smiling. "Sleepy?" she signed.

"Yes," I signed low and private to her. "Explain later."

After the lecture, there was a reception held for Ur. This was his last lecture and people had come to meet him. Ur didn't need me so Joy and I walked to her dorm to get her things. I explained to her why I was so tired and she said, "I will ask Ur if I can drive us back to Declo, and then you can get a nap."

"Do you have a driver's license?" I asked.

"Yes, of course. Why wouldn't I? And if you say it's because I am deaf, I'll slug you," she said a little defensively, mixed with teasing.

"I guess, I just never thought about it. I'll drive for awhile, but if I get tired I'll turn it over to you, okay?"

Just past Twin Falls I turned it over to Joy. I gazed at her while she drove, the dash lights illuminating her features in a greenish glow. "I like you," I signed. She caught my signs out of the corner of her eye and reached out and took my hand. She hooked her index finger into my index finger for the sign "friend" and then rested our hands on the seat between us. The next thing I knew, I was startled into consciousness as the car crossed the railroad tracks in Declo. Joy laughed at me for jumping.

After assisting Ur into the house, we headed for Oakley. At her place, Chet and Evelyn seemed disappointed when Joy said I needed to leave soon because I had to get up so early. Evelyn invited me up for Sunday dinner and I accepted.

On Monday night Ur and Mary asked me to go bowling with them. "This is part of your training," Ur said.

I couldn't, for the life of me, figure out how bowling could possibly help me wrestle. We pulled into the Y-Dell Bowl in Burley and you can imagine my surprise when Mary carried a bowling ball bag for both her and Ur. She acted as if nothing was unusual. After we entered the Y-Dell, I took Ur's hand to my face and asked, "How can you bowl?"

Smiling, Ur said, "A picture is worth a thousand words. Watch."

As I rented a pair of ugly bowling shoes and grabbed a heavy ball that wouldn't stick to my fingers, Mary filled out the score chart. Ur was the first up. I watched Mary maneuvered his chair onto the runway and set it just so on the runway marks. Locking his brakes she removed both armrests from the wheelchair and asked me to bring Ur his ball. With a dubious expression I dug in Ur's bag and brought him his ball. Then I backed away to watch.

He sat with the ball on his lap for a full minute, his head down as if he were trying to remember something. Then in one smooth motion he leaned over the side of the chair, swinging his arm back then bringing the ball forward in an easy graceful motion. The ball rolled slowly down the lane going first toward the gutter and then arching back to the center making a perfect strike. I stared in disbelief. No way, Jose, I thought! Mary jumped up, squealed and quickly made an X on his palm. He beamed in delight.

Mary was next. She made a good approach and delivery. Her ball rolled straight into the pins leaving a spare on the left side, which she knocked down with the next ball.

I had never really been much of a bowler. In fact, I probably looked more like a hog running on ice than a bowler, yet I enjoyed it just the same. Usually I bowled about 65 to 80. Once I even bowled in the 90's. I hooked my first one and barely hit one pin. With the second ball I blasted it down the lane, hoping to compensate for lack of skill with velocity. I nearly broke the pins but left three standing. That was about my average.

On Ur's next ball he took them all out except one. Mary explained which pin was still standing and he got it. Then Mary scored a strike. I rolled a gutter ball, and with my second try knocked six pins down. We went through several rounds with Mary and Ur doing excellent and me putting on my usual lackluster performance. It didn't bother me because I never aspired to star on Bowling for Dollars.

In the sixth frame Ur said, "Jon, now it is time to begin training."

Unsure of what he was driving at I said, "Ah...all right."

"Who has the highest score, you or I?"

"You, by far," I admitted.

"Does that seem unusual to you?" he asked innocently.

"Like a palm tree in Idaho."

Ur paused with a glint in his eye as he searched for my meaning then he nodded with a smile. "So what is the obvious question?"

"How do you do it?" I asked.

"Visualizing, I am visualizing it. I remember what bowling alleys look like. I bowled before my eyesight was taken, so that is easy. Mary sets me in the exact same place I am visualizing each time. By the way, we have practiced quite a bit since I moved here. Mary is on a league so we come often during the day to practice. What is important is that before each release I visualize exactly where I want the ball to go. I am sure I don't understand how it works, I just know it does.

I heard once about some research that was done with three basket- ball teams. All three teams were chosen to be as equal as possible. Then one team practiced an hour each day. The second team sat in a room and was led through visualizing exercises. They visualized passing, shooting and working their plays. Then they ran to keep in shape. The third team did nothing except run. At the end of several months the three teams played each other again. It was not surprising that the team who just ran was the poorest of the three. But it was surprising that the other two teams were still equal. The researchers concluded that visualizing was a powerful tool in improving performance and altering behavior."

I wasn't sure what this had to do with training or bowling, but I thought the research was interesting.

"I want you to do something. I want you to stand holding your ball in front of you, and before you make your approach to release the ball take a minute, close your eyes and visualize the whole process of running and releasing the ball. In your mind, watch the ball roll down the lane and hit in the right place to get a strike. See every pin fall and the big X appear above the lane. After you have done this, open your eyes and without thinking of anything else just walk forward and bowl your ball. Can you do that?"

By now, I had learned that when Ur was trying to teach me something, I was better off to just do it and try to figure out later what he was doing. "Yeah, I can do that."

I did exactly what he told me. In fact, I started my approach before I opened my eyes. The ball seemed to release the same as always except this time it went straight for the lead pin. I stared in disbelief as the ball rolled exactly as I had visualized. Every pin fell. I glanced at Mary. She made an X in Ur's hand. He grinned brightly and nodded his head.

I went back and sat next to Ur. "How did that happen?" I asked.

"Do it again—now."

I did it again. In fact I did it three more times, and each was a strike.

"How many strikes did you make tonight before you visualized?"

"None."

"And then you do four strikes in a row?"

"Yes."

"Jon, what changed?"

"I visualized."

"Was that all?"

I thought for a moment. "Yeah, I think so."

"You are right! Visualizing is a tool to change as well as enhance behavior. Now you need to begin visualizing the state championship. When we get home, I'll help you write an affirmation card.

"A what?"

"Don't worry about that now. Let's finish our game."

This would be an even better story if I could say that I bowled perfect strikes after that and went on to win Bowling for Dollars, but I didn't. Ur had said, 'Visualizing enhances our performance, it does not replace practice and determination.' Regardless, his point was well made and I was a *believer* in visualizing, or maybe a better word was a *knower* of visualization because I had experienced it.

After bowling we drove back to the house where Mary put some crisp sliced cucumbers in some kind of sweetened vinegar water for snacks, and Ur explained about affirmations.

He told me affirmations help keep you focused and they also help change your mind so you think differently. They are a powerful tool and need to be used with wisdom and great discretion. "It is like medicine: if you use it wrong it can harm you."

I listened, wondering how this tool could be harmful, but like before, I knew to wait and listen first.

"Affirmation is a positive statement written in the present tense about what you want to become. Say, for example, you want to become a better student. You write, 'I enjoy the satisfaction I receive by studying hard and receiving better grades.' You read this statement often during the day."

"That wouldn't be hard because I could memorize it," I interjected.

"No, that would not do. It must be read. The subconscious part of the brain seems to learn better through reading. It is your subconscious thoughts that controls most of what you do. If you want to change behavior, you must change your subconscious thoughts."

"Uh...I'm lost," I confessed.

Ur smiled, "I think, I am going too fast. Let me slow down. Jon, your brain has a conscious and a subconscious part. The conscious part is what you are aware of most of the time. It is the part you control, but the subconscious is the part that mostly controls you. It is the pattern of your soul, or in a more rural sense it is the ruts of your soul."

When he said ruts, I knew exactly what he meant. Some of the roads I drove on out in the desert, especially around Yost, Idaho, had never been paved or even graveled. They had deep ruts made by many trucks driving on them when they were muddy. If you drove in a rut, you pretty much could turn loose of the steering wheel and take a nap because the truck would naturally follow the rut. One time I slid into a rut so deep that the pickup high centered on the bottom. Kenny and I had to walk about five miles to a ranch and borrow a tractor to pull the pickup out. I hated driving on roads with ruts. I had to fight the steering wheel to keep the truck going where I wanted to go.

If I understood Ur right, he was saying there were ruts in our subconscious that made our behavior go a certain way even if we didn't particularly want to go that way. Now I understood what it meant when people say they are stuck in a rut. They are going a direction they don't want to go, but feel they don't have a choice.

You understand about ruts don't you, Jon?" Ur asked sincerely.

"Like ugly on an ape. I understand ruts."

"Where do you come up with these colloquial phrases?"

"Is that what they are? Well, I heard that one from Festus Hagan on *Gun Smoke* one time. I just pick them up here and there or I make them up myself. I think they explain things clearer sometimes."

"Well, they certainly are colorful." He put back on his teacher's expression and said, "Okay, affirming helps to smooth the road and then to make ruts to the places you want to go. People act like they do basically because of ruts they have, and the ruts are made by how people think. A proverb says, 'As a man thinketh in his heart so is he.' Just as a rut isn't made by one passing car, so a new way of thinking is not made by one passing thought. You must read the affirmation often, not memorize it. Now to make the process work even faster, you also visualize the thing you want to be."

"Visualizing is like rain," I interrupted.

Mary looked up from some knitting she was doing while Ur stared in blank bewilderment. "Rain?"

"Yeah, rain. When it rains, it is easier to make ruts in a road."

"Oh, rain. I understand. Sure, it is like rain." Ur smiled and Mary smiled. "You read the affirmation and you visualize exactly how you want things to be. Here, Mary, will you write this affirmation down for Jon, please?"

Mary put down her knitting, went to a cupboard drawer, and took out a 3 x 5 card and a pen.

Then Ur repeated the affirmation, "I AM FILLED WITH CONFIDENCE AND STRENGTH AS AN IDAHO STATE CHAMPION WRESTLER."

Mary slid the card to me. "Does that sound right to you?"

I read the words out loud, smiled and nodded. Ur encouraged, "Jon, read it often, and visualize you winning the state championship in as much detail as possible. See everything in the greatest detail—the mat, the opponents, and the crowd. Hear the cheering and the shouts. Smell the mats, the gym and the opponents. Feel in your mind the struggle and the power of preparation. See in the greatest detail the moves you want to make. Do this again and again and again. Visualize every chance you get—while milking, driving, or going to the bathroom, and especially before you go to sleep at night. Read your affirmation often too. We don't have much time, and we want the ruts to be as deep as possible before the state tournament."

"Wow, this is neat," I whispered. "Is there anything I should be careful about so it doesn't work?"

"Yes. Be careful about bragging or telling people what your affirmation says. It sounds boastful and will invite people to criticize you and try to hold you back—except, of course, those who are truly your friends."

Privileges are the sweet things we strive to receive. These are the things we value most and are willing to invest our time, talents and wealth to receive.

# CHAPTER 30

## I Have a Right to Feel Gratitude

S oreness had become a part of my life. Running every morning with Ur and then pumping iron on Mr. Johnson's bench meant that by the time I hit wrestling practice I was already more worn out than a fall-down fence. Coach Chugg didn't let up either. With just a torn T-shirt and gym trunks to cover his woolly body, he screamed drills at us. I drilled on everything he asked; and after practice, even though I could hardly move, I stayed and worked to perfect four moves. Coach Chugg had his own farm to take care of, but he always stayed and let me practice on him.

In two weeks the awful soreness was replaced by a continual squeaking of tightened muscles. My face was leaner; the thin layer of fat that had rounded and softened my features was gone. I was taking on a hard body, cut look. Even though I lost the fat, I had not lost weight. It was replaced with rock-hard muscle. Mr. Johnson started me skipping rope to improve my speed. In fact, Mr. Johnson started getting up an hour earlier to get the chores done and be available to coach me during weightlifting. He was relentless in pushing me, and his knowledge about weightlifting was amazing.

At first it was awkward working with him, but soon the employee-employer relationship turned into a real friendship. When I struggled on my last couple of bench reps, he'd say, "You're a Wuss! You're a baby! Come on, jelly arms, do one more!" and other ridiculous insults. Sometimes I would bust up laughing so bad that he had to grab the bar to keep it from crushing my throat. A couple of times we got to laughing so hard that his wife came downstairs to tell us to keep quiet before we awakened the baby.

As my fat started to come off and the rangy look began to appear, he would shout, "Be an ant!" At first I didn't know what he meant and then he explained, "An ant can lift and carry eight times its weight on those skinny little bodies. Be an ant!"

Those were weeks of the greatest happiness I had ever known. What Ur said was true: "Happiness really is cleverly nested in the process of attaining predetermined, worthwhile goals."

Even my relationship with Fred improved. One morning when I got up to run I almost stepped on him—he was in a sleeping bag at the foot of the bed. Later, when I asked him what he was doing, he said, "Well, little brother, your body is getting so darn hard that it's like sleeping with rocks. So, I figgered that I'd just sleep on the floor for awhile."

I slugged him on the shoulder and said, "Thanks, Fred. I know you're just trying to help me get a better night's sleep, and I appreciate it. Only a couple more weeks."

He nodded with a grin and then got serious and said, "Win it all! Do it for the family, Jon." That was the first time I realized that through me Fred was feeling some family pride.

Early in the third week everything almost ended in tragedy. It snowed about three inches during the night, and the air was cold and calm when I got up to run.

As usual Ur was sitting outside his front door when I arrived. "I guess it snowed last night," he said as I moved his chair down the ramp and onto the street.

I stopped and told him, "Yeah, about three inches."

It was hard pushing him, but by this time I knew a little more difficulty would be good for me. The roads hadn't been ploughed yet and with every step the powder-like snow crunched and squeaked under my feet. When the snow got really cold, like around 10 degrees, it squeaked, and you could get pretty good traction when running through it. The snow was so light and powdery that it was like running through feathers. I padded along, listening to my muffled steps and to the constant 'swish-swish' of my frozen pant legs. The sky had cleared and it seemed I could see for miles in the blue light of the winter night.

In the third mile we turned to head west. Through the crystal-clear air, I could see the south hills to my right patched in black and white. Dimly I heard a vehicle coming up behind us. It was making a lot of noise, but I dismissed it as a farm truck. I was not paying attention to the approaching vehicle. Instead I was in a deep visualization where I was spinning Luther high over my head, when Ur sensed the ground vibrating.

"What is that?" Ur asked, his voice full of concern.

Jerking my head back, all I could see was a 16-ton truck with a nine-foot wide iron snow plough rushing upon us. It was kicking up so much powdered snow that the driver only occasionally caught glimpses of the road. He must have been going 50 miles per hour. Without thinking and in a nits half-life, I plunged Ur's chair toward the barrow-pit and threw myself in after him. The snow plow hurtled past, peppering us with gravel and burying us in snow.

In a second I was up. Snow swirling everywhere, and for a moment I thought Ur had been hit and catapulted someplace. Then I saw him, still seat-belted to his chair, but toppled over. His arms flopped grotesquely to the side. His snow-caked blanket was covering his face.

I immediately up righted his chair and saw the cut on his head bleeding profusely where he had struck a jagged lump of ice. I dragged his chair out of the ditch and onto the road. As I quickly examined him, I could tell he was dazed from the blow to his head. Heart pounding, I looked east and west to determine which direction would bring me to the closest farmhouse. Darringtons' house was about 200 yards away and I sprinted for it pushing Ur ahead of me.

My lungs were burning and my legs cramped when I pushed Ur into the farmyard. I could hear the milking machine running and see a light on in the barn. Rather than waste precious time looking for Mr. Darrington, I charged into his house, startling Mrs. Darrington, while shouting for her to call Mary. Grabbing a dishcloth I rushed back out to attend to Ur. I carried him up the back porch steps, through the mud room into the house and laid him down on the sofa. I heard that Mr. Darrington had been a medic in World War II, so I went looking for him while Mrs. Darrington began cleaning off Ur's face.

I found Mr. Darrington throwing hay to the cows. He told me to slip into the barn and check the automatic milkers and then come to the house. He went to see how Ur was doing. In a few minutes Mary was there, her face full of concern. Mr. Darrington said Ur had a nasty cut on his forehead, but he didn't think he had a concussion. I carried Ur out to Mary's car and we took him to Cassia County Memorial Hospital in Burley. I sat in the backseat holding him since he still wasn't communicating very well.

I explained to Mary what happened, and cursed myself for not being more careful. I guess I got pretty emotional, and Mary put her hand on mine. "Jon, don't blame yourself. These things just happen. You didn't plan on it happening, and you did the best you could under the circumstances. I am proud of you."

After the doctor checked Ur he told us he would be fine, but he will need some stitches and should stay in the hospital for a few hours for observation. Ur was sleeping now.

I called Mr. Johnson from the hospital and told him what happened and said I wouldn't be there to work out. Mary drove me home and said she would see me for lunch.

I didn't get to school until the middle of second period since I stopped to comfort Mom and convince her I was all right. Thankfully, Edith had already hurried over and told Mom that I was okay and would be home soon. It always amazed me how Edith seemed to know everything happening in Declo. It didn't matter to Mom. She still was worried. It seemed Dean's passing had left her pretty fragile.

I walked up the broad front steps of the school and saw Moose, who worked in the front office that period, run out of the front doors to meet me. Her face reflected the concern I was soon to know everyone had. She threw her arms around me and cried, "Are you all right?"

"Sure, I'm fine," I said with practiced nonchalance. I noticed other kids looking out the glass doors and some watching out of the study hall window. "How'd you know so soon?"

"This is Declo; everyone knows everything in Declo. I am so glad you're okay. We heard that you were busted-up, and Ur was in critical condition."

"I'm fine. I wasn't hurt at all, and Ur will be fine. They're giving him a few stitches and keeping him in the hospital awhile for observation. He's got a cut on his head."

Mr. Black came out of the principal's office as we entered and wanted to hear the whole story. He said he would make an announcement so everyone would have the right story.

At lunch Mary said she brought Ur home about an hour earlier, and Ur wanted me to come to his bedroom and see him. Entering the room I noticed the lights were off, but the curtains were open and sunlight was filtering in past Ur's bedposts and onto him. Hanging above him was some kind of a contraption that looked like monkey bars. I assumed it probably assisted him in getting up. His head was wrapped in bandages, and his face was a little paler than usual. He looked asleep, but I gently took his hand and spelled, "Hi."

He smiled and stretched, "I guess I was just catching 40 winks. How are you, Jon?" he asked with tender concern in his voice.

"Oh, I'm fine. I feel a little stupid after almost getting us both killed this morning. I'm so sorry!" I declared.

"Were you visualizing?"

"Yes."

"Then you have developed your ability to visualize to the point that it may help you, and as we have seen this morning, it may hurt you . . . and me," he said with a chuckle.

I grimaced.

"Please don't fret about what happened this morning. It was a fluke, and we should not concern ourselves with it any longer. Keep visualizing! I'll have to miss our run for a few days, but Mary will have my substitute in the wheelchair tomorrow morning. Keep one ear free to listen for snowplows."

When arriving the next morning, I was surprised to see his chair sitting on the back porch with a 50-pound sack of flour dressed up like Ur. There was even a volleyball with a face slightly resembling Ur's stuffed into the hooded sweatshirt. A note was pinned to the front of the sweatshirt.

"UR SAYS TO PUSH THIS DUMMY AROUND UNTIL WE CAN GET THE OTHER ONE FIXED.
LOVE, MARY."

I laughed.

I wheeled my new friend off the porch and headed east through town, past Ross's and Gillett's grocery stores, and then past Chet and Minn's Café and Bar. Wheeling past the high school on a slight downhill slope, I crossed Marsh Creek and the last streetlight faded behind me. My new friend was lighter than Ur so I decided to change my running route and head up toward Anderson's hill. This would be a longer run than usual since the pass over Anderson's hill was three miles away. I felt I could pick up my speed and maybe finish about the same time as usual.

I listened to the steady slapping of my sneakers as I passed from yard light to yard light. Usually that rhythm was a comforting companion, but this day it seemed to say, "You Can Win! You Can Win!" Again and again the phrase slapped through my brain. When I hit the bottom of the hill I knew I had about a two-thirds of a mile climb to the pass. I focused on keeping a steady pace. "You can win! You can win!" I dug my chin deeper into the scarf to keep frost from burning my lungs, and pounded out the rhythm faster and faster. I hit the top at full blast.

"Win! Win! Win!" I shouted. "Do something with your life! Be something different, something great! Leap for it!"

While I was catching my breath, my feelings started to change to gratitude; in fact, I was so filled with gratefulness that I couldn't contain my emotions. All alone on that windswept pass overlooking both Declo and the Dewey Ranch, I choked out in tears, "Thank you, God, for my life, for my mom, for Ur, for Mary, Moose, Joy and Mr. Johnson. Thank you for Mr. Chugg and even for Fred. And I thank you most of all for the rights and privileges you have given to me, that have made my life so sweet and happy!"

Looking out from the pass, I enjoyed a quiet moment gazing at Declo, its cluster of lights plainly visible as it snuggled in the blue hue winter. I took a deep breath of the crisp air and started back toward home. Reaching the foot of the hill, I glanced over at the Anderson Ranch. Its majestic red barn with the "Cross-A" brand painted on its broad front once doubled for a stage stop on the run between Albion and Burley. It was there, down near the water trough, on September 30, 1957, that Fred and I were told by a much older and distant cousin that our dad had died. Trudy Dawn, Anderson's daughter who was our age, was with us.

"Boys, I'm sorry, but your dad passed away this morning," he said soberly.

While riding away on our horses, I asked Trudy Dawn, "What does 'passed away' mean?"

"It means he died," she said. Our eight-year-old innocence protected us from the pain of reality.

I wondered what my dad would think if he knew his son was breaking out and going to do something big, like be a state champion.

Suddenly, a loneliness came over me and I slowed my pace. I hardly knew my dad, but there was a gnawing in a little corner of my heart that loved and missed him. It was like a small, dry branch that scratches on a stone when the wind blows, never making a large noise, yet over time leaving its mark.

"Dad, I don't know if you can hear me," I spoke in a whisper, my speed starting to pick up as I crossed the first canal, "but if you can, I want you to know that breaking out doesn't mean I'm not grateful for what you've given me. It only means that I want to be able to bring greater honor to your name and memory."

To be real honest, I wasn't sure what I meant. I only knew I wanted more out of my life than my dad had enjoyed. I wanted better opportunities for my children and grandchildren.

In a few days Ur was back with me, and the training continued uninterrupted until the day before state.

BELIEF IS A CHOICE.

RIGHT OR WRONG, GOOD OR BAD, YOU CHOOSE WHAT YOU BELIEVE IN AND THEN YOU UNCONSCIOUSLY BEGIN COLLECTING EVIDENCE TO SUPPORT YOUR BELIEF.

WHY NOT CHOOSE GOOD.

# CHAPTER 31

## I Have a Right to Be Free to Do Good

I had a standing invitation for Sunday dinner at the Reynolds house. Evelyn said, "Jon, you don't need to ask or be asked, just show up. You know we always eat after church about two."

Three days before the state tournament on February 12, 1967, I sat at the familiar dinner table of the Reynolds. I trained myself to eat carefully, but today it wasn't necessary. Evelyn mothered and scolded me every time it even looked like I was going to take too much.

. "Jon, not so much. You'll be too heavy for your wrestling."

I smiled and quipped, "Heck, that's just what I want. I want to get away from Luther so he don't pound me again. I'm afraid if he does I'll lose my place at your table." She threw the dishtowel at me that she always kept on her lap.

After dinner, Chet asked, "Could I talk to you alone for a moment?"

We put on our coats and stepped outside. It was a cold, shimmering clear day with a slight breeze from the west that cut at our faces. We walked out toward the barn, and I sensed that Chet had something serious he wanted to talk about.

"Jon, I'm a little hesitant to bring this up, but I feel like I should."

My heart went colder than what a well-digger sits on and my imagination took off like dandelion seeds in a hurricane. I knew Chet was going to say, "You know we all like you, Jon, but I don't think you should see Joy any more." Or, "Jon, you know how sensitive Joy is, and she just couldn't bear to tell you herself, so she asked me to say she has started liking Luther." This ridiculous thought jarred me back to reality.

While crossing from the house toward the barn, Chet pulled on his Bull Durham string, retrieved his bag and started building a cigarette. We stepped into the barn as Chet struck a match on his Levi's, squinted his eyes and lit the twisted end of his cigarette. He shook out the match and flicked it into the frozen barnyard. Chet sat on a hay bale while I turned over a grain bucket and sat across from him.

He sat for a long moment looking out toward the open door as if gathering his thoughts. Finally, he drew deeply on his cigarette letting the smoke partially drift out of his nose before blowing the rest out of his mouth with resolve, evidently ready to discuss whatever was on his mind.

"I don't talk much about these things … I don't know why. I guess it's just too personal, so try to understand me as best you can." He paused again and massaged his earlobe. "Did you know I was in the war with Japan?"

"Yeah, Joy mentioned it once."

"I was 20 years old when I was landed on the black sand beach of Iwo Jima. That's a 5X8-mile island south of Japan. The U.S. wanted it for an air base or something. It didn't have any cover from Mount Suribachi on the south to the deeply gulched and trenched high ground on the north. The job was given to just us Marines. I helped take Mount Suribachi. I watched that photographer Rosenthal take that famous picture of the American flag going up. The wind was blowing hard. I could've been in the picture, but it looked like they had enough help. I knew Ira Hayes and the other guys in that picture…"

"Is that the same Ira Hayes that the movie and the song were about?" I interrupted.

"Yeah, same one. A great guy. I'm sure sorry about what happened to him after the war. I understand his feelings. Sometimes, I still feel guilty for living too." He coughed and pulled the back of his raw-boned hand across his mouth. I heard his whiskers scrape across his hand.

"I'd been fighting in the South Pacific for over a year by then. My two best friends were killed on Iwo: Jerry Robinson from Davenport,

Iowa, and Ruben Strauss from Brooklyn, New York. Jerry was built like a fighter—stocky, big shoulders and a flat nose. Ruben was just the opposite—tall, lanky, thin faced, with dark beady eyes. Fighting together makes you close, closer than you you'd ever imagine. Those were two of the finest boys this country ever sacrificed during that hateful war."

He took one last drag on the cigarette, dropped it between his boots and ground it out in the manure on the barn floor. I noticed his hands were trembling a little.

"My time almost ran out too." He made eye contact with me for a moment and then continued. "The whole island was honeycombed with tunnels and fly-specked with pill boxes. You never knew what direction you might get shot at. The week after Ruben got killed, Jerry and I were moving up a gulch when from a small rise, a volley of fire hit. Jerry was shot in the face; the hit completely tore his jaw off. The impact knocked him unconscious.

I felt something slap hard on my chest," he unconsciously rubbed an area near his second button, "and then I felt a sharp stinging sensation. The wind had got knocked out of me and I couldn't catch my breath. I thought I had taken one to the chest. Fighting to get my breath, I crawled to Jerry and tried to stop the bleeding. The wound was too massive—he was choking on his own blood. There were still bullets slapping the ground around us, but we had a little protection from a rock. Jerry took two more hits in his exposed legs before he died."

Chet was looking directly at me, hoping I was understanding him. I didn't know what to say, so I just looked back at him and waited for him to continue.

"We laid there for two hours while that battle raged around us. I soon realized that I must have been stung with a ricochet instead of a direct hit. As I slowly started getting my breath back, I started searching my chest for a wound.

I'd picked up an American flag at a Fourth of July celebration in Rupert just before I left for the war. I kept that flag folded in my chest pocket. The bullet had hit that flag and bounced off my dog tags. I was lucky it hadn't been a direct hit.

After Jerry died there huddled next to me, while we waited for the skirmish to end, I took that flag out of my pocket, beings it was all I had, and covered what was left of his face to keep the flies off. Some of his blood stained it. Later, when I washed it, I noticed it had eight holes— because it was folded when it was hit. No matter I never got the stain out, I carried that same flag with me all the rest of the war. When I see it, I am reminded of why Jerry, Ruben and all of the rest of those 5,800 died on Iwo, and of the other hundreds of thousands who died in World War II. Do you know why they died, Jon?" He looked right at me waiting for an answer.

"I want to say 'yes, Chet', but I'm not sure I fully know. I want to say 'to preserve freedom,' but somehow I'm not sure that is enough of an answer," I said carefully.

"You're darn right, it's not enough of an answer," he replied, his eyes picking up the fire of his voice. "They died so that people would be free to do good. Whenever I see bad men hiding behind freedom and saying they have a right to do bad, I think of Jerry's face and the blood on this flag."

Chet reached into the right pocket of his plaid shirt and brought out an old, tattered and stained American flag that was about the size of a sheet of paper. He handed it to me, and I held it with awe. I couldn't remove my eyes from the sight of Jerry's blood, which had been put there 23 years ago to the month. The feel of the dark stain interrupted the silkiness of the flag. I unfolded it and saw the eight elongated holes.

Chet's voice was husky when he said, "Jerry and Ruben were as good of men as I've ever known. They were honest and moral and fun to be around. They both loved life and wanted to live it out to the most. Neither of them ever married or had ever been with a woman, if you know what I mean. They had parents and brothers and sisters and friends who loved them. They died to give others a chance to do good and to live the life they couldn't."

I started to hand the flag back , but was stopped when Chet said, "Hang on to it for a week. Tuck it away in your wrestling uniform and take it into battle again," he smiled. "This deaf-blind kid, Luther, puts a bad smell on the reason Jerry and Ruben died. He mocks their deaths by his rudeness and arrogance. He takes the protection of freedom they died for and cowardly hides behind it so he can have his own selfish, insulting way and do whatever he wants, even hurting other people, as if it were his right.

"A Frenchy named Toquerville said, 'America is great because America is good, and when America ceases to be good it will cease to be great,'" he looked at me. "It is a small war, but heck, it would sure give me pleasure to see Luther whipped. Take that flag and kick his butt for Jerry, Ruben… and me."

As I was folding the flag he reached out and slapped my leg. "I sure like you, Jon. If you ever get tired of seeing my daughter, I hope you come over anyway and see me and Evelyn. You're a rare one. I don't know what it is about you…but, I guess you're the reason we fought and died."

A quiet feeling settled into the barn, like the feeling you get at a cemetery or a church. This was another of those experiences where I knew what I had heard, but couldn't comprehend all of it. Still, I was deeply touched and said, "Thanks, Chet. You've helped me put some things in order today that Ur's been trying to teach me."

On Monday, the day before the tournament started, I went to Johnson's for my last workout. After Mr. Johnson and I did a light workout, he asked me to come upstairs. Mrs. Johnson and all of the kids were waiting in the living room when we entered. Six-year-old Danny, the oldest son, was holding a brightly wrapped box. The children all squealed with delight and jumped up and down when they saw us coming. I looked questioningly at Mr. Johnson and then to Mrs. Johnson, but said nothing.

Their four-year-old daughter Elaine and the two-year-old daughter LaNae ran over and hugged my legs. "Are woo going to min?" LaNae asked.

I picked her up and said, "I sure hope so, little Nae-Nae." She beamed at the attention and then wiggled to get down.

"Here," Danny said, holding out the present.

"What's this?" I asked.

The little girls clapped their hands on their mouths then shrieked, "Open it!"

I began opening it slowly to tease the children.

"You folks have already done too much for me."

"Oh, heck-a-mighty," Mrs. Johnson exclaimed, "You're the one who has done so much for us. Don't you keep us in good clean milk?"

I cringed as I remembered the night Betsy stood in the bucket.

I lifted the lid off the box and saw a brand new pair of wrestling shoes. Not the Converse basketball shoes I usually wore, but real wrestling shoes! Written with a felt-tipped pen on the side was "Rover Rules."

"What's that mean?"

Mrs. Johnson laughed and said, "I heard that deaf-blind kid called you 'dog meat.' Well, when I was growing up on the Northside we had a gray dog called Rover. I don't know what breed he was, but he had short hair and a big slobbery face. One thing for sure was that he was gentle as a lamb till someone crossed him, then he was meaner than a cornered badger. I figure you're a lot like Rover, gentle as can be, but tougher than boiled owl when you need to be."

The little kids insisted I put them on and see if they worked better than my old shoes. As I was lacing them up, the thought came to me: Acceptance and love sure can make a road gentle to travel. With all of the help from my friends, preparing for the tournament had been a pleasant trip.

Soon though, the plow would bite into the furrow, and I would find out what kind of mettle I was really made of.

# CHAPTER 32

### I Have a Right to Believe in Myself

O n Tuesday morning, just before we loaded on the bus, Declo High School held its wrestling pep assembly. We all strutted out onto the gym floor wearing our lettermen's sweaters with our big "D" letter on the front, our gold wrestling emblems attached to the "D" like badges of courage. All 12 of us had placed in district and were headed to the state tournament in Twin Falls. Our small pep band played the school song, and everyone stood and while clapping out a rhythm sang:

*"We give you a cheer, Declo High,*
*For a free shot and basket we'll try,*
*Come on keep your pep do not die,*
*We are all behind you now ... "*

I wondered why they sang about basketball to the wrestlers. I guessed it was our school song and that's what mattered. Besides, the attention felt great.

While Coach Chugg individually introduced the wrestling team, my mind wandered. I knew I was ready. I was as ready as I could ever be. My body had become hard and lean. For the last two weeks I had to workout against the 183-pounder, Crash Bingham. He was over 40 pounds heavier than me and also favored to place in state. At first he just played squash with me, but this last week I stopped being intimidated and started attacking with the determination of a pit bull and slowly started holding my own.

Even Moose had noticed a difference, "Jon, your eyes are so weird."

"How come?"

"I don't know. They look peaceful and fierce at the same time. It's like . . . oh, I don't know, just different."

"You all know Jon Rhoades!" The coach shouted into the microphone, its tinny sound reverberating throughout the gym. I stepped forward, hands locked in front of me and my shoulders squared back. "He is probably our most improved wrestler, but he is in a real tough weight bracket, so we'll have to see what happens."

That was a pretty mediocre vote of confidence, I thought.

As the assembly ended, the pep band struck up our fight song again and we all grabbed our ditty-bags and headed to the bus idling in the frigid winter air out in front of the school. A plume of frozen exhaust enveloped the back of the big yellow beast. The cheerleaders had taped a big butcher paper sign on the side of the bus: "Sting 'em Hornets! Take state!"

The bus was unusually quiet as we headed for the interstate. We had been on the road about 30 minutes when the 130-pounder announced that he was sick and needed to hurl.

Coach Chugg's voice boomed from the front, "Sick! How come you're sick?"

"I ate a can of sardines before the pep assembly and I guess there must have been a bad fish in it."

The 183-pounder threatened, "You better not toss your cookies, ah . . . or fish, on this bus or I'll pound you into hog mash!" The whole bus erupted with pleas to stop the bus and let him out.

"Shut up, you guys!" The coach shouted. We're late for weigh-ins already. Just drop that window and put your head out."

We all glanced at the windows, which were laced with frost. Suddenly the 130-pounder, who was sitting near the front of the bus, leaped up and struggled to open the frozen window. Soon, other brave wrestlers were jerking and cursing as they worked to open the stubborn window. In the nick of time, the window slammed down and the 130-pounder thrust his head out the slit and blew bits of tiny fish into a 60-

mile-an-hour wind. The rushing air whipped and painted the regurgitated fish along the entire length of the bus's windows. We wrinkled our noses and collectively screamed, "Sick!" The 130-pounder pulled his head back in and started wiping the spray from his forehead, cheeks and neck.

"That is the nastiest thing I've ever seen!" said Jeff, the heavy weight. "Coach, stop the bus and let him wipe those little suckers off the windows." Coach Chugg stared resolutely out the front window and mumbled something.

The Twin Falls High School gym was the largest gym I had ever seen. It looked like a giant warehouse with open steel beams that spanned from one side to the other. The 106-pounder expressed all of our feelings when he said, "Gees, you could put all of Declo in here."

The smell of wrestling mats was strong as I stood there with our team gazing at the eight mats already laid out. We felt small and intimidated. We felt like a bunch of farm kids wrestling out of our league.

Remembering something Ur taught me, I stepped up on the lower bleacher and looked around the gym until I found what I was searching for. On the far end of the gym was the victory stand. Stepping down from the bleacher, I walked across the mats and stood in front of it. I touched its smooth finish reverently and then climbed to the top platform, which had "State Champion" printed under it. My team watched me in silence. This was the dream of all wrestlers—to be able to stand on the top! To be the best! There would only be twelve, one for each weight division. I wanted to be one of the twelve.

Over the head of my teammates I saw another wrestling team entering the gym and stop to stare at me. It was ISDB. Louis quickly signed something to Luther. I could see some angry signing from Luther, but I couldn't understand what he said. Then with powerful and determined steps, Louis brought Luther to the stand. Louis and Luther were "two peas in a pod" except Louis wasn't near the wrestler Luther was.

"Get your butt off that stand. That's mine, and you're dog meat!" Luther signed, with quick, sharp signs accented with vicious grunts.

I smiled without malice and thought, You're right, at least as far as the dog meat goes. I stepped down and took Luther's hands. "I'm sorry for how you feel. Just call me Rover from now on." I took his powerful hand, shook it, and then we stood there clasping hands. His face started to turn red as he applied pressure to my hand trying to squeeze it into juice. It didn't squeeze. I stared at his blank eyes and knew at least as far as hand strength was considered I was now his equal.

He threw my hand to the side and tried to thump me on the chest with the heel of his hand. I saw it coming and stepped back. That caused him to overextend and stagger forward. In humiliated fury, he took a couple of swings in the air hoping to connect with me, but I just kept clear of him. Then he showed me a sign you didn't have to be deaf to understand. Taking Louis's arm he turned and they left.

My team watched the whole thing in amusement, then they charged me throwing me to the mat, yelling, "Dog-pile on Rover!" The intimidation of the big school, the big gym and the state tournament was gone, and our fear of littleness dissolved into a laughing squealing pile of puppies. Then we were all on the stand together acting crazy as Coach Chugg took our picture before we headed out to weigh-in for the tournament.

Every match in state competition is serious business. These are all good wrestlers, and any one of them could get lucky and knock off a top contender. Lose one match and you're eliminated from becoming a candidate for state champion. I had seen outstanding wrestlers do something stupid and wind up getting pinned by mediocre opponents. High school wrestling was not like the fake professional stuff that glorified violence and rudeness. High school wrestling put highly trained and conditioned opponents against each other in three, two-minute rounds.

Every wrestler knows he is out there on the mat all alone. There is no one else to depend on or to blame if he loses. He has six minutes to do all he can to put the opponent's back to the mat for a second or outscore him on points. Points are awarded for take-downs (2 points), reversals where the wrestler who is on the bottom gains advantage by switching from bottom position to the top(2 points), escaping the control of the top man (1 point), and near-fall which was almost pinning the opponent by holding his back toward but not touching the mat for three seconds (3 points). A wrestler could also get points if his opponent was penalized for illegal moves (1 point).

I was seeded in fifth place and Luther was seeded first on the tournament brackets. That meant that the coaches who put the brackets together thought I was the fifth best wrestler in the state tournament. Because Luther was seeded first he would have easier opponents to wrestle until the last round.

I skimmed down the list of other wrestlers in my bracket. The guys seeded above me were wrestlers who had placed in last year's tournament, including a last year's state champion, Brent Foster, from Teton High school in Tetonia. The coach was right. I was in a tough weight.

I started to feel a little discouraged. My first match was Thursday morning. If I won that one, I would have to meet Brent Foster. Brent Foster was seeded second, and the coaches, who made the tournament brackets, clearly felt he was the one to go against Luther in the finals. It said something about what the coaches thought of Luther if they would seed him ahead of last year's state champion.

Luther had demolished every opponent this year, including Brent Foster in the Grizzly tournament in Idaho Falls. His uncanny feel for the sport and his unusual strength were both respected and feared. He destroyed everyone he wrestled and treated all of them with the same rude contempt, except me. He treated me with a special kind of rudeness and contempt.

All of the hoopla and bravado was melting inside me like snow before the January thaw. All of the visualizing and affirming started to shatter like a slow-motion rock crashing through a window.

Our team was staying in the Blue Lakes Motel on Blue Lakes Boulevard. My roommate was gone eating supper with some of the team. I sat alone on my bed, drooping from discouragement. I felt lower than a snail's belly in a well. Maybe I couldn't even beat the first guy in the morning, I thought. Flinging myself back on the bed at the thought of seeing Ur, Mary, Mr. and Mrs. Johnson, Chet and Evelyn and the whole school if I lost, I blew out my breath in a huge blast of disheartenment.

"This will never do!" I said, and went over and started pulling my black and orange wrestling uniform as well as my new shoes out of my ditty-bag. In the bottom of the bag was a plastic bread sack. Opening the sack, I pulled out a bullet-riddled American flag. I unfolded it and held it in my hands. I stared at it a long time, trying to imagine Jerry, Ruben and Chet during the war. Jerry and Ruben weren't much older than I when they laid it all down for this country and for our freedom to do good. Brent Foster had not beaten Luther and maybe would not beat him during this tournament. How could I disappoint Chet? I thought of what he said last Sunday in the barn: "Take that flag and kick his butt for Jerry, Ruben and me."

How could I kick his rear if Brent knocked me out of the tournament in the second round?

The discouragement started to lift as I thought of my cause. I had to win. I, in my small way, was helping to keep the good things alive that Jerry and Ruben died for—-not just by beating Luther, but by trying to keep good alive. As Ur said, "It may be the best thing for Luther." I resolved to do everything I could to help Luther as much as possible. I smiled at the thought.

I took my shirt off and stood in front of the mirror. I first flexed my arms and looked at them in the reflection. I looked at the front, the back, and then curled them. The muscles stood out like ropes of steel with blue mole runs where the veins lay along the arms. Then I brought my arms to the front and did a power flex with my neck, chest, arms, and stomach muscles. Everything started to bulge and ripple, snapping and popping like spring steel. I took a wrestling stance and visualized Luther opposite me. I shook my head and put a tough look on my face. I sneered and curled my lip. Then I laughed at the thought that it didn't make any difference what kind of tough-guy face I put on, Luther couldn't see it. The only thing that communicated to Luther was what he felt.

Then I bounced up like Cassis Clay used to and dared Luther to attack as I danced away out of reach. "I move like a butterfly and sting like a bee," I taunted. I thought I had heard Cassis Clay say that once. I was really getting into the match and feeling the confidence coming back. Bobbing and juking and dodging . . . That was when I heard giggling.

I had forgotten to close the curtains, and there was a crowd of five or six cheerleaders in green and white cheer jackets gawking and grinning through my motel window. My brain froze, and I wanted to crawl into my new wrestling shoes and tie the laces tight around my throat.

Instead, I turned to the window and did another power flex and shouted, "HORNETS RULE!" Then I smiled, what I hoped was a cute little Paul McCartney smile, and closed the curtains.

Flopping down on the bed, I shook my head at how ridiculous I must have looked to those cheerleaders. I wondered which school they were from, probably Wood River up near Sun Valley. I was feeling better about things generally in my life, and especially how differently I handled the incident that just happened. A year ago because of my embarrassment, I would have become angry and shouted at the cheerleaders. I guess when someone is happy, he cuts people a lot more slack, especially himself. I knew I was happy—happier than I had ever before been. Getting off high-center and making something happen in my life had been part of the key.

Before I met Ur, I was like a bumble bee I once found trapped inside my car. I rolled all the windows down and opened the wind wings, but the bee kept banging his head on the front windshield. Like the bee, I could see where I wanted to go; but some invisible, yet real, barrier kept me from getting there. I remember gently trying to guide the bee to a window, but it refused to be helped, and its buzzing only became more furious.

I had been like that bee, determined to get out my own way and refusing all assistance. The solution to the bee's situation was obvious to me, but like the bee, I needed someone else like Ur to help me out of my own desperate dead-end. I finally gave up on the bee, closed the car windows, and went into the house. The next day the bee was dead.

There was a gentle knock on the door. Grabbing a T-shirt I slipped it on and opened the door.

"Hi," I signed brightly, looking into Joy's beautiful blue eyes.

"Hi yourself. What are you doing?"

"Oh, I was just daydreaming."

"About winning?" she smiled.

"Let me grab my coat. Coach says no girls in our rooms, but we can go for a walk, or are you driving?"

"I'm driving. Dad let me have the truck for a few days. Come on. Let's go to the A&W for a snack. There is one over near where our school is staying."

"Well, I'm not sure that's a good idea. Luther and I had a little set-to earlier today at the gym before weigh-ins. I'm a little nervous about seeing him again."

"Oh, okay. I know where there is a diner," she suggested.

We piled into Chet's 1965 red and white Ford F-250. The heater felt good as Joy skillfully maneuvered the truck out of the motel parking lot and onto Blue Lakes Boulevard. She took us to a diner on Highway 30 called Thousand Springs.

It was obviously a truck stop, with a parking lot filled with Peterbuilt, Mack, and Kenworth big rigs. Sitting across from each other so we could see each other sign, we talked and ate for almost an hour.

"Are you nervous about tomorrow?" she asked.

"I was really nervous earlier tonight when I saw that I wrestle Brent Foster from Teton in the second round. He's last year's state champion." I took a deep breath, "I didn't get seeded as good as I hoped. I guess I'll have to get this state championship the hard way."

"You're not nervous now?" she puzzled.

"Yeah, a little bit. But most of all I'm afraid of disappointing all the people who have helped and supported me. A lot of people have given a lot of time to get me ready, including your dad. I know I'm as ready as I will ever be, but one little mistake against someone like Foster or especially Luther, and it's over."

"Then don't make a mistake. I heard you have a new nickname, Rover? Where did that come from?"

I told her about Mrs. Johnson's dog. "Oh, and they gave me some wrestling shoes with 'Rover Rules' written on the sides."

As if on cue, we fell quiet and looked at each other. She was truly the most beautiful person I had ever met. Her red hair haloed her sunshine-freckled face. I loved her features and the playful expressions that continually danced across her countenance. Then she turned her head a little and squinted at me out of the corners of her eyes as if to ask, "What are you looking at?"

"Joy, you are the most beautiful girl I have ever seen. I am so glad we are friends."

Her expression grew cloudy. "Just friends?"

"Best friends!" I signed emphatically, crossing my index finger with the middle finger in the sign. "Best friends for now. What do you think?"

She brightened, "That is good, best friends. All romance must start as best friends, is what Mom says."

"Do you talk to your mom about me?"

Before she could answer, two drunks came over and sat next to us. One, with a flushed face and bad teeth, put his arm around me; and the other, pot-bellied and greasy, sat across from me with his arm around Joy. Their sour breath reeked of strong whiskey. "What are you little dummies doing?" the one next to me asked.

Fear and fire filled Joy's eyes. "Get away from me! Your breath stinks, and you're drunk!" Joy shouted in her deaf voice. The sound of it startled both men and drew the attention of all of the truckers.

In spite of the seriousness of the situation, I had to smile at Joy's spunkiness.

I spoke calmly as if to a child, "Now you two please leave us alone. We were just having a private conversation that does not involve you."

I think my voice was a greater shock than Joy's because I guess they had assumed I was deaf too. Recovering, the drunk next to me started to squeeze my neck in the crook of his arm. My right arm was lying across the tabletop so I brought my elbow hard into his gut with all my strength. I heard the wind go out of him in one great smelly whoosh. Then he and the other guy were jerked out of the booth by a couple of truckers and slapped to the floor where they stayed.

The truckers both looked like they could have been bikers with a bad gang. Both men were over six feet with full beards and big bellies. "You kids go ahead and run along while we entertain these two for a minute," one trucker bellowed, his eyes flashing in delight.

I tossed a $5 bill on the table to cover our meal, stood and thanked the truckers. Joy jumped up and on tiptoes kissed each man on his hairy cheek. "Thanks," she said.

Both men laughed, embarrassed, I guess, and one said, "Well now, Walt, was that worth it?"

"Heck, yes! Maybe if we slap them again she'll give us another," Walt laughed.

# CHAPTER 33

## I Have a Right to Do My Best

On Wednesday morning I took the mat against a fine wrestler named Lance Richardson from Parma High School. Parma High School, like Teton High School, was a powerhouse in Idaho wrestling. Dressed in black, Lance looked formidable. I glanced to where my private cheering section was seated. Mary was seated on the lower benches with Ur and the Johnsons. Chet and Evelyn were behind, them sitting with Joy. Just before I got on the mat, Joy kissed the tips of her fingers and blew the kiss to me. I smiled in spite of my nervousness. I bounced a couple of times to loosen up and shook my head. Coach Chugg rubbed the back of my neck and whispered, "Watch your legs. This guy has a great leg take-down."

After the referee checked the length of our fingernails and for oil on our necks, we shook hands and he blew the whistle. The next thing I knew I was on the mat. This guy really did have a great leg take-down! The referee signaled two points for the Parma kid.

I built a base by getting to my knees and then stood. Pushing my hips from him, I clawed at his hands and started moving away. Then I turned quickly to face him. I was free.

"One point," The referee signaled for me.

Circling this time, I waited for him to shoot at my legs again. When he did, I countered with a quarter nelson which forced his head to the mat and eventually caused him to flip over to his back.

"Two points, take-down!"

I locked onto him like a dozen C-clamps, and he didn't move until I heard the referee slap the mat and shout, "Pinned!"

We stood, shook hands and then the referee raised my hand in victory.

"Whew," I thought, "The first one is behind me."

Coach Chugg shook my hand as I came off the mat and said, "That was pretty impressive." I grabbed my warm-ups and went to speak with my friends.

Chet slapped me hard on the back and said, "You ever thought of being a bulldogger? That was quite a throw." Everyone laughed.

Ur reached out his hand and took mine. "Nice job! Any surprises?"

"Just one."

"What was it?"

"That I didn't cry from being so nervous." Everyone laughed again. "Thanks for coming. It really means a lot to me. I wrestle Foster at about two this afternoon. It would mean a lot to me to have you here."

"What're you saying, Jon? You know we wouldn't miss it for anything!" said Mrs. Johnson. "And say, you sure have classy shoes."

"Let me see those shoes," Mary exclaimed. What do they say?"

I stepped back and turned my ankle to the side.

"'Rover Rules'! What's that mean?"

"Mrs. Johnson's idea…let her explain," I said as Joy pulled on my hand. We walked over to where Luther was warming up.

"I guess I have to cheer for him," Joy said without enthusiasm.

"You cheer good," I signed. "I don't want anything to happen to him until the final night."

She smiled in a way that told me she didn't understand. I watched as Luther totally destroyed and humiliated a wrestler from the nearby town of Filer. It was sickening to see how easily Luther played with his opponent. Everything he did was technically legal, but unsportsmanlike. I could tell the Filer wrestler was being hurt, and soon those watching— family and friends—were booing at Luther. When it was finally over the Filer wrestler's mom yelled at Luther, "You're the most disgusting wrestler I've ever seen!"

Totally oblivious to the crowd's reaction, Luther smiled and put both fists into the air to cheer for himself.

I heard the announcer call Foster's match, so I asked Joy if she wanted to go over to watch. She said she had a cheer meeting to attend, but when it was over she would come find me.

Foster was wrestling a boy from Wood River. Foster could be the "poster-child" of what a wrestler should look like. He was powerfully built, broad at the shoulders and narrow at the hips. I had never met him, but everyone who had said he was a decent guy and treated his opponents with respect.

I hadn't noticed, but the Wood River cheerleaders were standing behind me. I glanced back at them, and then I heard some whispering and giggling. I glanced again and one cheerleader, who had *Jenny* stenciled on her sweater, said, "Hey, Mr. Muscles, how ya' doing?"

I smiled, "You girls really embarrassed me last night."

They laughed, and Jenny said, "Do all guys do that muscle thing to get ready for a match?"

Embarrassed, I started to move to the other side of the mat and then said, "No, just the strong ones. The skinny ones, they look like defeathered chickens when they do it."

The cheerleaders all laughed and said, "good luck."

Brent Foster was a work of art on the wrestling mat. He was a straight-forward power wrestler. His moves were quick and strong. His technique was almost flawless. It was easy to see why he was a state champion. I began to wonder how Luther could have beaten him so easily. I noticed that his only weakness was that he left himself open for the fireman's carry takedown. I tucked that bit of information away in case I needed it. Foster pinned the Wood River wrestler in the first round.

By 1:30 p.m. I was dressed in my orange and black wrestling singlet, jumping a rope in the warm-up area. Pretty soon Foster joined me. Teton school colors were the same as Declo. Only the style of our wrestling suits and colored leg bands would help the referee keep us apart.

"How ya' doing?" I asked.

"Pretty good!" Foster said, reaching for my hand.

We shook hands and I said, "I'm glad to meet you. I watched you wrestle the Wood River kid earlier. You're pretty good."

"You're Jon, aren't you? From Declo?"

"Yeah."

"You're pretty good too. I watched you put the screws on that kid from Parma this morning. When you get hold of something, you're like a bulldog—you just don't turn loose."

It felt good to hear a compliment from someone of Foster's stature. "Thanks, Brent. Can I ask you a question?"

"Sure," he said, as we both dropped down to stretch.

"What was your match like a couple of months ago with the deaf-blind kid, Luther?"

He shook his head and grinned. "Well, I'm not sure. First of all, I think I underestimated him, and second, he has unusual skills and wrestling savvy. But I think the main reason he beat me was that he was meaner than me. To me this is just a sport, and I do my best. You'll see that in a few minutes." He smiled and then I did too. "But for Luther, it's like he unleashes all of his anger and hatred on his opponent. To tell you the truth, I don't look forward to wrestling him again."

I glanced at him and replied, "Well, I'll try to help you out there, so you don't have to."

He stared at me for a minute and then caught my meaning and laughed. "You know, Jon, you and I are going to have a great match. Let's go for it!"

We stood and shook hands, smiled and then went to different areas of the room to focus.

I sat in a corner and began visualizing the whole match with Foster. I visualized in the clearest detail each move and counter move during the match. I was so engrossed that I missed the call and Foster had to come and get me.

I didn't have a chance to see if my little group of fans was there, but I knew they were. The referee checked us; we shook hands, and the whistle blew.

Foster took me down almost immediately. As soon as my knees hit the mat, I reversed him with a hip switch, grabbed his leg and began to ride him to the mat. Then he stood and escaped. I took him down again with a chicken wing only to have him reverse me.

It was a match like I had never had, the purest of wrestling joys, both to watch and to participate in. It was two highly conditioned and trained boys giving it all they had. The match was so intense, so fast and so full of skilled wrestling that soon the entire crowd was watching us. Nobody knew who they were cheering for; they only knew that they were seeing a clinic in the best of high school wrestling. When one of us would get an advantage or do a good move, the crowd cheered.

One minute into the third round the score had changed so fast that the referee stopped the match to talk with the scorer's table. Foster and I were both pouring sweat and breathing heavy, but we were not tired. We were feeling a euphoria that clears the mind and fills the soul with power. As the referee came back, Foster looked at me and I looked at him, then we both smiled and gave a man-nod. No matter who won this match we had both enjoyed something that most wrestlers never experience, maybe something greater than a state championship. We had experienced the pure joy of hand combat with an equal whose skills and being you respect. It was the total letting go of inhibitions and letting instinct and training takeover.

The score was 20-21 in Foster's favor. There was one minute to go before one of us continued in the championship bracket and the other went someplace else. The whistle blew and we locked again. It was like nothing had stopped. We went from one move to countermove, changing from top to bottom, to escape, to take-down. We traded the lead with each move. Finally the match ended with me trying desperately to finish a single leg take-down. We were tied at 28-28. We rested for a minute before the overtime round.

Mary brought Ur to the edge of the mat where Coach Chugg stood. "Coach, may I speak with Jon?"

"Sure, go ahead."

"Jon, you have been wrestling a great man. Mary has helped, but I admit I have not been able to follow it all. It seems your opponent is an equal in goodness and skill." I rinsed my mouth out with water and listened. "It will be sad for either of you to lose. Let me tell you why I think you should win. You are the only one who can beat Luther ... and it will be the best thing for Luther."

With that the referee called us back for the sudden-death overtime round of one minute. I was filled with adrenaline and fire! All the spectators seemed to be riveted on our match. The lifting, running, jumping rope, practicing, visualizing and affirming were paying off. I was 10 times the wrestler I had been before. I loved this sport! I admired Brent Foster. He was truly a champion in every meaning of the word. Between him and me there was not any anger, hatred, or even dislike. We were just two boys matching skill, strength and stamina in a contest as old as man. I could hear Mr. Johnson, Chet and Mary screaming at the top of their lungs. Moose and the other cheerleaders were pounding the mat as they sat cross-legged along the edge. This was it. I took my position on the center circle.

At the exact instant the whistle blew, Foster shot for my leg and snatched it. Lifting it high, he stepped forward to trip my other leg. I could not have been in a worse position. All he had to do was put me down and take control and he would win the match. I was hopping on one leg trying to keep ahead of him as we circled on the mat. He hooked my leg with the heel of his shoe and I began to buckle before I caught my balance and hopped up. The next time Foster thrust forward he accidentally forced me out-of-bounds.

"No points! Back to the center!" the referee yelled.

We started in the middle again, circling like two cats, each ready to attack. I tended to wrestle with my legs slightly bent, my upper body more erect and my hands in front. Foster wrestled bent over at the waist, elbows lifted. I also noticed as he shuffled forward, he lifted his right arm higher than his left. I remembered when I watched him wrestle earlier that he looked open for a fireman's carry take-down.

I hesitated and glanced at the clock. Ten seconds. There is a counter to the fireman's carry and I was sure Foster knew it, but the fireman's carry was the take-down that I had perfected. I hadn't used it yet because I was waiting to take Luther down with it; however, if I didn't win this match there wouldn't be a match with Luther.

I start circled to my left which made Foster instinctively circle to his left. His arm elevated slightly and I shot my left hand out and took hold of his left arm and pulled it down. Then I dropped slightly and shot my right arm into his crotch and I was under him. Foster went crazy. Writhing like a yearling bull calf, he almost toppled me over. Five seconds. I shifted my weight forward bringing him past my head to the mat and latched onto him like a saddle on a bronc.

"Two, take down!" Shouted the referee as the towel sailed in, ending the match. I sprang to my feet and extended a hand to Foster. I had no desire to gloat over his defeat. He slowly stood, and then bypassed my extended hand and embraced me as the referee raised my hand in victory.

"Thanks for a great match, Jon," he rasped, barely keeping his tears of disappointment in check.

"Thank you, Brent, for being such a great wrestler and a great person." I turned and ran into the arms of Chugg, Chet, and Mr. Johnson, and about 10 million other people who wanted to congratulate me. I hardly knew any of the people, but they all seemed to want to pat me on the back and congratulate me. I noticed a similar crowd engulfing Foster. I felt two soft arms come across my back and two kisses land on each cheek before I could move. It was Joy and Moose, my two closest friends! Both were crying.

"Great match!" Moose shouted. "Now don't get a big head," she teased as she left to go cheer for Crash.

"You did great!" Joy signed and voiced, "I am proud of you!" She hugged me.

It took almost an hour to get out of the gym and into the dressing room. When I did get there, Brent Foster was just stuffing his gear into his ditty-bag.

"Brent," I said, "I wish it was you and me going for the state title Saturday night. That would be a great honor."

"Yeah, that would've been great. I hope you win. I know you'll have your hands full. Luther is the most skilled wrestler I have ever seen, but he wrestles to hurt people, not just to win. He is the worst kind of person to be a state champion, because he gives the sport a bad name. Jon, you be the state champion."

We shook hands, stared into each other's eyes for a moment, and then embraced and pounded each other's back.

I predict future happiness for Americans if they can prevent the government from wasting the labors of the people under the pretense of taking care of them.

Thomas Jefferson

# CHAPTER 34

## I Have a Right to Forgive

Mary and Ur stayed over on Friday night in the Blue Lakes Motel. I had asked Ur if he and I could go for a run on Saturday morning. He said he would be ready at eight and that he would leave the door open for me. Entering, I found Ur dressed and ready to go. I loaded him and his wheelchair into Mary's Fury III and drove east out of Twin Falls for a few miles. I unloaded the chair and then carried Ur to it and strapped him in.

For Ur and me, running was a ritual. We never talked until we had run about a mile, except a few maintenance words to get us going. Today was the same. I started rolling him along the rural road into the sun. The crusty snow sparkled like twinkling diamonds in the winter sunshine. Fence posts stuck up out of donut rings where the sun had begun melting the snow. The air was crisp, and my breath exploded in blasts of fog with each stride. After rolling along for about a mile and I settled into a breathing pattern that was comfortable, Ur started to talk.

"Jon, Mary and I are very proud of you and your success, both as a wrestler and as a citizen."

I turned to the right and headed toward the Snake River gorge. Ur was quiet for a long time. "Where are we headed?" Ur asked finally.

It was awkward to sign and push Ur, but he lifted his hand from under the blanket and reached back. I pushed with one hand and spelled into his hand, "Wait until you feel it."

He paused with a question on his face and then said, "Okay."

We plodded along for about a mile before starting a steep descent on a winding road that clung to the lava cliffs. Entering the gorge, the air became noticeably cooler, and the road dipped sharply down. At times it was all I could do to hold Ur's chair back from taking off and flying over a jagged lava cliff. Ur grabbed the armrests several times as he sensed the steep incline. Near the bottom I noticed Ur stiffen.

"Jon, what is this place? I feel like my bones are going to rattle off me."

I pushed the chair closer to the source of the vibrations, and Ur smiled at the feeling.

"I feel like I did when I visited Niagara Falls."

Stopping the wheelchair on the overlook, I locked the brakes took his hand to my frozen face. "This is Shoshone Falls. It's where the Snake River flows over a ledge of about 100 feet."

"Oh, Jon, I love this feeling. It fills and wraps me from top to bottom with sound. Describe it to me."

I was never very good at describing things, but I plunged in anyway. "We're down in the Snake River gorge, maybe 300 feet from the top. The gorge has black, jagged rock of lava stone. The river has a spray of water that has built up ice on the rocks immediately around the falls. Oh, and there is snow along the ridges of the gorge."

"Thank you, Jon. Why did you bring me here? I'll bet the climb out will be tough."

"I've been here before on a school outing, and I thought you would enjoy it."

"I do! I do! It is magnificent! But my feet are getting a little cold."

I reacted quickly to cover his feet. "Ur," I said, "you don't have any feet."

"Well, if I did they would be cold." We laughed. "Let's start back. I want to talk to you about something. No, wait, let me ask you something first. Why do you want to beat Luther tonight? Is it so you can be the state champion, or is there a more pressing reason? Now, I want you to think about it before you answer, so why don't you push me up the hill you nearly killed me on coming down."

While I labored up the hill, I asked myself why I wanted to beat Luther so bad. If I was going to be totally honest, I'd have to admit it was for a different reason than I wanted to beat Foster. With Foster it was the pure love of matching strength and skill against another of equal or greater ability. Luther was obviously a different story. I knew I wanted revenge. I wanted to hurt him and embarrass him the same way he had embarrassed me. I wanted to wipe that sneer and arrogant attitude off his face.

Thinking about Luther had made my blood begin to boil, and I began pushing Ur faster than was necessary. Ur could sense the unnecessary speed and said, "Whoa, Jon, you are going to wear yourself out before the match. Do you hate him?"

That was a good question. I really never hated anyone except Mom's old boyfriend. I shuddered at the thought of him. Facing the truth, I knew I hated Luther too. Afraid of burning out, I walked the last 200 yards to the top and thought about Luther.

At the top I stopped to stretch my legs and back.

"So, Jon, do you hate Luther?"

"Yeah, I do," I admitted. "I hate Luther."

Ur sat with his head down and thought for a moment. Finally he looked up as I started rolling him along again. "That is too bad, Jon. I'm not sure you can beat him tonight then."

I stopped dead in my tracks.

Suddenly feeling angry, I forced his hand to my face. "What are you saying?" I jerked away and spit on the road in frustration, "I don't need to hear this today. You know how much I value your opinion. If you don't think I can win, I won't win. It's your belief in me that has sustained me through these last few weeks. Why would you tell me this now? I can't believe this!"

"Push the chair and let me talk for a few minutes." I roughly started pushing the chair, hoping Ur got my message.

"If you stay how you are—hating, that is—then there won't be a nickel's worth of difference between you and Luther tonight. Both of you will be wrestling for revenge and driven by hate. The whole match will be ugly, and no matter who wins there will not be a true champion standing on the platform. Real strength and goodness flows from the heart. If the heart, like a tree, is corrupt, then how can the fruit be good? Hatred and resentment are like a sore tooth that craves massaging. The

305

only difference is, hatred and resentment can spread throughout your entire body and, like cancer, slowly destroy you!"

I swerved the wheelchair around a pothole, causing Ur to lurch to one side and then the other. I was confused and not sure why every time the subject of forgiving came up, I got mad. I reminded myself again of that three-legged dog only now I was going where I wanted, but I still felt awkward and disjointed.

Ur was speaking again with greater intensity. "I spoke with you before about what Abraham taught me. Remember, he said we have a right to forgive. What do you think happens if we waive this right?" He went on, not stopping for me to answer. "We become vulnerable. It is a weak spot in our defenses."

"Remember the city I told you about? Our rights are like a wall that protects the city from unhappy invaders. If you neglect or waive any right, it's like having part of the wall down. You may not get invaded right away, but you have to worry about it . . . you lose peace of mind. It is absolutely impossible to have liberty without virtue!"

I was starting to settle down, partly because I had been running too fast and partly because I knew Ur was right. I loved my mother, but I also knew that I would have a closer relationship with her if I forgave her old boyfriend, and I guess, consequently, her. I never realized until then that I also had some resentment for my mom. Ur was right; I had lost my peace of mind. Whenever I saw that man or heard his name, bile-tasting anger surfaced. The same was true with Luther. Whenever I thought of Luther, I wanted to hurt him—not just win the match but grind his face into the mat. As I thought of Mom's old boyfriend and Luther, I started running faster. I gripped the wheelchair handles tighter, my fists white with frustration and hatred. Finally I exploded, "I hate those filthy, maggot-infested slime pits! I hate them both!"

I stopped the chair and turned to face Ur. "When I think of Luther and one of Mom's old boyfriends I am filled with hatred. Why do I hate them so much?" I was crying now. For a fleeting moment I thought of how ridiculous I must look. Tonight I would wrestle for the state title, and this morning I'm crying like a baby.

"How do I stop hating them?"

Ur didn't say anything for a minute. And then to my surprise he choked out a cry. His shoulders shook and tears streamed down his cheeks. It took him a long time to recover. Not knowing what else to do, I started pushing him again at a slow trot. By the time we reached the car, he had stopped crying but sat with his head in his hands.

"Ur," I said gently, now feeling less concern about my own problem and more concern for him, "Can I help you into the car?" He nodded as he put a handkerchief to his face.

After we were in the car, I drove down to the falls again, and sat there with the car idling and the heater running.

Finally Ur turned and haltingly said, "Thank you, Jon. Our conversation brought up a long-forgotten incident that I need resolve."

"Do you want to talk about it?" I asked gently.

"Yes." He fumbled with his watch dial. "I guess we have enough time."

"I've got plenty of time. I don't have anything to do until the luncheon with you, Mary, the Johnsons and the Reynolds."

Ur's voice was tired but steady. "Okay, please forgive the personal nature of this story, but maybe it can help you with your problem."

I nodded my hand.

"There was something that happened at the death camp that I hadn't remembered until this morning. Our conversation triggered the memory. I…"

"I'm sorry," I broke in.

"No, no, nothing to be sorry about. Sometimes it is good for me to remember, even though it is often painful. I have often been asked how I lost my eyesight and hearing. I think you even asked me that question once. I always say I don't remember, and I think most people don't believe me. The fact is, I didn't remember. For all of these 22 years, I didn't remember—until a few minutes ago. There was a long pause while Ur again regained his composure. I think your frustration with your own hatred for Luther and the other man somehow struck a common chord with me and I remembered."

He laid his head back on the seat and gazed at the roof as if he was watching it happen again. "In January of 1945, rumors about the nearness of the end were flying around our death camp. As a result of this, Dr. Mengele's experiments on twins was accelerated, and daily I saw my little flock of twins shrink as they were killed, cut up, and hauled off to be burned. Anna, Toby, and I were among the last dozen or so. I don't know the reason for this, except I was doing good work taking care of the twins. I assume Mengele didn't want to lose me until the last, so he kept my children alive with me.

Mengele was trying to determine how to change eye pigment to blue. He had a wall covered with eyeballs removed from twins and others."

The thought of that gave me the heebie-jeebies. I shivered.

"On the morning of January 15, 1945, while I was telling a story to Toby, Anna and a few other twins left in my care, a guard came for me. The night before, we had heard cannon fire not more than a few miles away. I felt a stab of fear and uncertainty as the SS soldier told me to follow him. I . . ."

Ur's voice became husky and he couldn't continue for a minute. I reached out and touched his hand. Taking a deep breath, he continued. "I held Toby and Anna for the last time. Somehow I knew it was the last time. I tried to memorize every part of their features. I was afraid that I would forget what they looked like. Two little kids whose eyes looked larger than normal because they were so skinny. Anna's hair flopped over her eyes. Their frightened looks are burned into my memory . . ." He choked out a cry and then blew his nose and continued.

"I just hoped their end wasn't too . . ." He brushed his hand over his head in frustration. "There was nothing I could do for any of the little twins except make their young lives as comfortable as possible while they lived. The Nazi army was too big, and I felt powerless before them. I would have started hating except for what a friend, who also was a prisoner, had told me."

"His name was Viktor Frankl. He said, 'The last human freedom: that one may choose their attitude in any given set of circumstances.' Like all the other inherent rights, it takes concentration and dedication to maintain the last human freedom."

"Dr. Mengele was in a hurry. I suppose he had heard the order to evacuate the camp soon. It was like he and I had never met before. His eyes were cold and glazed over like a snake's before it strikes. He sharply ordered that I be undressed and strapped to a clinic table. Seven straps bound me to the cold table. My head was placed in a cradle board and strapped so tight that I couldn't move it. So there I was, left without any choices at all, except one. I couldn't decide anything. I couldn't decide when I got up or went to sleep; I couldn't decide when or what I would eat. I couldn't even decide if I could keep my modesty. I had lost all of my freedoms except one: I was free to choose my attitude.

I chose not to hate. It was not easy, especially when Mengele said to finish the work on the other twins and send them to the kindergarten, after which he would get ready to leave. To him I was like a slab of beef, without feelings. It was the end. I knew I was going to die soon and so were my children. I was powerless and helpless against a bully."

Those were the same exact feelings I had against Mom's boyfriend and Luther also. I felt powerless against them. My problem seemed to diminish when compared to Ur's, but they were essentially the same. I felt powerless.

Interrupting, I said, "You don't seem to be filled with hatred anymore. Were you ever? I mean, how could you go through that without hating?"

"Well, yes, you remember right after my wife was killed and I was separated from my children? I hated plenty then, but that was early on. This time I did not want to hate. I had learned that hating was like drinking poison and waiting for the other person to die. I answered this same question for you once before. Do you remember what I said then?"

I had to think for a minute. "You said I have to beat Luther in a fair match. Do you mean that if I don't win tonight I can never forgive Luther?" I smiled to myself, thinking Ur was stuck.

"I said you have to overcome the effects of his offense on you. If you wrestle with dignity and honor you <u>will</u> win, no matter what the score is at the end of the match. Besides, you overcame the effects of his offense when you went back into the gym and faced him in front of the home crowd. You have disciplined yourself and trained enough that you will probably win tonight if you let the hatred go out of your heart. You need to recognize when you have overcome the effects of someone else's offense."

"Wait a minute. If I have overcome the effects of his offense, then why do I still hate him?"

"Because you choose to," he shot back. "Between now and tonight, you'd better find some reasons why you shouldn't hate Luther. Even better, you should find some reasons why you should like him."

"Bull! I can't think of any reasons."

"Then you better find some," Ur said quietly.

"Sure, what reasons did you have to like the Nazis?" I was sorry the moment I asked the question. I could see the hurt return to Ur. His face clouded, and I knew I had dredged up old painful memories. "I'm sorry, Ur. I shouldn't have asked that."

"It's a fair question," he said flatly. "I think I can answer it, but you may have to listen to some pretty painful stuff first."

"Okay," I said hesitantly, a little uncomfortable at what I might hear.

"It amazes me to suddenly be able to remember so much of this in so much detail. It's like it happened yesterday."

Then Ur began talking in a way that reminded me of a doctor. He seemed detached, like he was describing something that happened to someone else.

" Mengele took a hypodermic needle and injected some kind of blue dye solution into my right eyeball. He had just developed a new dye to change eye color to blue and wanted to test it before he had to evacuate. When the needle pierced my eyeball I instinctively twitched my eye. The skin tore and the optic fluid gushed out. My right eye just went flat. Today my right eye is glass.

"He started to do the same thing on my left eye, shouting, *'Dummkopf!* Don't move!' I could feel fluid running into my right ear from my torn right eyeball. He had attached two hemostats to my upper and lower eyelids. A nurse held my eyelids open while Mengele said, 'Focus on something. Don't move.'

" Sitting on a medical cabinet was a family picture. I focused on that. There was a mother and a father sitting and smiling brightly with their children. The father in that happy family was Mengele.

"The needle stabbed in my eye. I clenched my teeth and curled my toes and stared at that family. Slowly the picture clouded over. My eyesight was gone. Mengele kept saying, 'What do you see? Can you see?'

"I couldn't answer. He slapped me hard and shouted, 'Don't waste my time. I am in a hurry. What do you see?'"

I shifted uncomfortably in my seat, having completely forgotten about my own hatred for the moment.

"I heard Mengele say to the SS guard, 'Go get the last twins and strap them down! Tell Dr. Kraner to load some hypodermic needles with chloroform for the twins.' Chloroform was used to kill the victims by injection into the heart. His experimentation with twins usually began with both twins being killed simultaneously this way.

"To the nurse he barked, 'Get the ear scope and that drill, hurry!' I felt a cold probe enter my ear and move, as if he was looking at something, then the whirring of a drill, followed by a piercing pain that caused me to cry out as the drill entered my ear canal and eventually the eardrum and my inner ear. I cried out in agony. It all happened so fast.

Then Mengele was probing in the other ear with the scope, followed by the whirring of the drill. Just prior to the drill destroying my hearing forever, in spite of the pain, I thought I heard Mengele shout, 'Where are those ... ' and then all was totally quiet. I felt detached, floating and in a slow spin. I vomited.

"There was working in the lab a Jewish prisoner named Levine, who ran errands and kept records for Mengele. He and I had become good friends over the time I was in that camp. I later learned that he was called to take me to the showers where I would be gassed with others and cremated. Instead, he walked me to the latrine house and forced me into a toilet hole. There was not any way, or enough time, for him to explain what he was doing. My head was pounding and I felt dizzy and nauseated as I slid into the ooze. I was forced to stand like that until the evening, hours later.

"I didn't want to live. I wanted to join Beth, and I wanted to join my little Toby and Anna who I was sure were dead, or would be dead soon. Still, for some reason I clung onto life. I lived and I stood for hours in that waste. There were 20 holes in that latrine. I found a corner and pressed myself into it. For three days, Levine brought food and water to me and helped me out of the hole at night and back into it in the morning."

"I kept asking him, "Where are my Toby and my Anna?'

"He always avoided the question and wrote letters in my hand saying, 'I D-O N-O-T K-N-O-W.'

"I guess he didn't want to tell me the truth for fear I would give up. In three days the Russian forces liberated our camp. I was discovered and cared for at a field hospital. I never saw my friend Levine again. I don't know what happened to him.

"I developed infection in my eyes and ears as a result of my injuries and standing in the latrine. It was nearly impossible to keep the sludge out of my face and hair. I was dizzy and sick from the trauma inflicted to my head. Also, standing for 14 hours a day in human waste before Levine could get me out all but killed me.

"I got to the place that Viktor Frankl spoke of, 'The last human freedom: to choose my attitude in any set of circumstances.' What good thing, for me, came from the Nazis? That."

"That, what?" I asked.

"I learned that I could choose my attitude."

"That's all? Is that enough for what you suffered?" I asked incredulously.

Ur's silence made me uncomfortable for a minute.

"If you mean, would I trade my family for that knowledge? No. But if you mean, was my personal suffering worth knowing that one thing?...then I must answer with a resounding yes! There is little, if anything, else that has the ability to empower a human like the knowledge that he has the ability to determine his attitude.

"I could not tell when we were liberated since I could not hear or see. All I knew were the hands grasping me and lifting me out of the mess. I didn't know if they were Nazi, American, Russian, or just camp prisoners. My clothes were stripped off, and I thought for sure I would be gassed. Then my bony body was washed all over with cold water and soap. It was then that I started to wonder who was cleaning me.

"I asked several times, but it seemed that either they couldn't understand me, or perhaps I had lost my voice at the same time I lost my hearing and eyesight. It didn't make sense to me that I would have lost my voice too. I could feel my voice box vibrating when I talked, yet there was no way to communicate with me. Only when I was placed on a bed that smelled clean did I finally accept that I had been liberated.

"You asked, 'What did I like about the Nazis?' Well, nothing, absolutely nothing. Yet, I have to admit that inadvertently they gave me a great gift."

"What gift?"

"The gift to see without seeing and to hear without hearing."

"What does that mean?" I asked.

"I am afraid I can't explain it, but some day you will understand. Jon, how much do you know about Luther?"

"I know he's a jerk!"

"Well, yes," Ur smiled, "but other than that, how much do you know?" Ur smiled.

"Not much," I admitted, "Other than he moved here last year from someplace back East."

"Okay, you don't know much about him, so how much do you understand him?"

"I don't understand him at all. I don't see how someone could be so rude and mean-spirited."

"Sometimes it is easier to forgive if you know something about the person. This afternoon before the match, try to find out as much as you can about Luther. Okay?"

I answered, "All right, I'll try."

Ur checked his watch. "I guess we'd better head back."

The democracy will cease to exist when you take away
from those who are willing to work and give to those who
would not.

Thomas Jefferson

# CHAPTER 35

### I Have the Right to Inspire and Help Others

After showering and changing my clothes, I rode with Joy and her parents to a Chinese restaurant called George Kay's. It made me a little uncomfortable to be the guest of honor, but everyone was having so much fun that I soon relaxed. The Johnsons, Ur, Mary and the Reynolds made up the party. Mary was the self-appointed master of ceremonies.

"Okay, everyone, I guess I should thank Jon for making this possible."

"Heck, yes," drawled Evelyn, in her gentle southern-Idaho accent, "Chet's so tight he squeaks. That's why I'm so happy to finally get to eat out at a nice place. Thank you, Jon!"

Everyone chuckled.

Mary continued, signing as she spoke. Joy sat with Ur and interpreted by signing into his hands. "Jon, we all want you to know what an impact you have had on each of us. Your dedication and persistence have been a blessing to all who know you..."

Mrs. Johnson cut in, "Lands sakes alive, I'd say so. Little Danny, who is only five, says he wants to be like you when he grows up." There was a lot of head nodding and gentle grunting of approval.

Once again Mary continued, "Jon, your cheerful attitude and willingness to learn and train have been an inspiration to all of us. You probably think you owe us something. You don't. You have given us something we can't buy—that is inspiration and the joy of seeing a good young man achieve. We all got together and bought you something. We

315

asked the coach and he said it would be all right." She handed me a large box wrapped up in orange paper with black ribbon. A card said, "To Rover, from your Fans."

I took it, and after Joy and Evelyn cleared off a place on the table I set it in front of me. Clearing my throat, I said, "Thanks. You guys sure mean a lot to me. You all know, I hope, how much I have depended on you to get me ready for this tournament. But your friendship is more valuable to me than any championship."

I stopped, suddenly choked with emotion. A twitch was pulling at my lower lip. "The last four weeks of heavy training have pulled all of us together into something like a family." I took a drink of water. "I've learned more during this last six weeks about succeeding than I could've ever imagined. My confidence in school, sports and being a friend has increased 10 times over. I'm glad to know that you've all got something from my training. There's a couple of other people, who aren't here, that I want to thank. One is my mother." A tear started to slide down my cheek. "Her trust and love, and her willingness to let me go and have the freedom to do this, is evidence of her great heart."

Everyone nodded in agreement.

"Also, I want to thank someone else who has made all of this possible for us, someone I don't understand, but I'm still grateful for his strange way of helping me. That is Luther. That guy sure gets on my nerves," there was a little laughter, "but if I am to be honest, I have to admit that if it wasn't for him, I wouldn't be wrestling for a state championship tonight." They all applauded and Ur was smiling and nodding his head.

"Open the package. Hurry!" Joy signed enthusiastically.

I untied the ribbon and slowly opened the package, deliberately teasing Joy.

"Hurry!" Joy signed again.

Lifting the lid, I still was not sure what it was until I lifted it out and unfolded it. It was a jet-black, satin warm-up robe, the kind those professional boxers have that look like a bathrobe. I had seen a few at the tournament and thought they looked cool.

"Turn it over and look on the back," Joy persisted.

Turning it over, I was amazed at what was embroidered on the back.

"IDAHO STATE WRESTLING CHAMPIONSHIP—1967" was embroidered in a half-circle like a rainbow in large white letters. Under that was embroidered "DECLO HIGH SCHOOL" in the same rainbow style. In the middle was a large orange, black and white fierce-looking hornet, just like the one on the wall of our high school gym. Under the hornet was embroidered "JON RHOADES." The last thing was the words "ROVER RULES."

"Put it on!" Joy insisted.

I couldn't stop beaming as I slipped my arms into the silky satin sleeves, overlapped the front, and tied the belt.

"How does it look?" I almost shouted with enthusiasm.

"You look like a world champion!" Chet crooned and slapped a brawny hand onto the table, making the dishes rattle. "Rover Rules!" he shouted.

Pretty soon the whole café was disrupted by "Rover Rules!" being shouted by my little fan club. I guess guys with larger families know what it feels like to be the center of attention. I never had. I only had one birthday party in my life and that was because it was the day after my dad died. Now I wasn't sure how to react, so I just stood there grinning like an idiot.

I arrived at the gym about an hour early to do some visualizing and stretching. I saw the ISDB wrestling coach stick his head into the warm-up room and then start to leave. "Hey coach, got a minute?" I asked.

He looked back in, saw me and started walking over. "What can I do for you?" he answered in a friendly tone.

"Well, I'm the guy wrestling Luther tonight."

"I know that. Good luck," he said shortly.

"Thanks. Could you tell me a little about his background? You know, where he's from and what his family is like—stuff like that?"

"How come?" he asked stone-faced.

"Well, personally, I can't stand the sucker," I stated honestly, "but a friend told me if I would learn a little about Luther then maybe I could find something good about him to like, other than his wrestling skills, I mean."

The coach stared at me for a minute and then said, "Well, I can't believe it. I heard from some people that you were a different kind of guy, but this does beat all. Let me see if I have this straight. You want to find something about Luther you can like, so you can change your attitude about him?"

"Yup. That's it. I've been told that I'll wrestle better if I don't hate his guts."

"Then telling you something about him might help you beat him," he smiled.

"Yup, that's probably right."

"Well, I guess you could use all the help you can get just to stay in for a round," he smiled again. "You know, nobody can beat him. I don't think he has ever been beaten in his life. In the summer he wrestles freestyle and has been national champion for four years in a row."

I gulped, "I never knew that."

"You're a good kid, and I would like to see you do well, but you're not in his class, son. Nobody is, especially out here in the west. Last year he won the nationals by outscoring his final opponent nine to zip, and then pinned the guy in the last 10 seconds."

"How come nobody knows this about him?"

"We wanted to keep it private so other teams wouldn't try to wrestle around him, you know, by having their good guys change weights to avoid him. You want to know something about his family? Okay, he never has had a family. He was abandoned at birth and put in a trash can in Pittsburgh, Pennsylvania. Someone found him and he went from foster family to foster family until he was six, then he was put into a residential school for the deaf and blind in Pennsylvania. That's where he learned to wrestle. And that is about all he has ever done well. I'll tell you something about him that maybe I shouldn't— he has never been loved. Not by a mom or dad or brother or sister or friend. I don't love him. I can't even stand him myself. He's arrogant and obnoxious. But boy, can he wrestle!"

"Why is he out here?"

"He got into trouble back in Pennsylvania, and my brother, who teaches in that school for the deaf, asked me if I wanted a state champion. I said, 'Sure.' If I had known what he was like, I wouldn't have agreed. Listen kid, I've got to go. Good luck tonight, but be careful; he is dangerous … and he has a particular grudge against you."

I went back to stretching and thought about what the coach had told me. My family wasn't perfect, but at least I had a family. I knew who my mom and dad and brothers were. We weren't close and never did things together, but we loved each other. Luther didn't know his family and had never been loved, never. I couldn't imagine it. I couldn't even comprehend a life without at least one person loving me. Wrestling had consumed his whole life. That was why he was so good. What would happen if he lost a match? Ur said it would be good for him. In what way?

PAIN IS INEVITABLE.
DON'T GO LOOKING FOR IT,
BUT DON'T RUN FROM IT EITHER.
LEARN FROM IT.

# CHAPTER 36

### I Have a Right to Rewards Whether I Win or Lose

"Fools rush in where angels fear to tread." I heard that in a song once. I guess that's why I was not discouraged after talking to the ISDB coach. I settled into a corner and visualized the entire match. I visualized my four perfect moves again and again. I was totally at peace with myself and Luther. I didn't hate him anymore. I didn't really know why, except that I was grateful that he had beaten me so badly at home and motivated me to prepare for this match. I had empathy for him and his life. I understood why he was like he was. I didn't respect his attitude on or off the mat, but I did respect his skills. Ur was right: I did feel better and more in control of myself, maybe more like a four-legged dog, more like Rover.

The other contenders for state champion were coming into the warm-up room. Everyone was stretching and wrestling with buddies to warm up. Crash and I were the only wrestlers from Declo to make it to the finals. He sauntered over and piled on me.

"Hey, little buddy, are you ready to rumble?"

Slipping from under him, I said, "Yeah. How are you feeling?"

"I'm up for it. I'm just glad I'm not in your weight. That deaf-blind guy is meaner than a stepped-on rattlesnake, and he is a good wrestler too."

"His coach said he is a national champion in freestyle. So, it is an honor to wrestle him, and it is a greater honor to beat him," I said calmly.

Crash was looking at me. "Do you think you can beat him?" he asked incredulously.

The announcer was calling for the parade of champions to begin as I got up. "I know I can. I know his weakness."

"What's that?"

"Hate."

The parade of champions was one of the most thrilling events a wrestler could experience. The wrestlers marched out en masse, like they do in the Olympic's opening. The lights were turned down and a couple of spotlights were sweeping the floor. In the center of the giant gym was one mat. The crowd was going crazy, and loud music from the Olympic games was rattling the rafters. I was so pumped! My body tingled all over. I couldn't see the Declo bunch, but I knew they were there because as I approached the center section I heard a chant start, "Rover Rules, Rover Rules, Rover Rules!" and "Crash Crushes, Crash Crushes!"

As Crash passed the Declo section, cymbals began to crash from the DHS pep band in honor of Crash Bingham. Just then I and the wrestlers around me were pelted with about a hundred foam rubber doggie bones. I caught one, and printed with a magic-marker was "Dog Meat" on one side and "Rover Rules" on the other. I shaded my eyes against the bright spotlight to see who threw them, but finally gave up and raised V- shaped hands over my head and then brought them down and signed, "Thank you." I knew Mary would tell everyone what I said.

I felt excited and proud to wear the warm-up robe. It made me feel loved and supported. After once around the gym, we lined up on both sides of the mat, Luther opposite me with Louis as his guide. I looked across at Luther and did not feel any animosity toward him. In fact, I felt compassion and a certain degree of gratitude for his opposition which helped me get to the finals. Ur had once said, "Opposition is often an ugly friend." As our names were called, we were to run out onto the mat to shake hands with our opponent.

When my name was spoken, the place went crazy and the ole' DHS pep band struck up a few bars of our fight song. The cheerleaders sang out, "Go, Jon, go!" I trotted to the center of the mat and waited for Louis to guide Luther out to meet me. I extended my hand as Luther was positioned opposite me. Louis had a stupid grin on his face, and

Luther was smiling mischievously. I couldn't figure out what they were up to so I kept my eyes on them. Louis guided Luther's hand to mine. At the last moment, I caught a glimpse of a plastic glove on Luther's hand, then I felt something squish into my palm. Pulling my hand back, I could smell and see a chunk of dog fertilizer smeared into my palm. Luther and Louis were laughing as they retreated to the line of wrestlers. For a moment I was seized with fury. I wanted to run after them and rub it all over their faces. Then just as fast, I thought, "The last human freedom." I smiled while I jogged back to the line and then over to the restroom to wash my hands. I would do my rubbing on the mat.

As the matches began, the lights over the bleachers came up a little and I saw the crowd. I was too nervous to sit so I paced on a warm-up mat behind the wrestlers' bench and studied the crowd, while the 98-pounders struggled to identify a new state champion.

The entire gym was filled with screaming wrestling fans. The crowd was a sea of rainbow colors, as each fan showed support for his or her local school by wearing the school colors. Scattered herds of cheerleaders wandered around the perimeter of the gym waiting for their turn to pound the mats and scream encouragement to their boys. I tried to spot Joy's little flock of red, black, and white clad cheerleaders.

Then my eyes found Declo's cheering section. In front was Moose, Trish, Sandy, Vicki, Nilene, and the others waiting anxiously for my match. I would be the first of the two Declo wrestlers to compete. The shiny instruments of Declo's pep band waved above their heads while they talked and teased each other. It looked like every resident of Declo had come out to the state wrestles wearing orange hunting vests, including the Osterhout brothers, whose massive bodies stood out like orange semi-trucks parked at a diner.

Huddled together in the middle of the orange and black Declo throng, were Mary, dressed in her hunter-orange stocking cap and vest; Chet, Evelyn, the Johnsons, and Ur. Even Ur had on an orange vest and orange stocking cap. Chet must have carried Ur up to his seat. Mary was hollering down the row of seats, evidently trying to get everybody to move down and make a couple more seats available. She kept pointing down toward the main entrance and yelling something. My eyes drifted down to see what she was pointing at.

My mom! Tears stung quickly when I saw Fred carefully escorting Mom through the crowd. I couldn't believe it! Mom, here at a match. She looked uncomfortable as she furtively observed the mass of people. I knew crowds and noise made her nervous. I knew she could not stand to see me pounded on, too. I worried about how she would react when Luther and I tore into each other like two enraged bears.

The crowd parted to allow Mom and Fred to hesitantly climb up to the two seats next to Mary and Ur. Mom smiled and sat down awkwardly. I was sure she was dying to have a cigarette or two to settle her nerves.

I was so intent on the crowd that I didn't notice someone slip up behind me and cover my eyes from behind with gentle hands. I reached up and pulled the hands down to my lips and kissed them. I knew whose hands they were, and I loved them. I turned around to see ... Elton Greasefark standing there, staring in disbelief at his kissed hands.

"Oh, crimendently, Elton, I thought you were someone else!" I burst out in total mortification.

"Uh, yeah ... well, good luck, Jon," he stammered, as he slugged me gently on the shoulder and walked off.

Someone tapped me on the other shoulder and I spun around to see Joy beaming up at me.

"Did you see what just happened?" I signed.

"No. What?"

"I just kissed Elton Greasefark's hands thinking it was you."

She put her hands to her face and burst out laughing so hard she had to turn away. "I wondered why you had such a funny look on your face." Then she got serious. "Are you ready?"

"Yes. Did you see? My mom and Fred are here!"

"Mom told me your Mother might come. I am so glad." She glanced at the other wrestlers' bench across the mat and said, "Luther has been saying some mean things," she signed, suddenly looking alarmed. "Jon, be careful. He wants to hurt you, not just beat you."

"Why does he hate me so much? It can't just be because he has a crush on you," I signed.

"Dad says it is because you are so good, and most of all, because he is intimidated by your decency." She popped her forehead with the heel of her hand and said, "Oh, I almost forgot, Dad wanted me to ask if you have the flag with you, whatever that means." I glanced up at Chet and saw he was staring at me intently. I patted my belly. There under my uniform I had carefully folded and placed the sacred cloth. Chet put two fingers up in a "V" for victory. Our eyes locked and I gave him a man-nod.

"I won't cheer for Luther tonight," Joy said openly, searching my eyes for a response.

I smiled and hugged her. "Good. Cheer for me. I'll need all of the help I can get."

Joy tiptoed and kissed me on the cheek then turned and bounced away, her red ponytail flip-flopping from side to side.

Two more matches and then I would be up. Twelve more minutes of wrestling or less if it was two quick pins.

I started visualizing while stretching. The first match was a quick pin. The next opponents darted onto the mat. The crowd roared.

I could see Luther on the other side of the gym. His coach seemed to be arguing with him about something. Glancing up to the Declo section I saw Mom staring at me with fear in her eyes. She probably shouldn't have come. I wanted her here, but there was so much she didn't understand about wrestling. Hopefully Mary would help her to understand that I wasn't getting killed. On the other hand, when wrestling with Luther one never knew. I peeked at the scoreboard—30 seconds left in this match. It looked like a Parma kid was going to be a state champion.

Coach Chugg came up and started massaging my neck and shoulders. "Jon, keep your head. Look for an opening and then seize it with all of the determination of a pit bull. There isn't one person in here that doesn't want to see Luther beaten. His arrogance and meanness have turned everyone against him. You are ready. Make no stupid mistakes. This is your day to win!" And he slapped me on my back as I trotted onto the mat.

Luther and his coach were still arguing while I waited for Luther. Then I saw Luther jerk loose from his coach and push him away sharply. As Louis escorted Luther onto the mat, I could see he was in a murderous mood. Someone in the crowd booed him.

Strangely, I wasn't afraid. Every muscle in my body felt like iron and my mind was clear and determined. The gym reverberated with the announcer's voice, "Jon Rhoades from Declo High School (cheering) is wrestling Luther Ledger from the Idaho State School for the Deaf and Blind (booing)."

This was like a melodrama, I thought. I felt a little uncomfortable being put in the hero role.

I watched Luther while the referee checked our nails and hair. I had never seen so much anger, hatred and contempt in any human face. The Declo and ISDB cheerleaders were in position along two sides of the mat, sitting cross-legged so they could reach out and beat the mat with their cheers. I glanced at Moose. She had a nervous smile, but tried to look confident as she clapped and shouted, "Get 'em, Jon."

Joy, on the other side of the mat, caught my eye and flicked her little finger, index finger and thumb out at me. That was the international sign for "I love you." Her face was pale with fright. The referee placed our hands together before the whistle blew and backed off a step. As he blew the whistle he reached forward and touched Luther on the back. If I had ever thought Luther was fast and strong before, I was wrong. He tore into me with such vengeance that I recoiled back several steps.

Luther dropped to one knee and felt the mat to know where I was. I circled him looking for an opening. Luther struck at me with the speed and strength of a giant viper, slapping me on the back of the neck and locking us together. He shucked my head up a little and in a blink threw me hard to the mat in a headlock pinning combination.

With my neck in the crook of his iron-sinewy arm, he held one of my arms and slid himself out perpendicular to my body. Then he just bore down, lifting my head and almost putting my shoulders to the mat. He now had five points, two for take-down and three for near-pin. I tried like a madman to get out, but I felt like a worm with a horse standing on one end. All the thrashing I was doing was not changing the situation.

He brought my back to almost touching and then wrenched my arm over my mouth and nose so I couldn't breathe. I guessed the referee was busy looking for the pin and didn't notice that Luther was suffocating me. The crowd could see it, and was going crazy trying to tell the referee. My eyes were bulging and my head pounding as I started thrashing in an effort to get my breath. Coach Chugg was screaming at the referee until the referee finally noticed my arm over my nose and mouth. I was so exhausted and weak from lack of oxygen that I couldn't struggle.

Then I noticed that Luther wasn't trying to pin me. He was holding my shoulders off the mat while squeezing with all of his might. I thought my head would squeeze off at the shoulders. A burning sensation jolted up the back of my head. He wasn't going to pin me; he was going to just play with me again until I was totally humiliated and then quickly pin me. I also knew he wanted to make me suffer as long as he could.

I tried to turn so as to see Coach Chugg, and when I rotated enough I saw the coach lying down holding Brent Foster in the same pinning combination Luther had me in. It took a second for me to realize that Brent was trying to show me how to counter it. First he brought his body around parallel with coach Chugg's and then hooked a leg on the coach. I started doing the same thing. Just as Foster hooked Chugg's leg, he immediately scissored it, grabbed Chugg's waist and bridged. This caused the coach to flip over with his back to the mat.

I glanced at the clock and saw there were 20 seconds left in the first round. I knew I had to score points on Luther to stay in the match. I hooked Luther's leg, scissored it, grabbed his waist and bridged. It was hard going because of Luther's strength, but he went, and in a second I had him on his back in a pinning combination.

"Two points, reversal! Three points near pin!" The referee shouted as the round ended. "Score is five to five."

I glanced over at Coach Chugg and Brent Foster and gave them man-nods in appreciation.

The referee flipped the coin and I called "heads." It was my choice to choose either up or down position. I looked at Luther; his blank stare was menacing. That was probably the first time anyone had put his back to the mat in years. Luther was still dangerous, but I thought I detected a slight change in his face. He seemed more cautious. Moose and the other cheerleaders were beating out V-I-C-T-O-R-Y. The ISDB cheerleaders were unenthusiastically cheering for Luther. I took bottom.

At the whistle, I exploded out from under Luther and escaped. I was glad I perfected that move. I was ahead six to five. I started circling Luther again, trying to get an advantage. I reached in and touched Luther's head, and he shot out and seized my ankle. Immediately, he elevated it above my head and shoved me completely off the mat toward the ISDB cheerleaders. I slammed into them, causing Joy to bump her head hard on the floor. I jumped up and nearly rushed him in anger, then checked myself.

Luther was smiling. He knew exactly what he was doing. He intended to hurt his own cheerleaders. He intended to hurt Joy. I wasn't the only one who noticed his attempt to hurt the ISDB cheerleaders. All of the ISDB girls got up and stepped back from the mat, refusing to cheer any longer. A few people shouted condemning things to Luther. Not even angry gestures would affect him. The referee went to the ISDB coach and warned him not to let Luther get out of hand. The coach came out on the mat and tried to talk to Luther, but Luther slapped his hands away and refused to talk to him.

I looked over at Joy and saw her hurt expression as she rubbed the side of her head. Looking back at Luther's face twisted up in anger, I realized that the only person who could make a difference in Luther's life would be me. His hateful bullying of smaller people, his blind indifference to other people's rights, was going to end—tonight. That is what Ur meant when he said it would be the best thing for him to lose. It meant that Luther was like a truck running away down a steep mountain road with an intersection full of children below. Someone had to stop him.

I touched the bullet-riddled handkerchief given to me by Chet. A resolve came into my heart that settled into an iron-willed commitment to win this match for all good people who care for other people and treat them with respect. That was what our freedom was all about. Just like Ur said, "We are free to do good. We are not free to do bad; we only have the power to choose it."

We both started in the standing position. When the whistle blew I attacked with the swiftness of a leopard. I slid under his arm and executed perfectly a fireman's carry, and just for show lifted him on my shoulders. The crowd went crazy as I slowly turned him in the air. I stopped long enough to face Declo and smile at my mom, who was standing and staring with both hands to her mouth. Dropping to one knee first, I brought him over my head and onto his back.

Like a cat on its back, he instantly flipped over and attacked me. Everything after that for the rest of the round was a blur to me. I was wrestling purely by instinct. At the end of the second round, I had to look at the scoreboard to see the score because I had totally lost track of it. I had a red line across my forehead from a fingernail scratch he had put on me. The referee ordered me to the corner to have Coach Chugg wipe off the blood before we began the third and last round.

Chet was there. "Jon, if you can throw that move I showed you that one night, he's wide open for it. Do it for Jerry, Ruben and me," he paused for a moment, "and for everyone who is sick of guys like him," he pointed his chin at Luther.

I noticed Ur was now seated in his wheelchair on the main floor with Mary near him watching me.

I was trailing by six points and Luther picked top position. I heard Mrs. Johnson start crooning, "Rover Rules, Rover Rules, Rover Rules . . .!" Soon it seemed everyone was chanting, "Rover Rules! Rover Rules! Rover Rules!"

Luther chose top. When the whistle blew, Luther clamped onto so tight around my waist that I couldn't breathe, and my ribs ached. He drove me forward off my knees. I sprung back up. It went like this for the next 90 seconds. He wasn't trying to pin me—only control me and torture me. I wondered what he had in mind.

Finally, with 30 seconds left he let up the pressure, encouraging me to stand. I did stand and he started to load up the soufflé. I knew immediately he was going to soufflé me in a dangerous way. He was cold and calculating. He didn't care so much for winning the state championship if he could break my neck instead.

Even though I never used the move Chet had shown me in a match, I had practiced it a hundred times and visualized it another thousand times so it came second nature to me. As we stood, I pinned his hands to my stomach, rotated my hips to the right, slipped my right foot behind his left foot and brought my elbow as hard as I could against his chest. He had no idea what hit him as he flew backwards over my leg. Before he landed I wrapped a reverse-nelson around his neck and was cinching it down with the power of a cable winch. He bellowed like a wounded buffalo and thrashed around with the angry power of a trapped beast.

"Two points reversal and three points near-pin!" yelled the referee.

I needed six points to tie, and seven to win. I could let him up and hope to take him down again, but that would give him one point for escape and me two for take-down. That would leave us in a tie and bring on an overtime match. I decided to go for the pin.

I watched the clock tick down: "fifteen . . . fourteen..." I felt like I was giving it all I had until I remembered Ur saying, *"When you think you've done all you can, you've only used up about 30 percent of your capacity. To unlock the other 70 percent, use your soul."*

"thirteen . . . twelve..." I visualized a huge hydraulic press pushing on Luther's shoulder. I let the air I was holding, out slowly. I saw the press move down a fraction of an inch. "eleven . . ." the crowd started chanting the time. "ten . . . nine . . . " Luther's anger, hatred and frustration frothed out of his mouth, as I felt hot saliva splatter across my face. "eight . . . . seven . . . six. . . ." Sensing the nearness of the end, he went manic; his screams and thrashing intensified to a horrifying level. "Five . . . Four . . . Three . . ." I kept watching, in my mind, the powerful press pushing down, and I could feel his shoulder lowering. "Two... One..."

The referee was shaking me, "Turn loose kid! Let him go. It's over. The round's ended. I slapped the mat. Didn't you hear me? You won! You're a state champion!"

I was so focused on the hydraulic press forcing Luther's shoulder down that I became oblivious to everything else, and had not heard the referee slap the mat just before the last second ticked off. I stood up as pandemonium broke out, and I found myself being mobbed by cheerleaders from Declo and ISDB. Coach Chugg, Foster, and Chet were pounding me on the back, and a hundred other people were mobbing me too.

The pep band was blasting, "We give you a cheer Declo High..."

The Osterhout brothers were rattling the bleachers by jumping up and down. I could see Mom and Fred standing on their seats, fists in the air, screaming. The Johnsons, Evelyn and everyone else seemed to be hugging and laughing. The whole building was roaring.

The referee broke through the crowd, yelling, "Bring the champion back onto the mat, I need to raise his hand."

Champion, I thought. It still hadn't sunk in. As the crowd parted, the gym suddenly fell into silence and everyone stared at the mat.

Mary had quietly wheeled Ur out onto the mat, and he was swinging down from his chair to where Luther was still lying, bawling like a baby. Ur found Luther's hand and spelled something into it and he sat up. Ur was signing and spelling into Luther's hands so fast that I couldn't understand him. Luther's whole expression now changed from pure hostility to what seemed like disbelief and contriteness.

Luther shook his head in confusion, not belligerence. Great after-sobs wracked his body. He looked weak and vulnerable, pale and childlike. Ur gently patted his hand and signed comforting, reassuring things to him and then gathered Luther into his arms and held him like a father would. I'll bet it was the first time Luther had ever been held like that.

I did not know how devastated Luther would be at losing; I think no one knew how broken he would become, except Ur. Ur looked around and then signed into open space, hoping I would see him, "Jon, come here, please."

The crowd was awestruck at what they were watching and the whole place became as quiet as an emptied outhouse. I walked over and took Ur's hand.

"Jon, Luther would like you to escort him back to center circle and then to his team," Ur spoke quietly while he signed to Luther.

I couldn't believe it. It was like Ur could see this whole picture weeks ago. He knew what I needed to do and what Luther needed to do in order for that scene to be acted out, right then. Ur knew Luther needed to be beaten in order for him to become humble enough to change. Ur's plan this whole time was to build me and Luther at the same time. Ur once told me that he always tried to do what is best for people.

I remembered him saying, "Jon, the best thing for Luther is to lose." Luther needed to be taken to the bottom, totally conquered and his arrogance destroyed, so he could be rebuilt on true principles.

Ur placed Luther's hand in mine and then reached for his chair. I signed, "Ready," to Luther and he wiped his eyes with the heel of a powerful hand and nodded. Someplace, someone started to clap as the referee raised my hand in victory, and when I raised my other hand that held Luther's hand, the crowd exploded in tearful cheers.

I am not sure everyone understood what was happening, but they all felt the swing from hate to gratitude.

I am sorry to say that after that everything seemed a little anti-climactic. Oh, the crowd cheered for their favorite sons, and wrestlers clashed for the state titles with the same enthusiasm. Crash won his match, but no one could get out of their mind the miracle of Luther's change, as well as the miraculous change in their feelings for Luther.

After things settled down and the next match began, I went up to see my mom. I climbed into the Declo section amid back-slapping, and "Way-to-go, Rover!"

"You... did... really... good, Jonny-boy," she spoke slowly while touching the scratch on my forehead. "Your...dad would...be proud...of you."

I know everyone must have thought I was such a boob, because I began to cry in my mother's arms. Maybe it was releasing the stress of everything, or maybe it happens to everyone who breaks out against overwhelming odds and does something really big. Maybe people who try to do good just feel more in life. Regardless, last fall I was a kid who had never done anything significant in his life, and probably never would, and now I had hundreds cheering for me because I had accomplished a great goal. I was a young man who had broken out and received a great privilege, while maintaining my inherent rights. Maybe I was crying because my dad wasn't there, or maybe I was crying because Ur had come into my life and filled the void. I sat there for about 10 minutes until Mom said, while looking down at Luther, "Okay, that's enough . . . g-go down . . . and t-talk . . . t-to that b-boy . . . make him . . . feel better."

I spent the rest of the evening talking to Luther while Joy rubbed my sore neck. The more we learned about him the more we understood him. We marveled at what he had accomplished in his life in spite of the odds being stacked against him. He was a pretty good student and tried to excel in everything he did. He apologized for how he treated me and explained that I was the first person he had ever met that he envied.

"What do you envy?" I asked thinking he would say Joy, or my hearing and sight.

"I envy how much people like and respect you. That is about all I have heard since I first wrestled you. I thought if I could beat you, people would talk about me in the same way."

I could tell that Luther still had some rough spots, but it was obvious he had taken a new tack in life.

When it was time to stand on the victory stand for the medals and pictures, Luther insisted that I guide him to the second-place platform next to mine. I leaned over and the presenter put the gold medal around my neck, and handed me the silver one which I put around Luther's neck. When I did, flashbulbs lit up so much that I was almost blinded. The crowd went crazy all over again. Every newspaper in the Mountain West and a few back East had that picture and the amazing story of the underdog beating the deaf-blind champion. One caption read, "Not every handicapped person is an underdog."

The next day I went up to Oakley and had Sunday dinner with the Reynolds. Evelyn had cut out the article about the state wrestling tournament. She had already framed the picture of me getting my first-place medal.

"You can have the article, but I'm keeping this picture." She walked it over and set it on the television next to the picture of Joy as a little girl holding a yellow rose.

In a private moment, when I walked outside with Chet, he lit a smoke and I handed him back his flag. "You done real good, Jon. Jerry and Ruben would be proud of you too." He looked off toward Birch Creek for a long time, his jaw silently working over some emotion. Suddenly he brought up the bullet riddled flag and rubbed each eye with it. "Thanks, Jon," he said again in a husky voice. "I think you scored one for the good of this country."

About then Joy came out of the house bundled in a heavy wool blanket. She walked over to us and, sliding her arms through ours, said, "Dinner's ready."

Chet flicked his Bull Durham out onto the hard-pack. I watched its smoky trail arch and then bounce a couple of times, roll and lay smoking. At that moment I was suddenly filled with a happiness that seemed too big to be real. I was a state champion and Joy was my girl. I felt loved and cared for by Ur, Mary, Chet and Evelyn. Moose and Kenny were best buds, and my relationship with Fred and Mom had never been better. Life was as sweet as it could get for a Declo kid. Joy lifted the blanket and wrapped the two of us into it as we walked. Chet put his hand on my shoulder. Evelyn came out and with mock anger yelled, "You guys, get your tails in here 'fore I wear you out with a switch! You know the rolls ain't never as good cold."

Later that evening I went to Mary and Ur's home. Before entering the house, I went over and tugged at my Cedar Post. It was still frozen tighter than the Snake River in January. I closed my eyes and let my hands caress its rough timber. I think for the first time I felt a genuine affection for my post. It was more than just an upright for a clothes line; it was a cheerful friend, a crying towel, and a quiet confidant. It seemed to whisper to me about pristine beautiful things recently uncovered in myself and in my world. It's funny that at that moment the thousand dollars seemed pretty inconsequential. I looked up and saw Mary moving around in the kitchen. I took a deep breath of the best air in the whole world, hugged the post and went inside.

While around Mary's kitchen table, I told her and Ur of my happiness. Mary smiled and then reached out and patted my hand in understanding. Ur spoke, "Always look to the hills, Jon, because that will give you hope to climb out of your valleys."

It is amazing to me, as I look back, how true that is—how one's life rolls along nonstop through the hills and valleys of life, sometimes enjoying magnificent vistas from the hills with a view as clear and big as the skies and fields of southern Idaho. Other times one cannot see the close and warm farmhouse for the snowstorm. It is those times I think that one's inherent rights are of most value. They are the steady, rock-solid and dependable course needed to ensure peace of mind and happiness in uncertain times.

# EPILOGUE

I look up from my laptop. The sun is starting to slide toward Burley. The echoes of evening chores are beginning. My attention is drawn toward the road passing in front of the new high school. A teenager wearing green LaCross irrigating boots, double folded at the top, a white T-shirt, and a ball cap turned backwards, rides by on a mud-covered red four-wheeler. He sits straddling the handle of his irrigation shovel, the blade sticking out from behind. He leans forward into the wind…and into life. As he passes, he looks my direction and our eyes lock for a moment.

For a millisecond, I saw myself 30 years ago driving Mr. Johnson's old red pickup. I saw my irrigation shovel stuck up in a rack-hole in the back, headed to change the water on Sam Richardson's old place. I smile—he waves and yells, "Great speech!"

I wave back. "Great ears!" I shout. He looks confused. "To hear my speech." He waves again and is gone.

There is so much more to tell. That spring and summer were too outrageous to believe. The time Ur and I fought a couple of drunks while he was learning how to fish. In fact, Ur and I found ourselves in a couple of scrapes that year. One fight was for our lives. That summer the Polish National Police chased us, and we became the focus of the world press. I became acquainted with the power of death and its invisible impact on the living. There was so much to tell that I will have to sort it out before I can write it. And Joy, oh sweet Joy! I cannot number the tears I shed for you. Tears of the greatest happiness as well as tears of the greatest anguish. Even now as write this, I cannot prevent my eyes from burning in the memory of you.

NOTE: Be sure to read the sequels to The Cedar Post. It is called *Tears of Joy, Fly Papaer* and can be ordered at www.americandreammakers.com

## CHAPTER 1

1. What did the dents in Jon's car symbolize to him?

2. What dents do you have that you think are hidden from public view?

3. How is it that your secret problems are like rocks in your pockets?

## CHAPTER 2

1. Do you ever find yourself thinking of all of your weaknesses?

2. Do you ever wish you had a magic clock so you could turn back time and start again?

3. What is the first thing you would change about yourself if you could start all over again?

## CHAPTER 3

1. Do your problems seem too overwhelming to you at times?

2. Do you sometimes feel powerless to change things for the better in your life?

## CHAPTER 4

1. Why do you think people with disabilities make some people feel uncomfortable?

2. What disability makes you most uncomfortable to be around?

3. Why do you think you feel this way?

4.  What disabilities do some people have that are not so visible?

## CHAPTER 5

1.  What kind of attitude did Jon have on his date?

2.  What recurring situations have you been in where a different attitude would have made the situation better?

## CHAPTER 6

1.  What does Mary mean when she says, "People are teased about things they can't change by those whose problems could be changed?

2.  What makes pride a grueling taskmaster?

## CHAPTER 7

1.  What specific things in your world would change if you suddenly became blind?

2.  How would the value of the following things in your life change?
    A.  Beauty
    B.  Cars
    C.  Clothes
    D.  Homes
    E.  Others.

3.  What things which you value today would not change?

4.  Of those things that would change and would not change, which is the most important and has the longest-lasting value?

## CHAPTER 8

1. Why do you think Ur put a $1,000 bill in the post?

2. What did Ur mean when he said, "Jon, you cannot see all I want to give you at this point"?

3. Why does Jon have to believe?

4. What could possibly be of more worth than hundreds of thousands of golden sugar beets?

5. Have you ever been asked to make a commitment that you knew would involve a lot of sacrifice, but in the end would be worth it?

6. What do you think it means when Ur says, "Real mettle is tempered by what you do after the emotion of the decision has passed?"

7. What does this mean: "Happiness is cleverly nested in the process of attainment of predetermined, worthwhile goals?"

## CHAPTER 9

1. What are privileges and how do they differ from rights?

2. What does it mean when Ur says that to be safe with one's privileges one must maintain his inherent rights?

3. Why would a parent or a political leader be a threat to others if they did not maintain their inherent rights?

4. Can someone have privileges without maintaining his inherent rights?

5. Name one privilege you would like to enjoy before you die.

6. Have you ever felt like Ur, knowing what was the right thing to do but unable to bring yourself to do it? What held Ur back? What held you back?

## CHAPTER 10

1. What does it mean to ride hatred?

2. What does this mean: "A guilty person blows up because the truth cuts him to his very center?"

3. When was the last time you felt at peace?

4. What does it mean to be totally honest with yourself?

5. What are some of the obvious solutions to your problems?

## CHAPTER 11

1. Summarize what inherent rights are and how our life is easier, safer, and filled with more peace of mind when they are maintained.

2. Like the grain combine, have you ever been confronted by a new idea that seemed just too big to understand at first?

3. What did you do to finally understand it?

4. Is this what you might be feeling about inherent rights and privileges at this time?

5. Why are inherent rights self-evident?

6. When compared to the ancient village, what is the big deal about inherent rights?

7. How is the wall around the city like inherent rights?

8. How does the waiving of our inherent rights cause us to lose peace of mind?

9. If you likened your life to the ancient city, how are your walls?

## CHAPTER 12

1. How does the maintaining of one's right to protect the health of his body give peace of mind?

2. What is a principle?

3. Name a principle of life that you understand?

4. What is your opinion of what Ur has taught Jon so far?

5. Why is desire more important that brains?

6. Have you ever felt mediocre and powerless to change?

7. Name one person whom you trust like Jon trusted Ur?

## CHAPTER 13

1. Summarize: How is life like playing golf in the jungle?

2. List a couple of bad places the monkey has thrown the ball in your life.

3. List a couple of good places the monkey has thrown the ball in your life.

4. The bottom line in life is I must _____ the _____!

5. How did you feel as you read this chapter?


## CHAPTER 14

1. Is it true that when a group of people maintain their inherent rights, there is little if any conflict?

2. Try to think of a circumstance in which two people are maintaining their inherent rights, but are in conflict.

3. What does it mean to infringe on inherent rights?

4. What does it mean to surrender or waive inherent rights?

5. How is one made more independent and free by maintaining his inherent rights?

6. What happens to a nation when the majority of its citizens waive their inherent rights?

7. Have you noticed that when you make a commitment to do something good, things come up to prevent you? How do you revolve this problem?

8. What lesson did Ur want Jon to learn when he sent him out in the rain to push on the post?

## CHAPTER 15

1.  What did Ur mean when he said that his mind was protecting him by not remembering what happened to his hearing, eye-sight and children?

2.  What inherent rights did Jon exercise by keeping in confidence the things that Ur shared with him?

3.  What inherent right did Ur's father exercise when he chose to embrace his son?

## CHAPTER 16

No questions

## CHAPTER 17

1.  Which inherent right does Dr. Smith waive that Miss Brandish maintains?

## CHAPTER 18

1.  Have you ever done something good for another person that was hard?

2.  Has anyone ever done something good for you that was hard for you to accept?

## CHAPTER 19

1.  When Jon sees Elton Greasefark sitting with Moose, he finds himself in a position where he feels he cannot stop himself from picking a fight. What rights did Jon almost waive?

2.  Does Jon have the inherent right to pick the fight?

3.  Which is the inherent right: to explode or to reason out the situation and find a peaceful way to resolve the problem?

4.  How does Ur define mightiness?

5.  Why does mightiness grow as one maintains his inherent rights?

6.  What is the path to peace of mind?

7.  Have you ever tried to explain this to other people? How did they react?


## CHAPTER 20

1.  What inherent right did Jon waive at the beginning of his match?


## CHAPTER 21

1.  Why would mourning be considered an inherent right?

2.  How does mourning bring us peace of mind?

3.  Is there any disappointment or loss that you have not finished mourning for?

4.  How would this chapter have been different if the good people in Declo had chosen to waive their inherent rights?

## CHAPTER 22

1. The most sacred right humans have is one Dean maintained. What is that right?

## CHAPTER 23

Dr. Richard Kinney, a deaf/blind man from Illinois, wrote two poems in this chapter. Read them again and again until you begin to feel what he is trying to say.

## CHAPTER 24

Now that you understand what your inherent rights are and are striving to maintain them, it is time to start thinking about enjoying the privileges of life. Privileges are the good, sweet, happy things in life. (material possessions, friends, wealth, parenthood, travel, employment, being loved by someone other than your mamma, teaching, good anger management skills, a forgiving heart, etc.) Privileges are the things people dream of doing or having or feeling. It always starts with a vision, or a dream. Take off your blinders and let your mind expand to great possibilities. Dream big! Dream good!

List 50 privileges you want to receive before you die. Take your time and savor the dreaming.

1. _____

2. _____

3. _____

4. _____

5. _____

6. _____

7. _____

8. _____

9. _____

345

10. _____

11. _____

12. _____

13. _____

14. _____

15. _____

16. _____

17. _____

18. _____

19. _____

20. _____

21. _____

22. _____

23. _____

24. _____

25. _____

26. _____

27. _____

28. _____

29. _____

30. _____

31. _____

32. _____

33. _____

34. _____

35. _____

36. _____

37. _____

38. _____

39. _____

40. _____

41. _____

42. _____

43. _____

44. _____

45. _____

46. _____

47. _____

48. _____

49. _____

50. _____

Of the 50 privileges you listed, prioritize the top 10.

Of the top 10 privileges, which do you now have the skills to accomplish?

1. _____
2. _____
3. _____
4. _____
5. _____
6. _____
7. _____
8. _____
9. _____
10. _____

1. _____
2. _____
3. _____
4. _____
5. _____
6. _____
7. _____
8. _____
9. _____
10. _____

List 10 privileges that you want to begin preparing to receive.

1. _____
2. _____
3. _____
4. _____
5. _____
6. _____
7. _____
8. _____
9. _____
10. _____

**HOPE**
A. **Pick** one privilege you want to start working on immediately.
B. Write a **plan** of how you can get it.
C. List what your **assets** are at this time for getting the privilege.
D. What are the **problems** that you see arising as you begin your quest for the privilege.
E. **Write** a plan for overcoming those problems.
F. Set a **timetable** for accomplishment of each step of the plan.

## CHAPTER 25

1. How would you waive your right to feel pure affection?

## CHAPTER 26

1. How did Jon maintain his right to overcome Luther's offense when Luther was at fault?

2. Ur said, "In life we don't avoid pain; we learn from it." What does that mean to you?

## CHAPTER 27

1. How can your attitude help you face your problems?

## CHAPTER 28

1. How does feeling pain teach you how to deal with it?

## CHAPTER 29

Go back to Chapter 24 and review the privileges and your plan for receiving them. The privileges should be great enough to generate their own motivation. If not, then you are not dreaming big enough! If your privileges are big enough to motivate you to get started, then you need to be able to generate a constant motivation. Success is the ability to accomplish the task after the thrill of the decision has passed. The following will help you keep motivated.

## BELIEF

A. Write an **affirmation** of the privilege you want. (Example: I enjoy the peace and happiness in my life from forgiving people who offend me. Or, I love traveling in Europe and staying in nice places. Or, I love the way people respect me because they know I am totally honest.)

    Always write affirmations in present tense, positive format. Never write, "I will or I want to ... " Think of it as if it already is yours. Never write negative things like "I won't get mad", or "I will never ... " This will only reinforce your problem. Write, "I enjoy peace from my ability to control my anger."

B. **Read** your affirmation as often as you can. Don't memorize it. Your brain must see the words to have the most impact.

C. **Visualize.** This is the best part. Visualize, dream, see yourself already doing or having that privilege. See yourself in the greatest detail—being that parent you want to be or having that dream house, or having a neat relationship with someone. Visualize yourself handling your anger or addiction.

D. **Assumption and assertion.** You have to be careful with this one because people will try to tear you down. You now assume yourself as having that privilege. In your mind begin to act like you already have the anger control or are on your way to wealth or education. Assert yourself! Get off your duff! Begin to do the dream. Don't delay one second from right now.

E.  **Share** your dreams and plans with someone you trust and who you know will support you. If you begin sharing with someone and he start discussing your plans, stop sharing. These are your dreams, and in the end you are the only one that it really matters believes in them.

F.  **REMEMBER**: "Happiness is cleverly nested in the process of attainment of predetermined worthwhile goals." Great trees take years to grow and great privileges take a lot of time to receive. These are not firecrackers you are letting off; these are great privileges you are receiving. Take your time. Enjoy the whole trip. There will be bumps and disappointments and once in while a detour. But there will also be great vistas, beautiful gardens and shady streams on this journey. You will meet wonderful new friends who will cheer you on. The important thing is you must enjoy finishing the game.

**KNOWLEDGE**

You are doing it! Keep it up! Go after other Pristine Privileges.

**CHAPTER 30**

1.  Why is gratitude a right?

2.  How does "breaking out" show more gratitude?

**CHAPTER 31**

1.  In what ways did Jon assume and assert himself toward receiving the state championship?

2.  Did you notice as Jon began to push himself toward his goal that others started to jump on his bandwagon?

3. Who were some who wanted to be part of his success?

4. Why do you think they wanted to be part of his life now that he was moving toward a goal?

## CHAPTER 32

1. What caused Jon to begin getting discouraged?

2. What did he do to turn his discouragement around?

3. What good things had come into Jon's life just because he began to exercise his inherent rights?

## CHAPTER 33

1. What rights did both Brent and Jon maintain before, during and after their match?

## CHAPTER 34

1. Have you ever felt like a victim?

2. Have you ever felt powerless and under the control of another human who wanted to hurt you?

3. Do you feel hatred for someone who has hurt you?

4. Is that hatred slowing you down or distracting you from receiving some of the privileges you want?

5. A person can't just say, "Okay, I forgive you," and it is all gone. How does Ur say we forgive people?

6.  How does one overcome the effects of the offense against us?

## CHAPTER 35

1.  What did Mary point out about Jon that was an inspiration to his friends and the whole community?

2.  What rights that you maintain in your own daily life could be an inspiration to those around you?

## CHAPTER 36

1.  How is opposition an ugly friend?

2.  What did Ur mean when he said, "Always look to the hills, Jon, because that will give you hope to climb out of your valleys"?

3.  What are some of the hills in your life that can and have inspired hope in you?

4.  What are some of the valleys that have taught you invaluable lessons of life?

5.  How can your knowledge of inalienable rights help you in your daily life now?

## FINAL

1.  Of the 36 rights in the book, apply 6 of them to your life.

2.  Find 6 other rights not listed in the book and write how they apply to you.

**American Dream Makers** is a unique concept in ethics education. It invites Americans to enjoy the amazing privileges this free nation offers, while being protected by their unalienable or inherent rights. Every business and school should teach inherent rights and how to receive the privileges of life. America seems to be on a  slippery slope of weakening virtue, and it is virtually impossible for liberty to exist without virtue.

**American Dream Makers** is an optimistic organization who still believes this direction can be turned around. We believe there are millions of people who go to bed each night hungering for some kind of endorsement of their rights to be good. So much of what we see and hear tells us that the wave of the future is self gratification by any means available. We as a nation have lost the understanding of unalienable rights and the hard work required to enjoy the privileges of life.

If you would like Jack Rose to present and inspiring and motivational speech to your organization about the power of our inalienable rights and the receiving of privileges then contact him at:

American Dream Makers
3305 Cobble Creek Lane
Heber, UT 84032
www.americandreammakers.com
jrose@americandreammakers.com

.

Take away the sacred sense of belonging to a family or community, and observe how quickly citizens cease to care for big cities.

Those of us who are business-oriented are quick to look for the bottom line in our endeavors. In the case of a value-free society, the bottom line is clear—the costs are prohibitive!

A value-free society eventually imprisons its inhabitants. It also ends up doing indirectly what most of its inhabitants would never have agreed to do directly—at least initially.

Can we turn such trends around? There is still a wealth of wisdom in the people of this good land, even though such wisdom is often mute and in search of leadership. People can often feel in their bones the wrongness of things, long before pollsters pick up such attitudes or before such attitudes are expressed in the ballot box. But it will take leadership and articulate assertion of basic values in all places and in personal behavior to back up such assertions.

Even then, time and the tides are against us, so that courage will be a key ingredient. It will take the same kind of spunk the Spartans displayed at Thermopylae when they tenaciously held a small mountain pass against overwhelming numbers of Persians. The Persians could not dislodge the Spartans and sent emissaries forward to threaten what would happen if the Spartans did not surrender. The Spartans were told that if they did not give up, the Persians had so many archers in their army that they would darken the skies with their arrows. The Spartans said simply: "So much the better, we will fight in the shade!" Neal A. Maxwell, An address given to Salt Lake City Rotarians, 7 February 1978

## AUTHOR INFORMATION

Jack Rose was reared in Declo, Idaho in a family of two brothers, Roy and Walter and two sisters, Brenda and Shirley. At age eight, his father, Roy died, leaving him and two brothers to be raised by his mother Wanda, who suffered the effects of a stroke. After high school he moved to Los Angeles where he became associated with the deaf and deaf-blind.

At California State University at Northridge (CSUN), he worked as a sign language interpreter while seeking his B. A. and M. A. degrees. It was at CSUN that he met and worked with several deaf-blind individuals who had a great influence on his life

For eight years he has taught ethics to incarcerated youth at a youth-correction facility. He has served his community (1982-2005) as a reserve police officer. He has also served as a Cub Scout Master, Boy Scout Master and as a Varsity Scout Coach. He has been involved in amateur wrestling in both freestyle and college style. He is also a runner and has run three marathons.

In 1973, Jack married his greatest friend, Ronda Babiracki, an elementary school teacher. They reared their six children in a beautiful valley in the Wasatch Mountains.

One of his great loves is lecturing. He has travels coast to coast for many years speaking at conferences and high schools in the United States and Canada. He is a popular speaker for both youth and adults, and has become renowned for his storytelling skills, using country wit and powerful stories to teach values.

Troubled by deteriorating ethical and moral standards in our society, as well as the insatiable and reckless pursuit of easy wealth, Jack set about seeking to understand the true meaning of the American Dream. What are the elements of true success in America? How does one attain peace of mind in a society that is never satisfied with enough? How does one build a solid foundation so that he might safely entrust himself with the privileges of power, wealth, and especially parenthood?

Pondering these question brought him to understand the meaning of inherent or unalienable rights. He has continued to research, write and speak about the power of peace that is obtained when these rights are maintained. Jack has discovered that except for the three famous unalienable rights—life, liberty, and the pursuit of happiness—most Americans cannot name any others. They cannot name a fourth, or indeed any others, yet these rights are their heritage, and they are powerful tools for successful living.

If you would like to read more about unalienable rights then go to
www.americandreammakers.com